VIOLET HICCUP

51 SHADES OF PINK

ANGUS SHOOR CAAN

Ordering Information:

Prime Seven Media
518 Landmann St.
Tomah City, WI 54660

Printed in the United States of America

*Since this is her favourite novel of mine, I'd like to dedicate
Violet Hiccup to my very good friend, Susie Williams.
Hope the volume is thick enough to balance
the wobbly leg on your table.*

xoxox

CONTENTS

Preface...9

Chapter 1: High...11

Chapter 2: As luck would have it 18

Chapter 3: Uniform day..................................29

Chapter 4: Doing a moonlight......................36

Chapter 5: Well and truly bedded in 44

Chapter 6: Fair exchange................................48

Chapter 7: A black promise...........................59

Chapter 8: Stranger Eight Ball 66

Chapter 9: Search me......................................74

Chapter 10: Thirty feet of rope.......................85

Chapter 11: Right time, right place................97

Chapter 12: Sour dough 105

Chapter 13: Good riddance............................116

Chapter 14: Chit chat.....................................132

Chapter 15: Touch and go..............................138

Chapter 16: Pet names...................................149

Chapter 17: The flying pig.............................162

Chapter 18: At the right time........................172

Chapter 19: Clocking on 180

Chapter 20: Quickfire promotions................191

Chapter 21: Raise and raise again.................201

Chapter 22: Back to the drawing board.........210

Chapter 23: Big boys' meccano set................219

Chapter 24: Banquet for one.........................231

Chapter 25: Kira nails it.................................241

Chapter 26: Money for old rope 251

Chapter 27: You can see our house from up there......almost....263

Chapter 28: A bad day at the office....................................273

Chapter 29: Painting with matchsticks................................282

Chapter 30: A domestic interlude. (Sideshow) 292

Chapter 31: A domestic interlude. (Showtime) 303

Chapter 32: Where did the day go?....................................315

Chapter 33: Return of the Prince......................................323

Chapter 34: An unenviable hat trick..................................331

Chapter 35: Scare tactics..343

Chapter 36: One more notch on the bedpost, and a narrow
escape..351

Chapter 37: A roomful of lovers..361

Chapter 38: Patsy takes an unexpected drop in wages 369

Chapter 39: Lightning strikes twice 378

Chapter 40: Two new brooms..393

Chapter 41: End of an era; a whole new slant on things............401

Chapter 42: Nine ten jack, a pair of spikes and a shattered
record..410

Chapter 43: One and two thirds sheets to the wind 420

Chapter 44: Funny how things turn out 433

Chapter 45: People in glass houses 440

Chapter 46: Time, gentlemen, please. Deserved.....................450

Chapter 47: Sandy: Rest in peace.......................................456

Chapter 48: A quarter the odds..466

Chapter 49: An introduction to The Movies...........................471

Chapter 50: Snap, snap, snap. SMACK. Snap, snap, snap.........478

Chapter 51: A whole new ball game......................................488

About the Author...499

Books by this Author...501

PREFACE

Pink Lynt, down on his luck and about to lose his squalid flat to a new supermarket development, hits the jackpot.

For once in his life he's in the right place at the right time, and his fortunes take a turn for the better.

More than one turn, in fact; many, many twists and turns.

Although he had never ever despaired, by his own reckoning the new good times came well deserved.

God alone knew he had waited long enough for them. Patiently, mind you. Always patiently.

Then, Violet shows up and he knows his life will never be the same again.

Eight Ball, Pink's trusty side-kick, can verify all this and more. Not to you or I, perhaps; but with Violet happy to act as translator, he's well worth an ear.

This is a romp through the late 70s-early 80s; with focus on the drug taking, music loving, sex obsessed scene of this particular period in time.

High

Pink shit, or rather he would have if he hadn't just been. His last place of residence had a cat-flap in the back door, and for the life of him, he couldn't get used to Eight Ball's comings and goings now that his means of access was different. The top section of the kitchen window opened just wide enough for him to clamber in and out without wrecking the place.

The reason for Pink's heart missing a beat was that Eight Ball had an uncanny knack for making an entrance between tracks, or maybe it was deliberate? He had a better chance of being noticed and subsequently fed; or then again, maybe he was being polite like he was at a gig, waiting for the song to finish before taking up his seat. That would be it, yes, he was being polite.

They both had a difficult time adjusting to their new surroundings. For a start, it was one floor up. No chance of putting in a cat-flap, either; the landlord didn't know of Eight Ball's existence. Pink had sneaked him in as soon as his furniture had found its place in the scheme of things. It was either that or let him fend for himself around his old stomping ground. Trouble with that was, the place was soon to make way for a supermarket.

So, Pink kept Eight Ball in for the first two weeks at the new flat, foiling many an escape attempt and locking him in the kitchen whenever he showed signs of contempt at being held hostage. He must have wondered what the hell was going on when Pink buttered his paws for him one day, then poured him out of the kitchen window. Forty five minutes and he was back, but only to let Pink know it had started raining. For the next four days he was in and out like a fiddler's elbow, mostly checking Pink hadn't disappeared on him.

Once it had been established they were both staying, Pink himself started going out again, venturing farther than the shops at the end of the road. That was as far as he had been since moving in, apart from signing on at the dole once a week.

He was totally self contained; shops on the doorstep for food and drink, his music and Eight Ball for company, and a lump of Lebanese gold the size of his fist, at least it had been at the onset of his self imposed exile. Now, he was finding it necessary to pack more and more into each joint he built in order to encourage the desired effect.

Time then for some horse trading. He left the radio on low and made sure the bedroom door was closed to give Eight Ball the illusion he was somewhere in the flat. Ten minutes later, he was at Donny Boot's back door and giving it the secret knock.

Donny's woman let him in. If she had a name, Pink had never heard it spoken. He followed her into the dark interior. Donny was spoon feeding his youngest child, his eyes sunk way, way back in their sockets. This was a good omen, it meant he had some decent shit on the go.

Pink refused a cup of tea, he always did when he came here ever since he found something unsavoury sticking to the bottom of a cup he had just been drinking from. Donny was genuinely pleased to see him, telling him long time no see. The television was showing cartoons with the sound down while the stereo pumped out some fine music, reverberating at a reasonable volume.

Donny pointed to an album cover on the coffee table adorned with all the makings necessary for skinning up, inviting Pink to get one going. He stuck his nose in the bag and inhaled deeply, grass was his favourite. Given the choice, he would plump for the grass every time. Grass was directly responsible for the recent boost to his circumstances, enabling him to afford the deposit for his present abode, clear all his debts and to be choosy about what he smoked for a change. He suggested to Donny that the weed was of Dutch origin and was quite taken aback to find it was Californian. No matter, it had a remarkable bouquet. Pink was soon toking away at a generous helping of it, knowing instinctively he would be set fair for the planets in the not too distant future.

He knew the album cover he was using as a worktop had nothing to do with what was playing on the stereo. He liked what he was hearing and asked Donny to enlighten him as he passed the joint. Donny couldn't remember exactly, someone else had recently laid it on him so Pink struggled to his feet at the second attempt and went to find out for himself. The house was untidy. All Donny and his woman did all day was sit around getting wasted. Pink couldn't see the point of flicking through Donny's considerable record collection looking for an empty sleeve, and instead approached the turntable. Rotating his head at thirty three and a third revolutions per minute, he tried to read the label, giving it up as a bad job just as the record finished. Deciding he wanted to hear more, he absorbed the information on the label, flipped the disc and played side two.

He assembled another joint, traded some of his Leb for a fair amount of the grass and sank into the couch to enjoy the sounds. Donny's woman found the album cover under the couch. Not that she had been tidying up, the child had thrown his teething keys at her and they sneaked under to where the cover was. Pink refused a drink for the second time. His tongue was sticking to the roof of his mouth as a side effect of the grass, but he couldn't bring himself to accept.

Thanking Donny for his hospitality, he headed for the back door, the copy of Nils Lofgren's 'Cry Tough' tucked safely under his arm. Donny made him promise to bring it back the following day;

it didn't belong to him, he forgot momentarily who it did belong to, but it definitely wasn't his.

He helped himself to a pint of pure orange juice from a stationary milk float, gulping it down like he was fresh back from the desert. After being in the gloom of Donny's dungeon dark living room, the spring sunshine almost blinded him as he meandered towards the High Chaparral; so named because it was higher up than his old place, or maybe because he had been high ever since he moved in, you could take your pick. That would have to wait a little while longer, he hoped to hell no one saw him enter the car, especially as it was driven by a policewoman in full uniform.

Eight Ball didn't take him on when he got home, preferring instead to sit and stare at his favourite wall. This was a new thing he had taken up. Pink thought it to be boredom at his incarceration, but the cat had stayed with it when given the option of going out.

First job was to set the mood by getting another spliff on the go, but not before he had picked the seeds out, he would keep these. Soon, it would be time to plant them out on an isolated stretch of the canal bank.

He put his new favourite album on the turntable, cranked up the volume and followed the words on the lyric sheet as Nils weaved his way through the songs. He had been in the habit of rolling single skin joints since taking up residence, but this stuff deserved at least three skins. He took some ice from the fridge freezer, dropped it into a pint glass, poured some Vimto over it, ran the cold tap for a few seconds and filled the glass almost to the brim. Instead of flipping the album over, he played side one again, this time remembering to set the tape recorder. Donny could have it back tomorrow, but Pink wouldn't be without it.

Finding his pestle and mortar, he crushed the tinder dry grass until it was a fine powder, added some loose shag from his tobacco tin and folded the two together. That was a thing about grass; in its rough form it tended to burn quicker than the tobacco it was usually mixed with, which often resulted in the joint burning down one side faster than the other and causing a lot of waste.

All this time he found himself picking up the lyrics and singing along. In a couple of days he would be word perfect. Two more days and the air guitar solos would be in the bag.

Another fine point about the flat, no heating bills. Being situated above an Indian bakery with three good sized ovens working almost twenty four hours every day, it was like having under floor heating. The aroma the bakery gave off wasn't unpleasant, either. The shop owner was his landlord, a true gentleman, a little apprehensive about letting his flat to a long haired, scruffily dressed individual until Pink produced a wad of notes as deposit. His sense of business took over then. He laid down a few ground rules, showed Pink round the premises, shook his hand and took his money. Two hours after he moved in proper, Mr. Rapati was at the door with a basket of his produce, telling Pink he had no need to buy either bread or pastries for as long as he lived in the flat.

He soon got to know Mr. Rapati's family and noticed a funny thing. He spoke to his customers in English, even if they were Indian; he spoke to his family in Indian and to his staff in a strange mixture of both languages, a true multi-linguist.

God alone knew what Pink would do in the summer, the clear days at present led to frosty nights and found him able to wander round in a pair of shorts, or less if the mood took him, without feeling the slightest bit cold. A warm summer would have it like a sauna, but with all the doors and windows open and being so lofty, he might coax a bit of a breeze to cool things down.

Side two was allowed three spins, recorded on the second and Pink found just one more spliff was sufficient to take the album to the upper echelons of his all time favourites list. In exalted company and no two ways about it.

All this time, Eight Ball had been staring at his wall. In his altered state, Pink worked it out that the animal was hypnotised by the wallpaper and mused on buying some paint on the morrow, see if that couldn't break his concentration. He could do without a cat with more behavioural problems than was the norm. He had never been a cat lover, not even remotely, but the old wives tale that the cat picks the owner proved to be most accurate. When he was poor and couldn't feed himself, he would very often visit friends right on the stroke of a mealtime, either lunch or tea.

On one such occasion, he was constructing a joint to share with his hosts when their cat decided to go into labour. The creature was exhausted after producing seven kittens and Pink had to help with number eight. Instantly recognisable from the word go, Eight ball was a bundle of black fur with a perfect white circle on the crown of his head; and a black dot in the middle of the circle.

Pink christened him immediately, being out of his tree on Temple balls all the way from Nepal, they had travelled very well. He checked on the kitten once a week, see how he was getting on; strangely, round about tea time on each visit. Of the seven survivors, Eight Ball was the only one of the litter who would go near him, quickly learning not to disturb him when he was concentrating on getting a smoke together. Subsequently, they became great friends, Eight Ball being quite chatty for a cat. Equally, he seemed to enjoy the ambience provided by the hash, going so far as to chase the smoke rings blown for him by Pink.

Now, no one wants a cat who has already been given a name. Finding a suitable handle for a new pet is a deeply personal, even emotional undertaking for whoever is taking on the responsibility for said pet. So, the rest of the litter found good homes quite easily. Eight Ball already had a name and the very family he was born into didn't want him either. Who, they wanted to know, should they sign the adoption papers over to?

So it was that Pink and Eight Ball teamed up and this was their fourth set of accommodations together. Some marriages don't last the course or stress of one flitting. Of the various females who had shared his flats and his beds, Eight Ball only ever showed an interest in one, Renee; but only because she spoke to him in French using the same throaty, sexy voice which had attracted Pink to her. When she packed her bags for France or wherever, Eight Ball moped around for weeks, going so far as to attack the next girl to share Pink's bed. He locked him out of the bedroom that night, but it was too late since the poor girl was traumatised by the psycho cat's actions. Pink later learned she joined a convent and had turned to Jesus.

He tended to just about tolerate Pink's friends after that, both male and female. In the previous flat he would come home to a houseful, ignore all attempts to pet him and announce his presence to Pink; always making sure he wasn't in the middle of something before landing on his knee. Now, they were content with each other for company, even going so far as to share the same taste in music

CHAPTER 2

As luck would have it

Pink rose, dressed and left the house without either washing or breakfasting. To be fair there was nothing in the larder. As for the wash, that would be sorted out at his next port of call. Today was Monday, Mondays and Thursdays he went to Bea's to wash his hair, take a bath, have his sexual urges attended to and eat breakfast, though not necessarily in that order. Bea was happy to give up these two mornings for him, such was their relationship she would have gladly jumped through hoops for him. He liked to wait until her mother went to work, very often passing her on the way. Then, he would find the key on the high window sill by the side door and let himself in, disrobing as he ascended the stairs. Bea would welcome him with open arms most times, allowing him to throw her all round the bedroom before attending to his other needs.

This particular Monday was bitterly cold and Pink was wrapped in an old army greatcoat as protection from the elements. He had no notion of the time, only knowing it was early, maybe too early for his jaunt, but Eight Ball had been all over him earlier looking for his breakfast and he was seldom wrong.

His route took him past the police station and he would pick up the pace for that part of his journey, being instantly recognizable to every man Jack of the drug squad. A common fallacy among his friends was that these people only operated by night, something Pink knew to be incorrect in the wake of a couple of early morning close calls.

Same again this morning. Turning to walk past the cop shop, he suddenly froze. D S Bland was parked by the door, he recognised the car and the back of the bastard's oddly shaped head; probably waiting for a colleague and with a dawn raid in mind. Pink took refuge in a doorway farther up the street and kept an eye on his arch enemy. Two minutes later, Bland was out of the car, leaving the engine running and making for the cop shop door. Pink saw his chance and made a bid to get beyond the car and the station. As he approached, he noticed the driver's window was open, a glance inside revealing a wallet on the seat. Now, Pink was as skint as his name suggested, with a surname like Lynt he had always been Pink Lynt, and he didn't hesitate. Snatching up the wallet, he made it to the corner and deviated from his normal route, turning out of sight as quickly as possible to avoid detection. Inside the wallet he found plenty of identification and fifty pounds cash money. His first thought was to rid himself of the wallet, then a brainwave, yes, he would try to stitch up the bad guy.

He wasn't a customer, but Red knew him well enough. A five pound wrap of speed, three fivers in his change for a twenty, advice for Red to keep his ear to the ground and he made himself scarce, picking up his route at the next corner. He almost knocked Bea's mother down in his haste and for once he was glad to see her. He gave her a fiver for herself, put another fiver in the wallet, stuffed the speed in behind Bland's ID and told her to hand it in at the sergeant's desk in the cop shop. She was to tell them she had found it just down the road a bit, and no, she hadn't looked inside.

She shouted after him, but he was so well wrapped up he didn't hear her, he was heading for a sure fire warm welcome with thirty five smackers in his back pocket and every intention of taking off for the planets later on.

He found the key and let himself in, usual script, shedding clothes on the way upstairs and bursting into Bea's room; the same room she shared with Jenny, her sister, who wasn't feeling too well and had taken a day off work. Bea's mum should have told him. Jenny was propped up in bed, wide awake and witness to the floor show. Pink shrugged his shoulders, he wouldn't let it spoil his day. Jenny half hid her eyes and watched him climb into bed with her sister, who in turn screamed with shock at how cold he was. She soon stopped complaining and welcomed him aboard; she was lovely and warm and fleshy and accommodating. Jenny pulled the blankets over her head to drown out their noise, surfacing twenty minutes later to ask Bea could she make her a warm drink when she had run the bath for Pink?

Pink asked her what the trouble was. Jenny told him she had been awake all night with a stinking cold, shivering and aching and suchlike. He told her to sweat it out, which she agreed was the best remedy, if she could only warm up in the first place.

Unselfishly, Pink hopped in beside her and cuddled up, his hands all over the place, groping and kneading and probing like he'd known her all her life. She only objected when her sister appeared in the doorway with her hot drink. Pink's reaction was to invite Bea to join them, help her sister work up a sweat. Bea told him his bath was ready, she would be in shortly to wash his hair for him, she would attend to Jenny when he was gone. Seeing how casual her sister was about what was going on, Jenny had wrapped her hand around the shaft of his cock and was massaging him gently back to life. Pink thought it prudent to escape her tender clutches. Bea was laid back, yes, but he didn't want to push it too far. He would no doubt catch up with Jenny at a later date.

He dried his scalp as best he could and let Bea brush his long, wavy hair. She said it was easier to plait when it was damp. She much preferred it down, but Pink sometimes dropped on the odd day's work on the roofs and it tended to get in his way. Jenny joined them for breakfast and by the kitchen light she did indeed look rough. Bea sent her back to bed, promising to jump in beside her when Pink had gone. Pink asked her to leave the door off the latch for five minutes while he ran to the shop, returning with a large box of Lemsips for Jenny, help her cold along.

The money in his back pocket was more than he had seen in months, but he was in no great hurry to spend it. Ten pounds was a debt to be paid off right away, then he could go back to the same place next time he was poor. That was to be his first move and he headed for the town centre to pay the man. That done, he wanted to score. There was someone walking towards him, a girl he had no wish to bump into so he ducked into the closest shop to hand. He hadn't been in a betting shop for over a year. Any newspapers he read were days old, but that didn't matter as he liked to do the crosswords. He was in no particular hurry to be anywhere, Donny rarely left the house so he took a few minutes to study the form. Straight away two horses jumped off the page and bit him on the bum. A further ten minutes contemplation gave him his bet, a Yankee, eleven bets at twenty pence each while he was flush, plus tax. He gave the lady a fiver, stuck the receipt and his change deep into his pocket and left the shop. A quick glance up and down the street to make sure the coast was clear and he was on his way.

He picked up half an ounce of tobacco and a couple of packets of papers before delivering the secret knock to Donny's door. It took a full five minutes for him to answer and the first words out of his mouth were that something was going on at the cop shop. Pink feigned surprise then asked Donny to tell what he knew. All he had heard was that DS Bland had been arrested, no details, but he offered Pink a wager he would get away with whatever he had done. Pink told him he wanted more facts before he would accept the bet. Donny had sent his woman to investigate, told her to put the child in the pram and wander around the town, see what she could find out. Pink decided to wait 'til she returned since he might as well be here getting warm and stoned as anywhere else.

An hour and a half later she fell through the door, frozen to the marrow, the baby was screaming its head off; either cold or hungry or in need of a change of nappy, or all of the above. Pink waited around only long enough to hear the tale, and what a tale it was. Bland had been caught with his pants down seemingly. He had dropped his wallet, which was immediately handed in by a stand up citizen. The chief inspector of all people was talking to the duty officer when the wallet was handed in and he himself emptied the contents onto the desk. Money, ID and a quantity of narcotics were found. Bland was sent for and Donny's woman witnessed him being escorted from the police station in handcuffs.

Three lepers came towards him, but Pink put his hand out first, asking could they scrape together the entrance fee so he could get into the pub where it was warm. They were about to ask him the same question, they would ask everyone they met that day and every day. The same three liked to borrow money, but disliked paying it back. Pink, on the other hand, always tried to pay his debts, that way he didn't fear rejection if ever he had to ask again.

The pub was abuzz with the big news and Pink played down what he knew, listening instead as the story gathered momentum until the entire police force was under investigation. He bought a pint, slipped the landlord the two quid he owed him from a week ago and sat in a corner of the pool room.

Clem, one of the roofers he did the odd day's work for, stuck his head in and gave Pink a wave. Pink asked him to mind the door while he rolled a joint and invited him to share it when he was done. Before they knew it, there were half a dozen round it, all looking for a toke. Clem set up the pool table and offered Pink a game and someone challenged them to a game of doubles. Mistake, big mistake, they ended up playing for pints and didn't put their hand in their pockets for the rest of the day. At one point two members of the drug squad stuck their heads in, but they took so much flak from the pub's regulars they didn't stay long. Pink was carrying, but he knew he could get rid of it if he really had to. Many a time the squad came in and found something on the floor, and strangely, no one ever held their hand up to owning it.

The pair's luck continued to the snooker table in the ex-sevicemen's club, then back in the pub when it re-opened later

Five minutes after he staggered home came a rap on the window, two acquaintances had been locked out, again. Pink let them in, he was getting fed up with it, but told himself it had happened to him and one or both had helped him out in the past; it was becoming a constant thing lately, though. Ten minutes later he had another visitor. Pink left a joint between them and went to bed, drunk enough not to care.

He slept fitfully. Something had him awake in the early hours, a banging noise. If it was someone else at the door he would leave it to the dudes downstairs to sort out, he wasn't finished with the sleeping yet. When he finally did surface, there was no one around. He soon found out why at the same time as he found the padlock on the gas meter had been forced off. In a way, that suited Pink since he had been on gas for ice for the past six weeks, so, all the robbers would have found was a tray of water where there should have been coins. A plasticine mould with six indentations the depth, size and shape of a fifty pence piece, lived in the freezer box of the fridge. The ice shapes created by these were a perfect fit for the coin slot and, hey presto, free gas. The building was due to be flattened for renovation. Pink would report the theft to the gas board, who in turn would report it to the police. He himself would also report it to the police to reinforce his story and to ensure no comeback on him.

He would kill three or four birds with the one stone, make his two reports, have a breakfast at the Greek café then treat himself to the hair of the dog; funnily enough, at the early drinker, the Canine Dog Club. First off, he rolled three joints and shaped them to the turn up on his bob cap. If he was pulled and searched, all he had lost was the three joints; the rest he stashed where no one would ever find it; at least none but the brave.

Thankfully, he only had the desk sergeant to deal with at the cop shop and it was a big relief to be in and out of the place quickly.

He dug his hand into a pocket to pay for his breakfast and came up with the betting slip, the drink had helped him to forget. The roofing gangs were recruiting, believing the weather was about to change for the better. Pink was offered work, but invented a doctor's appointment, he still had a good few bob in his back pocket. He borrowed a paper from an acquaintance and turned to the racing results.

Pale wasn't in it, another look was required. Must be some sort of a mistake, a misprint, even. No, it was there in black and white, four winners and all four at the rather attractive odds of nine to one. Deep breaths, Pink, deep breaths he told himself. Another look at the paper, it couldn't be denied, Grass Hand, first at nine to one, Solar Grass, first at nine to one, Keep on the Grass, the first horse to jump out at him yesterday, first at nine to one, and, last, but also first so to speak, Grass Skirt, first at nine to one.

He gave the paper back, let the roofing gangs go off on their travels then borrowed a pencil from the waitress. He had reckoned it up in his head, six doubles, four trebles and one four timer came to two thousand, nine hundred and twenty pounds exactly, maybe his luck had changed at long last. Seeing it worked out on a paper napkin helped him to digest it better. He destroyed the evidence of what he had been writing by blowing his nose into the napkin and throwing it in the bin at the café door. His next stop would be the betting shop.

Closed, the staff were inside, but the shop was closed. That suited him, he would be first through the door with a good chance of picking up his winnings away from the prying eyes of the riff-raff, who would make his life a misery if they found out about his windfall.

There wasn't enough money in the safe to cover his bet, not good enough, he wanted to speak to the manager. They were quick enough to take his money, they should at least have the decency to pay out on time. The manager apologised, he would be going to the bank in an hour, would Pink like to return then? A cheque would be waiting, made out for the full amount. Pink advised the manager he would be going to the bank right this minute; oh, and a cheque was totally unacceptable, cash money would be the order of the day. The manager didn't try to talk Pink out of it, he didn't know him, not one of his regular customers, but he recognised the menace in his voice and decided to comply with his wishes. A phone call, presumably to his superiors, and the pair walked the short distance to the bank.

The envelope fitted snugly into his inside coat pocket, then, he was down an alley, going into his superman routine. Word would soon leak out. He would be described as having a pony tail or plait, so he unravelled his hair and went home to change into his other outfit. Some other pony tailed dude could take the pressure off him. God only knew there were enough of them to go at.

He took a shortcut through the park to Donny's, lighting up one of the spliffs on the way. He could work things out better when stoned, only this time he would need to act on what he had worked out instead of letting it slide as was his usual trait. He had only just scored from Donny yesterday, time for a little subterfuge. He would say he had lost his hash, having had too much to drink last night, ask Donny could he have some on account, only a small amount so Donny wouldn't worry about giving it; an eighth or maybe just a sixteenth of an ounce. Slyly, that would remove all suspicion from him as to being the winner of all that money. Donny's house was like grand central station most days with people coming and going at a sometimes quite alarming rate. Donny liked a chat, he would be sure to tell one or two of his clients Pink had been round on the borrow. He used the toilet while he was there, slipping twenty quid from the envelope and stashing the rest where he was sure no one would find it, underneath the cleaning products Donny's woman kept in the cupboard below the sink. Two days max and he would be back to pay Donny and pick up his cash stash.

Now, he was thinking. There was no doubt he had to bail out of his present accommodation. Last night had put the tin hat on that one for him, so called friends helping themselves to the contents of his gas meter. They would be lying low now, disappointed there was nothing in the box and perhaps a little worried as to what Pink had in mind for them. He wasn't violent, had never started a fight in his life; finished a few, yes, but he had never ever started one. What his so called friends knew for a fact was that Pink knew some people who thrived on violence, people who owed him the odd favour, people who wouldn't hesitate if asked to avenge him. These were desperate times and if anyone was aware of that it was Pink. He was also aware these three dudes must have been pretty desperate to do what they did.

At home, he changed his clothes, fed Eight Ball and wandered back into town, still after that hair of the dog he had promised himself. Same pub as last night and he made a show of scratching around for his entrance fee, eventually borrowing five pence from the landlord's daughter. He knew she was sweet on him and she tipped up the shilling without fuss. Another marker had been laid down to bolster the view he was potless, so no one could point at him and say he was flush. No one. The girl was reading the local paper and he cadged it from her, retiring to the pool room for a look at the accommodations on offer. It was time to take stock.

The pub filled up with disconsolate roofers who had driven as far out of town as they were going, only to encounter bad weather. Pink put the hard word on one of them for a pint, telling him he was due his giro tomorrow, he would pay him back then.

One flat stood out from the others and it was a good ten minute walk out of town. He wanted to go now and put his name down for it, but he would stink of ale, not a very good first impression. He would lie low, go to Bea's for his rubdown on Thursday then straight to Donny's, pick up his cash and make a bid for freedom then. In the meantime, there was nothing to stop him from having a gander at the property, see if he liked what he saw.

The ten minute saunter worked out at nearer twenty, almost double his estimate, but it was worth the walk as he knew the flat would suit his needs the minute he clapped eyes on it. Situated on the edge of a predominately Asian area, and far enough out of town to put off unwanted visitors like the trio from last night, he would pull out all the stops and secure the lease if it was the last thing he ever did.

Scoring two hot pies on his way back to town, he had them down his neck well before entering the ex servicemen's club. The girl in the pie shop didn't ask him why he wanted his change in small silver and shrapnel, but if she could see him now, belly up to the bar coppering up for his drink, she would have sussed it. He was aware all eyes were on him as soon as he stepped into the club, but when he went into his routine with the coins, the background chatter picked up again, assuring him he was now off the list of suspects. At least half a dozen souls informed him of the mysterious big winner, although Pink couldn't shed any light on it, either. He did suggest one other person of like circumstances as the rest of them, only to be told that individual had also been discounted.

He still had two joints in his bob cap, but he wouldn't be sparking them up in the club. He needed this place like just about every other patron, to fill in the gap between pub hours. For the entrance fee, the price of a half pint of beer, it provided comfort, company, warmth and shelter so there was no point in upsetting the applecart.

He knew everyone there, if not by name then by sight. Drifting over to the card tables where Clem was playing, he got into conversation with the Waite brothers, Heavy and Light. Like everyone else, they were over the moon about Bland's arrest. Pink glanced at Clem, his opposite number raked in a decent sized pot with an outrageous bluff after the entire school had folded. On the next hand, Pink tipped Clem the wink with a deft hand single, the bluffer was at it again. Four hands later, he left the table, wondering where the fuck his luck had gone.

Clem interrupted the conversation with the Waite brothers, would Pink care for another pint? He refused .... unless Clem was heading for the Boulder when it opened, he would be glad of a pint in there. Settled, he had his entrance fee to the Boulder, maybe they could pick up where they left off last night on the pool table? That would be just dandy.

Light Waite continued with the tale he had been telling. His brother knew it only too well. It seemed one day they had been walking into town and Light, the younger of the two, spotted a ten bob note on the ground a few feet in front of them. As he bent to pick it up, Heavy kicked him in the nuts, picked up the note and gave his brother a shilling for his trouble. That was ten years ago and Light never forgot it. He never tired telling of it, either.

The brothers walked with him to the pub, you didn't get one without the other. They worked together on the knock, buying and selling gold, silver, jewellery or anything of value. They were always well turned out and never short of a bob or two. Heavy got the beers in after Pink mentioned he had a couple of joints on him. He would have shared them anyway, but this was a bonus. Clem joined them and they played pool for fun until the outclassed and defeated from last night rolled their collective sleeves up, determined to turn the tables. They lasted 'til half past nine before Clem went in off the black, but to be perfectly fair, he could hardly stand by then.

Determined not to have the same head as that morning, Pink scored chicken curry and chips from How Long's Chinese chippy on the way home and polished it off before he reached the front door. Managing to bind a spliff together, he smoked it in the dark with Eight Ball and the Grateful Dead for company. This was akin to putting a do not disturb sign on the door, no light, no one home. His chair shielded the glow from the gas fire so anyone passing would take the house to be empty.

Uniform day

Pink elephants marauded through his dream, but that didn't alarm him as he was astride the leader. Whoever was at the door had a knock like a policeman. It was the gasman, come to repair the broken meter. Pink asked him did he enjoy working nightshift and was surprised to find it was nine o'clock in the morning. The sky was black. As soon as the man had fitted a new padlock, Pink went back to bed. Some time later, Eight Ball padded in to let him know it was raining and that he was ready for a feed. Pink boiled the kettle and had a stand up wash at the sink, hoping his new place had a bath, or at least a shower; an inside toilet would be a big help, too. A luxury, in fact.

He was in good spirits as he whistled down the road, a large joint for breakfast will do that for a man. He thought about trying his hand with the horses again, then shivered as he remembered the last time he had the gambling bug. It cost him his house, his possessions and his relationship with a good girl who had been doing a fine job of looking after him. He said never again at the time and stuck to his word. No, he wouldn't be fooled into thinking his luck had changed; the other day was a one off, it was time to steer his life back on track, and with no detours.

He scouted out another couple of flats, deciding they were too close to town, it wouldn't take certain people too long in uncovering his whereabouts. By associating with lowlifes, he had become something of a lowlife himself; all in the name of survival, but he couldn't have sunk much lower. Now that there was a chance to get the fuck out of the rut, he would grab it with both hands.

The café was quiet, not the weather for roofing, they would all be sitting at home watching the clock and waiting for the Canine Dog Club to open. Pink ordered a breakfast from the girl who had loaned him the pen yesterday, he hadn't noticed then, but she was pleasantly attractive. With the place being empty, he asked her to join him for a cup of tea. A little younger than the ladies he normally set his cap at, but he wouldn't pass up the chance to corrupt her, that would be foolish of him. She was a student nurse, the café belonged to her uncle. Pink told her she didn't look Greek and she explained she was third or fourth generation. He steered clear of the uniform thing, besides, she looked good enough in the waitress outfit. If he could talk his way into that, the nurse's uniform would follow as a matter of course. She answered to Helena and he supposed that was Greek enough. She didn't smoke so had never tried hash; she would, though, given the right circumstances. Pink's imagination was running riot now, he would get her stoned, a big fat joint between her lips, then offer up the Cuban cigar he kept in his underpants. His reverie was broken when Helena leapt to her feet and threw her arms around a geeky looking young man's neck, there hadn't been any mention of a boyfriend, lucky bastard.

He was horny now, the hash had that effect, but mostly rendered him too lazy to do anything about it. He thought about sloping off to see Bea, but maybe that would give her the wrong idea. She would keep 'til morning.

On his way to the Canine he had to pass the Boulder. Sara, the landlord's daughter was washing the windows from the inside and Pink stopped to pull faces at her. She laughed and motioned for him to go to the front door. Her mum and dad were at the brewery for a licencee's meeting, she couldn't reach the tops of the windows, maybe Pink could help? There would be a pint in it for him.

It was one hour until opening time, how long would her folks be? They had only just left not five minutes ago, did he have a joint on him? She wanted to try it for herself, how could he refuse? He built a joint while she put the kettle on, they couldn't smoke it here, maybe they should go up to her room, would that be ok? One door closes was Pink's thinking on that, he knew she liked him and now, all of a sudden, she was very alluring to him. They smoked the joint and undressed each other at the same time. He stood her in front of the full length mirror and ran his hands all over her body as she whimpered and moaned. Maybe his luck was changing after all? The girl was a willing participant, dropping to her knees and, gently at first, nibbling and sucking at his cock then, coming up for air, asking him to please fuck her face, hard. Pink obliged. He hadn't heard anyone mention they had been with her and word usually found its way round about that sort of thing. Mind you, her father, the landlord, was an ex paratrooper and big with it. Maybe he would be wise to keep this little interlude to himself? She was soft and warm and had curves in all the right places, the smoke had heightened their senses. Positioning her on her knees, he rode her hard until they came together, collapsing in a heap of arms and legs, pretty much exhausted with their efforts. She wanted another smoke and he obliged, but only if she would make another cup of tea, the earlier cup was stone cold. She asked could they do it again sometime and Pink told her he would check his diary. Not really what she wanted to hear, but then again, he didn't exactly say no, did he?

There were two or three early birds on the doorstep so he went to the toilet while Sara opened up, thus making it look like he had just come in when he eventually went belly up to the bar.

The first pint was on the house, and not because he had washed the windows. He hung around the bar and watched her bend and stretch as she worked, telling himself he would revisit with her, but only when it suited him; she was a good looking girl all right and it would be rude not to.

He sloped off while her back was turned, just to keep her guessing, deciding he should go to Donny's and pick up the money and hoping his woman hadn't suddenly picked up the spring cleaning bug. It was where he had left it; he didn't need to score, but Donny informed him there was a bit of a drought. According to his supplier, there was nothing coming in for a few weeks after a big bust on the coast. Pink had already decided to go out of town for his next buy. If he scored the flat, he planned to lie low for a while. Donny would have talked if he scored heavy, there would be no hiding place.

Twenty minutes on the train and it was like stepping into another world. Bigger, louder and busier, three colleges here so a healthy supply of what he wanted. Where there were students there was dope. Straight to the Flat Iron, real name the Foundry, but nicknamed the Flat Iron for its shape. The barmaid he was after wasn't working today so he ordered a pint of cider while her friend looked for her phone number. As he looked through the juke-box, he spotted another dealer. He dropped his money in and made three random selections, they were all good songs on this particular machine so he couldn't go far wrong. Joining the dealer, he made enquiries as to what was available, but there only seemed to be Moroccan. That's all anyone had, and not too much of it at that. The barmaid gave him a shout, telling him she couldn't find Gwynneth's number, maybe he should call round and see if she was in. He knew where she lived, didn't he?

He knew alright. The last time he had been through he had tried it on with her, making good progress until she brought the vodka out. He woke up alone in the morning, Gwynneth had gone to work, that was when he realised vodka and hash didn't do it for him. He could hammer the beer all night and get stoned at the same time with no adverse reaction, but vodka? Forget that.

Gwynneth answered the door in her dressing gown and dragged him in by his jacket front, she was pleased to see him, mentioning the vodka briefly before inviting him to put a joint together, she was glad of some company.

He knew as soon as she passed him the makings it wasn't Moroccan, too fluffy. He guessed at Leb Gold and hit the nail on the head. Gwynneth told him she had half a weight of the stuff, she could let him have five ounces, but only if he could afford to pay up for it there and then, the rest was spoken for. They agreed a price, she made a drink then settled back for a smoke, the movement under her dressing gown giving him the horn for the second time that day.

Gwynneth confessed she had taken advantage of him on that last occasion. He had fallen asleep with a hard on and she had climbed aboard. Now, she wanted more, with him on the same planet this time. No argument, she was a looker and for the second time that day his tea went cold.

He wasn't to tell anyone where he had scored the dope from, Gwynneth knew there wasn't much about and she didn't want every dealer and smoker in the shire at her door. He had to promise to go back soon before she would let him leave and he did so with hand on heart, but he didn't specify when, exactly.

The train was busy on the way back. A policewoman walked past him towards the front and he gave her the once over, fantasising yet again. Next thing, she was back and sitting opposite him in her tight blue uniform. What the fuck, he engaged her in conversation, asking did she enjoy her work. She was very pretty with a gorgeous smile and he told her as much. Then he told her she had a fair pair of legs, even in those flat shoes; which made her blush, adding further to her allure. He was seriously considering going for the hat trick when she stood up to leave the train. As he checked her legs out again she turned, took his hand in hers, wrote her name, Louise, and her phone number, 999; scoring that out then adding her proper number. It was good she had a sense of humour. he was fantasising again, a pigess in full uniform. Now that was a challenge.

He would have gone straight home to stash the hash if Jenny, Bea's sister, hadn't given him a shout. She wanted to thank him for the medicine and was doing so when the heavens opened. Pink led her into the nearest pub, a place he wouldn't normally frequent, but any port in a storm. He bought the drinks and let Jenny continue with her thanks for his thoughtfulness. She was nothing like her sister. Pretty, in a different way and curvy in a different way. The more they talked the more he felt the hat trick was alive and kicking. Jenny let it be known she had the house to herself tonight and Pink took the hint. Only trouble was, the rain didn't look like it was about to give up. Not to be outdone, he bought another round in and asked the barman to order him a taxi. He couldn't let the opportunity go, not while it was being served up hot on a plate.

Jenny wasn't a smoker, never had been, but she looked on fascinated as Pink rolled a joint and asked just what exactly it did for him. Pink laid it on thick about how it raised awareness, yet was relaxing at the same time; how it heightened the senses when listening to music, and sex .... sex was something else when stoned. That was it, she was interested. She had to try it, coughing and spluttering at first, eventually taking to it like a duck to water. Two joints later it was striptease time, any inhibitions she may have had simply evaporated as the drug took effect and soon she was as naked as the day she was born. Pink took his time, admiring her body and savouring the first contact; she had a lovely figure and for now it was his to play with. Jenny was just as adventurous as her sister, maybe it was the dope, but somehow he didn't think so. He couldn't stop himself from comparing them as she gorged herself on his cock, making as much eye contact as she possibly could and obviously enjoying what she was doing. When he finally slipped it to her, she gave out a squeal to let him know he had hit the spot. He was right about the dope, too. She had never felt so aroused. Her orgasm was the loudest he had ever heard, she liked to broadcast the fact she was having a good time. Pink wasn't far behind her in coming, she begged him not to do it inside her, pleaded with him in fact. She wanted it all over her face, she felt wanton, she felt like a whore, she asked him was it the drugs that made her feel that way? Pink was in no hurry to be anywhere in particular and suggested they have a cup of tea, try another romp and see if it carried the same sensations as before. Jenny wandered into the kitchen, still naked, and put the kettle on. When the tea was made she asked him to show her how to skin up; slowly, not at light speed like he did earlier, but stage by stage, slowly. He was glad to, then let her try. She was a quick learner, building the perfect joint at the second attempt. Then, she was all over him again and yes, the sensations were as intense, maybe even more so than previously. She was so loud the neighbours knew she was having a good time, multiple orgasms accompanied by multiple decibels. Pink managed to quieten her by feeding his cock into her delicious mouth while she played with herself.

The rain had died to a light drizzle by the time he was allowed to leave, another promise of a return match having been begged of him. No matter, the rain was light. By the time he bought his supper, was stopped and searched by the drug squad and took himself home, he was soaked to the skin. Nonetheless, he was grinning like a Cheshire cat, thanking his lucky stars he'd had the foresight to stash the hash and the cash in the airing cupboard after his romp with Jenny. After all, he would be back in the morning to sort her sister out then straight to the flat above the bakery, maybe his luck was on the turn after all?

Eight Ball positioned himself at Pink's feet. He knew there was fish wrapped in the newspaper before it had even been opened. Pink stripped the batter from one piece of the fish, necked it and put the bare fillet on a plate to cool. The rest of the meal was shovelled hungrily down his neck. Eight Ball made short work of his when it was put in front of him, the last thing Pink was aware of being the cat's loud purring as a contented Eight Ball settled on the pillow above his head.

CHAPTER 4

Doing a moonlight

Pink eyed up the policewoman he was following down the street. Not as good looking as that Louise from the train, but definitely shagable all the same. She disappeared into the police station, leaving him almost face to face with Bea's mum, who was on her way to work.

Before he could begin telling her off for not warning him about Jenny, she jumped in first. Someone had told her about the detective being arrested. She had left her name and address when she handed the wallet in and now they wanted to interview her. She might even have to go to court to give evidence. Trouble being, her memory wasn't what it used to be. Pink took the hint, dug into his pocket and came up with two fivers. Her eyes lit up, it was all coming back to her, yes, it was clear in her mind now. Pink handed her one of the fivers, called her a scheming old witch and told her she could have the other when she had given her evidence. Then he kissed her on the forehead and told her to fuck off to work before he reported her to the cops for trying to blackmail him. She cackled as if to prove she was indeed a witch and went on her way, whistling to herself through the gap in her front teeth.

Bea was in a good mood. Happy to see him of course, but there was something else. It didn't take her long to spill. Last night she went to the bingo with her mother and they won ninety quid between them. Now, they could afford to go and visit her aunt on the coast for a fortnight, would he miss her? Pink told her he would call for a bath when Jenny was in, she wasn't going with them to the coast, was she? Bea was in two minds now about taking the trip. She trusted her sister implicitly, but she wouldn't trust Pink as far as she could throw him.

Pink put her at ease, he was after a new flat since they were pulling his present accommodation down, he would be busy with that for a good while. She was to make sure she brought him back a stick of rock. With that settled, she made a fuss of him, taking up every position imaginable. Cheekily, at one point, he even had her on her sister's bed.

She spoiled him at the breakfast table too, rustling up as big a meal as he had faced in some considerable time. Looking at it, he couldn't make his mind up whether to eat it or climb it.

His scalp was almost dry when the knock came to the door. A neighbour was in hysterics, something wrong with her baby. Pink told Bea to go and have a look and to take her house keys with her, he would be getting off soon.

He dried his hair as best he could then ran the brush through it. Shit, today of all days he needed it in a plait. He couldn't risk leaving that flat for another day or someone would surely snap it up. With his hair tied back and stuffed down his collar, it looked like it was short, especially with the bob cap on.

Gathering up his hash and cash stash, he decided to try his luck anyway, nothing ventured and all that. Digging deep in his coat pocket he came up with an old wallet he had uncovered at the bottom of a drawer, it had been a long time since it saw any banknotes; not much point in carrying a wallet when you're on the dole. He transferred some of his winnings from the envelope to the wallet, then stuffed the rest down the front of his trousers to keep his hash company.

The girl behind the counter in the baker's shop didn't know what to make of him; she was Indian, and beautiful with it. All jet black hair, big brown eyes and full, kissable lips; nice figure, too. Pink asked about the flat upstairs, was it still available? She flashed him a huge smile and went through the back to the bakery, presumably to ask whoever was in charge.

The little man who appeared from the back of the shop had doubt written all over his face from the word go. Undeterred, Pink gave him what he hoped was his best, reassuring smile, extended his hand for the customary greeting and immediately engaged him in conversation.

How long had the shop been here? It had been some time since he was round these parts. He had been attracted by the wonderful aroma from the bakery and, reaching for his crammed wallet, was two months in advance sufficient to secure the lease on the flat?

Mr Rapati was on the back foot, basically charmed into showing him around the place; and what a place. It was spacious, clean and airy. Pink knew he was home as soon as he entered. Two doors between him and the outside world and room enough to swing a cat, not that he would subject Eight Ball to such torment, not unless he asked him nicely. Mr Rapati had a few words to say, mainly about no parties and stuff like that. He shook Pink by the hand, took his money from him and handed him the keys. Pink told him he would be taking up tenancy right away and by tomorrow, all his furniture would be moved in. Mr Rapati left him to it; any problems, he could be found downstairs at the bakery.

Pink sat at the breakfast bar, rustled a spliff together and planned how to arrange his furniture, such as it was. His bed consisted of two double mattresses, no bedstead, just the mattresses in good condition and comfortable, so they would be moving in. The coffee table was decent enough, too; he could leave the chairs, they were on their last legs, as was his stereo, he could buy second hand. The bathroom was big enough to house a bath, but only had a shower, not a problem, easier to keep clean. The bedroom was to the front and had built in, spacious wardrobes. A quiet neighbourhood like this, he wouldn't be disturbed. Already, he was thinking he had landed on his feet; yes, as of this moment he was home.

He stashed the drugs and most of his cash, plans for a moonlight flit taking shape as the minutes ticked by.

Transport, since he didn't want anyone to know where he was he would have to chance a visit to Doc Thistle's place. Doc's van had remained parked up on his drive since he was sectioned over a month ago. Trouble was, his woman had a thing about Pink and had never tried to hide it, not even from Doc. To be fair, Doc would never have recognised the signals she gave off, being at all times tripped out of his gourd on acid; the reason they eventually carted him off to the house on the hill. Two tabs a day will do that to a man. Pink had always assumed his woman did all the driving and was shocked to learn it was Doc. How the fuck he managed that while being so far out of his tree was a mystery, no one could explain it.

His luck was definitely holding. As he walked up the path to the house, Doc's so called best mate was swapping spit with his woman, right there on the doorstep for all to see. Pink had no qualms about confronting her now, they knew he had clocked them. Rizla, Doc's best mate, scurried up the path and away. Pink didn't even have to enter the premises, neither did he have to pay for the hire of the van. The guilty party handed him the keys and begged him to keep quiet about what he had witnessed.

The van wouldn't start. God alone knew how long it had been since anyone had bothered to turn the engine over. The drive was on a slope so Pink released the handbrake and bump started it in reverse. Thick black smoke belched from the exhaust as he revved the engine, but he didn't hang around long enough to taste it, he had too much to do and he wanted most of it done today.

Eight Ball wanted to know what the fuck was going on. The bed was stripped and the bedding bagged up and carted round the corner to the launderette, along with a bag of clothes gathered from here, there and everywhere in the house. Pink paid an old lady to take care of it for him, he would pick it up before closing time.

The van was clean inside. Doc used it for removals and suchlike, but never anything dirty such as roofing materials. Pink dragged both mattresses downstairs, slipped one along the inside wall of the van, put the television in next and made a sandwich of it with the other mattress. He didn't watch much telly, maybe the news or a decent documentary; sports, yes, some sports. Oh, and sight and sound in concert on a Saturday night prior to going round to the Albatross for the rock disco when he could scrape together the entrance fee. A chest of drawers, a battered old suitcase, the beanbag, coffee table, two lava lamps, the old battered sheepskin rug from in front of the fire and the stereo; should he take it? No, fuck the stereo, it was on its last legs and needed a good thump every now and then to remind it of its function in life. It was downright dangerous. Leave the fucker, let someone else get electrocuted; take the albums, though, they were his pride and joy.

Eight Ball had disappeared so he locked the van up and went to the shop for a local paper, see what was for sale. No sign of Eight Ball when he returned. He looked all over the house, spotting he had forgotten to take the wigmaker's dummy head he kept his spare bob cap on.

Three ads caught his eye. A bed settee, hardly used with matching easy chair, eight pounds or nearest offer, buyer collects. He circled that one and wrote the number large at the top of the page. He would be using a public phone-box. They all had lighting inside, but they didn't all work.

Next, one music centre, still in box, unwanted gift, any demonstration, twenty pounds; circled likewise. The last one was for separate components, no brand name and no reason for sale. Priced at eighty quid or nearest offer, it was a bit steep, he could easily afford it, but thought it a bit too extravagant. He circled it anyway and headed for the phone-box.

The bed settee was as the advert said, looked like new and light enough for him to manage it into the van on his own. The old man who sold it wanted it out of his way, the space it created would be just right for his new aquarium.

The music centre had never been used. Pink took it from the box, connected the speakers, plugged it in and ran through the radio stations. He didn't have any tapes, but he had a shit load of albums in the back of the van. The woman who was selling it seemed determined to give him her life's story. She had bought the thing for her ex, a birthday present. He hadn't known about it and had fucked off two days before he was due to be presented with it. Pink sympathised, told her to put the kettle on and nipped to the van for an album.

He asked was it ok if he rolled a joint and she didn't object, watching intently as his fingers flew all around the makings. She lit a cigarette and cocked an ear at the music centre. Who was singing she wanted to know? It was John Martyn's 'Solid Air' album, a long time favourite of Pink's. He hadn't chosen it for any particular reason, it was the first to come to hand, but half an hour later he was glad it had. Sonia, for that was her name, tried a smoke for the second time in her life; the first time she smoked dope it did nothing for her, but she asked Pink to roll another one, by which time side two was enjoying an airing. He knew what was on the cards now; she was thirty five, ten years older than him, but very well preserved. A little shy at first or maybe she was teasing him, but either way, they went at it like rabbits; no finesse, no fuss, just honest to goodness fucking. He told Sonia her ex must have a screw loose for leaving her like that and it was obviously what she needed to hear.

Pink thanked her for a good time, she thanked him for the smoke. In a further show of gratitude, she let him have the player for fifteen quid, a double result and no question.

He was in a hurry now, the launderette would be closing soon, he wanted to be rid of the area. His laundry and Eight Ball were all that was tying him to the old place now. Just in time, he caught the old lady about to lock his clean bedding and clothes up for the night.

To save time, he dumped his laundry on the passenger seat of the van and went to look for Eight Ball. The cat was playing hard to get. No amount of chee-chee-cheeing would bring him so Pink left him to work it out for himself. He didn't particularly want to come back round this way, but he would for Eight ball.

It took him an hour to empty the van and hump his worldly possessions up the stairs, having had to stop halfway through for a joint, he wasn't used to this physical shit. Another hour and a half of arranging and rearranging what furniture he had and the place looked and felt comfortable. One more joint and he would return for Eight ball, wait for him to show up if necessary; he was a cat, his curiosity would be sure to get the better of him soon enough.

The guy on the radio said it was time for the news at three a.m. Pink had been sitting there for two and a half hours and was not in the least bit amused. Luckily, he had left his old stereo there and plenty of ice in the gas meter, otherwise it would have been a long, cold night. He was just about to give up when Eight Ball crashed through the cat flap, turning back towards the door like something was chasing him. He didn't bother to look around the almost empty room, which told Pink he had been back while he was out.

Placing the old stereo against the cat flap, he decided he wanted the speakers from it and ripped the wires from their sockets. He would splice them to the speakers on the music centre, create a better effect. Transporting Eight Ball was his immediate problem. He tore one of the small kitchen curtains away from its rail, scooped the cat up before he knew what was going on and bound him up in it. He couldn't very well let him bounce all over the van, that would have given him big problems when it came time to introduce him to the new flat. As it was, Eight Ball didn't struggle and was still well and truly wrapped up when they reached their destination.

He wasn't tired now so he put a spliff together and set to work splicing the speaker wires together. Yes, good idea that, it definitely gave the music something extra, a better sound, more body and it filled the room perfectly. Eight Ball was restless, nothing he could do about that other than make a show of it being home for them now and hoping the cat would catch on quick. Finally, he settled. He wouldn't lie down, though; just sat there at the long, bare wall, but at least he was quiet.

Five fifty five according to the radio and Pink decided it was bedtime, then, a knock at the door; don't say someone had found him already? Mr Rapati was on the doorstep, welcoming him to his new flat and offering a basket of freshly baked goodies, he had spotted the light. Pink thanked him very much, thinking to himself his luck was definitely on the upturn.

CHAPTER 5

Well and truly bedded in

Pink showered, made a list while his hair was drying and decided to make further use of the van while he still had the keys. A run to the supermarket, fill the kitchen cupboards and the fridge, stop off for some blank cassettes, drop the van off and hole up at home for a session of well earned relaxation.

He wasn't gone above an hour and a half, but going by Eight Ball's attitude you'd think he'd been in orbit around the moon for a week. Talk about sulk. Even his favourite cat food couldn't bring him round. Pink didn't let it show he was the least bit bothered, telling him to eat it or starve, and to stop staring at that fucking wall.

He reversed the van onto the drive. The curtains twitched, but Doc's woman didn't bother coming to the door; embarrassment probably, so Pink posted the keys through the letter box.

Eight Ball finally relaxed when Pink kicked his shoes off and sat down to roll a joint. Jackson Browne's dulcet tones had him stretched out on his belly, paws out in front, but still facing that bare wall.

It was Friday, the weekend; he had made his mind up to put the socialising on the back burner for a while, which meant no rock disco at the Albatross. That's all he would miss, it was one of his favourite places. Many a time, with just enough in his pocket for a half pint of beer, he could enter the Albatross and get stoned from the atmosphere. That, combined with a clued up landlord who would flash the houselights whenever anyone who looked remotely like the drug squad showed up, made for a very pleasant evening indeed. Of course Pink's reputation for being able to put a joint together in a hailstorm ensured he would have more than the atmosphere to go at. People would hand him the makings and be rewarded with a swiftly rolled joint, minus the first two tokes as payment for the architect. The DJ, Brat, was a personal friend of Pink's and would lend him albums as well as providing the makings from time to time. Brat claimed to have worked as a disc jockey in Germany, that's where he picked up his nickname. A German with a sense of humour had picked up on his surname, Wurst, he could only be Brat after that, or before that, or .... you know what I mean.

Now, Pink was determined to adjust to the fact he could eat whenever he wanted, have a wash whenever he chose and generally suit himself as to what he did with his time. No one to answer to but Eight Ball, and then only when Eight ball was civil with him. Worked both ways.

A trip to the fridge found one of his large bottles of cider to be sufficiently chilled enough to partake of. Previous sessions on the stuff had often ended up with him in trouble, either for something he said, or did, or both. So, moderation was the answer, it wasn't his favourite tipple, but as a thirst quencher it couldn't be bettered. He had to drink it straight from the bottle, so, when he took up socialising again he would bring a few glasses home with him from the pub.

Whether it was the calorific value of the cider or the heat from the ovens downstairs, Pink had to change into his shorts after a while. Twenty minutes later he was stripped to the waist; not perspiring as such, but definitely warmer than he had been all winter.

Eight Ball only shifted himself to use the litter tray and to eat, checking between the two functions to make sure Pink hadn't abandoned him. He took up his position facing the wall again and had a catnap, ears twitching whenever Pink dared to change position in his chair either to reach for the makings or to make himself comfortable. All of this should have been covered by the noise coming from the speakers, but he was still highly suspicious.

Pink was high enough now to contemplate getting his head round the recording side of the new music centre. Tuning the radio to the most popular music station, he set about recording the odd song or two. After ten or twelve attempts he gave it up in frustration. It wasn't that he didn't have the know-how, more that the so called DJ spoiled his efforts by either talking over the beginning of the songs or the ending, or both. Verbal diarrhoea being the best way to describe it because this guy seemed to love the sound of his own voice. To compare notes, he scoured the stations until he came across one playing classical music; not his cup of tea, but the presenter treated it almost reverently, allowing both the beginning and the end to be heard uninterrupted, what a difference it made.

Pink didn't have a watch, or a clock for that matter. He played the tape back, one complete side of a C 120, which meant an hour's worth of recording. There was eleven songs on it at, say, three minutes per song, leaving twenty seven minutes of inane waffle. Who on earth cared a shite if the guy burned his fingers on his boiled eggs that morning, or that he was having his hair permed at the weekend? There was room for another nine songs in that hour; mind you, most of the songs Pink liked to listen to ran a good bit longer than three minutes, and all without interruption.

He kept it all to himself since Eight Ball was too engrossed in that wall to bear witness to his criticism. Pink didn't want to say it out loud, that would be too much like talking to himself. If he started with that, how long before he took to answering himself back?

Another spliff and a flick through his album collection, stopping at ' Solid Air' and remembering Sonia. Going to the blank tapes he had bought, he selected a C 90 and recorded the album onto one side. As the album played, he re-ran their romp in his mind; he would shove the tape through Sonia's letterbox, she would know who had left it.

Hunger, he hadn't eaten for a while and now he had the munchies. A mountain of hot buttered toast and another bottle of chilled cider had him feeling a whole lot better. Following that up with a well fashioned joint and the mellow sounds of Dan Fogelberg's 'Souvenirs', he couldn't think of anywhere else he wanted to be. His mind wandered back to Sonia, she had made a big impression, maybe she would like this album too? If it wasn't for the ten year age gap he could see himself getting very interested indeed. Surely, at thirty five, she was far too old?

CHAPTER 6

Fair exchange

Pink pricked up his ears. He had opened the bedroom window a crack in the middle of the night and now, the neighbourhood was being called to prayer. Deciding he would give it a miss, he stuck his head between two pillows and promptly went back to sleep. Some time later, Eight Ball made his presence felt, letting him know his food dish was empty; oh, and perhaps a drink, too.

The milk was off, he had left it out on the worktop and the rising heat had done the rest, time for a foray into Indian territory, locate the nearest shops.

Sneaking out while Eight Ball was eating seemed like a good plan, less hassle if the animal was unaware he had left the building.

The small row of shops had everything he needed; post office, chip shop, newsagent/grocery/off license, launderette and what looked like a bric-a-brac sort of second hand shop. All he needed was a newspaper and a pint of milk, but what he ended up with was two bars of chocolate, a daily paper, a music paper, the New Musical Express and his pint of milk. Walking past the second hand shop, he spied a box containing six pint glasses and decided to price them. It turned out the box of six was a box of four, or more accurately, a box of six with two missing. He haggled over the price and secured them for five pence each. An old pestle and mortar caught his eye and he stumped up fifty pence for that. On his way out, he spotted something that would be ideal for Eight Ball and added it to his haul. One little problem solved.

Mr Rapati was outside the shop when he strolled back and gave him a wave. Pink joined him for a chat, he liked the little man, not because as his landlord he had to keep him onside, more that he seemed a genuinely nice person. Mr Rapati asked had he settled in ok, did he have any problems, if so he was to go directly to him. What about bread, did he have enough bread?

Pink thought that was very kind of him, he just knew he was going to enjoy himself here, he passed a good ten minutes with the man, talking about his family, his business and the neighbourhood. A glance up at the bedroom window brought the conversation to a close, Eight Ball was giving the curtains a hard time of it, he would have to go to their rescue and make the room off limits while he wasn't on the premises.

He went upstairs, dumped the shopping, shooed Eight Ball from the bedroom and closed the door. Putting the milk in the fridge, he spotted the plate he had piled his toast onto last night, maybe he did need bread. A quick check and he was downstairs at the bakery where the lovely Mira, Mr Rapati's eldest daughter, was in charge of the shop. Flashing her bright white teeth at him, she took his basket and sorted him out with a couple of loaves and some biscuits. Pink wanted to hang around and chat, but the shop filled up suddenly and he had no choice but to abandon his plans to charm her.

Eight Ball made a bolt for freedom when he re-entered the flat, only escaping as far as the bottom door. Pink let him sit there and yowl until he was hoarse, turning the music volume up and closing the top door when it became over plaintive. The cat calmed down when he heard the top coming off the milk bottle, he didn't want to miss out on his cream. Pink stripped off, deciding he was in for the day, probably the next couple of days. A bowl of cereal followed by a quick tidy up of the kitchen and he was ready for the first joint of the morning. Putting his new pestle and mortar to work, he powdered a fair chunk of his hash, easily done with Leb gold as it was less compacted than most other brands.

Then he settled down with the paper, reading it from back to front, sports news first and rising to look for a pen when he came to the crossword. Ten minutes later he scanned the news and then the television page. Seven o'clock, sight 'n' sound in concert, Frankie Miller's Full house; essential viewing and listening, something to look forward to.

Eight Ball lapped up his cream then assumed his position facing the wall, that would be him for the day now that he'd calmed down a bit. Pink experimented with the tape recorder on the music centre, he wanted it just right so he didn't have to fiddle with it when the concert started; sight 'n' sound meaning it was broadcast simultaneously to the radio. A raging thirst sent him to the fridge for a bottle of cider and when he returned Eight Ball was rubbing himself all over the same part of the wall as before. Pink selected one of the gifts he had bought for him, a ping-pong ball, and threw it in the cat's direction. It missed by a whisker, but that was close enough for Eight Ball to do a backward somersault at the shock. Then, regaining his composure, attacking the ball with murder in his eyes, but at least it took his focus away from the wall. He soon tired of it and found his place in the middle of the floor. Pink gave up, he would soon grow out of it.

The New Musical Express was a mine of information, although just lately, Pink had noticed a lot of punk and glam rock outfits were finding their way on to the pages. Not really his cup of tea, but there was still enough of what did interest him to hold his attention. He completed the prize crossword and decided to enter the competition, see how his luck was holding out, telling himself he would learn to play the Fender Stratocaster if he won it. The closing date was the following Friday. He would post his entry on the Wednesday, that would put it towards the top of the pile and give him an altogether better chance of winning.

Time for sport on the telly, most of which he could watch with the sound down and play his own accompanying soundtrack.

Horseracing, athletics and tennis, he could easily follow these without the need for commentary. Rugby League, however, was a different kettle of fish; his favourite sport by a long, long way. From the first time he ever watched it he was hooked, with Wigan as his favourite team for no other reason than they were the first team he laid eyes on, quickly adopting them as his own. As luck would have it, Wigan were playing today, the third round of the Challenge cup, a mouthwatering tie against their local rivals and sworn enemy, St Helens. The commentary was essential for this particular event. For one, Pink wasn't quite up to speed with the rules, secondly, one Mr Eddie Waring, a man with a vast knowledge and enthusiasm for the sport and a penchant for throwing the odd spoonerism into the dialogue of his commentary.

A fresh joint and a fresh bottle of cider heralded the start of the athletics coverage, the heats for the womens two hundred. A big favourite with male viewers, Pink was sure a prerequisite for being a cameraman at these events was that he had to be some sort of a letch. Close ups of the ladies in the tiniest of shorts, cutting into their flesh like wet bikini bottoms with plenty of buttocks and front bumpers on show. Then of course the piece de resistance, a slow motion replay.

The game lived up to all of his expectations. Fast, furious action, a veritable mudbath, two mass brawls involving almost all twenty six players on the field and the narrowest of victories for his team. Eddie's observations were to die for. Pink was familiar with a number of the players names and field positions. Eddie spoke like he knew each and every one of them personally, passing on his great knowledge of the game to anyone who cared to listen. He didn't let Pink down with his spoonerisms either. The river Douglas runs past Wigan's Central Park ground and on one occasion the ball was punted over the stand and out of the ground. Eddie Waring, bless him, said. "He's kicked it into the Dougie riverless." Classic.

Pink also found a new use for the batch of ping-pong balls he had purchased for Eight Ball, hurling them at the telly when he disagreed with a refereeing decision since they did no harm to the telly and allowed him to vent his anger admirably.

A cup of coffee, a mountain of hot buttered toast, half a packet of chocolate digestives and a large spliff, it was time for Frankie Miller. Pink waited until the introductions had been made then pressed the record button on the tape, that way he would be sure to record the whole gig on one side of the C120. The only time he sat throughout the entire performance was to put a joint together. Eight Ball joined in at one point, allowing himself to be scooped up and waltzed around the room. He soon resumed his position again when Pink reeled dizzily and let him go back to what he was doing.

He rewound the tape to make sure it had recorded ok and ended up listening to the entire gig once more, pleased as Punch he had managed to do it properly.

He held a ping-pong ball ready to throw as Eight Ball approached the wall again. He stopped about a foot short of it this time, sat down and stared straight ahead, cocking his head from side to side like he did when Pink conversed with him; strange cat or what?

His dancing and air guitar frenzy had him all of a lather so he jumped in the shower to cool off, turning the music up a notch so it could be heard above the noise of the running water. Of course he knew every word of the Bob Seger album he was playing and felt compelled to sing along at the top of his lungs. When he turned the shower off, he could hear laughter coming from outside. With the bathroom window open to let the steam escape, he had inadvertently been serenading the girls downstairs in the bakery. Along with the laughter there was applause, maybe he could take it up for a living? He didn't bother to put clean shorts on when he had towelled himself dry; there was no point, no one could see him, only Eight Ball.

Searching through the radio stations, he came across the news at ten o'clock. The announcer told him a 'live' Reggae broadcast would follow the news, that had to be worth a couple of spliffs and another couple of notches on the volume control. The show wasn't live, definitely prerecorded, how else could they bleep out the random expletives employed by the bands to put their message across? Hugely enjoyable all the same. Pink made a note of one or two names, he would keep an eye out for them in the second hand record shop.

He could smell something, it wasn't bread. Curry, that was it, but from the same source as the bread; maybe Mr Rapati was branching out? It must have been nearly midnight, all the take away places would be closed by now and besides, he was sure there wasn't an Indian take away in the area. The aroma had him salivating so much he felt the need to investigate so pulled his jeans and a t-shirt on and followed his nose downstairs. The shop was closed so he went round to the back of the bakery. The back door was ajar and he stuck his head round, coming face to face with the night baker. Introducing himself, he asked was Mr Rapati knocking about, being given a negative response and the question as to why he wanted Mr Rapati. The baker was about Pink's age, his nostrils had picked up on something and his eyes fixed on the joint in Pink's hand. Pink mentioned the curry and the baker grinned, could he have a toke of that joint? In return, he would sort Pink out with a taste of his curry. The two started talking. The baker, Johan, was an Indian chef to trade. Nightshift at the bakery suited him as he could sign on the dole without suspicion and make a fair wage at the same time, helping towards his three or four trips to Goa every year.

Pink was impressed, surely Johan could bring some decent dope back with him?

He had tried it once. No problem smuggling it out of India, but sniffer dogs on this side of his trip caused him to lose his bottle and jettison his stash. It hadn't cost him much to purchase, but compared to what he could have sold it for here, he had lost a small fortune. He seemed like a decent guy so Pink suggested he should post the dope to himself, or to someone he trusted. It would have a fair chance of getting through, especially if wrapped within a consignment of Indian spices. The plan was hatched. Pink nipped upstairs for another joint and laid a chunk of his stash on Johan, who promised a batch of curry in thanks. The radio was playing in the bakery, just above the hum of the ovens and during the course of Johan's nightshift the pair became firm friends, finding they shared a liking for the same type of music, which is always a bonus.

Pink didn't hear the call to prayers that morning. The window was open same as yesterday, but he was dead to the world, even Eight Ball gave up on trying to rouse him.

A bowl of cereal, a couple of rounds of toast, orange juice and a large reefer, Pink was ready to accept whatever the day had to throw his way. Maybe another joint and a cup of coffee, just to be absolutely sure. Eight Ball made a move towards the wall, realised what was coming, turned, and saved the ping-pong ball like a goalkeeper diving for a penalty kick. He then chased the ball all over the living room in a rare flurry of activity, which had Pink highly amused for as long as it lasted. When he finally calmed down, he took up his favourite position facing the wall, thinking he was being clever by keeping the ball between his paws.

The athletics meet was into its second day with almost four hours of coverage on the telly. Pink replayed the concert from last night and settled down to watch the ladies work up a good sweat.

He found himself in the kitchen, standing in front of the open fridge door and wondering what the fuck he had come in for. Selecting a bottle of cider, he shrugged his shoulders and rejoined Eight Ball in the lounge. One joint later, he remembered what he had gone to the fridge for. He had two pork chops in the freezer compartment and had intended thawing them for his Sunday dinner. The television news told him it was six o'clock, then, a loud knock told him someone was at the door. He pulled a t-shirt over his head and padded downstairs, it was Johan, no, he wouldn't come in, one of the girls had come down with the flu and he had been asked to do the extra hours as cover. He gave Pink a full pan of chicken Madras and told him to call at the bakery later. Pink thanked him for the curry, what a stroke of luck, Sunday dinner would now be chicken Madras, mopped up with some of Mr Rapati's Roti bread. Bring it on.

There was too much for one sitting so he decanted some in to his own pan, put it to one side for tomorrow, or more likely his next attack of the munchies, and got stuck into the rest of it, delicious.

If he was warm before, the sweat was pumping out of him now. The cider did very little to cool him down and he vowed to purchase some rice as accompaniment to his curry at his earliest convenience; he liked it hot, but there was hot and there was hot.

He helped the Doobie Brothers take it to the streets while he was in the shower, drying himself again to as much rapturous applause as three people could muster. Even so, he laid the blame on Michael McDonald for a couple of bum notes halfway through the song.

Around midnight, he rolled a couple of joints and went down to see what Johan was up to. He let himself in the back door to the bakery just in time to catch the Indian building a joint with his back to the door. Placing his hand on Johan's shoulder, he yelled in his ear he was the police. Hard to believe a dark skinned man could turn so pale. A lesson Pink had learned a long, long, time ago; never skin up with your back to the door unless someone you can trust is keeping a lookout for you.

Regaining his breath and his colour, Johan eventually saw the funny side of it, accepting a ready rolled joint from Pink and allowing him to finish building the one he had been disturbed at.

Pink let him talk about his travels, he had been all around the globe from an early age. Having had the choice of becoming a fisherman like his father and uncles or going away to sea on the cruise liners with another uncle, he chose to travel. It was hard work, all the dirty jobs you could imagine and low wages; slave labour, in fact. They worked through an agency which took a chunk of their earnings, and had to supplement their meagre income by doing laundry and cleaning crew cabins for a couple of quid per week. All the same, they were relatively rich men whenever they landed back home because they worked all the hours God sent, didn't ever go ashore, and put all their hard earned in the bank. So, although it was true he was well travelled and had been twice around the world, he didn't actually get to see much of it. Pink confessed he didn't even own a passport and had never been above forty miles from home in his entire life; he did all his travelling in his head, mostly to outer space.

Between them, they concocted a plan to smuggle some heavy duty shit into the country, make an obscene amount of dosh by selling it off then Johan would show Pink around Goa. A place, he assured him, he could live like a millionaire; he wouldn't believe how far his money would go over there.

They talked until three in the morning, time for Johan to switch the ovens off, he would sleep now 'til half five, six o'clock when the boss turned up and took over. Most of what he had made would be shipped out to various outlets, Mr Rapati would then fire up the ovens again and bake for the neighbourhood." All day Fresh Bread" the sign in the shop window said.

About a dozen joints and six hours of chat, the two men felt they had known each other a lifetime; they knew instinctively they would make excellent business partners.

Pink slept until noon, the call to prayers went unheeded again. Eight Ball threw a tantrum, but failed to make an impression on him. Still, the evidence was there when he finally did surface. The NME had been well and truly shredded and the side of his new chair had been used as a scratch pad. As luck would have it, he had cut his competition entry out so no harm done there. Pink put it down to cabin fever and didn't even raise his voice to the bugger, merely letting him know in a calm, firm voice if he ever did it again he would sell him to a Chinaman.

If it wasn't for his trips to the dole and the shops, he would most likely suffer from cabin fever himself. He didn't know much about cats, only that they were notorious wanderers with some having the need to belong to more than one household. Pink was sure no one else would have Eight Ball, but he wasn't prepared to take the risk; he would hold him hostage for a while yet, then it would be up to the cat himself if he wanted to stay or not.

Mira was at the shop front when he came back from the dole. Because he had changed his address his cheque was handed over there and then. The post office was closed for lunch so he planned to cash his Giro in the morning. There was no rush for the money, but he reckoned if he let the Giros accumulate without cashing them, it might look a little suspicious to the benefits people. He offered to help Mira wash the large front window, slyly volunteering to hold the ladder steady, that way he could take in her aroma without arousing suspicion. While she washed, she told him she and the other girls liked his singing. She slinked down the ladder and into his arms, albeit with her back to him. She giggled when he didn't move and he told her she smelled wonderful, almost as good as her dad's baking. This earned him another giggle, along with one of her dazzling smiles. He took the ladder from her and washed the rest of the window himself. When he backed down the ladder, Mira didn't move this time; she whispered in his ear that he had a hole in the arse of his jeans. He asked how she was with a needle and cotton and she told him to take his jeans off, she would patch them for him, howling with laughter as he made a show of unbuckling his belt. She told him to to hand them in at the shop, he could pick them up tomorrow. She was puzzled as to how he knew the ladder belonged round the back of the shop and he explained he was friendly with Johan. Her dad thought a lot of Johan, treated him like the son he didn't have, but she and her two sisters had been warned off. Although her dad had taken on a lot of western ideals and traits, there was still a class or caste distinction which was somehow carried through the generations. Johan was of lesser class, decent as he might be he was off limits. Shame that, one of her sisters really fancied him.

He stole a kiss, only on her cheek, twice in the matter of a few hours he had witnessed a dark skinned person change colour as Mira blushed, adding further to her beauty.

Eight Ball gave out a growl as Pink did a quick change and headed for the door again, he was only gone for a matter of seconds this time, not long enough for Eight Ball to get up to any mischief.

As soon as he returned he stripped off, signalling his intention to stay at home so the cat relaxed and settled down to keep an eye on his wall.

He couldn't find any cartoons on the telly so he switched it off and concentrated on the music, giving his favourite blues album, Savoy Brown's 'Hellbound Train' a spin. With his air guitar very much in evidence, he soon whipped up a lather and the shower beckoned, he had never been so clean.

After his shower things became more relaxed to the accompaniment of J.J. Cale, then Jackson Browne; he was so laid back he was almost comatose. Only one way to wake himself up, 'Next', The Sensational Alex Harvey band, he could never play this album without first directing the stylus to 'The Faith Healer'. The hypnotic intro heralded the band onstage when he saw them live, a night he would never forget, a stunning performance mixing theatrics with raw, powerful rock music. So, 'The Faith Healer' it was, followed by the whole album and suddenly he was wide awake.

The rice mellowed the curry somewhat, or maybe his palate had become accustomed to the fire; either way, it was delicious. Eight Ball accepted a taste from his fingertip and skedaddled into the kitchen for a drink, he didn't come back for more.

Pink must have fallen asleep, the smell of curry was still lingering when he woke, then he realised it was different. Still curry, but a sweeter aroma. He dressed and went down to investigate, armed with a couple of spliffs. Johan was using the bakery to concoct another batch and teaspooned a small amount for Pink to sample. He wanted more, but was advised to let it stand for a day, he would appreciate the difference tomorrow. So, they shared a joint and chewed the fat. Pink learned how to control the ovens and blended the ingredients for a batch of bread, expressing surprise at how precise it all had to be. Now, he was yawning his head off. He sparked up his other spliff, shared it with his friend and retired from the fray, a large freshly baked loaf tucked firmly under his arm. All that air guitar play had taken it's toll on him.

CHAPTER 7

A black promise

Pink cashed his Giro at the post office, bought a paper and had a mooch round the bric-a-brac shop. Some old battered albums caught his eye and he had a rummage through them. One or two would have been worth a spin, but they hadn't been looked after, visible scratches rendering them unplayable. Asking the lady who ran the shop to keep any further albums to one side for his inspection, he headed for the door and was distracted by a drinks tray emblazoned with the Guinness logo, just the job for keeping his makings all in one place with the added bonus of a lip to prevent spillage. The tray and a matching ashtray, the type used in pubs, cost him twenty five pence, a bargain.

He called at the bakery to see if Mira had sewn his jeans, that, and to have another look at her being as she was so pleasant on the eye. She was busy, but found the time to shout through to the back of the shop. A younger girl, who could only have been her sister, brought out his jeans in a carrier bag and passed them over the counter. She wasn't quite as pretty as her sister, but pretty all the same. Pink thanked her, watched her turn back to the rear of the shop, blew Mira a kiss and was rewarded with that wonderful smile which lit up both her face and the shop at the same time.

Eight Ball hadn't moved, he was still staring at the wall and only left it to weave in and out of Pink's legs as he opened his cat food. While Eight Ball cleaned his plate, Pink inspected Mira's efforts as a seamstress, laughing out loud when he took the jeans from the bag. The patch was perfectly sewn, Mira had used a piece of pink denim to conceal the hole. She had also washed and ironed his jeans for him

He tried them on, no mirror, there was one at the shop near the post office and he made a mental note to haggle for it tomorrow. Nothing to do but go down and let Mira have a look. The shop was busy again, but she indicated he should go round to the back door and joined him a few minutes later. He thanked her and told her if he could ever do anything for her, she shouldn't hesitate to ask, he emphasized his offer of *anything*. Mira inspected her work, he felt sure she was doing so only as an excuse to fondle his backside, but not one word of complaint left his lips. She had to go back to work. Pink stole another kiss and this time she turned her full, soft lips towards him. It was only a peck, but it set his pulse racing, along with his imagination.

Building his first joint of the day, he ran it through his head just what he would like to do to Mira. Bearing in mind he hadn't been with a woman since moving in, not necessarily a long time by his standards, but in light of his more recent track record, long enough.

Eight Ball padded in, crouched facing his wall and gave himself a good wash. Pink thought of asking him why, he certainly wasn't going out. After his wash he chased a ping-pong ball round the living room floor, probably keeping his eye in for when he could go hunting again. Pink set another spliff going and relaxed back to watch the fun.

Eventually, Eight Ball tired of his game and settled down to his sentry duty. Pink picked through his record collection, coming up with an album he only ever played when there was acid around. The album was 'First Utterance', by a band called Comus; the blurb on the back said it was folk music. Pink understood folk music to mean someone standing with his hand cupped to his ear, singing to little

60

more than a foot tap. This Comus might have had such a person involved, but the accompaniment was like something out of Bedlam. He gave it a spin, remembering with relish the looks on his fellow trippers' faces as they wondered just what the fuck they were being subjected to. There was fear on show; abject horror would have been nearer the mark, and relief when it was all over. One or two actually fled the scene and weren't heard of for weeks.

Halfway through side two, Eight Ball tried to run up his wall. If Pink had been tripping he would most likely have tried to follow him. As it was, he threw another ball at him and watched again as he batted it around the room; this was easily better than the cartoons on the telly.

The pork chops had been stuck together when he released them from the freezer. He bent one knife trying to separate them so he decided to eat both. Spuds, carrots, peas and a fried onion made up the rest of his meal, he was living very well now. When he was poor, he went for days without food if he couldn't manage to knock on the right door at the right time. Now, he could see his way clear to cut a generous piece from one of the chops and leave it on Eight Ball's plate as a treat; how times change.

A bottle of cider and a spliff, a single skin spliff; he would only build bigger if there was someone to share it with, otherwise it would burn away in the ashtray if he was distracted.

Feeling a little drowsy after his feed, he looked out some wake up music, allowing Dr Feelgood to take over the turntable for a while and giving Wilco Johnson a run for his money on the air guitar.

His exertions ended with him in the shower again, substituting the air guitar for a back-scrubber, a fair imitation of a microphone and giving Fogelberg some back up on 'Souvenirs'. He barely heard the applause, the volume was set as high as it would go.

The outside temperature hadn't risen above freezing all day; yet here he was, comfortably warm in a pair of shorts, the only chill he felt was when he put the tray on his knee to roll a joint. He could put up with that.

Eight Ball had his hackles up, still facing the wall but growling like a dog, a deep, throaty rasp ending in a high pitched yowl. Pink turned the volume up again, he had no wish to listen to that cacophony, no wish whatsoever. The animal quietened down after a few minutes, but Pink noticed he had edged about eighteen inches closer to his wall. Best to ignore him.

Putting off an attack of the munchies wasn't easy, but he contented himself with the knowledge it would soon be supper time. Johan's curry had stood for the obligatory day. A listen to side one of Boz Scaggs' 'Silk Degrees' and he would dress to eat.

While the music filled the room he built a couple of joints, found a t-shirt and pulled on his newly patched jeans. Eight Ball threw him a disapproving glance and went back to his study. He knew there was no point in protesting, it wouldn't do him any good.

The first two spoonfuls brought his palate to life, coconut based and not as spicy as the Madras. When he shovelled the third spoonful in he couldn't feel his tongue. Worse than that, one side of his face was numb. Johan laughed, signalled for him to take his time and stopped him from drinking from his bottle of cider. After a few seconds his taste buds sorted themselves out and it seemed he could sense all the flavours as the lamb melted in his mouth. Using fresh baked naan bread to clean the bowl, he heaped praise on his friend. Johan refused to give any hints as to the recipe, only saying the cider would have spoiled the sensation. They shared the cider and a spliff then set about mixing the ingredients for another bake, stopping just long enough for Johan to accompany Carlos (see how long I can hold this note for) Santana on the radio with a fine display of air guitar virtuosity.

Pink let Johan fire up the other spliff and ran upstairs for another bottle of cider, his friend had been promised some best black for today, but his supplier hadn't materialised. He promised to chase it up when he finished work and Pink offered to split the cost with him. It was decided he would order twice as much, there hadn't been any black in circulation for quite some time. Needless to say neither of them would be running around telling the world they had some.

Paki black, to give its proper street name, was the hash of choice for the majority of smokers, but only if you were prepared to be laid low. With most other forms of the drug you could get about, do shit, function. With good black, best Paki black, you had no choice but to make yourself comfortable and let it wash all over you for as long as it lasted. Many a time, in a room full of people stoned on Paki black, not one of them could find the wherewithal to turn the record over, sitting in silence until either someone mustered up the energy or until someone who wasn't stoned entered the room. That same someone was instantly nominated to get the next joint on the go, but only after he or she had done the honours with the music.

Pink mixed the next batch as Johan emptied the ovens, he was yawning his head off, time to call it a night. Johan handed him tomorrow's dinner, reminded him to eat it slowly and not to have a drink with it.

When he opened the top door, Eight Ball shot between his legs and galloped downstairs, only to find the bottom door locked; he came back up straight away, a look of dejection on his face.

Pink dreamed of sharing a huge spliff with every woman he had ever known. Surprisingly, they were all happy to see him. He put it down to the fact that he had come up with the goods, everyone was happy when there was a joint of black on the go. Even Eight Ball was smiling, grinning like a Cheshire cat. The harmony didn't last long, half of the women turned into witches and Eight Ball sided with them. Pink woke up in a sweat just before they finished casting their spell, he would have to keep out of certain ladies' way and he would be keeping a close eye on that fucking cat, too.

The mirror was more awkward than heavy, full length and with a stand so it could could swivel. He left the stand in the shop saying he would pick it up tomorrow and humped the mirror the five hundred or so yards home. The winter sun was hanging low in the sky and he almost blinded a lorry driver, forcing him to slam on his brakes as the mirror reflected the sun into his eyes. A young Asian lady at the bus stop was checking her make up using a little compact mirror. Pink tapped her on the shoulder and had her doubled up with laughter when he offered to let her view the bigger picture. Unfortunately, her bus came before he could get properly acquainted, but he was glad for the chance to be of assistance.

Eight Ball liked the look of himself and Pink thought he had managed to deflect his attention from the wall. Sadly, that didn't turn out to be the case because five minutes later he was back in his usual spot. Pink moved the mirror to the bedroom.

Two joints, half a bottle of cider, an hour's air guitar practice and he was ready for his afternoon nap. He must have needed it because when Eight Ball landed on him it was dark. The lava lamps didn't throw out much light, but through years of practice he could have skinned up in a coal mine. In under a minute he had another spliff on the go.

With no idea of the time he put the radio on. The announcer said the next news would be at nine o'clock, which would make it just after eight. He put his curry on a low light, selected some wake up music and threw a couple of joints together for later. The food was out of this world, Johan could certainly put a curry together; it had been a fair portion, but it left him wanting more. Not greed as such, more appreciation; yes, that was it, appreciation.

He knew Johan had scored as soon as he laid eyes on him, his eyes were at the back of his head. He had to tell Mira he had a bit of a head cold as an excuse for his appearance. His source could only come up with the original amount ordered, that's how scarce the stuff was. Johan tossed the small foil wrapped wedge to Pink and told him to split it in two, he had promised to share and that's what he would do. Pink ran the black under his nose, his face giving out signs of approval, there was real strength here. Johan backed his instincts up by telling him to go easy with it, describing it as potent; very, very potent.

Pink had to smoke the single skinner by himself, Johan confessing he wouldn't get any work done if he were to join him. Almost immediately, Pink could see what he meant, sinking into the chair by the radio and watching his friend go about his business in slow motion. This was good shit, top class shit; no word of a lie, no shit.

There was little or no conversation. Johan took rest on the chair in the opposite corner and cried with laughter as Pink tried to struggle to his feet when Wishbone Ash let rip on the radio. Giving it up as a bad job, he contented himself by moving his head to the groove, making a mental note to look out his copy of 'Argus' when he went home.

A full hour later, he shared a joint of the Leb with Johan and even managed to empty a couple of ovens for him.

Three o'clock, he went to bed. He remembered to look out his copy of 'Argus', but left it ready to play in the morning; a second single skinner of black had knocked him for six.

Eight Ball joined him on the bed, his vigil at the wall over for another day. The loud purring lulled Pink to sleep, a sleep which brought with it the same dream and the wake up at the same point. He didn't know what to make of it, a recurring dream, he would ask Bea's mum next time he dropped on her; witches knew about these things.

CHAPTER 8

Stranger Eight Ball

Pink found a set of compasses on his way to post the competition entry, must have fallen from some kid's schoolbag. He bought a paper and a pint of milk then collected the stand for his mirror.

Mira caught up with him, she had escaped from the shop for an hour, but only so she could visit the dentist. She opened wide to show him the filling and he became instantly aroused, he could get lost in that beautiful orifice; only a matter of time, he told himself. Mr Rapati wouldn't be too chuffed, but he and Mira would. He let her carry the stand for him; after all, it was a mirror stand.

Breakfast cereal at one in the afternoon, nothing wrong with that, he could have it for supper if he so wished. Eight Ball got the top of the milk by demand, prowling round it and having a good sniff before imbibing, ultra suspicious since the incident with the curry.

Pink let the radio play while he put a joint together, a cocktail with equal amounts of black and Leb. Suitably stoned, he gave 'Argus' the full volume treatment. Between tracks he could hear Eight Ball yowling and jaberring to himself, or to the wall. It had come to something when a cat starts talking to himself; maybe it was the effects of the dope, then again, it could be the cabin fever.

The days began to meld into one until Pink no longer knew where he was in the week without consulting the newspaper or someone he met in the street. Eight Ball's behaviour became stranger and stranger, inching ever closer to the wall and yowling for hours on end. Pink continued to flirt with Mira when he wasn't out of his tree. The dream came at least three times over the next week and he always woke at the same point. That was it, he was alive to the world, he wouldn't go back to sleep in case the dream picked up where it left off. He was definitely going to consult the witch about that. He had never been one for remembering his dreams before, very seldom anyway.

The woman in the bric-a-brac shop gave him a shout one day. Someone had landed fifteen albums on her, did he want to have a look? Two caught his attention. He had never heard of them, but one album title looked interesting and he bought them on sale or return. Five bob each wasn't about to break the bank, but he had been frugal with his money when he was poor and old habits died hard. The albums sat in a corner until he was well and truly out of his head on cocktails of black and Leb. The title which had took his attention was 'In one eye and out the other' by the Cate Brothers; the other album was by the same outfit and self titled. On that was a picture of two men, obviously brothers, stocky, muscular arms folded. They looked like a couple of night club bouncers, definitely not musicians. Pink didn't really know what to expect, certainly not what he heard. They sang and harmonised like angels, looks can be so deceiving. Their music was a delightful blend of soul, funk, blues and rock, unlike anything he had ever heard. He played both albums until he knew them intimately, someone's loss was definitely his gain. He put them on a tape for Johan, no names nor song titles. Johan reported back two nights later demanding to know everything Pink knew about them, remarking, when shown the album covers, that those two bruisers couldn't be responsible for such enchanting music.

Pink missed one night in the bakery, sitting on the toilet all night with a severe dose of the shits. Something he had eaten, but he couldn't say to Johan, just in case it had been one of his curries. He told him he had slept round the clock which was why he was a no show. Johan told him it was the longest night he had spent in the bakery for some time.

One night, Pink left the butter out of the fridge and the temperature in the flat caused it to melt. He was almost to the end of his tether with Eight Ball, the cat was getting on his tits with his odd behaviour. By then he was no more than two feet away from his favourite wall and talking non stop. Pink scooped him up, coated the pads of his paws with butter, another old wives tale; the cat should remember where his home was when this was done according to the folklore. He then fed him through the kitchen window. He settled down to watch a play on the telly, but couldn't concentrate, hoping the butter treatment would work. He needn't have worried, as soon as the play was over Eight Ball scrambled in through the window, checked all was as it should be and clambered back out again. That was the script for the next twenty four hours or so, in and out like a fiddler's elbow, checking nothing had changed. Pink thought he had conned him when he went down to see Johan, closing the bedroom door and leaving the radio on, but Eight Ball was perched on the low roof of the bakery and let him know he had been sussed. Hopefully things would settle down now, Eight Ball would go out on the prowl, check out the local talent and forget about that fucking wall. Not so. When Pink came home from the bakery the cat had taken up position again, closer than before, he didn't even bother to look up when Pink returned; that's when the decision to paint the wall became a definite.

Three quarters of a tub of magnolia would fit the job perfectly. The woman in the second hand shop found him an old roller and a small brush for the fine lining along the skirting board and ceiling. Eight Ball was curious, Pink waited for him to disappear and closed the kitchen door to prevent himself from being disturbed. The wallpaper was flat, not embossed. Pink spread some old newspaper along the length of the wall and got stuck into the job at hand. It soon became apparent he would need two coats to cover it and he was sorry now he'd started.

It looked an absolute mess after coat one. He opened all windows and doors except for the kitchen, changed the record and rolled a joint of Leb while he waited for it to dry.

One joint led to another, he was aware of Eight Ball talking to himself in the kitchen, but refused to let him in, determined the wall would be completely different when he next saw it.

The second coat covered the wall to his satisfaction. He left the papers down, sheer laziness, he had one joint of black left and now was the time to set it alight.

No sooner had he fired it up than there was a knock on the front door, the postman, second delivery. Whatever it was it certainly wasn't a guitar, more the shape and size of an album.

A compilation, runner's up prize in the NME competition and only three hundred copies pressed. Pink hadn't heard tell of some of the artists, but it was free so he gave it a spin and sat back to finish his joint. It wasn't half bad. One of the songs stood out above the others and he realised it was from his only other success in the same crossword competition. He hadn't played it for a while and was afraid it might have gone AWOL like so many others. He was mightily relieved when it came to hand quite readily as he rifled through his collection. So it was that Graham Parker and the Rumour were afforded the next slot on the music centre. He had reasoned it to be more punk rock than anything else when he won it, but soon came to realise it was something else, social commentary being his best explanation and now a big favourite.

He found himself staring at the wall now. He wasn't happy with it, he decided, too plain. He would see what Eight Ball made of it. One thing was certain, he couldn't very well put it back to the way it was.

Eight Ball came in and gave his verdict, the only difference to him was the newspaper spread along the base of the wall where Pink had left it. He padded to the edge of the paper and took up where he left off, staring and mewling at the wall. Now, Pink didn't know what to make of it. Eight Ball had all the freedom he could wish for, but still came up with the same strange behaviour, stranger if anything. Also, his new habit of bursting in between tracks made Pink jump out of his skin on more than one occasion, he was sure the animal knew what he was doing.

He left the paper where it was and went to see Johan, the black was finished, maybe he could score another lump from the same source. No joy, the Leb wasn't doing much for him now, time for some dope hunting, he would have an early night and call on Donny around noon. Eight Ball knew where he lived now and Pink was getting increasingly horny. Bea's house would be his first port of call, she should be back from the seaside by now.

The dream came again and he woke at the same place, just in time to hear the call to prayers. Eight Ball had joined him on the bed when he retired, but there was no sign of him now. Pink went for a piss and saw the cat in front of the wall; this was doing his head in, he was determined to get to the bottom of it.

He went close to Sonia's house on his way to Bea's so he looked out the tape he had recorded for her and shoved it through her letterbox, she would know who had left it.

Bea's mother, the witch, crossed the main road above the cop shop so he knew she was home. The key wasn't where it should have been so he gave the door his best policeman's knock. Bea appeared a minute later and he fondled her backside as he followed her upstairs. At the top of the stairs, she started to speak, but Pink covered her mouth with his own and steered her towards the bed. Since it had been a while, it didn't take him long to take care of business. Bea saw her chance and found her voice. What she had been about to say before she had been set upon was that she had met someone while on holiday. Searching Pink's face for clues as she related her tale, it seemed the guy was very keen on her, very keen indeed. Not only that, she was quite taken with him, they had spent a lot of time together and she was thinking of moving to the coast to be with him.

Ideally, she would like to hear Pink's views on it, if he had any that was.

By this time she was running his bath, force of habit, telling him to jump in so she could wash his hair. Pink took both her hands in his and looked deep into her eyes. He would be sad to see her go, he wished her every happiness, he hoped this new dude would look after her. He could never promise her more than what they had now, so yes, she should grab it with both hands and have a stab at it. Just one thing, could he have a blow job for old time's sake?

Bea thought he was joking, but he wasn't. She obliged him this one last time, allowing him to come all over her tits, she knew he liked that. They had a bath together then she plaited his hair and cooked him his favourite breakfast, thanking him for his kind words and his understanding. After breakfast he went upstairs to use the toilet and slipped a piece of the Leb under Jenny's pillow, sort of like a calling card, she would know he was thinking of her.

Smoking a joint with his second mug of coffee, he asked Bea what her exact plans were and more about her new boyfriend. Not that he was particularly interested, merely making small talk while he finished the joint, no point advertising he was carrying as he made his way through the streets. He kissed Bea goodbye and wished her all the very best for the future, he really meant it, she knew when he was being sincere.

There was a spring to his step as he bowled along the road until he heard his name being called, a female voice which could have been a good thing, it could also have been a bad thing.

Sonia, standing on her front doorstep and waving like someone demented. She all but dragged him into the house, thanking him for the tape and asking him could she please have another taste of his drugs. Pink was in no particular hurry to get to Donny's, happy to oblige her in fact and quietly delighted to see her. The kettle was on, which meant he was staying, Sonia remembered how he liked it and one joint later she remembered how he liked a lot of things. She played her new tape while they went at it, telling him she would think of him every time she played it in the future. He thought better of letting her know he would do the same, had already done so truth be told. She wanted to know where he hung out and he saw no harm in telling her about the Albatross.

Back on the street, he argued with himself. Did two goes with Bea and one with Sonia count as another hat trick? The debate was up in the air, maybe he could ask a few opinions; without, of course, mentioning any names.

His business successfully concluded at Donny's, he let himself out of the back door. A car horn sounded as he rounded into the street. Cowboy, Donny's older brother, a painter and decorator to trade and a damn fine one at that. Pink walked back to where Cowboy had parked up, shook the man's hand and scored a two week tenure in his employ. Out of town, cash in hand and, knowing Cowboy as he did, he wouldn't need to bring his own dope to the party. Arrangements were made, ten o'clock start, overalls provided, they would see each other in the morning.

Another car horn, passing the cop shop this time. Pink thought his number was up until he recognised Louise, the policewoman, and in her own car at that. Why hadn't he called her? Pink explained he had just moved in to a new flat and had been decorating non stop. Changing the subject rather deftly, he told Louise she looked tired. She agreed, night shift then overtime can do that to a girl. Pink suggested she could do with a massage to relax her and found himself in the passenger seat being whisked towards her house, wherever that might be. He ducked below the dashboard once or twice on the way, not one of his peers would look upon it as fucking a policewoman, more like fraternizing with the enemy. Pillow talk could be held responsible for a whole lot of jail time over the years.

Louise didn't object to a relaxing joint before her massage. Pink insisted she should keep her regulation stockings and suspender belt on as he administered his special brand of treatment. Her handcuffs came into play at one point, she loved that, she loved everything he did to her. After she had cooked them a snack and smoked another couple of joints, she let him fuck her in full police uniform. The skirt was a bit tight around his waist, but the blouse fitted perfectly, it was the highlight of his day, his week, his month, his year. Fuck it, it was the highlight of his entire life so far; two hours to be remembered and stored forever.

He was relieved to see Louise was in her civvies when it came time to drop him off at the end of his street, it wouldn't have looked good otherwise. She let him walk about a hundred yards then pipped her horn. There she was, a policewoman, waving a lump of dope out of her car window for all the world to see. He jogged back, collected his hash, stuck his head through the window and put the lips on her.

He worked alongside Johan until half past midnight, thinking he had better try for some shuteye, it was work in the morning. He left a note for Mira to give him a knock about nine o'clock in case he overslept.

CHAPTER 9

Search me

Pink managed to catch the eight o'clock news on the radio, it was going to be a long day; a bowl of porridge would keep him going, give him the energy to work through it. After breakfast he went down to the bakery to let Mira know he was knocking about. She had something for him, an alarm clock of the wind up type. He hated clocks. Not clocks as such, more what they represented, being tied to time, something he hated more than anything. Mira told him she didn't mind waking him up, but sometimes she could be mowed out at that time of the day in the shop. Pink thanked her, thinking he should get her a key cut, then she could give him a shake every morning, halfway down. The thought made him horny; he threw her a wink, blew her a kiss, thanked her again and carried her beautiful smile with him for the remainder of the day.

Cowboy picked him up as arranged. He had been saved a seat in the front of the van, the reason becoming immediately obvious when he was passed a tobacco tin containing a lump of moroccan, tailor made cigarettes and a packet of skins. Of the three dudes riding in the back, Pink knew one of them, Ronnie, very well. Another, Patrick, he knew to nod to and he had never met Skip before. In the front, sandwiched between Cowboy and himself was Bongo, Cowboy's right hand man. Pink took two tokes out of the first joint and passed it to Cowboy, three tokes from the second and passed it back to Skip, who was nearest to him. Forty minutes later they turned into a huge mill and Pink wondered what he had taken on.

Cowboy explained it had been converted to a catalogue goods depot and their job was to paint the inside from top to bottom. Two gangs of three were formed. Pink stepped into his overalls and set about emptying the van of paint and equipment, brushes, rollers and dustsheets. He had Skip pegged as a lazy bastard from the word go since he stood and watched as the others got stuck in to the unloading, maybe he had never been on a big job before? He would keep an eye on that situation, probably have a word with him at an appropriate moment. There were lifts and it was decided to work from top to bottom, Pink's suggestion. That way they had less chance of fucking up their work as they went along. Cowboy agreed, four levels, a gang of three on each of the the top two levels to start with, the mill's staff would be kept out of their way so they could hammer on with it.

Pink, being the shortest, was volunteered for the ceilings, he could clamber onto the top of the shelving, use a roller fixed to a pole and throw emulsion to his heart's content. While he was up there he could gloss the top sections of the metal columns which held the building together, easy peasy. Half an hour into the job he could have kicked himself, he had missed a golden opportunity; not a word to his colleagues, but he wouldn't be making the same mistake tomorrow. He was getting a good rhythm going, sending Bongo for the plank he had spotted in the back of the van and using it to bridge the gap between the racks of shelves. When Bongo disappeared, Skip downed tools, sat on his arse and took on a vacant look. The streak of lavender paint Pink deposited on his head actually suited him. The lazy bastard rubbed at it vigorously with a rag and promptly sat back down again, jumping like a scalded cat when Bongo returned with the plank. Bongo had him sussed and threw Pink a wink as he passed the plank to him. A betting man would put a lot of money on Skip being redundant the following day. These jobs ran to a tight schedule and one bad apple could play havoc with the profit margins.

Pink would be paid no matter what, but he didn't like to see Cowboy being shit on. Cowboy had come up with a few soul saving jobs for him in the past, he wouldn't find it necessary to say anything this time knowing Bongo had it all in hand, but if the need had arisen, he would have opened his mouth.

Lunchtime and Pink was so far ahead of his colleagues on the floor he decided he would back up a bit and gloss the columns, let them catch up. Cowboy came round taking orders for the chip shop and handing Pink the makings. He would be back in fifteen minutes, would Pink do the honours and fashion a couple of joints?

What people didn't realise, whether it was in the pub or in company or like now at work, the skinner up gets more stoned than anyone else, and not by clever placement of the drug when adding it to the joint. Consider the facts. Burn the dope to soften it for crumbling, spread it along the prepared canvas and, what to do with the residue on the fingers? Sacrilege to wipe it on one's jeans or overalls, sacrilege to even consider washing it off so straight into the mouth, lick it off. If it's stubborn, scrape it off with the teeth; either way, ingest it and end up twice as high as anyone else.

The food helped accelerate the dope through their collective bloodstreams. Skip looked like he was ready for a kip when Cowboy rose to his feet and declared lunchtime was well and truly over, the odds against him catching the van in the morning were shortening by the second. Half an hour later the book was closed, no more bets please. Skip had washed his hands of the job, realising what the rest of the gang were already aware of, he and hard work just didn't mix. Cowboy paid him for half a day and told him to catch a fucking bus when he had the temerity to ask for a lift home.

The day seemed to go a lot faster in Skip's absence, the gang of two covering just as much of the mill's surfaces as the gang of three one floor below. Pink suggested a couple of names for the next day's play and left it with Cowboy to decide.

He knew he had done a day's work when he landed home, muscles he didn't even know he owned were aching and crying out for rest. If Mira had called round and begged him to fuck her he would have told her where to get off. Then again, that was never going to happen, was it?

A big feed and a couple of joints eased his pains. Eight Ball must have missed him because he prowled around the kitchen, talking nine to the dozen while circling underfoot as Pink prepared both their meals. As soon as he had been fed he was back to his old self and back to his wall; must have been a case of cupboard love.

Pink made it to the couch after his meal, put the hour long Frankie Miller tape on and stretched out with a large spliff. He managed to finish the spliff, but not the tape, the tape played on as he snored his head off.

It was dark o'clock when he woke, but then, the skies had been darkening when Cowboy dropped him off. The flat was silent, only the low hum of the ovens, that and the sound of hiccups, did cats suffer from hiccups? Must do. There was just the two of them in the room and he certainly didn't have hiccups. He rolled off the couch and struggled to his feet, put the radio on to find an idea of the time then remembered the clock Mira had given him.

Wait a minute, wait a goddamn fucking minute. Eight Ball wasn't at his station. A quick search told him he wasn't anywhere in the flat, so who the hell had been hiccupping? Must have imagined it. The clock said ten forty five, that was a good sleep; and no dream, excellent.

He blended a bit of Cowboy's rocky with his own Leb and built a couple of joints to cover his part shift in the bakery. People sneered at rocky, or Moroccan to give its full name, but it had always been a good standby, enabling one to do shit and be stoned at the same time. Cowboy had kindly donated some in thanks for Pink's efforts on the work front. He knew he was guaranteed a good day's work out of Pink.

Eight Ball was on the bakery roof with no sign of having hiccups. Johan was out at the dustbins and spotted the cat. He was just about to shoo him away when Pink appeared and stopped him, explaining he was a friend of his, besides, he would keep the vermin to a minimum.

Johan was beside himself, more animated than usual. Obviously, something had occurred and he couldn't wait to relate whatever it was to his friend. Pink calmed him down and drew the information from him. He had only gone and secured a date with his boss's middle daughter. What did Pink think about that?

Pink shook the man's hand, telling him he wouldn't let on to his good friend Mr Rapati as long as he was given a blow by blow account of the date. Johan asked how his day's graft went and advised the intake of a couple of bananas for the aches and pains, something in the bananas administered to muscle pain.

Eight Ball must have heard his master's voice and came strolling into the bakery, bold as you like. Johan made a fuss of him, and to Pink's surprise the animal stood there and let him. Johan had the royal seal of approval, or the feline equivalent.

The dream left him alone that night; he was spark out as soon as his head hit the pillow, possibly before then truth be told. Not even the new sound of the ticking clock registered as he put some zeds in.

Different scenario at eight o'clock the next morning. He was on his feet like a boxer starting a round, standing in the middle of the bedroom floor with his dukes up and wondering what the fuck was going on. Since he'd had a three hours or more nap after his evening meal, he only went to bed at about three-ish. Surprisingly, he felt quite refreshed, still aching, but it was a good ache, an honest ache.

He needed milk and nipped down to the shops, helping himself to a couple of dozen plastic carrier bags and winking at the woman behind the counter, she was used to him by now and didn't question his motives as she watched him stuff them into the same bag as his milk.

Cowboy was late and Pink was freezing. He knew from going to the shops it was a cold morning, but owing to what he had observed the previous day, all he was wearing was his overalls and an old pair of trainers, he was naked underneath. Draped around his neck in the style of a kid carrying his football boots was another old pair of trainers.

The van turned up at long last. Pink was frozen to the marrow by this time and was glad of the heat in the front seat when he clambered in. He had rolled two large joints after breakfast and lit them both from the same match. One of them he passed to Cowboy in the driver's seat, the other, he took three tokes from and passed it behind him to the back of the van.

A familiar voice thanked him and he grinned when he heard it. Everyone had said their good mornings at the same time, which was why he didn't hear it earlier, but he recognized it right away now. Mad Frank, a very good friend and well named, probably the best shoplifter in the northern hemisphere and stories of his prowess were legendary. Pink's favourite involved him personally. He had been scoring out of town one day and was walking past Woolworths when he heard his name being called. Mad Frank exited the shop, a music centre under his arm, and motioned for Pink to follow him down a side alley. Frank then left him to look after his haul, returning five minutes later with a speaker under each arm; cool wasn't in it. His name wasn't Frank, but that was what he answered to, Mad Frank.

So, he thanked Pink for the joint and for putting a good word in for him about the job. One of the security guards opened the back doors for them and Pink engaged him in conversation, offering him a sniff of the old trainers he had hanging round his neck. The guard reared back like someone had poleaxed him and the rest of the paint crew had a good laugh.

The morning breezed by with Mad Frank impressing Bongo with his work rate. Again, Pink picked up an early lead on those on the floor, stopping at one point to gather up the empty emulsion tubs, taking them down in the lift and throwing them in the back of the van. Lunch time saw him putting another couple of joints together and catching up with what Mad Frank had been up to.

He was due in court in three weeks time. Some guy had tried to glass him for chatting to his woman. Mad Frank took the glass from him and demonstrated how it should be done, leaving the guy with twenty three stitches. It would have been more if a mutual friend of theirs hadn't leapt between them. Of course Mad Frank was pleading self defence. Pink hadn't been there at the time, but was aware of the incident. The others looked at each other and wondered what the fuck they had taken on. By the end of the day, Mad Frank had them all eating out of his hand, his stories were the stuff of legend and no one ever got hurt, there was no harm in the guy; unless you tried to glass him, that was.

The same security guard checked them out of the building when they had done for the day. He kept his distance from Pink in case he was offered another whiff of his shoes. Cowboy swung by the council tip and Pink was glad to jump out and toss the empty tubs, he was sweating like a stuck pig even though the evening temperature had dropped below freezing.

At the High Chapperal, he undid his brand new Doc Marten's, stripped off his overalls, unbuttoned the three Ben Sherman shirts and slipped out of the two pairs of Levi's he had acquired over the course of the day. He hadn't left a scrap of evidence either, since that was all safely tucked into the empty paint tubs. No one gave him a second glance when he knocked off ten minutes early, slipping into the toilets with his stash and squeezing into his new boots and clothes. He was upset though. If Cowboy had explained about the ins and outs of the job he would now be on his second day's worth of freebies.

He was aching again, not as badly as last night, but noticeable just the same. He had asked Cowboy to pick up a hand of bananas when he went out to the chip shop, now he would put Johan's theory to the test. One banana while his curry was warming and another when he had eaten it. An hour and two joints later he was completely pain free, but the jury was still out. Everyone knew hashish had certain healing properties.

Swearing he would listen to the entire taped concert tonight, Pink fell onto the couch. Eight Ball joined him, bouncing about trying to catch the smoke rings; he only flaked out for two and a half hours this time.

Darkness again, and again the sound of hiccups. Eight Ball wasn't present, but he could definitely hear hiccups. Sitting and concentrating in the dark, straining his ears and failing to hear it again, he put it down to his imagination and headed for his stock of records.

Using the Graham Parker and the Rumours' Live at Marble Arch album as wake up music, he jumped into the shower, knowing most of the words, which enabled him to join in and appreciating the applause from downstairs as he towelled himself dry. Eight Ball had reappeared and was eyeing up his favourite spot. Pink strolled between the cat and the wall for badness, picking up a badly scratched ankle for his trouble. This was getting weird, very weird indeed.

Johan was still in bouyant mood, looking forward to his date with Sira which prompted Pink to ask the name of the youngest sister. His friend wasn't sure, he only had eyes for the one sister, but now his curiosity had been aroused; he promised to find out. Pink told him about his catalogue shopping spree and took orders for a pair of brown brogues, size nine, a size bigger than Pink, and a couple of pairs of Levi's, he was fussy about his shirts, he would need to have a look at them before committing himself.

Another dreamless night and no aching muscles when he woke before the alarm. Porridge for breakfast, central heating, otherwise he would catch his death of cold from wandering about with nothing under his overalls.

Thankfully, the van was on time this morning, no hanging about, a couple of joints on the way and the day was set fair. The security guard hardly gave them a second glance. This suited Pink, no shoes round his neck today, but they would be there at the end of play, he had orders to fulfil

For security guards, they weren't very observant. Pink strolled into the mill as thin as a whippet and waddled out in the evening like a Sumo wrestler. Today, he had added three pairs of underpants, two t- shirts and wore five pairs of socks to make up the extra room in Johan's brown brogues. Again, the evidence of all the wrapping had been secreted away via the empty tubs. His outfit was finished off with the trainers draped around his neck, by now a familiar sight to the guards.

They were given the option of working the Saturday with the vote coming in at four to two against. At least three out of the six would be in the Albatross, possibly Bongo, too, if his missus let him off the leash. Pink added another six shirts, six pairs of underpants, four pairs of jeans, four t-shirts and two pairs of trainers to his haul of booty. Next week, they were in the electricals section, and a new game plan was called for.

Pink didn't make it to the Albatross. Instead, he filled in for Johan while he escorted Sira to the pictures, the Indian picturehouse near the Stockade, another one of Pink's haunts, although he was barred from the place after a bit of a disagreement with the landlady.

The bakery ran itself. Pink had all the batch mixes committed to memory. A couple of spliffs, the crossword from the paper, decent music on the radio and he didn't mind putting his feet up after a quite hectic week. Eight Ball joined him for about an hour, then, around two o'clock, Johan relieved him, grinning from ear to ear. No need to ask him if he'd had a good time.

At the Albatross, Brat put out an APB on him. A young lady had been enquiring as to his whereabouts. Mad Frank had put him wise as to Pink's good health then escorted the young lady, Sonia, home; although he wasn't allowed over the doorstep. All he made on it was a peck on the cheek for his trouble and a message for Pink to get in touch.

He saw the shift out with Johan. The evening nap had been almost four hours, but now he was tired, sleep would come instantly as soon as he retired.

Seven twenty nine and he was wide awake, no alarm this morning, no need, the dream was back, but that wasn't all. He was sure he heard the hiccups again.

Saturday, nothing to do but relax and recharge the batteries. Thing was, the week's work had triggered something in his brain whereby he felt the need to be active. A large joint and ten minutes of staring at the wall with Eight Ball had him on his feet. He had brought home a quarter of a tub of the dark brown emulsion with the intention of putting a sort of border round the bare magnolia wall, but now he had changed his mind. He let Eight Ball go out for his constitutional, closed the kitchen door, rooted out the compasses he had found, inserted a pencil into the instrument and described several different sized circles on the blank wall. Another spliff and he described several more. They were coloured in by the time the wrestling started on the telly. He liked the effect, he didn't mind looking at the wall now. He wouldn't mind Eight Ball sitting in front of it now, now there was something to look at.

The aroma of roasting chicken brought Eight Ball clambering through the kitchen window. The entire meal was roasted to save time and washing up, potatos, carrots and an onion. The chicken, a gift from Johan, was done to a turn, Eight Ball's share being left to cool where he couldn't reach it. He knew it was there, he also knew he would have to wait for it so he bided his time by sitting in front of the wall. No mention was made of the change in decor.

The tape was set for the evening concert, the Steve Miller band, coincidence or what? Last week Frankie Miller, this week Steve Miller. Pink sat back to enjoy and was on his feet almost from the first note to lend backing with his air guitar.

Shit, shower, shave and shampoo, he was ready for the Albatross, telling Eight Ball not to wait up. Good job, Sonia showed up again. Mad Frank handed the reins to Pink when he saw she only had eyes for him. Brat played two tracks from the Cate Brothers album and asked could he take it home. Pink had no objections, seeing it as a sure sign he was on to something.

Sonia had turned into something of a dope fiend, she couldn't get enough of the stuff, she couldn't get enough of Pink, either. He stayed the night with her; she was insatiable, but he tried his best, well into the wee small hours. Not a bad cook, either, but all of a sudden a bit too clingy for his liking. He told her he was late for church and took himself out of there; he would revisit yes, but on his own terms; he hoped he wasn't going to be sorry he had let her know about the Albatross.

Church turned out to be the Boulder. He would have walked on by, but Heavy Waite spotted him and wouldn't listen to any excuses. Light was at the bar and Heavy shouted for him to order up another pint. Heavy wanted some hash, but there was nothing around, could Pink help him out?

Half an hour later they were in the car and heading out of town to the Flat Iron, see if Gwynneth could fix them up. Sunday was a slow day for her. The pub's clientele, students, had a tendency to lie in until well after lunchtime to compensate for their excesses of the night before. Gwynneth took her break, the Waite brothers had to wait in the living room for half an hour while Pink helped her to look for her stash. Going off the sounds they heard from the bedroom, he found it several times over.

Pink refused another drink when they drove back to town, preferring to go home and take some rest, but his luck was out, or in, depending on your perspective. He had no sooner stepped out of the Waites' car than he was in Louise's. A few joints, a Sunday roast and more sex than he thought himself capable of. His by now customary evening nap couldn't come quickly enough.

It was only once he was home he realised another hat trick had been achieved; this was becoming monotonous, a new ambition would have to be a four timer.

Later, Johan was most helpful, telling him he looked as rough as a bear's arse then beseeching him to look after the place while he sneaked off with Sira. Three hours later he was tucked up in bed and he didn't care if the dream visited, he was past that.

CHAPTER 10

Thirty feet of rope

Pink heard the hiccups in his sleep. Either he was going mad or he was imagining it. Lying in the dark, he strained his ears, nothing, silence, apart from the ticking of his alarm clock and the hum of the ovens. Monday morning comes round all too fast for a working man, and he was no different, telling himself it would only be for another week or so. He could have refused this job what with having a few quid stashed away, but saying that, he was glad he hadn't. Orders for jeans and t-shirts had flooded in from friends at the Albatross, so, like the previous week, he was naked under the overalls.

Bongo passed him a bag of home grown grass as soon as he landed in the van and thirty seconds later he had to open a window as the sweet smelling smoke threatened to cause an accident. It left a smooth, mellow feeling and Pink was invited to build another two before they reached their destination.

There was maybe two hours worth of work left on the top floor. Pink made good use of it by stashing his chosen apparel near the toilets and getting rid of the wrapping at the same time.

A change of colour on the second floor, Sunfire yellow, whatever that was. He opened the lid of the first tub and was momentarily blinded. Cowboy came round to see how everything was going and Pink asked who had chosen the colour scheme. Cowboy gave him a sheepish grin and admitted it was down to him. On signing the contract, he had negotiated with a bankrupt firm and bought a job lot. Pink took a break. Mad Frank was on the third floor finishing off the last wall, the same colour as Pink had been using on the top floor. A quick mooch round and he found what he was after, sunglasses, Foster Grants no less. He advised Mad Frank to help himself to a pair, he would find out soon enough why he would need them.

Suitably attired, he got stuck into his work, choosing his moments to inspect the covered shelves. On the third nosey he hit the jackpot, Sony Walkmans, or was it Walkmen? He wasn't too concerned about the correct pluralisation. The boxes were bulky for all that was inside, probably only one to a tub. Stripped of all packaging and safely sealed in one of his stolen carrier bags, he managed to secrete four units per tub. The packaging could be flattened, folded and squeezed into another tub. The security guards didn't give him a second glance as he used the lift to take the 'empty' tubs to the van. Since it was his job to throw the rubbish onto the tip, he was careful to keep his swag separate from the waste. He would take two tubs per evening home with him and tell Cowboy they were for his pot plants. Good idea that, he could use them to start his seeds going, the heat in the flat would bring them on a treat in readiness for planting out in the summer.

Mad Frank paid him a visit before lunchtime, as ever, always on the look out for something to help himself to. Pink didn't encourage him, he had his own little scam going. Still, he could see Mad Frank trying to figure out how to liberate one of the large stereos and ghost it past the guards; if he could manage that, he then had to get it past Cowboy and Bongo.

When Cowboy stopped at the tip that night, Pink jumped out, ran to the back doors and dragged the rubbish out. Mad Frank's keen eye picked up on the fact that he seemed to have piled a whole lot of weight on since he last saw him, but he didn't say a word, merely grinning his understanding. Pink just knew there would be a lot more stuff missing from the mill over the next four days.

While his curry was warming, he opened the tubs and carefully removed the Walkmans, making sure they didn't come into contact with the paint. Eight units, complete with headphones were individually wrapped and stashed behind the couch. He would claim one for himself, Johan could have one as a gift and the rest would be converted into cash money or goods to the value of. He was thinking hash.

His nap lasted two and a half hours. Eight Ball used that time to stare at the wall, making sure Pink was sound asleep before rubbing the length of his body along it, purring loudly as he did.

Johan was delighted with the Walkman. He wanted to know how much he owed Pink, but since he had always refused payment for the curries, Pink told him it was fair exchange. The two tubs he had brought home were washed out using the bakery hosepipe. Ten minutes and they were spotless. Johan eyed them up, he could use a couple of those for storing shit in. Pink told him he could have two tomorrow, but he could wash the fuckers out himself.

Sira called round, this was getting serious. Pink told Johan he would look after the place for an hour, but Sira wasn't staying, she was only running an errand for her dad. When Eight Ball strolled in she let out a scream and both men doubled up with laughter. Eight Ball ignored them and went straight to Sira, allowing her to make a fuss of him, much to Pink's bemusement. This was the cat who totally ignored everyone but for his lord and master; yet here he was, lying on his back, having his belly rubbed and purring his head off. Stranger and stranger.

Pink decided he wasn't tired when he went upstairs, maybe another spliff would knock him out? The radio was playing low as he inhaled deeply and counted the balls on the wall. A recount gave him a different total, eight more than the first count, the third attempt left him somewhere in between and that's when he knew it was bedtime. He left Eight Ball to count the balls as many times as he cared to, maybe he would come up with an accurate figure.

Hiccups again through the night. No dream, but definitely hiccups; thing was, when he concentrated on listening for them they simply weren't there, weird.

He almost left the flat without his change of clothes, it was dole signing day. Like last week, Cowboy would lend him the van for an hour, he knew it made sense.

Home grown to start the day, Bongo was quoting prices now he had everyone interested. Pink ordered a quarter then changed it to a half ounce, Johan liked it, he could bake all night and day if necessary on this stuff.

Mad Frank helped him unload the van, he had cottoned on to what was available from the mill, he too was naked under his overalls except for a thirty foot length of clothes rope wrapped around his waist. Pink didn't ask, he really didn't want to know, but somehow, he felt sure he would find out before the day was over.

He couldn't get to the shirts so half a dozen t-shirts were set aside for later, eight more Walkmans found their way into the back of the van by lunchtime and all was well with the world.

Mad Frank raised a few eyebrows when he produced a soup flask at the lunch break. While the rest of them were eating shit from the chip shop, he was tucking into home made rabbit stew; smelled good, too.

They congregated and ate on the floor Pink was working on, Bongo handing over the makings so Pink could roll a couple of boosters. Mad Frank went to the toilet to rinse his flask out and winked at Pink on his return, something was afoot. When the others went back to work, Frank opened the flask, fished four pairs of underpants from his overalls pocket and stuffed them in, Pink liked his style.

Halfway through the afternoon, Mad Frank sneaked onto the floor Pink was working on. Pink was perched on top of the racking and caught him out the corner of his eye. He disappeared from view for about twenty seconds and reappeared with two bin liners, tied at the neck and connected to the clothes rope. Pink looked on as he opened the largest window and fed his swag through, letting the rope run almost to full length before peering out to make sure he had reached ground level. Pink tiptoed up behind him and put his hand on his shoulder, forcing a surprised yelp from him, coupled with the resigned look of a trapped rat. His relief when he saw it was Pink was a picture in its own right, although he soon regained his composure, doing a run with the empties and stashing the booty in the back of the van. Cowboy and Bongo had no reason to look there until the following morning, but Pink was still curious as to how Frank proposed to sneak his stash out without them seeing.

It took him almost fifteen minutes to get dressed in the toilets. He'd be well and truly fucked if anyone looked at his feet, three pairs of socks and a pair of Jesus boots, summer was approaching, he had left his sandals at the old place in a very poor state of repair.

At the tip, he jumped out and started getting rid of the day's rubbish. Another van pulled in alongside them, at the same time, Mad Frank pushed his two packages towards the door and winked at Pink.

He had only arranged for them to be picked up. Pink knew the guy well, Reg, a confederate of Frank's. He gave Reg the nod and placed the packages gently to one side for him.

The heat inside the van, combined with all the clothes he was wearing and the effects of the home grown almost had him nodding on the way home.

Mira happened to be walking past with her youngest sister when he left the van. She wanted to know what was in the tubs and he told her it was black paint, he was decorating the flat and black was all he could get on the cheap. Mira introduced him to Kira and he told them he couldn't wait to meet Bira. Kira was still at school, but already Pink could see she would be as beautiful as her sisters. Mira linked his arm and asked how his job was going. Kira noticed the contact but said nothing, deciding it was none of her business. Mira gave his arm a squeeze and whispered goodnight when they parted. Pink called her back, he had a few pairs of new jeans, the legs were about four inches too long for him, could she possibly adjust them for him? Mira was only too glad to help, she told him so. He was to bring them down and if she wasn't in the shop he could leave them in the back with Johan. Then she realised he would need to try them on so she could gauge the right fit, result.

Eight Ball was all over him as soon as he landed, he had food on his mind. Pink obliged him, then rid himself of all his clothing, putting Little Feat on the stereo and jumping straight into the shower; he had worked up quite a sweat at the mill. He separated the clothing he had worn next to his body, it would need a wash before he could wear it again. He wondered if Mira took in washing and ironing as well as sewing. No harm in asking.

His nap was interrupted by the hiccupping again, he heard it above the sound of the music. Eight Ball either ignored it or didn't hear it; yet cats were supposed to have so many times better hearing than humans, this was becoming all too weird.

Johan had something for him besides a pan of curry, four batteries for his Walkman; it only needed two, but they didn't seem to last long. Pink resolved to seek some out at his place of work, he would probably need some for his next project.

He tended to the ovens while Johan washed the paint tubs. Sira showed up when he was almost finished and they disappeared for an hour. Eight Ball padded in and spent fifteen minutes curled up near the base of the ovens, then he was off on the prowl again. He came back in with Johan, having met him half way along the street and tagging along in the manner of a faithful dog. Both men were highly amused by his behaviour, he never failed to surprise.

Johan had been promised some Thai sticks, Pink had ordered a load of home grown, the word was that the whole area was suffering a drought. No one had told them, but they seemed to be doing alright.

No dream, but a disturbed night, and where was that fucking hiccup sound coming from? It was beginning to drive him up the wall. Could be Crickets in the wall cavities, or Bats in the belfry. The building didn't run to a belfry, Crickets were more your outside creatures and probably more tropical than this part of the world; whatever it was, he would get to the bottom of it.

Cowboy had forgotten to mention it, the catalogue company bosses planned to inspect their work tomorrow, Thursday, not that he was unduly concerned; he himself was well pleased with his crew's efforts, but he thought they should be aware of the visit.

As they unloaded the van, Pink suggested to Mad Frank maybe they should keep their hands in their pockets tomorrow. Frank agreed, no point upsetting the applecart, but today, today was open season.

Pink wasn't too bothered about not being able to access the shirt section, he now had more shirts than he had ever owned and he only very rarely wore one. Grandad T-shirts were all the rage and he helped himself to a couple of long sleeved and a couple of short sleeved, stashing them with his two pairs of dress trousers, three pairs of socks and another pair of Jesus boots, Johan had taken a shine to yesterday's pair, but he needed one size up, maybe Pink could pad them out with another couple of pairs of socks?

Fourteen Sony Walkmans should be enough to be going on with. Today, he had his heart set on cameras, finding he could fit three Polaroids, complete with instructions and two smaller instamatics into a tub. All tucked away in the back of the van before lunch, five pairs of the Foster Grants made up the contents of each tub. Pink was looking ahead to the summer again, he had become quite used to wearing them as protection from the glare of the Sunfire yellow.

True to form, Mad Frank lowered another double binlinerful of goodies and assisted Pink with the empty tubs, stashing his booty at the same time. He asked Frank to keep an eye out for batteries.

During the afternoon break, Bongo passed out the goodie bags. Pink had a half ounce of the stuff tucked safely into his overalls pocket, but all five other members of the crew tried to hand him their own bags so he could skin up for them. Life just didn't get any better than this.

The same van pulled in alongside them at the tip. Pink carefully placed Mad Frank's swag to one side and tipped Reg the wink, no words were necessary. Before he could close the doors, Mad Frank caught his eye, indicating a carrier bag tucked down beside his own booty. Pink reckoned Frank had found where the batteries were kept, what a star, mutual back-scratching was the order of the day.

Pink landed home, stripped off all his new clothes, pulled on a pair of his Levis, emptied his tubs and took them down to the back door of the bakery, signalling through the shop window to Mira as he walked past. She knelt in front of him and they both knew what he was thinking. She blushed ever so slightly, looked up into his eyes, smiled that wonderful smile and made him fall head over heels in love with her; as if he hadn't done so already. Sira interrupted them or who knows what might have happened, there was definitely an attraction here, strong on both sides. He told her there were six pairs of jeans and she said she didn't mind, she was happy to do anything for him. He promised himself he would give her every opportunity to be as good as her word. He washed the tubs out while he was there and Mira kept him company, Sira didn't complain. Pink was good to her, her and Johan.

Upstairs, he divided the home grown straight down the middle, singing along with Jackson Browne while he did so and catching a whiff of his curry as it warmed on the stove. The tape lasted long enough for him eat and wash up after himself.

Sticking the phones in his ears, he laid himself back on the couch and played Frankie Miller through his new Walkman. Eight Ball did the decent thing and left him alone; he was more interested in his wall, anyway. No dream and no hiccups, his nap lasted all of three hours.

Grace Slick joined him in the shower. He didn't care who was listening as he sang along at the top of his voice. There was applause between tracks, but he was limbering up for the next song.

Johan had been sampling the Thai sticks and by the look on his face they had been awarded the thumbs up. Pink did the trade with his home grown and promptly blended a cocktail together, smooth as silk. In his hurry to get hold of the new stuff, he had forgotten to bring his Levis for Mira and the Jesus boots for his friend. He nipped upstairs for them and caught Eight Ball rearing up against the wall like he was begging for food, he couldn't ignore it and kicked a nearby ping-pong ball in the cat's direction. He had thought of moving the bed settee in front of the wall, but it would have looked out of place. He told himself there was still time for the animal to become bored with his shenanigans, although he wouldn't be holding his breath while he waited.

Johan tried his sandals on, a perfect fit, he wouldn't wear them for work, better to save them for the summer or his next trip to Goa.

For all it was excellent grass, the Thai sticks were fiddly. Most people discarded the stems, but not Pink; he would soak them in a cup of water for a day or so, then boil the water and add it to a tea bag. Waste not want not.

Another spliff and Pink was nodding. He blamed it on the heat from the ovens, but whatever it was he couldn't stay awake. Eight Ball walked into the bakery as he left, he could finish his shift for him and by the look of Johan, he could finish his for him, too.

The dream was there again, with a slight twist. Hiccups, fucking hiccups, the bane of his life lately and no clue as to why.

He was at the pick-up point before he remembered about the inspection, dressed as usual in his overalls and little else. Thankfully, the van was right on time. He passed round a pre-rolled cocktail of a joint which drew favourable comments from all present.

Lunch came and went with no sign of the inspection crew. Pink had helped himself to a new boiler suit, snugly fitted under his loose overalls and with a high necked t-shirt to hide it from prying eyes. Mad Frank stuffed his empty flask with a couple of shirts and had just put it to one side when the inspection started.

Pink let on he hadn't clocked the men in charge and carried on throwing paint around with his roller and at least two of the men ended up with Sunfire yellow flecked suits before Bongo could stop him.

He grabbed up a couple of empty tubs and headed for the lift. One of the security guards took it upon himself to check them out while the bosses were around, the first time this had ever happened. Pink had nothing to declare for a change. On the ground floor, he made sure Mad Frank had informed Cowboy about the imminent arrival of the inspectors then carried on out to the van.

There was an hour and a half of the day left in which time Pink managed to fill a tub with Foster Grants, he knew he wouldn't be stopped again. He didn't like to leave the place empty handed, or empty footed for that matter. A new pair of comfortable slip-on shoes, black, his old trainers hanging round his neck.

On the way home, Cowboy informed them they were up for a bonus, the bosses were most pleased with their efforts. At the tip, Mad Frank pushed all the tubs towards the doors and was surprised when Pink pushed one back in. He hadn't taken anything other than the shirts in his flask where Pink on the other hand had decided to take the risk. Mad Frank shook his head, more in admiration than anything else, there was always tomorrow.

Kira walked him home, chatting away like she had known him for ever and dropping it in to the conversation that Mira had worked all evening at sewing his jeans. Pink picked her brains, what did Mira like? Did she like chocolates, flowers, music? Her reply took him aback. All she knew for sure was that Mira liked Pink, both her sisters liked Pink; in fact, now that she had met him she could say, hand on heart, that all three sisters liked Pink.

The same three sisters were gifted with a pair of Foster Grants each. Pink presented them to Mira when he went to pick up his jeans and have his basket filled with baked goodies. Sira thanked him and blew him a kiss, Mira squeezed his arm as she passed him his jeans, Kira tried her new shades on and knocked him out with her dazzling smile. Quite honestly, he didn't know where to look. He actually blushed when Mira asked him to have his shower soon so the girls could hear him sing.

He didn't disappoint them, giving his interpretation of 'Crazy Mama', with J J Cale strumming away in the background.

Johan was impressed with his Foster Grants, he had tried to talk Sira out of her pair, but she wasn't for giving them up. They had a few spliffs, put the world to rights, did a bit of baking and breezed through 'til three thirty, Pink's bedtime.

He was up early, no disturbance, no dream and no hiccups, just wide awake and raring to go. Last day at the mill, they were looking at a possible lunchtime finish. Cowboy wanted to put him on standby, he had a couple of tenders in for similar jobs, even further out of town, but Pink wasn't too sure. During the fortnight he had been mulling over the idea of finding a proper cards in job, feeling he was secure and settled now at the flat, something he hadn't felt for a long, long time. The few quid he had behind him, coupled with a regular wage coming in might just be the making of him.

He treated his fellow workers to another grass cocktail and when asked, let them know he wouldn't be showing up at the Albatross, not tonight and maybe not all weekend. No one asked for further details, but Mad Frank's eyes lit up, maybe he would have half a chance with that Sonia woman if Pink wasn't there?

The morning seemed to fly past. He had all his clothes and cameras sorted out before he had even applied a lick of paint. The ceilings were all but finished, but he'd had the sense to save a couple of empty tubs for the final push. Mad Frank lowered three units of whatever electrical equipment he had found buyers for, Pink hadn't bothered to ask, he didn't really need to know since it wasn't interfering in any way with his own business.

They worked through the lunch break to finish the job. Cowboy tipped up their wages and thanked them for their good work, telling them if he ever went legit he couldn't ask for a better crew. Mad Frank made a call from the payphone in the office foyer and Pink knew he would see Reg at the tip, as sure as night follows day.

After the tip, Cowboy pulled into a pub car park, it was bonus time. The pub was connected to a small restaurant at which they ate and drank until they were fit to burst, slipping outside between courses for a smoke. Pink was kept busy handling dope from all directions.

He was dropped off at the end of his road a mere forty minutes earlier than had been the norm. Cowboy and Bongo laughing their heads off when he gave them their overalls back. There he stood, half cut, stoned as a rat, resplendent in his new navy blue boiler suit complete with factory labels and of course, a so called empty paint tub in either hand. It took them a full five minutes to regain their composure, by which time Pink was sprawled all over the bed settee and throwing out a few zeds. He had big plans for later, but first, rest.

Right time, right place

Pink had no problems in securing the keys to Doc's van for the weekend. He made sure Eight Ball had enough food, leaving a spare tin in the bakery for Johan to feed him if necessary. One tub full of cameras and another full of Walkmans, a holdall with a change of clothes and a few pairs of sunglasses, he set off for the Flat iron. The students would snap the Walkmans up, he was sure of it.

Gwynneth was pleased to see him and only too happy to punt the Walkmans from behind the bar, she knew who to approach.

An hour and a half later, he could have kicked himself. All eight had flown from the shelves, why oh why hadn't he brought the other six? Not to worry, it was all profit, except for the one Gwynneth had put aside for her friend's son's birthday. He wouldn't be charging her for that one; besides, she was looking more and more appealing to him as the night went on. Not that he needed it, but a free Sony Walkman would charm him into her knickers later. The Foster Grants didn't last long, either. This had been a fact finding mission, test the waters. He should have loaded the lot into the van, gone with his instincts and made a real killing. He told her about the cameras and she promised to take him to a guy she knew in the morning. He was staying the night, wasn't he?

They shared a joint in the back room of the pub. His beer was free, that went without saying, a long standing arrangement since their first ever drug deal. Gwynneth had some black at home, tasty stuff she told him; another reason for staying over, the weekend was taking shape nicely. She cancelled her taxi, Pink could drive her home. He really wanted to leave the van outside the pub, but she advised against it, he would have found it on bricks in the morning, if he found it at all.

So, he slowed down on the beer and helped her clear up at last orders, she had stowed a few cans in the fridge when it was decided he was staying over. Pink could resume his drinking at her place.

She almost had them off the road through giving him a blow job on the way. Yes, the weekend was shaping up very nicely indeed.

A can of beer, a joint of best black and a more than willing woman, Pink was in his element. Gwynneth was all over him, ripping his clothes off and straddling him without undressing herself. He didn't mind, he liked it when the lady took charge sometimes, besides, the black had all but left him rooted to the spot. She rode him for all she was worth, letting the neighbours in on the fact she was having the best of times.

He woke in the middle of the night to find her rolling a joint with a large block of Paki black taking prominence on the bedside table. He took his time with the lovemaking, exploring every inch of her body with his fingers and tongue, teasing and probing until Gwynneth begged him to get on with the main event.

At breakfast he decided to go home for the rest of his swag, flog it off all in one go. Gwynneth didn't want him to leave, she had a day off and had made plans in her mind, she hadn't had any fun in a long time. Pink promised to be back in an hour and a half, surely she could manage without him for that long? Reluctantly, she released her grip on his cock and took a knife to the lump of black. She didn't weigh it, there was a lot of trust between them, she didn't count the bunch of pound notes he handed her in payment, either.

Eight Ball was in front of his wall. He turned and miaowed something to Pink, but it was a half hearted attempt at conversation and he ignored it, they could catch up later. He checked the food bowl, gave it a wash and replenished it. Gathering up his swag and another change of clothes, he bit a piece off the hash and carefully stashed the rest, Johan was in for a treat. Then, he was out the door and away.

Turning in to Gwynneth's street, he spotted a familiar looking car about a dozen doors away from her house. He checked the registration and parked up opposite Gwynneth's. Running inside, he snatched up her stash, told her the drug squad were raiding further up the road and advised her to destroy any evidence, he would be across the road in the van and keeping an eye on things.

Five minutes later they hammered on her door, one of them slyly heading for the back door. They were in for twenty minutes and Pink watched what was going on over the top of his newspaper. The raid wasn't anything new, but considering there was a drought in the area, someone must have squealed to the fuzz about where there actually was some dope to be found.

They came out scratching their heads. Pink ducked further under his paper, but still managed to observe their movements. Gwynneth, bless her, was giving them both barrels, arms folded across her ample breasts and letting the coppers know just what she thought of them.

She was trembling when Pink went to her. He had prepared and lit the coal fire while Gwynneth cooked the breakfast, she asked him to bring a shovelful of dross to dampen it down and, although puzzled at the request, he did as she asked.

That done, she reached up the chimney and produced another lump of black, Pink had only saved half of her stash. If the drug squad had taken any longer the whole neighbourhood would have had a free doping session as the heat from the fire would have sent it abroad via the chimney.

They had a good laugh about it, more nervous relief than anything else. Gwynneth was black from the soot so they ended up in the bath together and had some fun while soaping themselves clean.

Pink rolled a joint of his home grown, he had to drive to Gwynneth's friend's place and didn't fancy attempting it on the black. She gave him directions and soon he was turning into Fester's street. Pointing down the road a bit, she told him to pull in behind another white van, but Pink stopped about twenty yards behind it. He jumped out of the van with Gwynneth hot on his heels, turning up at Fester's front door just in time to meet Mad Frank and Reg, he had recognized the van. They were shaking hands with a huge bald guy who Pink guessed would be Fester.

Reg saw him and gave him a wave, followed by Mad Frank, who was grinning from ear to ear. He immediately told them of the drug squad's activities, both men would most likely have a stash to look after. They thanked him and allowed him to introduce Gwynneth. Frank couldn't place where he knew her from until it clicked with Reg, the Foundry, the Flat Iron, by the look on their faces they approved wholeheartedly of his choice of companion.

Fester grabbed Gwynneth in a bear hug and motioned for Pink to follow them inside. The place was like an Aladdin's cave with all manner of electrical goods and shit lying around. Pink spotted the bin liners Mad Frank had wrapped his goodies in, all open just wide enough at the neck to show him the fruits of his friend's labours. Now it was his turn. They reached a fair price on his goods, shook hands and repaired to the kitchen for a cup of tea and a joint. Fester's place was kitted out with all mod cons, all the latest gadgets. On Sundays he loaded up his own van and drove for about a hundred miles. Pink knew the place, it was reported you could buy just about anything you had set your heart on, and at a reasonable price. Fester would sell off most, if not all of what he had purloined during the week.

Pink drove out to the pub the paint gang had stopped at last night, Gwynneth insisted on buying lunch as thanks for him saving her drug dealing career, among other things. It was leisurely, neither of them in any particular hurry to be anywhere. Between courses they sat in the van and had a spliff, home grown again, the black being much too heavy to drive on.

It was siesta time when they drove back to Gwynneth's. Two hours kip, a joint of the black, a romp of sorts on the couch and they both agreed they should have a night out. She didn't want to go to the Flat Iron so Pink decided he would take her to the Albatross, but he didn't fancy driving, he had every intention of getting absolutely wasted. Gwynneth rustled up a snack while he rolled half a dozen joints, cocktails of home grown and black, he would end up in orbit and he would take a few others with him. Gwyneth nipped to the house next door for a bus timetable, the bus would drop them about a hundred yards from the Albatross.

Another spliff on the top deck of the bus, shared with a couple of like minded souls. Pink had forgotten about Sight 'n' Sound in concert, he didn't want to know who had been on in case it was someone he really wanted to see.

They floated down the hill to the pub. He took Gwynneth to Brat at the decks and introduced them, but they already knew each other, Brat had played at the Flat Iron on more than one occasion. Brat was given a joint to be getting on with and Pink found a seat by a table, it was time to relax. He had no sooner sat down than a couple of girls asked him to skin up for them, thrusting the makings and their chests in his direction. He duly obliged them, putting their noses slightly out of joint by allowing Gwynneth to spark it up. They didn't bother him again over the course of the evening.

A murmur of approval hit the atmosphere as Brat played a track from one of the Cate Brothers albums, it had taken no time at all in becoming a firm favourite of the Albatross's clientele.

Sonia stuck her head in the room, saw he was with someone else and turned on her heel. She didn't stay for a drink, she didn't look too happy about something.

Pink informed anyone who would listen of the drug squad's activities, they tended to concentrate on one area at a time, wouldn't be long before they were round this way; forewarned is forearmed.

Quite a few people visited at his table over the course of the evening, he seemed to be the only person with anything worth smoking, some wanted to score and were disappointed not to. Others simply wanted a toke and he was only too happy to oblige, he had done enough hovering of his own in the past; swings and roundabouts.

It had been his intention to drag Gwynneth back to the flat, public transport being totally unreliable after a certain time of night. He really wanted to keep the place exclusive to himself, but had decided Gwynneth didn't pose any real threat to his privacy, she lived far enough away to ensure she wouldn't be a regular visitor. His plans changed for the better when Brat joined them to share the last joint and mentioned he was going Gwynneth's way at the end of his gig, problem solved. Pink would help him load the van and Gwynneth would sort him out with some of the black when he dropped them off.

Brat actually ended up on the couch, the black having restricted his movements to a series of nods and the odd arched eyebrow as he tried to follow the limited conversation. Gwynneth threw a blanket over him and manhandled Pink upstairs. They managed to undress but sex was off the menu, totally incapable the pair of them, all they could do was spoon. Several hours later, Brat stuck his head round the bedroom door to say thanks and goodbye. Pink heard Gwynneth telling him to make sure he closed the front door properly and to keep quiet about the source of the black then went back to sleep. No dreams, no hiccups, maybe he should move in with Gwynneth?

The clock on the bedside table said ten past eleven, Gwynneth had him in hand and was getting a good rhythm going. He turned towards her and returned the compliment, probing gently at her moist pussy and making her moan then purr like a contented cat. They wrestled for what seemed like hours, although when Pink next looked at the clock it was only five to twelve. Gwynneth told him to stay where he was, returning with an album cover and all the makings. Five minutes later he could smell the bacon. This was the life, a good fuck, a joint and breakfast in bed. He could get used to this.

Gwynneth had work later, seven o'clock start, Pink would drop her off and head for the High Chapperal. One more joint of black and they would stick to the home grown after that. A couple of Gwynneth's friends called to score. Pink did the honours and couldn't resist a toke or two. Both dudes sank into the settee, immobile for about an hour. Brat had left his Cate Brothers albums and he impressed them all when he gave them a spin at high volume, Gwynneth wanted him to leave them with her, but he wouldn't, promising her a tape instead.

Between them, they managed to rustle up a Sunday roast, chicken and everything that goes with it, sponge pudding for afters, but no custard. An ice cream van bellowed its jingle to let them know it had pulled up outside to save the day.

There was no time for a nap so they let their meal digest, had a roll about on the floor in front of the fire, jumped in the bath and then it was almost time to go. He had enjoyed his weekend and told her so. She thanked him for his company and asked could they do it again soon. He promised to consult his diary, she was plaiting his hair at the time and gave it an extra strong yank, telling him if he had a diary he would have fuck all to write in it.

He was tempted to call in for a free pint when he dropped her off, but decided it would be more prudent to head home. One free pint would surely lead to another, and another night with Gwynneth. He didn't want to outstay his welcome.

If Eight Ball had missed him, he made a good job of disguising it, barely looking up from his sentry duty. Johan, on the other hand, was delighted to have his company, and doubly delighted when told about the black. He wanted to try it, but not until he had finished work for the night. Pink told him about his weekend, flogging his swag, messing around with Gwynneth and the drug squad's raid. He had been fortunate, by pure chance being in the right place at the right time, proof positive if he needed it his luck was holding out; had been for some time.

He left just as Mr Rapati arrived, a basket of fresh baked goodies giving off its wonderful aromas. Both men laughed as they spoke at the same time and were drowned out by the call to prayers being hailed over the rooftops. Pink said goodnight while Mr Rapati wished him good morning and both men laughed again.

Before falling into bed, he banished the alarm clock to a cupboard in the kitchen. It had run down and stopped over the weekend; it would show the correct time twice a day, but no one would witness it.

He heard the hiccups as he lost consciousness, but he was much too tired to consider doing anything about it.

Sour dough

Pink eyed up the envelope suspiciously, no address, sealed, definitely something inside, though. Neat handwriting, Mr Rapati would like to speak to him as a matter of some urgency. Funny, he had only shared pleasantries with the man some seven hours earlier. The reason he knew this was he'd been for some milk and a paper, clocking the time in the post office window and finding the note when he returned.

In the shop, Mira showed him her perfect smile and shouted through the back for her dad. He in turn shouted through, she was to send Pink round the back. Mr Rapati shook his hand, a worried look on his face. Just after he had arrived this morning, Johan received a phone call, a relative was in trouble, he had no choice but to go to his assistance. Thing was, he had recommended Pink as a stand in while he was away, would he be willing to fill in at such short notice and if so, could he please demonstrate his knowledge of the ovens and batch mixes? Mr Rapati had to go somewhere on business, but Mira, his eldest daughter, would conduct the interview. He would be most grateful, most grateful indeed if Pink could help him out.

Mira was all business until her father drove off, she knew full well Pink was up to speed with all things bakery. They spent half an hour in each others company anyway and when another member of staff came through to the back she would fire a question at him. Pink suggested it might be an idea if she were to work the first couple of hours with him, make sure he had the hang of it. He could see the idea appealed to her, they were interrupted again and she told him he was to be there, ten o'clock sharp.

It was a lovely spring day so he slotted some batteries into his Walkman, rolled a joint, half black, half home grown and wandered off to the local park with Frankie Miller for company. The park was deserted but for a couple of dog walkers and a jogger, a female jogger, a familiar looking female jogger. Louise, she didn't live anywhere near here, what the fuck was she doing? She wasn't stalking him, was she?

Louise stopped when she recognised him, smiled sweetly and explained she had a compulsory medical coming up soon and was trying to get into shape. Pink told her she looked in good enough shape to him, with very little room for improvement. Louise saw the joint, had a good look round, led him into the bushes and let him run his hands all over her toned body as she toked furiously on the spliff. He didn't tell her how strong it was and watched her eyes glaze over as she sucked greedily on his cock, her suggestion, but no argument from him. He had to assist her to the car at the edge of the park and all the while she was insisting he should call her. Her driving left something to be desired as he watched her return to work. She was definitely his favourite police person by a long, long way.

Feeling pleased with himself, he walked beyond the park, headphones on and singing along with Frankie. At the top of the lane end he decided to check his grass growing site for the coming summer. To get there, he had to pass by a cluster of allotments, all fenced off and protected by barbed wire. Some of them were dilapidated, their owners having died off or moved away. The majority were well tended with large wooden sheds, cold frames, neat little vegetable gardens and poultry. Turning the corner leading to his destination, the canal bank, he saw the Blunt family, a semi Neanderthal tribe of knuckle scrapers. Six brothers and assorted cousins, he could handle any one of them individually, but collectively, forget it. If you stood on one brother's toe they all limped, Pink wasn't alone in suspecting a definite hint of interbreeding among them. Their allotment was probably the biggest of them all and the untidiest, no vegetation in sight, more like a rubbish tip. He stayed where he was and observed them, building a joint of home grown as he did. They were unloading a large van full of boxes. He couldn't make out what was in them, but they were in a hurry to finish the task, scurrying in and out of the large shed and chasing each other up.

Ten minutes later they were gone and Pink resumed his walk, almost shitting himself when a large Alsatian launched itself at the fence as he strolled past.

Everything looked different when he came to the canal bank. The sewage plant was still there, he knew that for a fact before he left the park, the wind direction being what it was had wafted the obnoxious stench in his direction. Two hundred yards away, at the exact spot Pink liked to use for his planting out, the land had been razed, flattened beyond all recognition. A huge hoarding heralded the imminent arrival of a new water treatment plant. A new road of sorts had been hewn into the site, but he wasn't in the least impressed since this upset his plans somewhat. On a more positive note, it would bring employment to the area. Another worry, the existing sewage or water treatment plant was a source of income to Pink. Once a week from late Spring to mid Autumn he would wedge the rotating sprinklers to a stop, throw a plank across each section and collect mushrooms from the beds then sell them to local merchants. As long as they were thoroughly washed, no harm would befall those who dined on them. Across the canal, an open field, often used by Gypsies to winter their horses was another source of income. More mushrooms, of the magic kind, nature's bounty, the horseshit bringing them out in their thousands.

His immediate concern was to find a new spot to raise his grass, the horses would munch on it if he planted in their field. Venturing beyond the sewage plant, he came to the wall of an abandoned scrap yard, the base of it protected by a dense patch of, for the moment, dormant bramble bushes. It was tinder dry and sheltered. He found some old newspaper, checked the wind direction and cleared a decent area by use of fire. Another visit with some sort of implement and he would clear the roots to stop them from choking his own plants. All was well, but a good job he had decided to come down.

The Blunts' dog gave him a hard time again as he passed their allotment. Whatever was stored in the shed would be as safe as houses, the animal looked like it was part wolf. Of the Blunts, Mick was the one Pink got on best with. He was short, stocky and with a long, flowing beard. Last summer Mick knocked at his door and asked could he borrow his oven and some tin foil. Producing a large bag of magic mushrooms, he baked them until they could be powdered. Pink warmed up a tin of lentil soup and Mick added a generous helping of the powder. After sharing the soup they arranged to meet up in the Boulder at opening time and Pink walked the mile and a half to the Marlborough Club to talk over some business with the Waite brothers. When he arrived there was a crowd in the foyer, gathered around a new space invaders machine. Pink had never seen such a thing and came face to face with it just as the mushrooms kicked in. Everything was green, he was hysterical with laughter, the Waites manhandled him out of the place before they were all barred. Pink explained about the mushrooms and Heavy decided he wanted some so they walked into town with Pink, hoping to score for themselves. On the way, he saw a green fire engine, spewed up some green worms and bayed loudly at the full green moon. At the Boulder, Light bought the beers in and Pink went to look for the Blunt brother. The pub was empty only for Mick, who was sitting in a corner of the pool room, the image of a green garden gnome. As soon as they spotted each other they were helpless with laughter, eventually agreeing they had overdone it ever so slightly with the mushies. But Mick could be as nasty as his relatives, Pink had borne witness to that on more than one occasion; when it all boiled down, they all pissed in the same pot.

Mr Rapati himself turned up shortly after ten and watched as Pink went through his moves. By eleven he had seen enough, leaving him to get on with the night's baking. Pink wondered if he had spotted the interaction with his eldest, was that why he had shown up and not Mira? He let the notion pass, if that had been the case he wouldn't be where he was now, working for the man. Eight Ball must have waited for the bossman to leave, strolling into the bakery as his car left the street. Pink had the impression he was only looking for Johan or one of the girls, they had all subscribed to his fan club, especially Sira, even after he dropped his gift of a dead rat at her feet. An hour was all he was prepared to give up for Pink, sloping off into the night when his back was turned.

The shift passed quite quickly. He thought he had misheard when the radio announcer said it was time for the news at four o'clock. All of his quotas were done and dusted, the two early deliveries dispatched on time. He relaxed and made a mental note to save his paper for this time tomorrow morning, pass the last hour on. Five o'clock on the dot and he heard footsteps approaching, heels, not Mr Rapati. Mira, looking fresh as a daisy; her smile more than compensating for the semi darkness he was sitting in having dimmed the lights when the work was done.

She was chatty, wanting to know how he had coped, had there been any snags? Pink noticed a hint of sadness in her demeanour, something wasn't right. Patiently, he managed to coax it out of her and it wasn't the best of news.

Mira was engaged to be married. It wasn't sudden, having been arranged some seventeen years ago when she was four years old. A distant cousin being her intended, they had never met, she had known from aged ten and had managed to put it out of her mind and now it was coming on top of her. It had made her ill last night when her parents sat her down and put it to her, this being the reason she didn't show. She had wanted to come, it was important that Pink should know that, she liked him. Of course he knew that, didn't he?

Now Pink was upset, and not only for himself. Sure, he would like nothing more than to get into her knickers, but his feelings ran deeper than that, a lot deeper.

There was no way out of it for her, these arranged marriages were a time honoured tradition, her parents had an arranged marriage and their parents before them; both her sisters were spoken for as well. Pink wondered if Johan was aware of that fact. Mira didn't want to talk about it, nor did she want to think about it, she had heard tell of girls in her position going off the rails, shacking up with the first guy to wink at them. It released them from the arranged marriages, the prospective grooms deeming them to be sullied, spoiled goods. It also found the girls to be ostracised from their families, something else Mira couldn't bear to think about.

Pink couldn't comfort her, he couldn't even tell her he wouldn't be attending the wedding, if invited. He did ask when her cousin was coming over from India and was surprised to learn he only lived a hundred and fifty miles away.

That other cultures should try to preserve their traditions was their God given right, but in Pink's opinion, some of those traditions were totally archaic.

Mr Rapati arrived and Mira put her brave face on, telling her dad he could have had a lie in, Pink had prepped his first batches for him. Maybe he could take over the day to day running of the place? Mr Rapati shook his hand and thanked him, Mira stood behind her dad with her fingers to her lovely lips, asking Pink to say nothing about her predicament.

Eight Ball poked his head in the back door, saw the boss there and turned tail. He must have known the score.

When Pink went upstairs, Eight Ball was already positioned in front of the wall. Pink ignored him, he was too tired to either argue or pass comment, tired and upset for Mira.

Three hours sleep found him in better humour. A trip to the shops and the launderette, he knew the lady well enough that he could leave his laundry and pick it up the following day; he was on fist name terms with all of the shop owners and their staff. In the bric a brac shop he uncovered an almost mint condition copy of Carlos Castaneda's 'The teachings of Don Juan, a Yaqui way of knowledge'. He had previously read three quarters of it before it mysteriously disappeared. For fifteen pence he could continue on his journey.

After eighteen months or so of a gap, he found it surprisingly easy to immerse himself once more in a world of transcendence, a good spliff of best Paki black lent wind to his sails and he picked up where he had left off. He only put the book down to feed himself and build another joint, it was another warmish spring day. After eating, he took his joint and his book and found a spot in the park; if anyone else was there he didn't notice, he was tripping with an old friend.

An hour and a half later it was all over, the woman in the shop had been charged with keeping an eye out for other tomes by the author. Until she came across some, he would revisit this one by going back to the beginning again.

It had certainly taken his mind from his problems, or rather Mira's problems. He sat crosslegged in the middle of the floor, closed his eyes and entered meditation. No music, just a blank canvas and a dab of Tiger balm on his forehead; an old girlfriend had put him wise to that, she called it the third eye.

He was aware of Eight Ball taking up residence in front of him, he was also aware of a feeling of complete, blissful calm.

No way of knowing how long he had been sitting there, his meditation had taken him on a tour of vividly coloured South American landscapes. There was music, no, not music, vocals only, one of his favourite Boz Scaggs songs 'Harbour Lights', but it wasn't Boz singing. He had no knowledge of a female having recorded it, but he was snapped out of his reverie when the singer hiccupped at the end of the piece.

This was so weird, he had definitely heard it, the hairs on the back of his neck stood to attention and he shivered as if someone had walked over his grave; walked on it and stopped to piss all over it.

His eyes were open, Eight Ball was asleep in front of him, there was no one else in the room, or was there? He had the feeling he wasn't alone, it was almost dark so he did the only thing he could think of.

"Who's there? …. is this a joke? …. is anybody there?"

Silence, then giggling, then the hiccups. Now, he was looking towards the door. If he had to get the fuck out he wanted to know his path was clear, but strangely, he was rooted to the spot, unable to move anything but his head. All of a sudden he had to use the toilet, then, a shadow on Eight Ball's wall of choice. This was unreal, considering what he had been reading this was totally unreal. The hiccup again then the giggle, a female giggle, then more definition to the shadow. Eight Ball was on his feet. He didn't even look at Pink, rather he padded over to his wall and purred loudly, then arched his back like he was greeting an old friend.

Pink was in an agitated state now, he could clearly see the outline of a lady, a young lady. Long flowing hair; mostly shadow, but eyes, piercing green eyes, no colour anywhere else, only those eyes. He was mesmerised, not scared now, realising if this apparition meant him any harm he would surely be in deep shit by now. He found his voice again. "Who …. who the fuck are you? …. and where did you come from?"

The giggle again, softer this time, interrupted by the hiccup, then the voice, soft and gentle like no other voice he had ever heard before.

"I'm Violet …. hiccup …. my name is Violet hiccup."

Eight Ball looked at Pink, realising he too could see his friend, he said something in cat language but it washed over Pink. He was transfixed, he was sharing his flat with a ghost, a real live fucking ghost …. and a cat of course, he laughed to himself nervously.

"Why, hic, why are you hic laughing?"

"Violet Hiccup, what a strange name." He said, unsure if he should be talking out loud to a ghost on the wall; it felt strange, very, very strange.

112

But, she was answering him back so it was ok, wasn't it? It was ok to talk if there was someone, or something to answer him back, he tried to convince himself.

"Violet .... hic. My name is Violet, but .... hic .... My surname isn't hiccup."

"Sorry, that was my little joke, it was a nervous reaction to be honest, it's not every day a ghost appears on your wall and starts up a conversation."

"You started the .... hic, the conversation .... hic."

"Are you dead?"

"Of course I'm, hic, of course I'm dead, hic. How, hic, how else do you suppose, hic, I can appear like this?"

She had him there, he was all out of ammo, he was struggling, but he couldn't leave it there. Quick as a flash, he came up with the ice breaker.

"How did you die? Your voice sounds so young, you must only be twenty .... ish?"

That giggle again. "Why, ... hic. Why don't you .... hic, just come right out, ... hic, with it?"

"Sorry. I can't find the words. I really don't know how to react to this, I've sensed for some time there was something more to this place than the four walls. Eight Ball has known about you from the word go."

"Yes .... hic .... He likes me .... hic .... He talks to me .... hic .... But Eight .... hic .... Eight Ball, why Eight Ball .... hic?"

"Never mind that for now." Said Pink, regaining some of his composure. "Answer my question. I want to try to understand all this. Just how did you die and did you die here in this flat?"

"Smoke inhalation, yes .... hic .... it happened here .... hic. I was drunk after a row with my .... hic, sister,. She didn't like me smoking. That wasn't .... hic, what the argument was about. I .... hic, I fell asleep with a lit cigarette in my .... hic, hand. Something in the. hic, pillow was toxic. The foam .... hic, I think. I just didn't .... hic, wake up."

"I'm sorry." Said Pink, his razor sharp repartee keeping the conversation fizzing.

"Stop apologising …. hic. It's not …. hic, your fault."

"I'm sorry, carry on please, I don't know what the fuck to make of all this, what's with the hiccups?"

"Hic, I don't understand …. hic, that one myself, I …. hic, I only started with them the …. hic, the day after you moved in …. hic, you walked in from the …. hic, shower to change the …. hic, record. You were …. hic, naked and I must have …. hic, I must have …. hic, been shocked. hic.

Pink was blushing pink now and Violet giggled again, he was beginning to like that sound, then, there was someone at the door. He ran downstairs to find Mira, wondering why he hadn't shown up for work. He thought of dragging her in to show her his resident ghost, but stopped himself short, telling her he would be five minutes. Back upstairs, he told Violet not to go away, he had to go to work, she wasn't to dare go away. Violet giggled again and Eight Ball rubbed himself on the wall at her feet. Pink came over all weak at the knees, this was just incredible.

He was fifteen minutes late, but that didn't matter, Mira had made a start for him. He wanted to pry about her upcoming nuptials, but instead decided to pick her brains about the flat.

Mira told him about the girl suffocating, it had been six months ago, her dad had told her not to say anything to prospective tenants, even after they moved in. She knew about Eight Ball staring at the wall, she didn't believe in ghosts, she knew Pink would be ok, but why the sudden interest?

Pink deflected the question, cleverly changing the subject to Mira's own problem, volunteering to take her virginity and run away with her. She gave him her best smile, no, she wasn't offended, in fact she had already thought of that one and was sorely tempted.

Changing to serious mode, he suggested she should jump on a train to where her intended lived and check him out, maybe he would turn out to be someone she could develop a relationship with.

Mira cupped his face in her hands and kissed him full on the lips, telling him that was the best idea anyone had come up with. She would do it, but only if Pink would go with her; after all, it was his idea, he had started the ball rolling so to speak.

She worked 'til midnight with him, making a fuss of Eight Ball when he strolled in and reluctantly taking her leave of them when Sira came to pick her up. Pink was awarded another full on kiss before she went, and with a wink from her sister.

The girls were no sooner gone than he was bounding upstairs for another look at Violet, just to make sure he wasn't imagining her. He put the big light on, only the second time he had done so since moving in, having decided it was much too bright for his needs. Violet was talking to Eight Ball, hiccupping after every few words. He could see her features better now, telling him what he already knew, or imagined he knew. She was a stunner. She giggled again as his chin hit the floor and he was glad she couldn't read his thoughts. Why oh why did she have to be dead?

CHAPTER 13

Good riddance

Pink couldn't concentrate on his crossword. With the night's work over, he had an hour to kill and he didn't want to leave the bakery for fear of Mr Rapati turning up early to relieve him. The crossword was supposed to keep his mind off developments upstairs, but he hadn't even put pen to paper, his head spinning with all manner of conundrums. This was all new to him. He had always kept an open mind about all things spiritual, supernatural, now this had been landed in his lap he was going to have to open his mind a whole lot wider.

The bossman came by at five on the dot. Pink, having been in the flat for a month, offered up his due rent. Mr Rapati took it from him, counted it and split it down the middle, half each, for services rendered. Johan would be travelling back later this evening, if Pink could do the first half of his shift he would be much obliged.

The men shook hands before Pink took his leave with his basketful of baked produce.

"HONEY .... I'M HOME" He yelled as he entered the top door. For all this was new to him, now that he was over the initial shock he was determined to have some fun with it.

Violet giggled, a delightful sound, maybe she had decided to have some fun herself? Eight Ball looked like someone had put his nose out of joint since Violet was no longer exclusive to him. Pink told him to get over it.

He got a spliff together, deliberately leaving the music off, determined to find out all he could about Violet. However, Violet had a mind of her own.

"Those are …. hic, funny cigarettes you make."

"It's a joint."

"Meat?"

"Ha-ha. Not meat, hashish, dope, blow, resin, grass, weed, puff, marijuana. Combined with tobacco, it's known as a joint, reefer, spliff, African Woodbine. I could go on at length."

"They all mean …. hic, the same thing?"

"Yes, it comes in all those names and more."

"What does it do? You seem …. hic, to smoke a lot of it?"

"It's for relaxation, stress relief; plus, it heightens the senses, especially listening to music, and touch." As soon as he said that he wished he hadn't, touch would surely be off the menu for her.

If she noticed, she didn't say.

"Why …. hic, why do you have to …. hic, smoke so much of it?"

"Depending on the strength of it, you reach a certain plateau, you want to stay there so you top up from time to time; it becomes a bit of a habit, although it's actually non addictive."

"Will you play …. hic, some music for me? I'm …. hic, sorry. I don't even know …. hic, your name?"

Of course, no one else had entered the flat since he moved in. He would have to introduce himself.

"Pink …. My name's Pink."

There was that delightful giggle again.

"Pink? …. hic. What sort of …. hic, a name is Pink?"

"It's from when I was a kid, rhyming slang, everyone had a nickname. My surname is Lynt, so I became Pink Lynt, skint, d'you see?"

"Yes, it's good. Pink …. hic, yes, it …. hic, suits you."

He felt a warm tingle down his spine when she said his name.

"What would you like to hear?"

"You choose, I can't say I've …. hic, heard anything I don't ….
hic, like. I'd never heard any of them …. hic, before, but I love ….
hic, love them all."

Pink played what Violet had been singing when she entered his
consciousness, Boz Scaggs' 'Silk Degrees'. She immediately started
singing along and there was no sign of those irritating hiccups when
she sang. He excused himself and went for a shower, singing along as
he washed away the night's sweat.

Violet was talking to Eight Ball, he could hear her above the
noise of the running water. Slipping out of the bathroom with the
shower still running, he leapt between the pair with a loud roar. Eight
Ball scampered for the kitchen while Violet let out a nervous giggle.

"Why did you do that, Pink?"

"I thought Eight Ball was bothering you."

"He's never bothered me, such a beautiful animal. I've always
liked cats and he's the most gorgeous specimen I've ever laid eyes on
so shame on you, Pink, for frightening him like that. You should go
and see if he's alright."

"I will in a minute, there was another reason for me jumping
between you like that."

"To show me your thingy? C'mon, Pink, I've seen that countless
times now."

He had forgotten he was naked, but continued anyway.

"It was to cure your hiccups. If you care to take notice, I do
believe it worked."

"I think you're right. Oh my God, thank you, Pink. Well, good
riddance to them, I say. Thank you, thank you, thank you."

Pink reckoned she was pleased. He pulled some shorts on and
built another joint. Eight Ball settled down between them and had
Violet giggling as he chased the smoke rings, all friends again.

Today was dole signing day, he would need a nap before going
there; not in bed, though, as he was enjoying the company. He nodded

off on the couch and the last thing he heard was Violet singing along to the Cate Brothers. She had a beautiful singing voice.

"Why didn't you wake me, Violet?" He demanded.

"You should have said. How was I to know?"

"Ok, we won't fall out about it. I'm supposed to be signing on about now. I'll have to tell them another story."

"Another story?"

"It happens every week. I'm sure they think I'm working."

"You are working."

"Unofficially. It's all cash in hand. On the QT, you know?"

"Oh, yes I see. Well, tell them you've been haunted." The giggle followed and he waved goodbye.

"Bye bye, Pinkeeee, don't be long. It gets very lonely here without you."

Heavy Waite was wrestling with a pushbike, trying to extricate it from the back of his car. Pink gave him a hand and between them they managed to free it. Heavy had picked it up on a country road, he couldn't see anything wrong with it; now, it was more trouble than it was worth, did Pink want it? No charge, just buy him a pint next time he saw him.

Never look a gift horse and all that, thought Pink, jumping aboard and pedalling in the direction of the dole. The traffic lights at the crossroads changed and he hit the brakes. Nothing. He tried again. Nothing. Shit, too late. He was halfway across the junction by now and how the petrol tanker didn't pulverise him he would never know. There could only have been inches in it. He had a good story to tell them now, if he ever made it to the dole.

On inspection, the brake cables had been cut, relatively easy to replace them, he was just happy to have the chance after his near miss.

On the way home, he bought the necessary equipment. The guy in the bike shop told him he would need certain tools, which amounted to three times what he'd spent. He negotiated with the guy and had the cables fitted there and then, saving himself some time and money.

Mira saw him riding past the shop window and met him out the back. Next thing, she was on the crossbar and being aimed along the street, squealing and laughing her head off. Mr Rapati met them when they returned, arms folded across his chest, a stern look on his face. Pink took the blame, but the little man wasn't convinced, telling Mira he would speak to her later. Pink let her go back into the shop and again said it was his fault, then asked Mr Rapati could he make use of the empty bin shed to house his new bike. Mr Rapati mellowed, nodding his head in agreement and wagging his finger in Pink's direction to let him know he wasn't best pleased with his antics.

He was ready for a joint after his horrendous ordeal. Eight Ball and Violet were getting on like a house on fire; he was glad he hadn't said that out loud, too.

She broke off from her conversation with Eight Ball. "Pinkeee....Would you do me a favour, please?"

"Name it." Said Pink.

"I've been having a word with Eight Ball. We both like music, so next time you go out do you think you could leave the radio on for us?"

"Can do." He replied, busily folding his spliff together.

"Is there something wrong?"

Pink told her of his lucky escape and she gasped. "I knew as soon as you walked in."

"I had visions of coming to join you."

"Don't joke about it, please, Pink." She implored. "I died in my sleep and didn't know a thing about it. You would have known all about it if that lorry had hit you."

"That's right. I'm very lucky, I know it, Violet. Thanks for your concern."

"Ok, that's ok. Why don't you have a nice joint and relax, take your mind off it?"

"Good idea." Said Pink. "Now, why didn't I think of that?"

"Don't be funny or I'll"

"You'll what? …. Haunt me?"

Another fit of the giggles did more than enough to relax him, of course the joint also helped.

"Anything you want to listen to?"

Violet sang a few bars of a Bob Seger song and he slipped it on the turntable. Old Bob picked up some uninvited backing vocals and he didn't once complain.

Between sides, the conversation picked up again.

"Why the baskets of bread and such?"

"It's free,"

"Huh, he didn't give me free bread. Mind you, I wasn't here long enough."

"Explain."

"I rented this place with my sister. We scraped the deposit together and picked out some furniture, then she told me my boyfriend had been trying it on. I didn't believe her and we had a massive fight. I was raging mad, hit the drink and you know the rest. I was here for two days before Mr whatsisname opened the door and found me."

"Shit, you died your first night in the flat?"

"Yes, there was only the bed and some pots and pans. The furniture was due the next day, but obviously they didn't get an answer when they knocked."

"That's so sad. I bet your sister feels bad about it."

"Not half as bad as me." This brought a fit of the giggles, like she had just caught the absurdity of what she said.

Pink joined in, the giggling was like music to him, sounding unforced, free and relaxed. He felt compelled to ask.

"Are you happy, Violet?"

She took a moment to consider. "I haven't given it much thought. The couple who were in here before you only seemed to be together at weekends, then they were always arguing. There was always an atmosphere and they split up eventually."

"Nothing to do with you?"

"No, they argued from day one. Neither of them seemed to be particularly happy."

"And now?"

"Am I happy? I'll say. Almost as soon as you moved in, you and Eight Ball. You lightened the mood immediately, like when you wander around naked, sing along to the records while pretending to play guitar and drums and piano. It was a breath of fresh air and Eight Ball, he's a sweetie. He was going mad when you wouldn't let him out, you know. I did my best to explain because I had a good idea as to why you were doing it."

"I was going mad myself, wondering why he was so fixated with the wall. He knew you were there, didn't he?"

"From the word go, he sensed me, he's very perceptive. It was all I could do to stop myself from laughing at you with the ping-pong balls, but he and I understood each other from the start."

"He's always been fussy with who he takes on, you should consider yourself honoured."

"I do. I really do, Pink."

"Did you show yourself to the last people?"

"No, it didn't feel right. They were too uptight, they would have run a mile."

"So, why me?"

"I knew you were getting annoyed about Eight Ball and the wall. I was wondering how to introduce myself because, if it's got to be like this, I would rather it was with someone I liked. When I got used to your music and started singing along, you couldn't hear me because you play it so loud, but Eight Ball could. He started edging closer to the wall. I wanted to let you see me, but I wasn't sure how you would react. Then the hiccups came. I knew then it wouldn't be long before you guessed I was here. I think now it worked out fine, don't you?"

"I'm still trying to get my head round it, Violet. I'm not in the least bit freaked by you. I think you're great company; but like I say, I'm still getting my head round it."

"Will you play me the one where he sings 'Darling'? Not just the one song, the whole album. The one that plays right through, the one with the audience."

Pink put the Frankie Miller tape on and stretched out on the couch, he had half a shift later; it would end up as a full shift since he hadn't seen Johan for a while and they had some catching up to do.

"Will you wake me up in an hour if I fall asleep?"

"There's no clock, do you want me to guess?"

"The tape lasts for an hour, could you wake me when it finishes?"

"Ok, you have a nice nap. I really like this one, night night, Pinkee." Giggles, then singing backing vocals, or more like duetting with Frankie.

He was aware of Eight Ball landing lightly on him and curling up like he used to do. He remembered nothing else except for being on stage with Frankie, sharing a microphone with Violet, gazing into her deep green eyes and serenading her.

She had to ask for Eight Ball's help. Pink didn't seem to want to be shaken from his dream. Eight Ball did as she asked and jumped all over him, tupping him on the side of the head for good measure.

"You must have needed that sleep. I've been shouting you for ten minutes."

Pink rubbed his eyes and put the radio on, hoping to catch a timecheck. Straight away the nine thirty news came on and he went to the bathroom to splash his face.

"I feel like shit. I'm sorry I agreed to this now."

"Why don't you have a joint? You might feel better, and play some pretend guitar, that always seems to raise your game."

"Air guitar."

"What what?"

"That's what it's called. Air guitar."

"Well, whatever you call it, it always seems to buck you up a bit."

Pink had to agree, she was right, what the fuck, he had nothing to lose. Taking centre stage, he played alongside Nils Lofgren and Violet harmonised delightfully. Eight Ball found the warm spot Pink had left for him on the settee and had a catnap, he would catch up with Violet later.

"I LIKE THE WAY YOU SHAKE YOUR BUM." Shouted Violet above the sound from the speakers.

Pink either didn't hear her or ignored her, too busy squeezing the last few notes from the neck of his instrument.

He had to admit it, she was right, he really felt refreshed.

"That wasn't a bad idea at all," he told her. "I'm going to enjoy having you around, Violet."

"You don't have to say that. It's good that you did, but I don't seem to be able to go anywhere else so it looks like you're stuck with me."

"What's it like?"

"What?"

"Being brown bread?"

"Huh? Oh, you mean being dead? It's weird. Really weird, I guess."

"I mean, going by all that religious stuff they battered into us at school, you should either be in heaven or hell."

"Or limbo? I think I'm in limbo, somewhere in between, I take it you're not religious, Pink?"

"I try to keep an open mind on the subject."

"I'd say you keep an open mind on a lot of subjects."

"Well, it reduces the chance of surprise. I mean, take you for example. I soon got over your appearance because I kept an open mind on the subject of ghosts."

"That's very clever, not a bad philosophy that. You should take it to the masses."

"Start up my own religion, 'the Church of the open mind'? I can see it now. People would throw money at me to hear me tell them not to give a flying fuck about anything."

"Hmmm ..... needs some work .... Speaking of work .....you'll be late if you don't hurry."

"Shit, you're right, shit shit shit. I'm off, see you later, don't wait up."

The delicious sound of her laughter followed him all the way downstairs. Mira met him on the corner and asked what he was grinning at, she had been on her way to rouse him. Again, Pink changed the subject. He wasn't ready to go public about Violet, maybe he never would. What did her father say about her antics on the crossbar?

Mira smiled, she had talked her way round him on that, she could get round him in most things. The smile dissolved. If only she could do it with this marriage thing.

Pink put his arm round her shoulder to comfort her and inhaled the smell of her recently washed hair. Mira slipped her arm around his waist and gave his backside a squeeze. If her father were to walk in now she would be divorced before she could get married.

Pink managed to keep her mind off her troubles for the couple of hours they had together until Sira picked her up. He knew if he put his mind to it he could probably avail himself of her delightful charms, but he wouldn't; partly out of respect for the girl and her family, but mostly because of his own fear of commitment. No one had ever pointed this fear out to him, he knew very well it existed, had never tried to rationalise it; believing it was just something he would have to live with.

Mira put the lips on him before she went home and thanked him for being her friend. He sensed he was going to have to fight hard against his feelings or he wouldn't be able to keep his hands off her.

When she left he stretched out and made himself comfortable, time for a catnap, the oven timers would wake him. The feeling he was coming down with a cold had returned with a vengeance.

When he opened his eyes, Johan was framed in the doorway, with Eight Ball tucked under one arm.

Pink felt a bit better for his nap and went to work on the batches for the next bake while Johan emptied the ovens. Eight Ball curled up on the flour sacks Pink had fashioned into a makeshift bed for him.

He had been thinking. Johan should be made aware of Sira's future intended before he found himself in too deep. There was no easy way to broach the subject so he jumped in with both feet, telling his friend what he knew. To his relief, Johan was aware of it, was in fact resigned to it. He and Sira were just mates.

Pink left it at that, not wishing to rock the boat by pointing out they looked a lot more than just friends to his well trained eye.

The reason for Johan's absence, his uncle, the same uncle who had brought him to this country had been the victim of a racially motivated assault, skinheads. Now, he wanted to come and live near his nephew. Johan had been charged with finding him accommodation and work, no mean task in this deprived area. What Johan didn't want was his uncle living with him, he was so used to his own space. His uncle wouldn't want that either since he too valued his independence.

Pink was sorely tempted to let his friend know of his ghost, but stopped himself. Might be best to talk it over with Violet first, ghost or not she was first and foremost of the female persuasion.

If a decent smoke was hard to come by in this part of the world, there was a true drought where Johan's uncle lived; people he knew there had been going short for six months or more. Not a problem for the two friends, they had quite enough between them to be going on with.

Pink lasted until three o'clock, his aches and pains had returned; a good night's sleep would sort him out, he hoped.

The radio had wandered off the station and Violet's face was contorted, letting him know she didn't like what she was having to listen to. Pink had a look, it was on the medium wave band, he changed to FM and retuned. Violet let out a sigh of relief, closely followed by a gasp when she noticed his pallor.

"Do you have any Lemsips, Pink?"

"No, I was thinking of dosing myself with whisky and sweating it out."

"Lemsip's best. It's the paracetamol. Takes away the muscle ache."

"You do it your way and I'll stick to mine."

"Oh, ok, but at least go to bed and get wrapped up warm."

He boiled the kettle, poured a generous measure of whisky into a glass, added a teaspoon of sugar and was just about to pour the boiling water in when Violet shouted.

"STOP!"

Pink froze, she was on the kitchen wall now. "What? .... What is it."

"Put the teaspoon in the glass or the water will shatter it."

"Oh yeah, I knew that, but thanks. How did you get in here?"

"I can move around."

"What, outside?"

"No, within the flat."

"And downstairs, to the shop and the bakery?"

"No, only the flat."

"So why stick to that one wall?"

"I like the space. It might sound a bit silly this, but I feel hemmed in by too much furniture."

"That makes sense .... I think. So, that's why Eight Ball always sits in front of that particular wall?"

"Drink that down, Pink, and go to bed. You look terrible, honestly." "You mean like death warmed up?" He joked, then regretted it. Violet laughed anyway. He was pleased she had a sense of humour. She sure as shit would need it.

As warm as the flat was, he fed his sleeping bag between the sheet and the blankets, wriggled in, zipped it up fully and slept like a baby. Nothing disturbed him; no Eight Ball, no dreams and definitely no hiccupping.

Violet was there when he opened his eyes, watching over him. Watching over him literally from the bedroom ceiling. He was becoming quite used to her presence now. He could make out a little more of her features in this better light and he liked what he saw, cursing his luck that he couldn't get a grip of her. If it ever happened that he somehow could hold her, he was sure he wouldn't want to let her go.

"How long have you been there?"

"All night and all day."

"How long did I sleep?"

"Hours and hours. I would say it's three or four in the afternoon."

Pink wriggled in the sleeping bag and felt decidedly uncomfortable, it was wet through. He unzipped it and grimaced at the stench of sweat. He would have to take it to the launderette, but not today, he would make sure he was rid of the aches and pains first.

"The postman's been."

"Thought you had been up there all night?"

"I heard him."

"Probably only bills. I'll have a shower first."

"I didn't like to say."

Pink laughed. There was that sense of humour again. This was marvellous, his own personal ghost, complete with funny bone.

"This is where I miss a bath. Shake in some salt and soak those aches away, shame."

"Yes, Radox, that's what you need. It's good stuff that."

"You always want to spend money when you don't need to."

"What do you mean, Pink?"

"Earlier you suggested Lemsip when a hot toddy does the same job, then, Radox when ordinary salt is just as good. Were you rich?"

"Never heard that one. The whisky, yes, but salt? And no, I wasn't rich. I had to work for a living. You're cheeky, you are."

"I'm for a shower, d'you want to wash my back?"

"He-he, I'd love to. I really would, Pink."

He sorted some music out and headed for the bathroom, naked as the day he was born. Violet tried to whistle, but couldn't. Instead, she sang along with the stereo and Pink did the same.

She was in the bathroom when he stepped out of the shower, just visible through the steam, still singing. He cracked the window open and the room cleared quickly.

"My, Pink. You are pleased to see me, aren't you?"

Pink followed her gaze and realised he had a lazy lob on; nothing unusual in that, the warm water and thoughts of what he would like to do to Violet combining to get him aroused. Even more so now that she had noticed. He certainly wasn't ready for what she came out with next.

"Play with it, Pink, please. Make it hard. I know you really want to."

He hesitated momentarily then thought, what the fuck? He had enjoyed mutual masturbation with more than one of his lady friends, but this was different. It didn't take him long to get a hard on. With Violet's more than helpful encouragement, he proceeded to pull the head off his cock, increasing the tempo when she begged him to go faster and told him she wanted it in her mouth.

When it was all over she thanked him, asked him did he enjoy it as much as she had and invited him to do it whenever he felt the urge. She would talk him through it anytime, anytime at all.

There was a spring in his step now, he felt good, a whole lot better than he had yesterday. The radio said five o'clock, about an hour's worth of daylight left, just time enough to prepare his little patch of land.

Jumping on his bike, he cycled through the park and down the lane towards the allotments. He stopped to borrow a spade which had been propped against an allotment fence, then pedalled on down past the mad Alsatian at the Blunt brothers' land and onto the canal bank. Half an hour later, he stood back to admire his work, a job well done. He stashed the spade in the bushes. By the time conditions were right for planting out, the brambles would probably be trying to spread themselves over his plot. It wouldn't take him long to clear them.

On the way back, he ran over a young rabbit, couldn't do anything about it. Picking it up, he teased the Blunt's dog with it, noticing how quiet and almost docile he had become at the notion of some food. Pink lobbed the rabbit over the fence and watched as the animal made short work of ripping it apart to get to the flesh; it was almost clinical.

Mira met him as he stowed his bike in the bin shed, she had a day off on Friday, would he go with her for a look at her intended? She would be very grateful.

How could he refuse? Of course he would take her, did she want him to borrow the van? That would be ok, it would be cheaper than the train and she would pay for the petrol.

As luck would have it, Johan had been round with a pan of chicken Madras, he hadn't thought about food with having been ill. He knew as soon as he caught a whiff of it warming his appetite would kick in.

"Who makes the curries?"

Pink was rolling a joint, crosslegged in front of the wall. "Johan, the night shift baker downstairs."

"Is he foreign? Dutch, or something?"

"Foreign, yes, but not Dutch. Indian. Goanese. Come to think of it, I'm sure it might have been a Dutch colony at one time. I'm not positive on that, I'll ask him, I'll tell him you want to know."

"Don't you dare, Pink. Don't you dare."

"Why? You've let me see you so why not my friend?"

"It took me a long time to even consider letting you see me. I'm not sure I could handle anyone else, it could turn into a circus. Please, Pink, don't let that happen."

"Whatever you say, Violet, but you'll have to explain it to Eight Ball, you know what a chatterbox he can be."

Violet giggled, possibly his favourite sound, at least it was high up there on his list of favourite sounds.

"Thank you, Pink. I'll have a word with him."

"Now's your chance," he told her as Eight Ball clattered in through the kitchen window like someone, or something, was chasing him. "It's time for my nap."

He put the radio on low and flopped on the couch. Two minutes later he was asleep. Violet put her concerns to Eight Ball, accepting assurances the secret of her appearances was safe with him.

He knew it was late when he heard Violet calling his name, telling him it was nine thirty and almost time for work. Pink rubbed his eyes, he wouldn't be doing a full shift with Johan tonight, what he needed was another good sleep. Splashing his face, he decided he would spend two hours with his friend downstairs then try to sleep round the clock again.

He rolled a couple of joints, stood up, sat back down again and decided it was bedtime. Whatever had been hanging about him was still hanging about him. Next stop was the kitchen, a hot toddy then zipped into the still smelly sleeping bag. He forgot to turn the radio off, not that it had any chance of keeping him awake, but he was tucked up now. Violet could enjoy it, he didn't have the energy to struggle out of his cocoon.

Chit chat

Pink heard the rain hammering on the window and Eight Ball came into the bedroom to confirm the weather outside was indeed inclement. Well, maybe not for that sole purpose, Violet was on the ceiling so he was probably looking for her.

"You've slept a long time again, Pink. Are you sure you're ok?"

"I'll know better when I get out of this puddle I'm lying in. Whatever was in me must be sweated out by now. What d'you think?"

"Are you hungry?"

"Don't tell me you've started breakfast going?"

"He-he. No, silly, but if you're hungry it's a good sign. It means you're on the mend."

"Well, I could eat something nice. Nip in the kitchen and see if there's any curry left, will you?"

"You know there isn't. You couldn't get it into you fast enough last night."

"Maybe a fry up will sort me out."

"Have your shower first."

"What are you trying to say?"

"Nothing, Pink, really, you said you were all sweaty."

"I think you just want to see me naked again. Am I right, Violet Hiccup?"

"If you must know, yes, that's the real reason. He-he."

The cooked breakfast disappeared in record time. He was feeling better, but he had rallied yesterday, only to fall flat again. Today, he would take it easy, a few joints, a lot of good music and maybe a nap. Yes, a nice leisurely day, that would bring him back to something like.

But first, he had laundry to pick up. He would take the sleeping bag to be cleaned, see if it could be salvaged.

"You're not going out in that weather, are you?"

"It's only down the road a bit."

"You've been ill for the best part of two days. Going out will only make you worse."

"You sound just like my old mum, God rest her."

"Well, she was right. It doesn't make sense to aggravate the problem, does it?"

"But this sleeping bag will stink the place out, it already smells like a week at Knebworth."

"Knebworth?"

"Music festival. All tents and wigwams, drugs and music, fast food and poor sanitation."

"Sounds awful."

"Actually, it can be a lot of fun if the right bands turn up and the right drugs turn up. A whole lot of fun."

"Put it in a bin liner."

"Huh?"

"Your sleeping bag. Put it in a bin liner and tie it up until the rain stops."

"Ok. But what about milk?"

"What about milk?"

"I need some for Eight Ball. He likes the cream."

"He'll understand. Your health is more important."

Pink gave in and did as she asked, rolling the sleeping bag up, feeding it into a bin bag and tying it at the neck. The old lady at the launderette wouldn't thank him when she got the chance to open it.

"Now, put it between the doors and forget about it until the weather breaks.

"You'll have me washing the windows next."

"Wait until you've got your strength back. Look! You've two joints lying there from last night. Why don't you light one up and relax? They won't have gone off, will they?"

Pink's turn to laugh, interrupted by a coughing fit. Where had that come from? He thought he was better and now, here he was, barking like somebody's dog. Two tokes on the joint stopped the coughing, three more tokes and it started up again.

"Have a drink, Pink. Hey! I'm a poet. He-he. Have a drink, Pink."

"It was your idea to have a smoke. Maybe a drink will fucking kill me."

"Try anyway, Pink. You've turned a funny colour. Have a drink, please."

The cool cider soothed his throat. The joint burned away in the ashtray until he caught a whiff of it and decided to give it one more try; managing to finish it without doing himself further harm.

"Feel better?"

"A bit."

"Well, why don't you play that nice Bob Seagull album? Then you can sit down and relax."

Pink fished out the 'Stranger in Town' album, turned towards Violet and pointed to the cover.

"Seger. Bob Seger and the Silver Bullet Band."

"That's what I said."

"You said Seagull."

"Well, you must have known who I meant. You picked the record up straight away so you must have. Play it, please, Pinkee."

He couldn't argue with her logic, neither could he dispute her choice of music. Falling onto the couch, he closed his eyes and listened to her singing along with Bob Seagull. She let side one finish before picking up the conversation again.

"Have you any Steely Dan, Pink?"

"Where do you know them from?"

"The radio. I've heard the same song twice and each time the DJ gave the name of the band, but not the song."

"How does it go?"

"Something about ringing in the ears."

Pink didn't bother to correct her this time. He found his copy of 'Can't buy a Thrill' and made it back to the couch before the music kicked in. Lighting the other joint, he relaxed back to listen, wondering why he hadn't played it since moving into the flat. Another one of life's great mysteries.

Of course there was no female harmony part and no backing vocals since Violet had only heard one track, and that only twice. He would play with her head now. 'Reelin' in the Years' started off side two; she would be hanging on every word and waiting for her song to begin. The joint was half black half Leb and he knew it after only one hit. Now, he was feeling better, settling back into the couch and letting Steely Dan wash all over him.

"What happened to my song?" She demanded as side one finished.

Pink didn't bother to answer her, simply flipping the disc and warming up his air guitar. Violet squealed as the opening riff hit her ears and Pink strutted his stuff as only he can. All too soon, the first track was over. Pink built a couple of joints and they listened to the rest of side two in silence while Eight Ball sat between them and purred his furry little head off.

"What would you like to hear now?"

"Cry Tough."

"Excellent choice."

"You must've played it four or five times when you brought it in. That's how you get to know them, isn't it?"

"Clever girl. You're very perceptive."

"I've nothing better to do ….. er …. I didn't mean it to sound like that, Pink. What I meant was, I don't have any choice in the matter.

Really, I'm enjoying myself. I would never have had the privilege of listening to all this beautiful music if …. if"

"I know what you mean, Violet. It's nothing to worry about. I'm pretty sure I'll put my foot in it at some point, if I haven't already done so."

"You're very kind."

"I know."

"You don't seem to have a girlfriend. Why is that?"

Pink considered her question for a moment. "It's because I'm so painfully shy."

"Fuck off, Pink."

"Violet Hiccup. Where oh where did you get that bad language from?"

"From you, of course. You're a bad influence. I'd never have dared to say that word, but I think it's ok with you, Pink. Isn't it?"

"As long as you don't make a fucking habit of it."

Violet giggled. Pink pulled on his jeans and headed for the door. It was still raining, but he was only going downstairs.

"See you later, Violet."

"Not if I see you first. Oh, Pink. The radio please."

Johan told him he looked like death warmed up, but he felt a whole lot better than before. He poured two glasses of cider, lit a spliff and settled into one of the chairs. Johan was highly amused when he told the tale of the bike, wishing he had witnessed it and assuring Pink he appeared to be riding his luck. Over the next couple of hours he learned two things. Johan's real name was Mohammed Tisk Atiqur Fatorpa Bogmalo. A fisherman uncle had given him the nickname when he was a boy, for the simple reason Johan was easier to say than ' Mohammed Tisk Atiqur Fatorpa Bogmalo! Get off my fucking boat.'

After that couple of hours, Pink was feeling tired again. His bed was beckoning and he took his leave along with a basketful of baked goods.

"You weren't long, Pink?"

"Tired, me. It hit me all of a sudden. I virtually crawled up those stairs. Let's go to bed."

"He-he. But I hardly know you …. Ok, you charmed me into it you sweet talking man."

"By the way, Johan is a nickname. He has about eight names, but gets Johan for short. Which suits me because I could never remember all those other names."

"Is he descended from the Dutch, then? Did you ask?"

"Portuguese. Wait. He's not Portuguese. He's from Goa, so he's Goanese. But Goa was under Portugal for a long time. I think I got that right. There are almost as many Christians living in Goa as any other religion. I think Johan was brought up as a mixture of them all."

"So, what does that make Johan?"

"An immigrant."

"He-he. You are silly sometimes, Pink."

"Silly and tired. Night night, Violet."

"Night night, Pink. No hot toddy tonight?"

"Not unless you make it. I'll fall asleep standing up if I try."

He was out for the count before his head hit the pillow, knocking ot zeds like a bumble bee.

CHAPTER 15

Touch and go

Pink had maybe the most vivid, erotic dream he had ever heard
tell of. No multiple partners, no multiple situations, only his friendly
ghost for company; and in his own bed at that. It had started off
innocently enough. His hair had been flying free for a couple of days,
tied back only for the purpose of baking with Johan. He decided
it needed a thorough wash and jumped in the shower, working up
a good lather and making sure he got rid of all the flour dust. He
wrapped his head in one towel, turban like, and dried himself off with
the other. Thinking the towel would dry his hair while he slept, he
rested his head on the pillow and soon nodded off. Violet appeared,
he was used to that by now. This time, however, she was dancing to
the music, but in the middle of the floor. Now, she was kneeling on
the bed, inviting him to sit up so she could dry his hair. He reached
for her, expecting his hand to pass through; but it didn't; she was real,
real enough to touch, to caress. He could feel the fabric of her dress
and the fact she was naked underneath; then, the aroma of flowers,
lavender, that was it. He remembered thinking it should be violets,
but he wasn't complaining. Inhaling deeply, he reached behind her
and tweaked a double handful of firm young buttock, kneading and
fondling for all he was worth. Violet continued to dry his hair, quite
roughly, but that didn't bother him; he was busy himself, burying

his nose between her firm, perfect breasts and working his hands under her dress to reach the flesh he had craved since he first set eyes on her. Where did she go? Now she was behind him. He relaxed, feeling her hot breath on the back of his neck as she plaited his hair. Moments later, she stood in front of him and slowly disrobed, a shy little smile on her lips as she watched him devour her with his eyes. He told himself to take his time, to savour the moment; mostly, he told himself not to even dare think about waking up. Violet leaned in for the kiss and he made contact with her naked body, running his hands where he could reach and gently turning her on to her back. He nibbled her ear, her neck, one nipple, then the other, then back to the first and Violet let out a delightful purring sound to let him know he was pressing all the right buttons.

Rolling her onto her stomach, Pink took a moment to absorb what lay before him then ran his hands up and down her back, lingering to pay homage to the finest backside it had ever been his pleasure to gaze upon. God, she was beautiful; beautiful and uncomplicated, what a combination. He kissed each cheek in worship just as Violet reached for him, clasping him with a featherlight touch and slowly gliding her hand up and down the length of his shaft, just enough to let him know she had him where she wanted him. To be honest, he didn't want to be anywhere else himself, quite happy to let her dictate the pace. Still with that soft and gentle grip on him, she turned onto her back and guided his hand between her legs. To say she was ready for him was something of an understatement, hot and wet and inviting. He had to have a taste and plunged his tongue as far inside her as he could possibly reach, drawing a loud gasp of pleasure from Violet, followed by that satisfied purr again. He didn't want to stop, Violet was desperately trying to draw him into her mouth and all but made his mind up for him. Sixty nine wasn't his favourite position, he found it hard to concentrate on both giving and receiving pleasure at the same time, feeling either one or both partners would end up missing out somehow. Violet seemed to understand and guided him into her, giggling as he gasped at the sensation. The giggle turned him to jelly, turned most of him to jelly. Violet arched her back to accommodate him and they gyrated in unison, picking up on a silent signal from somewhere and increasing the tempo until they both screamed in orgasm. She was sobbing now, and purring, with tears of joy and pleasure streaming down her face. Pink kissed them away, he had often wondered what lavender tasted like and now he knew; he could live on it if he had to.

He only closed his eyes for a moment. When he opened them he was in bed alone, although there was an indent in the pillow beside him which had him thinking maybe he hadn't dreamt it. Sliding to the edge of the bed, he felt something cold, cold, damp and sticky. Violet was on the ceiling, eyes closed, smiling sweetly, moving her head to an imaginary song and giving nothing away. In the bathroom, he caught sight of himself in his shaving mirror, a red mark on his shoulder. Closer inspection showed it to be remarkably like teeth marks; a bite, no broken skin, but a bite all the same. Maybe it did happen? He didn't want to ask in case it broke the spell, took away the memory. He slipped back into bed, kept away from the damp patch and watched Violet, watched her for an hour or longer. Still she gave nothing away, singing softly and smiling that sweet, innocent smile. He didn't dream again that night, maybe he didn't have the energy?

The sound of purring woke him up. He opened one eye and was disappointed to see Eight Ball curled up on the other pillow. That might explain the indent, a wet dream would explain the damp patch, leaving only the bite to ponder over. Eight Ball hadn't bitten him, he would have taken a chunk; besides, by the size of the mark it could only have been a human. He was human, but he couldn't possibly have bitten himself there, no way. Then, the hairs on the back of his neck stood to attention with the realisation his previously loose locks had been plaited to perfection.

"Good morning, Pinkee. You were very restless in your sleep." This was followed by her giggle.

"Funny that, I feel totally refreshed."

"That's good to know, I'm so pleased. Maybe you could wash the windows today, then?"

It sounded more like a command than a question, either way he ignored it, between adjusting his balls and rubbing his eyes at the same time he had quite enough to concentrate on.

The rain had stopped so he stripped the bed, but not before he had put some music on for Violet, she was as bad as him for that; music morning, noon and night. Again, no complaints.

Eight Ball was making his demands known now, cream, more or less indicating he should run to the shops and hurry back. Pink had other plans. These started with a spliff and a drink of some sorts; coffee; he preferred it black and sweet, the way the cowboys drank it.

When he went into the bedroom for his sheets he caught a faint whiff of lavender; bringing thoughts of his dream, if indeed it was a dream, flooding back to him.

His giro was at the back of the door when he bounced downstairs, that was handy, he could cash it and pick up some groceries without having to disturb his stash. The old woman in the bric-a-brac shop knocked on the window as he came out of the post office, she had something for him. It turned out to be an album Brat had been playing for a while, he had intended borrowing it from him this past couple of weeks, but hadn't got round to it. Close inspection found it to be in almost mint condition, which pleased him no end since the sleeve was well and truly damaged. Fifty pence was a reasonable price to pay for such a prize. He kissed the old woman on the cheek and told her to keep her eyes peeled.

"What have you got there?"

"Milk, cream for Eight Ball."

"Under your arm, silly."

"Patience, woman. Let me sort the cat out first."

"Hurry, is it good? Have you heard it before?"

"Yes, to all of that. Give me a minute."

From the first few notes she was mesmerised. Pink put a joint together and watched her as she listened intently, waiting for side one to end before daring to speak again.

"Who is it, Pink? It's so different, almost sleazy. Who is it, tell me?"

"Tom Petty and the Heartbreakers. It does sound sleazy, doesn't it? You picked up on that right away, you're very perceptive."

"Only since I've been listening to your music collection. I can't say I took much notice before."

"What did you listen to then?"

"Oh, mostly the top twenty, the radio, you know?"

"That explains it. I only really use the radio for background unless it's someone who knows what he's talking about and doesn't jabber over the music. Then I pay attention."

"Or she."

"Huh?"

"Or she. There's a woman on sometimes. I've heard you talking to her like she's in the room with you."

"You mean Annie Nightingale? Yes, she knows her stuff, she's turned me and millions of others on to things I otherwise might never have heard. My mate Brat does that as well to some degree, it's the sign of a good DJ that, always on the lookout for something new and having the gumption to feed it to people."

"You really love your music, don't you, Pink?"

"You noticed. Yes. It's kept me alive in the past."

"Explain, please."

"Some other time. Let's have a listen to the other side."

Another smoke, all black this time, he was going for the stupor effect, something that would knock him out for a couple of hours and force him to rest. It worked, the music finished and Violet called his name, but he was immobile. All he could move were his eyes and his right foot, which had been keeping the beat and had carried on when the needle lifted from the record.

"Are you alright, Pink? What's wrong? Don't you want to listen to music with me?"

He forced himself to roll off the chair, hopefully towards the stereo. This earned him a nervous giggle from Violet, then a gasp as his head bounced off the carpet. Now he was laughing helplessly, another sure sign he was out of his tree, as infectious as a yawn in a crowded room. Before long, Violet joined in and his heart leapt with joy to hear that wonderful sound coming from her.

He managed to reach up and change the function of the music centre, filling the room with the inane banter of a DJ he imagined to be preening himself in a mirror.

"What was in that joint, can you tell me? Is it so strong it can do that to you, Pink?"

"Uh-huh." He managed to mumble, at the same time slavering out of the corner of his mouth.

The DJ was still talking. It must have been five minutes, maybe more and he hadn't come up for air. Pink couldn't stand it any longer and managed to drag himself up onto his knees, laughing again at how ridiculous he must look to Violet. Eight Ball was watching him, too, but he had seen it all before; he did keep his distance though, past experience telling him Pink could topple over at the drop of a hat. Once bitten twice shy and so forth.

Pink worked it out all on his own, the tape deck would be the easiest of the stereo's functions to bring into play. Flip a switch, press a button and Fanny's your aunty. Nothing. Click, click, click. The tape had run its course. With a superhuman effort, he managed to turn it and set it in play before succumbing to Eight Ball's prediction and collapsing in an untidy heap once more on the carpet.

Violet was having a lot of fun with this now, howling with laughter along with Pink and shrieking whenever he tried to get something going with his helpless frame. The main thing was, they now had some decent music to accompany the sideshow, his one regret being that he hadn't had the foresight to build another joint for that very moment.

Pink flaked out on his chair again after taking a good ten minutes to manoeuvre himself into it; a failed attempt to accompany Steve Miller on air guitar having interrupted the fluidity, or lack of, his movements. All this to the great delight of his audience, Violet, who squealed and called encouragement, providing Eight Ball with a running commentary.

Forty five minutes later he was in the kitchen, making hard work of undressing a cauliflower. Whatever he was having to eat, he was having cauliflower with it.

"Careful, Pink. You'll have your fingers off with that knife."

"If it isn't sharp enough to cut into this cauli, it sure as shit isn't sharp enough to cut my fingers off OUCH."

"See, I told you to be careful. Let me see, have you drawn blood?"

"No."

"What then?"

"I stood on my toe."

"Is that all? …. I had visions of a bloodbath. You should make a cheese sauce to go with that."

"Sounds good …. but I don't know how."

"I can help."

"I'm game …. is it easy?"

"You've got cheese and milk, haven't you?"

"Yes."

"Powdered mustard?"

"What does that do?"

"Gives it a bit of a kick, a bit of bite."

"No mustard, yes, it's in a jar, though."

"Might spoil it that, and flour, do you have some flour?"

"No …. but I know a man who does."

With that, he was halfway out of the door before being stopped in his tracks.

"Wait …. wait a minute. Take a cup with you."

"Why?"

"Because that's what neighbours do. Borrow a cup of sugar or milk, or salt."

"But, I need flour."

"You are silly sometimes. Take a cup with you, and put something on your feet."

The sisters were pleased to see him. Sira went through to the back for his flour and Mira whispered she was looking forward to spending the day with him on Friday. Pink told her he couldn't get the van, but they could still go .... on the pushbike. Mira's smile had him transfixed, she knew he was joking, she hoped he was joking.

The potatoes and cauliflower were bubbling away on the cooker, a large pork chop under the grill on a low light, now for the sauce. Violet took him through it stage by stage until it looked perfect.

"Is that it?"

"Yes, have a taste."

Pink stuck his finger in and let out a yelp of pain.

"Why did you do that?"

"I've seen that woman on the telly taste her sauce like that."

"She's a cook, a chef, you are silly. All chefs have asbestos fingers from spending so long in the kitchen. You shouldn't copy. Run your finger under the cold tap .... and keep stirring that sauce."

The meal was delicious, a large pan of fried onions and a bottle of cold cider adding the finishing touches.

Sparks flew from his eating irons as he made short work of it, pausing only once to tell the irritating DJ on the radio to shut the fuck up and play some decent music. Sadly, his tirade fell on deaf ears.

"You'll give yourself indigestion, Pink."

"That bastard on the wireless will give me indigestion more like."

"Don't speak with your mouth full, please."

Pink ignored her and concentrated on the plate in front of him, then gulped greedily from his glass of cider, belching loudly to test the waters, see if it invoked further comment. There was none.

The next joint was of a lesser calibre than its predecessor; the last of the home grown, bolstered with a little bit of Leb. This would let him catnap; not like the black, the black tended to let all manner of thoughts run amok through his brain.

"It's nap time, isn't it?"

"How do you know that?"

"I can read you like a book."

"That's all I need, a mindreading ghost."

"Not your mind, Pink, It's your body language."

"Oh, ok. Yes, it is nap time. Care to join me?"

"Ooh yes, I'd love too. Can I?"

"Sure you can, but after you've done the dishes, eh?"

Her laugh made him break out in goose bumps. They both fell silent and listened to Frankie Miller, allowing him to sing on his own for a change.

The tape was nearing its end when he woke up; an hour must have been all he needed to recharge, a sure sign he was on the mend. It was too early to go downstairs so he passed the time on by putting a Cate brothers album on either side of a C90 cassette, reminding himself to buy some more tapes; that way he could preserve his vinyl collection, so easy to drag the stylus across every track when stoned.

"The more I hear this band, the more I like them."

"It's a good job that, Violet, because I can't get enough of them. I've got Brat looking out for anything else they might have done. I swear if they ever tour this part of the world I'll be first in the queue for tickets."

"Do you think they will tour?"

"Nah, I very much doubt it. You see, none of the radio stations have picked up on them so I don't think it would be in their best interests to come where nobody knows them."

"We know them, Pink."

"True, very true. Ok, I'll get on the phone to them in the morning, see if I can arrange a private gig. We can offer them accommodation, pay them in empty cider bottles, and feed them all the curry and baked goodies they can eat."

"He-he. D'you think they'll do it?"

"I really don't see how they could possibly refuse, Violet. That is one very tempting offer."

"I'll leave it with you then, shall I?"

"Ok, I'll keep you up to speed with how it's all going."

"Please do, Pink. He-he-he. Please do."

Johan kept looking at his watch, Pink wouldn't ask why although he had a good idea. At eleven o'clock Sira appeared in the doorway and he knew his hunch was spot on, just good friends indeed. This was a love match, and a dangerous one at that, dangerous enough for Pink to worry about the outcome. He chased them out into the night, advised them to keep their heads down and told them not to be late. Who was he to stand in the way of love's young dream?

Eight Ball showed his face, had a quick word then curled up on his flour sacks. He was still there when Johan came back, showing perfect timing as Pink had put a light to a very large joint that very instant.

Already, Johan had fixed his uncle up with employment in a friend's restaurant. The same friend had been enlisted as recipient and addressee for their upcoming import business. Pink was to meet him tomorrow, get acquainted; as soon as the goods arrived he would be required to rid the premises of them quick smart.

He lasted until three thirty, suddenly he was dog tired. Arranging to meet Johan at the restaurant the following afternoon, he said goodnight and made his weary way home.

"Tuesday's gone."

"Yes, it's Wednesday. No, Thursday now."

"No, no, silly. It's a song. Do you know it? Please tell me you know it?"

"Yes ..... from the first Skynyrd album. I don't have it. I mean, I used to own it, but it walked."

"Walked?"

"Disappeared, vanished, evaporated. One day I had it, the next day some tea leafing bastard had it."

"You're funny, Pink."

"It wasn't funny at the time, believe me."

"Will you buy it again?"

"For you, Violet, of course I will. Already on my list of things to do."

"He-he. Thank you, Pink. I think you're just wonderful."

"Me too. Did you hear it on the radio?" "Yes, it's a really beautiful song."

"The whole album's a bit special. I'll have a good look round for it."

"Tomorrow? I mean, later today?"

"Can't promise that, but soon. You've nudged it to the front of my mind so definitely soon. Now, I'm ready for bed, are you?"

"Yes, Pink, he-he. I'm ready."

The scent of lavender filled his nostrils, Violet was in bed with him, no acrobatics, but lots of caresses and cuddles. The best night's sleep he could ever remember.

Pet names

Pink was all alone when he woke up, another indent in the pillow beside him and the lingering aroma of lavender. He wouldn't ask Violet outright if it was her favourite scent, he would make her tell him herself; make a game of it, a challenge. Putting the radio on for the time, he had a quick wash and started on the breakfast. Porridge, followed by toast and marmalade. The only objection he had to having porridge was that he had to clean the pan when he was done, not his favourite job.

The guy on the radio said it was two o'clock, breakfast had turned out to be a late lunch. Pink rolled a couple of joints and lined the turn- up of his bob cap with them, he was due to meet Johan in half an hour.

"Why do you put your joints there?"

"If the drug squad stop me there's a good chance they won't search my hat. They can be as thick as pigshit at times"

"You say the funniest things sometimes. Be careful, Pink"

"Later, Violet. I'll leave the radio on for you."

"Thank you, you darling, darling man. See you later."

The restaurant was a twenty minute walk or five minutes by train and Pink opted for the latter. Two reasons, the sky was black with rainclouds for one; the second, after his recent illness he really didn't want to overdo it.

The place was closed when he arrived, but he could smell cooking. He rapped on the side door and a huge Asian filled the doorway. He informed Pink they were closed and made to shut the door again. Pink mentioned Johan's name and a huge grin spread over the man's face, then they were shaking hands and Pink was being escorted to the kitchen. Introducing himself as Ashwatthama, or Ash for short, he invited Pink to sit at what must have been the staff table in the corner. Pink told him whatever he was cooking smelled delicious and was invited to sample it just as Johan let himself in. The two men greeted each other and conversed in their native tongue for a few seconds, then resorted to English for Pink's benefit. As they ate, they thrashed out all the permutations of a three way partnership. Agreeing each of them were taking equal risks in one way or another, it was decreed the profits should be split evenly. The finer points were kicked around over the next two hours, during which time Pink must have sampled everything on the menu.

The handshakes were genuine, he was sure of that. The bearhugs were a little too personal for his tastes, but different strokes and all that, he could probably get used to it. Ash insisted he should dine there on a regular basis at his expense and he just knew they would be good business partners and good friends.

With the deal done and dusted, the three men sat around the table, good naturedly getting to know a little more about each other. Pink uncovered one interesting little gem about Ash, something he seemed a little sheepish about and, giving the impression he had said more than he wanted to, was reluctant to discuss further. The arrival of Ash's staff brought the meeting to a close, but not before they were all introduced to Pink, just so they knew his money was no good if ever Ash was absent from the restaurant.

Johan had promised to go in to work early as cover for Mr Rapati. Pink left him at the railway station and went to pick up the van, he and Mira would be making an early start in the morning, ten o'clock being deemed early enough for him.

He caught Doc's woman at it again. The guy was a stranger to him this time, but she knew him very well going off what he saw through the net curtains. When she passed the keys to him he suggested she should either turn the light out or close the curtains. Net curtains were of no good use if the interior light was on.

Taking a gamble, he turned up at Louise's house, the two joints he had rolled earlier remained unsmoked. The night was young, who better to share them with?

Louise all but dragged him into the house. He had the impression she was happy to see him, even more so when she began tugging at his clothes. They passed a pleasant hour together with Louise dressing up in her uniform and Pink helping himself to her charms. She thanked him for calling, he thanked her for being there; the arrangement suited them both, uncomplicated and undemanding.

When he returned to the bakery, Sira had arrived to pick up Mira so Pink offered to drive her home so the lovebirds could have a little time on their own. On the way, Mira told him Sira's intended husband was a first cousin to her own future husband. She had a photograph of them both together which was how she would know him tomorrow. Pink asked was she not worried about Sira's relationship with Johan, to which she replied, Sira wouldn't dare defy their father, just the same as she wouldn't. He held his own counsel on that one. Knowing Johan as he did, it wouldn't be too long before he was trying to nail her, if he hadn't already. He dropped Mira off on the corner, that way she could sneak in without having to explain her sister's absence. She nuzzled his lips before slipping out of the van. He got as big a thrill from that as he ever did, but his mind was on Violet. For all Mira was flesh and blood, Violet seemed more accessible somehow.

Johan asked for his opinion on Ash when Sira went home. Pink admitted to taking an instant liking for the man, especially since he was a much better cook than Johan was. Seriously, he reckoned they could trust him, he had a lot to lose if it all went down the Swanee, not least his liberty; but then, that applied to each of them. Johan had worked for Ash in the past, had discussed such a venture before, but had never come across the vital third party they thought they could trust. Pink felt honoured to be regarded in such a light, at the same time realising what he had imagined to be his brainwave had in actual fact been on the back burner for quite some considerable time. This sudden knowledge did nothing to put him off. On the contrary, it gave him the resolve to see it through.

Eight Ball joined them, having marked out his territory without encountering any problems. He let Johan make a fuss of him for a few minutes before reclining on the flour sacks and listening in to their conversation. Neither man felt the need to hide anything from him, they knew it wouldn't go any further than those four walls. Pink left his friend to it at one o'clock. With his early start in mind and aware he had missed his nap, an early night was called for.

Violet greeted him with. "Go your own way."

"Well, that's just charming."

"He-he. No, it was on the radio. Fleetwood Mac sing it. It's from a new LP."

"What's it called?"

"Go your own way."

"The album?"

"Oh, I didn't catch that."

"You're going to have to start writing these down, Violet. Lynyrd Skynyrd, Fleetwood Mac, what next?"

"I can't write them down, silly .... but you could....

You can write. Can't you Pink?"

"After a fashion, but you wouldn't be able to decipher it, not unless you're a chemist. Shit, even I can't make it out sometimes."

"Are you serious? I never can tell."

"One day I was very, very stoned and wrote out a shopping list. When I returned from the market I had nothing from the list, but I did have a load of shit I didn't need, and some of that I didn't even like."

"Poor Pink. You need someone to look after you."

"Are you volunteering, Violet?"

"I'd love to, believe me. Mind you, you're almost domesticated as it is."

"Yes, I'd make someone a good wife."

"He-he. It's a bit early for you to be going to bed, isn't it? Are you tired, Honey?"

"I've got an early start. Did you just call me Honey?"

"Yes, don't you like it?"

"Oh, I like it fine….Kitten."

"Oh, Pinkee. My dad called me that."

"I'll stick to Violet if you'd rather."

"No, no, no. It's ok, really. It just strikes me as strange you should choose Kitten."

"I have good reason to call you Kitten," said Pink, remembering to wind the clock up and set it to the right time as the news came on the radio.

"Do tell."

"I've heard you purring, it could only have been you. Eight Ball was nowhere in sight."

He was sure she blushed, a look of horror on her face like she had been caught red handed at something. However, she did make a remarkably quick recovery.

"Better get to bed if you're up early, then."

"Only if you come with me."

"Ok. He-he."

Violet was as good as her word, appearing naked against the curtains and slipping between the sheets. Pink didn't have to do anything, well, hardly anything; just make sure he didn't wake up while Violet dived head first under the covers and expertly brought him to a shuddering climax with her beautiful mouth. On the one occasion he lifted the bedclothes to see how she was getting on, he spotted something he hadn't noticed before. Under her left arm, almost in her armpit, Violet had a strawberry birthmark; a small, perfectly formed circle.

She stayed with him, snuggling up to his back and letting him feel her warm breath on the back of his neck. That, along with the reassuring sound of her purring gave him cause to dream of what else he could do with her. Somewhere in the night he turned to face her and was welcomed to her embrace, making love for what seemed like hours. Again, he spotted the birthmark and remembered wondering if it was some sort of a sign. A sign of what he couldn't begin to hazard a guess at.

No Violet when he woke up, at least not in bed with him; there were the same tell tale signs she had been, the indent in the pillow and the faint trace of lavender in the room.

"Oh good, you're awake, Honey. Can we have some music on, please?"

Pink obliged then headed straight for the shower. He was towelling himself dry and walking towards the bedroom when the alarm clock went off. Eight Ball shot between his legs like a scalded cat and Violet gave out her delightful laugh. Pink joined in, he had no choice, the sound was so infectious.

The laughter came to an abrupt halt when he entered the bedroom, The pillow, the one with the indent had been shredded. On closer inspection the actual pillow was still intact, but the pillow case was ruined. Pink went looking for Eight Ball, but he he was nowhere to be found, perhaps it was just as well. Violet was in the room with him now, tut tutting. He couldn't see her, but he could imagine her, arms folded across her chest and shaking her head, speechless.

"I'll kill the fucker when I get my hands on him."

"Why do you think he's done that?"

"You know as well as I do Violet, the bastard's jealous. Wait 'til I get hold of him."

"Don't say that, Honey. Let me have a word with him please?"

No doubt about it, she had a mellowing effect on him. He fried a couple of eggs to go with his bacon and toast, made a cup of coffee, rolled two joints and headed out to meet Mira.

Halfway downstairs he turned back, switched the radio back on and said, "Make sure you sort him out, Violet …. or I sure as shit will."

"Ok, Honey. Don't you worry about a thing. Oh, and thank you for the radio."

"Ok, see you later. Bye bye."

"Bye, Pinkee. Enjoy your day."

If Mira hadn't waved he would have driven on by. She was in traditional Indian dress complete with Dupatta, or veil. All he could see was her eyes, which he had gazed into more often than her father would be comfortable with. That's the only way he could recognise her, by those gorgeous almond shaped eyes.

Her mother had helped her to dress while Mr Rapati was out and about on his day to day business. It was she who had found the photograph and had decided to give her daughter a head start. So, she knew where Mira was going, helped with the disguise and gave her blessing, as long as she didn't get caught. If that happened she was on her own.

When he filled the tank, Mira tried to give him what it cost, but he would only accept half, telling her he too was having a day out. He told her she looked beautiful in her sari, her future husband was a very lucky man. Mira blushed a lovely shade of pink and fluttered her eyelids at him, almost having them off the road.

She sang along to all the pop songs on the radio, which made them almost bearable to Pink; when a song came on he knew himself it would be his turn to sing along. They only sang together twice throughout the entire outward trip. It was plain to see he would have to educate her. Not that he would ever decry anyone's taste in music, but to him, there was music and there was real music.

They stopped off at a café for a drink on the way down and drew some funny looks from the clientele. The girl behind the counter let her jaw drop to the floor when they walked in. Pink asked her did she have a problem, loud enough for everyone else to hear. No one said boo to them and he sat Mira at a window table, attracting more odd looks from passers by. They were probably seventy miles from home yet he could sense the difference in attitude. At home, no one would have given them a second glance, but here, they were Martians. He saw Mira could also sense it and told her not to worry. She wasn't in the least bit worried she told him, she knew he would look after her.

The area they found themselves in was predominantly Asian so Mira did the asking for directions. Her intended ran his father's textile factory assisted by his cousin, Sira's future husband. Pink parked the van opposite the main gate and watched as about twenty staff filed out for lunch. Mira had her veil covering all but her eyes and gave Pink a nudge as the cousins left the ground floor office. She let them walk a few yards up the road and hopped out to follow. Pink tailed a few feet behind her and saw the two men stop on the corner. A few seconds later they split up and Mira followed her intended, Pink would have gone after her, but she indicated he should tail the cousin.

Trusting she knew what she was doing, he did as she wished and followed the cousin into a busy market place. He momentarily lost him and realised he had ducked into the public toilets. Five minutes passed and Pink wondered if he had been mistaken about the whereabouts of his quarry. Deciding he had to pee himself, he made his way into the conveniences, just in time to see the cousin leaving a cubicle. He knew it would appear suspicious if he were to leave right away so he turned to the urinals and had a piss. To his surprise, another Asian came out of the same cubicle the cousin had been in and now Pink got the picture. Poor Sira, she was only engaged to an iron hoof, a queer. He wandered the market trying to pick up the trail, only to be distracted by a second hand record stall; game over, he had to have a look.

Two copies of Lynyrd Skynyrd's first album, but they didn't stand up to inspection. He was about to give up and go looking for

Mira when he came across a mint copy of Leonard Cohen's 'Songs of Love and Hate', an old favourite and, after bartering, snapped up at a decent price. A pack of five C90 cassette tapes were bagged up for him, and mysteriously, another pack of five found their way into the bag when the stallholder turned to get his change. The next stall along had a good selection of joss sticks and it took him two minutes to find what he wanted before deciding it might be time to get back.

No sign of Mira when he reached the van. He climbed aboard and started the engine, the workers were drifting back through the gates so lunchtime was almost over. Then, her betrothed turned into the street, followed discreetly by Mira.

She seemed buoyant and thanked him for bringing her. She had followed him to a large house about three streets away and watched him interact with his parents, she presumed, while they ate lunch. He appeared to be a dutiful son who respected his parents, very important that, and quite handsome, didn't Pink think so?

Pink passed on that one, he wasn't the one to ask such a question, but maybe if she were to approach his cousin, put it to him so to speak. He spilled what he had observed, Mira was his friend, Sira was his friend and Johan was his friend. He thought it only fair they should be aware of the facts.

Now she was upset, and rightly so. He apologised for being the bearer of such awful news, but she shushed him, he had done the right thing by telling her. The problem was, what to do about it? Something would have to be done and, by the tone of her voice, it looked like Pink was to be involved to some extent. He had opened up a real can of worms; and not only that, he had thrown away the lid.

Mira put her troubles aside and concentrated on enjoying the rest of her day, singing along to the radio, flirting with Pink and showing annoyance when he pretended he was about to turn into the same café they had used on the way down. Five minutes later she was wishing they had turned in, she wanted to pee. Pink told her he had an empty pocket she could use, which only served to make her need all the more urgent. Mira had never been in a pub so he pulled into the next one they came to. She didn't want alcohol, only to use the facilities. Pink told her it would be rude not to stay for a drink, besides, he was thirsty now he was here. Ordering up a pint for himself and a soft drink for Mira, he directed her to where she wanted to be. No sooner had the door to the ladies closed behind her than a slavering idiot at the bar told him they didn't want her kind in there. When Mira returned, Pink was helping the bigot back onto his stool and advising the barmaid to put some sort of an ice pack to his swelling eye. No one bothered them as they enjoyed their drink and Mira invited Pink to put his thinking cap on, find a solution to her problem. Refreshed, Mira headed for the door while Pink took the empty glasses to the bar. Under his breath, he called the bigot an arsehole, winked at the barmaid and took his leave.

Since her mother had aided and abetted their trip, Pink told Mira to let her know what she had discovered, maybe she could throw a few ideas into the pot. This suggestion drew a favourable response, now she was more upbeat. If anyone knew what to do about it, her mother would.

They were at Mira's street corner in what seemed like no time at all. Seeing her dad's car wasn't parked outside the house, Pink was dragged in to meet her mum. He had met her once at the shop, but only briefly. Now, it was the formal introduction, closely followed by Mira's revelations about her intended's cousin, her sister's future husband; this girl didn't believe in hanging about. Pink had to relate, in detail, what he had observed in the toilets. Moraji, Mira's mum, was visibly shocked by what he had to say. She made a pot of tea while her daughter ran upstairs to change her clothes, thanked Pink for looking after Mira and swore him to secrecy about the other. She calmed down while they sipped at their tea and he could see the wheels turning. Plans were being formulated there and then.

Mira wanted to go to the bakery and Moraji warned her to say nothing to Sira, not until she'd had time to think things through. Then she saw Pink's swollen knuckles. He explained he had trapped them in the van's sliding door, no real damage done. Mira, clever girl that she was, put two and two together and melted him with her glorious smile.

At the bakery, she clambered over the driver's seat to get to him. A simple thank you would have been sufficient; but the embrace, along with the lingering kiss, would serve just as well.

Upstairs in the flat, Eight Ball kept a wary eye on him, watching as he removed the wrapping from the cassettes.

"Hi, Pinkee. I've had a word with the cat. Seems it was a rush of blood caused him to attack the pillow. I'm sure it wont happen again.." "Tell him if it does he can choose his window, and I wont open the fucker, either."

"What's the record?"

"Oh, you wont like it, Kitten. Definitely an acquired taste."

"If you like it, I'm sure I'll like it."

He fired up one of the joints he had rolled earlier. Two days running he had taken ready rolled out with him and didn't partake. He put it down to the scintillating company of each occasion and put it out of his mind. Uncle Ned started off with 'Avalanche', and he waited for Violet's expression to sour. She closed her green eyes, appearing to absorb the slow, dirge like song. It had been almost three years since Pink last heard it, but like everything else he took a shine to musically, he remembered every word and every note.

Violet swayed to 'Diamonds in the mine', by now, spellbound. She wagged a finger in Pink's direction to say. "I told you so. I told you I would like it."

Pink gave her his best smile, he hadn't needed the reverse psychology after all.

"Will you play it again, please?"

"Listen to side two first."

"But, you always play them a few times when they're new."

"It's an old one. Tell you what, I'll stick it on again and go down for my bread. How does that sound?"

"Thank you, Honey. Thank you, thank you, thank you."

Pink put the needle back to track one, made a lunge for Eight Ball, just to keep him on his toes, grabbed up his basket and tripped downstairs to the sound of Violet's giggles.

Mr Rapati was in the shop and indicated he should go round the back. Nothing more than a chat. Mira was training a new girl, another cousin, on the ins and outs of the business; Mr Rapati felt in the way so they had a cup of tea and put the world to rights for half an hour. When business picked up, Pink helped himself to some fresh baked goodies and made good his escape, blowing Mira a kiss over her dad's shoulder as he left and catching her best smile as a reward.

Violet was treated to side two while he settled down for his nap.

Friday night, the Albatross beckoned.

Waking up to silence, Pink rolled off the couch and put the radio on for a timecheck.

"What was that you burned earlier, Pink?"

"Joss stick, why do you ask?"

"Was it lavender?"

"Yes, your favourite?"

"I've never told you that. How did you know?"

"When you're in the bedroom with me, it's almost overpowering. Maybe that's the wrong word, but there's a very strong presence of lavender."

"It is my favourite scent, always has been. You must like it if you bought the scented sticks. Do you?"

"Only since you started sleeping with me. It's a bit of a turn on. I'd like to know how you do it."

"Do what?"

"Get into bed with me, make love with me and how you manage to be there, but not there when I wake up in the morning."

"You've sensed that, same as me? I couldn't be sure you had. Did you enjoy it as much as I did?"

"I'd be the biggest liar in town if I said no, but it feels so real, so physical. That's what I don't understand."

"I think it works because we both want it to. At least I hope it's what you want. Please tell me you do, Pink, because it's what I want."

"It feels so natural, so real. Not only do I want it, Violet, I want more. I want as much of you as I can get."

"Oh, Honey. I'm so glad you said that. Thank God for lavender or we might never have made it this far."

The radio dude said eight thirty. Pink had his second shower of the day, rolled a few joints while Violet did her homework on Uncle Ned and quietly readied himself for his night out.

CHAPTER 17

The flying pig

Pink heard the news as soon as he entered the Albatross. Mad Frank had been stitched up in court by two witnesses who claimed he had started the fight in which he used the glass. His self defence plea flew out of the window, along with his liberty.

He was sentenced to eighteen months at her majesty's pleasure. As soon as sentence was passed, Frank vaulted from the box and got the fuck out of there. Word was, the two coppers who were standing either side of him in the dock blinked and missed it. Typical mad Frank, never a dull moment, he saw his chance and snatched at it. The story was about third or fourth hand. Pink vaguely remembered saying he would be there in court, but the chance to spend the day with Mira had erased it from his already poor memory.

Now, Frank was on the run. Pink would have had a visit if the cops had known where he lived so Frank could be anywhere. One thing was certain, he wouldn't be going back to jail, he had bad memories of the place. One reason he had grown a beard was to hide a facial scar he earned in a fight when he was inside.

Pink was sorting out a loan of Brat's copy of the Skynyrd album when the DJ's eyes almost popped out of his head. He turned to see none other than Mad Frank, trying his best to blend in with the wallpaper in the darkened room. He asked Pink to go with him, keep lookout while he picked up his passport and threw a few clothes in a bag. Pink obliged, Mad Frank was a mate, of course he would do what he could for him. He lived no more than five minutes walk from the Albatross. Pink stuck his head out of the pub door, saw the coast was clear and gave his friend the nod. The Albatross sat more or less on the canal bridge. Two thirds of the way across, three coppers; a sergeant and two constables, recognised Frank for who he was. Pink happened to be a few paces to the rear and saw the sergeant make a lunge for Frank, he probably still has nightmares about it. Next thing Pink knew the sergeant was flying over the bridge wall and Frank was high tailing it in the opposite direction from his house. There was a huge splash and the constables went to the sergeant's aid, leaving Frank to get on with his Olympic training.

Pink moved faster than he had done for a long, long time. He knew Frank wouldn't have been stupid enough to go where the coppers would look for him. Already, he had waited for the cover of night before showing his face. The direction he had run off in told Pink he was in one of two places; an old railway sidings shed where they had shared many a joint and many a story, or Gloria's place. Frank had taken up with her when he sussed Pink wasn't over interested. He went home for the van, having intended to load up with groceries and such before returning it, then headed for the sidings, his first hunch.

Mad Frank didn't make a sound until Pink was almost upon him, then he exhaled loudly and dropped the iron bar he had raised, ready to use on someone he didn't know or trust. Between them they thrashed out his options. He had little or no money, Pink could help him out there. He wanted to get out of the country, so, he would need his passport. Pink offered to go to his house, fill a bag with clothes and pick his passport up. Frank wouldn't have it, bad enough he himself was in the shit without involving anyone else. No, if Pink could take him home, see if the coast was clear he could be in and out in the matter of a few minutes.

He dropped Frank at the bottom of the long back entry then reversed the van and parked where he could see the upstairs bedroom window. The signal was one blink of the light. The street was quiet, with no evidence of the house being staked out. Ten minutes later, two unmarked police cars entered, one from either end of the street. Pink caught sight of another, running without lights and creeping up the backs. He was helpless, all he could do was observe, make sure there was no foul play when Frank was captured. The coppers were all in plain clothes. To Pink's surprise, Frank opened the door to them at the first knock and invited them in after a brief chat on the doorstep. Five minutes later, they left without Frank and Pink scratched his head in amazement. The police cars had no sooner left the street than Frank was in the back of the van, telling Pink to get him the fuck away from there and laughing his head off.

Pink stopped at the flat, went straight to his cash-hash stash and made a withdrawal for his friend. He nipped up to the flat for a couple of bottles and some food. Telling Violet he would explain later, he was out the door and heading for the ferry terminal.

Tears of laughter streamed down his face as Frank detailed what had happened at the house. Two or three minutes after Pink dropped him off, he was ready to go. He then had the bright idea of getting rid of his beard and his unruly mop of hair. He was just about to go upstairs and signal Pink when he saw the car headlights. A quick glance out the back window told him the game was a bogey so he came up with an outrageous bluff of pure genius. When the coppers knocked on the door, he answered in his underpants and vest, told them his brother, Frank, had been in court that day and he hadn't heard anything since. He had no objection to them searching the place, as long as they were quick, he was up early in the morning for work and it was well past his bedtime. Luckily, they didn't look behind the front door where they would have found his packed bag and the jacket detailed in their description. At one point Frank saw the chance to make good his escape, only one sentry at the still open front door. Not a problem to a man of Frank's calibre, but he decided to see his bluff out, play the cards he had in his hand.

An hour and a half later they were at the ferry terminal. Pink left Frank in the back of the van and scouted the area out. No sign of any police presence, the next sailing was eight fifteen, time for a joint and a nap. The build up of traffic woke them. Pink fired the van's engine up and told Frank to listen out for a timecheck while he sorted the breakfast out. Ten minutes later, they were tucking into bacon and egg rolls, washed down with ice cold milk. They watched as the night ferry from Rotterdam docked. This would be Frank's ride out of Dodge.

Pink wandered off and purchased a single ticket, checking out the security as he went. Nothing, at least nothing obvious; the only uniforms on view belonged to customs officers.

Mad Frank was still crouched in the back of the van, keeping a low profile so Pink wondered what the fuck was going on when he reached beyond him and started honking on the horn, drawing all sorts of attention to them. Then, it became all too obvious. Striding towards them from the recently berthed ferry was one Dave Thom, newly arrived back from one of his adventures. Dave was a good friend to both men, having introduced them at the very railway hut Frank had sought refuge in. Dave howled with laughter as Frank told his story and cheered his own good fortune at dropping on a lift home.

Between them, they decided all three would approach the gangplank, with Frank in the lead. Pink and Dave would make sure he boarded ok and run some interference if the cops showed up by realising they had left their passports in the car. As they queued, Dave hunted out a couple of addresses in Belgium and one in Amsterdam where Frank might find mutual friends.

They sat in the car park and made sure Frank sailed with the ferry. Dave produced a lump of black from inside his shoe, he had nothing else, no papers and no tobacco. Pink helped him out and rolled a joint, but refused to partake; if it was anything like the black he had been smoking recently he wouldn't be able to take them home for a good few hours. The two men caught up with each other on the drive, laughing at Frank's exploits. His vault from the dock, which he himself had verified when he told Dave the tale, was immediately the stuff of legend.

They found Reg at home, filled him in on Frank's whereabouts and on what he didn't know of the story and were invited to have breakfast. Dave handed the black to Pink and all three took to the skies. Reg abandoned any notion of doing a day's work, there was best black to be smoked and stories to tell. Dave had heard via the grapevine that his favourite drug squad officer was due in court for possession, could either of the two substantiate this? Pink went one better, he was among friends so he told the tale as it happened and was warmly congratulated. Reg prompted Pink about the painting job at the mill and Dave was enthralled at Mad Frank's guile. Reg had to fill in on what he had liberated as Pink only saw the bin liners, the contents were a mystery to him, except for the one he saw lying open at Fester's place. He then told of what he had helped himself to. Frank knew he was taking clothes, but he'd had no idea about the shoes, the Walkmans or the cameras. None of his co-workers knew; the only thing Cowboy saw was the boiler suit on the last day. More laughter and congratulations. Pink told Dave there was another mill job in the offing, he would put in a good word for him.

Reg went for a piss and returned to find Dave flaked out across his settee. Pink took that as his cue to leave them, but not without Reg's copy of the first Skynyrd album safely tucked under his arm. They made arrangements to meet up for the copper's trial with the intention of making a day of it.

The plan was to have a nap, fill the van up with shopping, return it to its rightful owner, have another nap, eat something; shit, shower, shampoo and shave then have his night out at the Albatross. That was the plan, set in stone. Wrong. After another couple of joints, several spins of the Skynyrd album and one more of uncle Ned, the shops were closed and Pink was out of it.

"Sorry I've not been much company."

"You looked bedraggled when you came in. Is everything ok?"

Pink told her more or less all that had gone on while trying to chase up some decent music on the radio. He knew he had missed his programme on the telly again. Fingers crossed it wasn't someone he wanted to see.

"You seem to have some colourful friends."

"That's one way of looking at it."

"And of course, you're very colourful, too."

"How d'you mean?"

"Pink."

"Huh?"

"Pink. It's a colour, get it?"

"Ah, yes, very clever."

"Well, I thought it was funny."

"Violet."

"Yes?"

"That's a colour, too."

"Touche."

"Bless you."

"He-he. No, Pink. That's French, for, I don't know what it means exactly."

"No good asking me, you lost me when you sneezed."

"I didn't sneeze. I .... oh, what's the use? .... You going out?"

"Got to, Kitten. I want to know what stories are circulating about Frank. C'mon, you can wash my back for me."

He sang acapella. Violet hummed along and giggled at the applause from downstairs.

"Do you think they heard me, Pink?"

"Who cares?"

"I do. You know I do."

"I forgot how shy you are, sorry."

Dave hadn't been home, his bag was by his feet, no one was expecting him. The funny thing about that was, his folks lived a stone's throw from the Albatross. Pink brought him a fresh pint and gave him a joint to spark up. He had carried the joint in his hand, not knowing what to expect. The fuzz would be smarting at Frank's guile and looking at everyone who associated with him. Four more joints were stashed nearby, no point in taking any chances. As luck would have it, he knew everyone in the place, but that could change. Reg and his woman joined them and they had a good laugh at recent events. Visitors to their table were invited to tell what they knew and were given nothing in return. Sightings of Frank in all manner of strange places were manyfold, and stories of his capture abounded. One ridiculous tale was that he'd handed himself in, unable to survive in the wild. The narrator obviously didn't know Mad Frank very well. Not many people were aware of the true story and that's how it would stay. Pink was pleased there were so many variations, that would keep the cops chasing their tails for a while.

Dave, wisely using his loaf, had left his stash at Reg's, taking a leaf out of Pink's book and rolling a couple of joints for the evening. It was heavy duty shit. Being somewhat jetlagged from his trip, he didn't want to fall asleep again and have either someone or the cops help themselves. Pink nipped to the bar to buy the round in and slipped outside with the intention of picking up his own little stash when he was apprehended and roughly manhandled to where he was facing the wall. He didn't know them, but he did know them. Drug squad. He knew he was clean and protested his innocence, then, noticing he was under the disco room window, proceeded to bang on it for all he was worth. By the time the seven narcs entered the room and had the house lights turned on, everyone in the place was clean. A couple of half smoked spliffs lay about the floor, but surprisingly, no one had a clue as to how they managed to be there. One officer picked Dave's bag up, unzipped it and emptied the contents all over the table, regretting his actions almost immediately. Dave had been travelling for three and a half days, the bag held probably three changes of clothes. He had slept on two trains and a ferry, plus overnight on the docks in Holland. He was as clean hygenically as anyone Pink knew and had changed his clothes after each mini trip, where possible; so everything, including the clothes he stood in needed a good wash. Quite rightly, since the officer hadn't found any contraband, Dave was adamant he should re-pack his bag for him.

The squad left with their tails between their legs, much to the delight of those present. Pink was offered more free drink than he could possibly cope with as thanks for the warning, but he didn't refuse it, there were four of them at the table. All night long they raised their glasses to absent friends, or at least to one absent friend.

Pink and Dave went back a long, long way. Room mates when they found some work once in a rather unfriendly part of the country. They had digs in a pub of all places, but not for long. Two days into their stay, Pink rinsed the bed, an untreated kidney infection blocking out the signals to his brain, which meant after a good drink he didn't wake for a piss. The cleaner, who also took care of the breakfasts, gave him a friendly warning; don't let it happen again, so noted. The following day was a Sunday. Pink and Dave went for a Chinese meal, found a taste for the beer again and fell in the side door of the pub more than a little the worse for wear. Walking through the kitchen, Dave spied what he took to be a plateful of scraps and made short work of it. Unfortunately, it turned out to be the landlord's dinner. That night Pink rinsed the bed again so both men had to pack their bags before work and find alternative accommodation. Then there was the time they woke up in the same bed, in all innocence and fully clothed. They had gone to score, managed to get completely wrecked and slept it off in a spare room. Their best story was of the time they spent as cellmates, loosely speaking. Dave had sought out Pink to ask his advice. The dole had inadvertently awarded him a double giro and he knew fine what his options were, but wanted to clarify them with Pink, a man who's opinion he valued highly. Pink gave the matter some serious thought. There were two post offices in town. Dave cashed his weekly giro in one, Pink used the other. Both men were well known to the people behind the counter of their respective post offices, so if Pink could cash Dave's cheque at his own post office, Dave could claim not to have received it and so put in for another payment. The plan was executed without fuss, the girl behind the counter only checked the amount and not the name of the payee, their day was looking better by the minute. Dave then had an idea of his own to pitch, they should make their way to the next town and drink a hole in their windfall. Pink saw the sense in that, too many hangers on where they normally drank; yes, an awayday sounded just the ticket.

They were as good as their word. Whisky followed beer followed whisky. Pub followed pub, then a club and back to the pubs. By chucking out time they were wrecked. Things become a bit sketchy at this point due to the state they were in. It seems either one or both men felt the need to relieve themselves and ducked down a back alley. Next thing they knew there were police everywhere, complete with dogs. Bewildered, both men were dispatched to the local cells, allowed to sleep it off and in the morning, formally charged with attempted burglary. They were whisked off to the magistrate's court, entered a quite reasonable plea of not guilty, with the hastily engaged brief asking for bail to be approved. They had been accused of attempting to burgle a chemist's shop, but neither could remember there ever being such a shop in the vicinity. Earlier, when they were charged, Pink gave his address as no fixed abode. He was living with friends at the time and the last thing they needed was a visit from the law. Not to be outdone, or in a show of solidarity, Dave also claimed no fixed abode. The magistrate refused bail on the grounds they might do a runner, remanding them in custody for a week. Both men shuddered with the shock of it. The grizzly remand centre had a terrible reputation as a not very welcoming place.

After processing, Dave was banged up with a schizophrenic. Pink heard him beseeching the screws to get him the fuck out of there. Pink himself ended up sharing with a forger, a bit of a know all, but harmless enough. That week was the longest of their young lives. They had enough money between them for some tobacco and skins, which helped a little. Their solicitor visited to brief them. He had taken photographs of where they had been arrested and assured them it would have been a physical impossibility for them to access the chemist's. There was a twenty five foot drop to the level the shop in question was located at. If that wasn't enough, it was protected like Fort Knox with an alarm, bars on the windows and more locks on the door than Houdini could have coped with. They weren't to worry, their next court appearance would see them released.

Wrong, remanded for another week. The brief had informed Dave's dad, who stood bail for him and offered to do the same for Pink. Dave was allowed home while Pink was sent back to the centre. Luckily, Dave's dad had brought cash and tobacco in case it all went pear shaped and this was donated to Pink without further ado, with Dave promising to visit and let him know how the case was shaping up.

Another long week for Pink. Besides being laid low with flu, his only visit was from the lawyer. He was surprised and upset Dave had let him down. He should have known better. Dave had picked up the same flu bug and found himself confined to bed, same as Pink. One good thing about having the flu was that he had lost the craving for a joint, which had plagued him in the first week.

At the next hearing they were advised to plead guilty. Dave had been threatened with further incarceration so they put their heads together, agreed to plead guilty and walked away with a fifty quid fine each; the double giro had cost them dearly. It wasn't anywhere near funny at the time, but looking back, it had become hilarious and turned two good friends into brothers.

Banking on the Albatross being police free for the rest of the night, Pink made it to his stash and everyone had a good time. At the end of the evening he had the good sense to join the queue for the Chinese chippy; his belly was complaining, thinking his throat had been cut.

CHAPTER 18

At the right time

Pink slowly opened one eye, where was he, who was he, what day was it? With the other eye open, he found himself staring at a huge balloon. When he tried to sit up, the balloon's string worked free and it floated towards the ceiling. He was at home, fully dressed and on the couch with no knowledge of how he managed to be there, automatic pilot being the only answer he could come up with. The radio was on low, all chat and very little music. He struggled to sit and came face to face with Violet.

"You were in a proper state when you got home last night, couldn't put two words together that made any sense and with something disgusting all down the front of your jacket and T shirt."

One thing he was sure of, there was humour in her voice so he wasn't being told off. That made a change, any other woman would most probably have kicked the shit out of him where he lay. Sniffing at the offending jacket, it all came flooding back to him. His company from the Albatross joined him in the queue at the Chinese and Reg mentioned he had beer in the fridge at home. Vito, a taxi driver and friend to all three men, had just dropped a fare off and gave them a free ride to Reg's, calling in for a joint and a beer while he was there. The last thing Pink could remember was Dave complaining he had left his bag in the taxi before collapsing on the settee. Vito was long gone by then, the bag would be sure to find its owner. Dave had been home for two days yet he hadn't been home. Pink went blank after that, vaguely remembering Reg's woman throwing a blanket over Dave and telling Reg her patience was wearing thin. He took that as his cue to leave the lovers to it and hit the fresh air. It was a good two miles to the flat, but he made it somehow.

"It's curry .... curry sauce."

"Did you manage to put any of it into your mouth?"

"That's my favourite jacket. I believe curry's a bastard to get out."

"I'll help. You'll need some glycerine."

"Glycerine? What's that when it's at home?"

"Something to do with soap. Like a by product, I think."

"Ok, but don't forget it's my favourite jacket. I don't want it ruined."

"Trust me, Honey. It'll come up good as new. Just like you when you have a shower and put some decent music on."

Pink found 'Cry Tough' and stumbled into the bathroom, wishing he hadn't as soon as he caught sight of himself in the shaving mirror. Rough wasn't in it. His eyes were bloodshot, hair everywhere and what could only have been curry from his nose to his chin. "Never again," he lied to himself. Violet had joined him and giggled like only she could, lifting his spirits somewhat.

He was ravenous, the milk was off and the shops were closed. Mr Rapati was in the bakery by himself and gladly gave him a pint of milk, the shop also catered in dairy produce so the day was brightening by the minute. Asked why he was on his own, Mr Rapati explained the girls and their mother had gone to visit relatives. When he mentioned where, Pink made his excuses and left. Very soon, he thought, the shit was going to hit the fan.

Corn flakes followed by bacon, eggs and toast, followed by even more toast and he was in much better shape. A joint of Leb, side two of 'Cry Tough' and a cold bottle of cider, Sunday was there for the taking. He had clocked the time in the bakery, that would be half an hour ago, making it round about noon. He toyed with the idea of showing his face at the Boulder then remembered it was Sunday, dog day; a time honoured tradition whereby everyone who had a dog would bring their pet to the pub on Sunday afternoon. No one knew how it started, but it allowed some of them out of the house for a couple of hours. Pink decided to give it a miss, it looked like a nice day, not too cold when he went for his milk. He would have a bike ride, take in some fresh air, find a quiet spot and smoke a couple of joints.

Change of plan, the front tyre on his bike was low; not punctured, but flat enough that he would do more harm than good if he were to ride it. He was well wrapped up so he opted for a walk, no point in letting a lovely spring day go to waste. Finding himself halfway through the park, he carried on down past the allotments in the direction of the canal. The Blunt's dog barked loudly as he approached, but quietened when he saw it was Pink. He must have remembered the free rabbit.

The noise of the heavy machinery hit his ears at the same time as the stench from the water treatment plant hit his nostrils. Obviously, work had started on the new site. Turning the corner, he was amazed at the transformation. The bigger firms had their own travelling workers and a rough camp of caravans had assembled. Fifty yards farther along, a stand of six portacabins were circled like a wagon train under siege.

The nearest caravan was the size of a bungalow, with an awning attached to form a front porch. A window was open and Pink could hear soul music. On a whim, he knocked on the caravan door and was greeted by a woman in her early thirties. He asked where he could find whoever was in charge and was directed towards the portacabins, which served the site offices. From there, he was directed to the canteen, another, larger portacabin. If the foreman wasn't there, he would be somewhere on site.

The foreman stood out a mile, a hulk of a man, six foot six if he was an inch. He was standing between two huge holes in the ground with his back to Pink, directing a crane driver and a JCB driver at the same time. Neither man would ever forget how they met. Mac, the foreman, was rugby tackled to the ground; Pink had no choice, the crane's hook was on a beeline trajectory towards his head. If Pink had shouted a warning, the hook would have killed the man so they ended up in a heap on the ground.

For a big man, Mac was fast. He had Pink by the throat and was about to unload a fist into his face when the JCB driver intervened, closely followed by a very pale and very shaken crane driver. All three men repaired to the canteen where the story unfolded. The crane driver had something trapped under a foot lever and was trying to free it. He looked up just in time to see Pink go into the tackle. Quick thinking, which in all probability saved Mac's life. Over a cup of tea, Pink was taken on as a labourer, he was to turn up in the morning at eight o'clock sharp.

The lady in the canteen was about to throw a tray of sausage and bacon in the bin when Pink stopped her, he knew a dog who would be glad of them. So, he set off for home, glad to be in full time employment and with a doggy bag for the Blunts' Alsatian, which had looked in need of a good feed.

Again the dog barked as he approached, then quietened when he came into view. Pink fed him the titbits through the mesh fence. He was right, the food didn't touch the sides as the animal made short work of it. When he had eaten up, he followed Pink the length of the fence, making appreciative noises and wagging his tail.

"You look pleased with yourself?" Suggested Violet.

"I just scored myself a job."

"Where?"

Pink explained what had gone on, his luck was holding out, if the tyre on the bike hadn't been flat he would never have been in the right place at the right time. Of course there was the knock on effect; Mac would be in hospital and the dog might not have eaten for another week.

"You deserve a nice joint after all that, Pink."

"You're not wrong, Kitten. Let's have some music on."

"What will you be doing?"

"The spadework starts tomorrow so it will probably be backbreaking hard work."

"I've never been on a building site. Is it dangerous?"

"Can be. Today was a good example of that. This is the biggest site I've ever been on and it looks like they're running a railway track through it."

"You are joking, aren't you, Pink? That can't be right?"

"I didn't get round to asking, but I saw sleepers and what looked very much like rails, all stacked in neat piles."

"Oooh, I'm excited now, me. You can come home every night and tell me all about your day."

"We'll see. Maybe we can find something else to talk about?"

Violet told the newly returned Eight Ball the good news while Pink sorted his dinner out, it was early, but the dope had given him a fierce dose of the munchies.

After his meal he hunted out the new overalls from the job at the mill and set about making them less new looking.

"What on earth are you doing?"

"I can't turn up in brand new clothes, it just wouldn't feel right."

"Explain, please?"

"I want to give the impression I've been around a few sites, blend in easier."

"Oh. Well, I suppose you know what you're doing, Honey."

He felt a tingle when she called him that, he wouldn't tell her so, but it did make him feel good.

When he put the radio on she knew it was the signal for nap time, she didn't state the obvious this time, but howled with laughter when Eight Ball used his head as a springboard to reach the trailing string from the balloon. It wasn't long 'til he was fast asleep, with Violet massaging his feet. How did she know he liked that?

"How long was I out for, Kitten?"

"About an hour and a half, the man just said it was a quarter to six."

"Time for some 'Night Moves'," said Pink, reaching for Bob Seger and realising his socks had been removed.

"Yessss," squealed Violet. Would that every woman was as enthusiastic about good music as she was.

He flipped it over to side two and designed a joint which would take him into orbit for a couple of hours. Violet sang along softly, she had picked up the lyrics in no time at all. Eight Ball sat at her feet as she serenaded him, stock still, hanging on every note. He only left when the music stopped. Pink was staring into space, aware only of Harry the spider, who was making his way across the ceiling, probably to investigate the balloon.

"There's another Ship of fools."

"Where, where?" Pink made a show of looking all around him for the ship in question, the sound of Violet's laughter like music to his ears.

"No, silly. Another song called 'Ship of fools', isn't there? Is it Grateful Dead?" She offered, answering her own question.

"More than one other I would say since the bible thumpers picked up on it. In fact, and don't quote me on this, but I'm sure it's a phrase from the bible. Like I say, I'm not too sure. The last bible I leafed through I used the cover for roaches."

"Roaches? Cockroaches?"

"Ha-ha, no. Have you seen the cardboard filters I stick in the end of joints? They're called roaches. They ensure you get every last hit out of your joint."

"Shame on you, using a bible for that, Pink."

"Needs must when the Devil drives."

"He was sitting on your shoulder that particular day."

With the mention of The Grateful Dead, he dug out his copy of 'From the Mars hotel', gave it a spin and snatched the balloon away from Harry before he reached it. When Violet joined in with the singing, he bit into the balloon, inhaled the helium and trilled along like Pinky and Perky. Eight Ball gave him a funny look, Violet was having fits; the helium was gone before 'U.S. Blues' finished, but the damage had been done. Eight Ball would never be the same.

Violet waited until side one was over before asking. "That thing with the balloon, where oh where did you discover that?"

"At a friend's divorce party."

"Your friend had a divorce party?"

"She was so relieved to be rid of her husband she threw a big party. Music, booze and a huge mountain of food laced with all manner of drugs. It was a real hoot, what I remember of it."

"And the balloons?"

"Ah, there was a debate on how some of the cartoon voices were created and someone, I can't remember who, demonstrated with the helium. The party fell into chaos after that with people throttling each other to get hold of a balloon. Best party I've ever been to."

Pink put his Jesus boots on, switched the music centre to radio and went to visit with Johan.

"Don't forget you've got work in the morning, Honey."

"I'll be ok, I had a nap earlier. See you later."

Mira was in the bakery, doing an extra hour so Sira could spend some time with Johan. Pink was given chapter and verse on the visit with the relatives. Moraji hadn't wasted any time, a discreet word in one or two ears, an hour and two cups of tea later she had the answer to her enquiry. It was all true, common knowledge, in fact. Mira was again sworn to secrecy, at least until her father had been informed, but one thing was for sure, no way was Sira marrying this fellow. Moraji would be telling her husband right about now. The shit, as they say, was edging ever closer to the fan. There was bound to be a backlash. Knowing her father as she did, Mira reckoned he would have more than a few choice words to dispense on the matter. Pink told her about his new job and how he came about it, being rewarded with a cuddle and a kiss by way of congratulations.

Johan was pleased to see him, Sira too, giving him her best smile and a kiss on the cheek when told about his new job. She smelled like her sister, not an exact likeness, but close enough that he wouldn't be able to tell them apart in the dark. What chance?

Neither the girls nor Johan had a bicycle pump. He had a twenty five minute walk to the canal bank, or under ten on the bike. Sira suggested he should take it to the garage on the main road, better still, she would take it tomorrow, walk it there and ride it back. Pink closed his eyes and imagined being the seat of his bike, the shock of Mira nipping his bum to say goodnight snapping him out of his reverie. Sira asked for the key to his bike shed and was shocked to learn the door was open, he just knew there would be a padlock on it tomorrow.

Johan laughed when told the tale of how he came about the job, then he quietened when he realised his nights were about to get longer again in that he would be devoid of Pink's company; still, he was happy for his friend, no question about it. A couple of spliffs later and Pink was ready for bed. He was sorely tempted to let Johan know about Sira's intended, but he had given his word to Mira and her mum. Johan would find out soon enough. The clock on the bakery wall told him it was midnight, he hadn't set his clock for the morning, now he had an idea of the time he would do so.

He lay awake, how long he didn't know, then, Violet was in beside him and they were making love. Slowly at first, then increasing in tempo as their passions combined to an urgency he had never experienced before. This was very special, he didn't want it to ever end. He told Violet as much, gasping it out in his breathlessness. Violet put her fingers to his mouth then kissed him goodnight. The last words he heard were, "I love you, Pink. I really do."

In his dream he was looking down on everything. All of his needs were to hand; hash, music, but only the radio, and a cup of coffee, he couldn't work out how he had managed to get so high. Not floating, sitting. He could see for miles, he had never minded heights, but this was fucking high.

CHAPTER 19

Clocking on

Pink had slept like a baby, despite the interlude and despite the dream, well aware of Violet's presence in the bed beside him. Yet, when the alarm went off she was back on the ceiling. The space beside him in the bed felt warm, though. He knew he hadn't been restless so the only explanation would have to be that Violet had definitely slept with him. He had a good wash at the sink while his porridge simmered on the stove, that had been Violet's suggestion, get a good meal inside him to set him up for the rest of the day.

"Are you nervous, Honey?"

"Nah, not a bit of it. More looking forward to it if anything."

"Good, but be careful, please."

"I will. Do you want the radio on?"

"Thank you, Pink. Have a nice day."

"You sound like a yank."

"He-he. I do, don't I?"

Seven thirty exactly, he left the flat with Tom Petty and the Heartbreakers for company and carrying a doorstep sized slice of bread soaked in leftover gravy from last night. He didn't know the Blunt's dog's name, so christened him Towser off his own bat.

Towser knew his footsteps by now and didn't raise a fuss, meeting Pink at the top of the allotment, wagging his tail and following him all the way down. At the bottom, he was rewarded with the bread. Pink thought the tail would drop off him at the rate he was wagging it.

The timekeeper took his details and provided him with a clocking on card. Pink knew him vaguely, another hash head. They were only nodding acquaintances before, but now they had names to go by.

It chose to start raining the second he clocked on and Mac told him to join the others in the canteen, get himself a cup of tea. Patsy, a red headed Irishman, shifted along the bench to make room for him. The crane driver from yesterday pointed him out as the guy who saved Mac's life and the comments flew thick and fast, most of them comic, but one or two bewailing the fact he had stepped in. Pink had an idea they were kidding around.

Mac filled the doorway and called for the drivers. Patsy explained they were the only ones expected to work in the rain since they were under cover.

A pack of cards was produced and a game of bastard brag broke out. Pink didn't know the rules, but soon picked it up by watching Patsy. He was about to say something about the strong language which was being used freely, thinking it might offend the lady in charge of the canteen. She soon put his mind at ease, demonstrating she could probably teach the men a few new words when she came to clear the table next to them. Pink had a quiet word, asked her not to throw any unused food away, no point in it going to waste.

The rain continued to hammer on the canteen roof and he played cards for about an hour and a half, ending up with exactly the same amount of money in front of him as when he started. The drivers came in for their morning break and he picked up on a few more names. Apart from Patsy, who lived locally, they all seemed to be travelling men, moving from site to site and from town to town with the company. He was able to recommend which pubs they should frequent and those they would do well to avoid.

Nipping outside for some fresh air, he saw the door to the storeroom open and wandered in. There wasn't much to look at, the job had only just started. A guy he hadn't met yet asked him to pass three large boxes over the counter to him, they were more bulky than heavy. When he passed the last of them over he was rewarded with a pair of wellingtons, size eight, they would come in handy if this weather persisted. He was bored now, wishing he had brought a book or a newspaper. He made a mental note to swing by the newsagent's in the morning, otherwise the days would be interminably long.

Abby, the canteen lady, must have noticed the boredom in his face and asked if he would like to help with the lunches. Most of the men were happy with a fry up for every meal, but she tried to get them to eat healthily, although everything was served up with chips. When work started properly, she would bring her daughter in to help; meantime, she could just about manage.

Pie chips and peas was reward enough for his labours, he had been employed for five hours and hadn't done a hand's turn for the firm, instead, he had to go looking for work.

At two o'clock the day was given up. Mac sent everyone home, clock out and be paid for a full shift. So far it was money for old rope.

Pink collected his doggy bag, stashed his wellies in an unused cupboard in the canteen and headed for home. Tom Petty stopped singing while he was feeding Towser so he fumbled under his jacket to turn the tape, trying to keep it dry and trying to remember what he had put on the other side; a huge grin covering his face as Jackson Browne eased into his favourite album of all time, bar none, 'Late for the sky'. The cold and the rain were completely forgotten, God was in his heaven and all was well with the world

He called at the shop to see if his bike had been mended. Sira handed him the keys to his new padlock and Mira disappeared into the bakery, meeting him at the back door.

Mr Rapati had been informed of Sira's intended's sexual preferences, that's where he was now; along with Moraji, who would have more than a few words to say herself. Mira half hoped her own wedding would be called into question, if not, she told Moraji she at least wanted to meet the guy before it went any further. Pink put his arm around her shoulder, reassurance and the chance to drink in her scent. He tried the padlock, it was good and strong. He hadn't thought of it before, but the bike shed would make an ideal stash for his hash. It was dry and airy; most importantly, there was now a fucking great padlock securing it. Further thought had him stashing his cash there too, a precautionary measure. After all, he had the only two keys to the place.

Kissing Mira, he skirted round the front of the shop, stopped to pull faces at the sisters through the large front window and went home.

"It's only three o'clock."

"I'm so sorry. I'll go out again and come back later, shall I?"

"He-he, silly. What I meant was you're early, I only expected you home around half five."

"Got an early dart, been rained off all day, sat in the cabin playing cards and getting paid for it. Not bad, eh?"

"Let's get you out of those wet clothes, Honey, but first, could you play some decent music, please? You choose. I've had enough of that radio for one day."

Pink took 'Late for the sky' from the Walkman and inserted it into the music centre. He had switched it off when he went into the shop, he couldn't not listen to the rest of it.

No applause from downstairs while he showered, but that was forgivable, it was a dirty day. The sky was so black it was more like night time.

Violet begged him to dig the album out and play it from the start, she just had to hear 'Fountain of sorrow'. Pink didn't have a problem with that.

Eight Ball scrambled out of his window and returned five minutes later to let him know it had stopped raining. He put his shoes on and jogged round to the bric-a-brac shop; if his memory served him right, there was a bicycle pump on offer at a very reasonable price.

He was glad he did, the butcher asked him could he use a pound of pork sausages? He was closing the shop tomorrow to re-decorate and the sausages would only end up in the bin.

They ended up in the frying pan as soon as he returned to the flat, sizzling on a low light while the spuds and carrots boiled. One large onion, chopped and fried to finish the meal off. What sausages were left would keep Towser quiet in the morning, the Blunts didn't seem to be overkeen on looking after him. He took the makings into the kitchen and rolled a couple of joints while the food cooked. Today was the longest he had gone without a smoke for quite a while. He would have fired one up as he walked home if it hadn't been pissing down. Now, he could relax and let it all go to his brain.

Eight Ball eyed his plate up when he sat it on the chair, he'd only turned his back on it to change the music. Violet chased the cat, being well aware of the consequences if he had made a play for it.

"Thanks, Kitten. He never seems to learn, does he?"

"I think he likes to live dangerously. Good job he listens to me."

"True. The way he's going he can't have many of his nine lives left."

"He should know as well as I do just how much you like your food. I shudder to think what you'd do to him if he had set about it."

"Doesn't bear thinking about, Violet, but he used to be so well behaved. It's only since he met you he's started acting up. I think you're a bad influence."

"He-he. A couple of weeks ago I would have taken you seriously on that one."

Pink applied the stylus to the Doobie brothers, signalling an end to the conversation for a while. Violet sang accompaniment as he went to war on the plate. A bottle of cider and a spliff complemented the meal, he felt bloated. A couple of glugs from the bottle and a good belch had him feeling a whole lot better.

"You won't need a nap if you've done nothing all day?" suggested Violet when the record had finished.

"Don't be too sure. It can be exhausting doing nothing, more tiring than physical work sometimes. I think I'll have that nap, besides, I want to go and see Johan later."

"Will you play the Cate Brothers for me then, please? I'll wake you when it's finished."

He must have been tired, the first song had barely started and he was out of it, although he did enjoy the foot massage.

Violet let him sleep for half an hour after the tape stopped, using the time to have a word or two with Eight Ball. Pink only caught the tail end of the conversation, but Eight Ball paid attention to every word. It would remain to be seen just how much notice he actually took of it.

"Oh, you're awake. I was putting Eight Ball right on a couple of points. You don't mind, do you?"

"Be my guest. He's as much your cat as he is mine now. Maybe more so since he at least seems to listen to you."

"That's so sweet of you, Pink. You really don't mind? I mean, I'm not stepping on your toes am I?"

"I wish you would, or could …. Like I said, be my guest."

"Oh goody, Eight Ball! Go and see if it's raining."

To Pink's surprise, the cat did as he was told, returning moments later to let them know it was indeed raining. They had a good laugh about it until Eight Ball gave himself a good shake and treated Pink to a shower at the same time. Violet couldn't hide her pleasure at that.

Gathering up his cash/hash stash and the bicycle pump, he glided downstairs to see Johan. Both sisters were still there and by the look on Johan's face he had heard Sira's news and was sporting a grin which would have put the Cheshire cat to shame. Pink immediately sank his boat by reminding him he still had Mr Rapati to contend with. Even if Sira was hell bent on selecting her own husband, Mr Rapati's approval would have to be given. All three fell silent at his words of caution, then brightened when he let them know he had a cunning plan.

He strode past them and into the bakery. The oven timers had gone off and they had all chosen to ignore them. Pink dropped the doors and set about extracting the contents, pies, while his friends stood there with their mouths open waiting to hear his plan. Realising they wouldn't be privy to a single word of it until he had finished what he was doing, it was all hands to the pumps. The next batch was installed. Pink looked up at the clock and told them he was for an early night. All three managed to step between him and the back door, he was going nowhere, at least not for a while.

Taking centre stage, Pink explained how Ash, Johan's friend, had planted the seed of an idea. Recent findings regarding Sira's intended had fanned the flames until the idea became something more substantial. Indeed, with a little help and a little cunning, Mr Rapati would be offering up a dowry and begging Johan to choose one of his daughters.

Taking his captive audience back to the inception of his idea, Pink told how Ash claimed he was able to trace his ancestry back to the days when the name of Kadamba ruled Goa. In effect, he was descended from Goa's equivalent of royalty. Sadly, Kadamba rule fizzled out during the Portuguese occupancy, although the name was still fondly remembered and respected throughout Goa.

Three pairs of eyes followed him to the ovens and watched as he checked the timers. Warming to his theme, he presented his plan.

As things stood, Johan wasn't good enough for Sira. Put bluntly, he was inferior.

Three heads nodded in agreement.

Now, what if it were to slip out, quite by accident, that Johan was a direct descendant of this Kadamba tribe? What if Ash and a couple of his waiters were to turn up, and in full view of Mr Rapati, all but throw themselves at his feet, at the same time showering him with gifts? What if Johan were to remonstrate with Pink for giving his secret away before discovering it was his uncle, recently moved to these parts, who let it slip; totally unaware of the fact that Johan wanted to play it down in order to live a normal, humble life? What if Moraji were to go to the library, Pink had noticed all the reading material when he had visited with Mira, and read up on Kadamba rule? What if Pink were to reveal Johan had indeed sworn him to secrecy, wishing to underplay his royal blood?

Silence, three jaws were on the floor. Pink had the feeling he may have offended one, if not all three of them. Then, smiles as they looked at each other, then at Pink. It wasn't perfect, but it was feasible. Give Mr Rapati time to get over the fact he almost had a fruit for a son in law, then to realise one of his daughters could easily end up as a spinster. Sira could work on him, get him worried she was about to say yes to the first man who asked her. Moraji would be the icing on the cake, Pink knew she had more than a little sway where her husband was concerned; a lot more sway than Mr Rapati would readily admit to.

They all agreed Pink's plan was a good one, not too complicated. The timing was the most important part of it, there was every possibility it would work. One thing was certain, they wouldn't know unless they gave it a try.

Pink was popular. Mira was kissing him, Sira was hugging him and Johan was pumping his hand until it felt like it would work itself free from his wrist. He wriggled away from them and tended to the ovens again, the timers had fallen on deaf ears for the second time that evening. It was time for him to tell how he had fared on his first day at work. He told them it was very like the bakery, the place would fall apart if he weren't there to keep an eye on things. No one argued with him.

The girls went home happy and smiling, asking each other why they couldn't have come up with such a simple solution to Sira's problem.

Johan would rehearse Ash and his uncle, make sure he could coax a performance out of them. Of course, his uncle would also have to be a direct descendant of the Kadamba family.

Pink gave Johan a joint to fire up and went to stash his stuff in the bike shed. As they shared the joint, Johan wondered was it ethical to lie to his employer. In return, Pink asked was an arranged marriage strictly ethical. If Sira and Johan were to marry, Mr Rapati would have prior knowledge of his son in law's attributes. He would know he was a good worker, punctual, polite and, although he wouldn't be able to brag about it, a Prince. Johan had a couple of weeks to think about it. As far as Pink could see it was the only possible way he could slip his feet under the table.

Johan would put it to his uncle and his friends. No disrespect to Pink, but he would have to get them onside. It was an excellent plan, his heart was racing with the prospect; yes, he would do what he could to sell it to them.

Pink hadn't had any curry for a while so Johan promised to bring some tomorrow, along with news of his progress.

"Don't forget to wind your clock, Honey."

"Shit, what time is it?"

"Just gone one o'clock before you came in."

Pink set the clock to the right time, rolled a quick single skinner and told Violet of his wedding plans for Johan.

"They're lucky to have you for a friend, Pink. That's a wonderful thing you've done for them. I just know it could work. Is the girl …. what was her name? Sira, yes. Is she up for it? I bet she is?"

"They all seemed to like the idea, but let them sleep on it, already Johan has shown some signs of doubt. I think …. I hope it's because the plan is so ridiculously simple. Then again, that's why I think it can work."

"I would go for it just for that reason if I found myself in that position. I would jump at it."

"I'm for my scratcher. You coming, Kitten?"

"Scratcher? Oh, you mean bed? I'll wait up for Eight Ball. He went out at the same time as you and he's not been back since."

"Probably on the prowl. He didn't visit the bakery, unless he's with Johan now."

"Night night, Pinkee."

"Night, Kitten. Don't make a noise when you come to bed."

There was that giggle again, a truly delightful sound.

Sleep came easily, No dreams, no disturbances until he heard his name being called. It was Violet, who else? Eight Ball hadn't showed yet.

Pink looked at the clock, quarter past four. What the fuck, he needed a piss anyway.

"Shout out of the window for him."

"He's a cat, not a dog, Cat's don't come when you call for them."

"Shout anyway, please. Do that chee chee chee thing you do."

Pink felt like a fool, but obliged anyway.

"He's probably miles away, probably sorting one of his girlfriends out. Sometimes he disappears for days on end."

"Not since he's been here he hasn't. I'm worried, Pink."

"I'm sure there's nothing to worry about. I'll have a mooch round for him in the morning before I go to work. How does that sound?"

"Oh, ok. I'm sorry I woke you, but it's just not like him to stay out."

Pink went back to bed, thinking he wouldn't sleep, or wouldn't be allowed to sleep, but Violet kept her vigil and left him alone. He was up before the alarm went off, though, feeling slightly guilty about not doing more to appease Violet. She hadn't moved from the kitchen all night and he almost asked her was she not tired, but managed to bite his tongue in time. Still, she wasn't at all talkative, maintaining her position facing the kitchen window; much like Eight Ball used to do with her at the wall.

Pink had his breakfast and told her he was going to have a look for the cat. Violet responded with a grunt, one of those 'not before time' grunts.

The call to prayers startled him as he left the flat, it was seven o'clock, cold, dark and damp. He had little or no chance of finding Eight Ball, especially if he didn't want to be found. He went straight to the bike shed, might as well utilise some transport to help in his search. He heard the miaow before he could open the padlock and realised Eight Ball must have followed him in last night when he stashed his valuables. The dumb cat found himself to be locked in, all down to his nosiness.

Since Violet was keeping watch on the window, Pink decided to sneak Eight Ball in via the front door and nonchalantly sit skinning up a couple of joints, see how long it took her to suss he wasn't missing after all.

Eight Ball scuppered his plan right away by making a dash for his food. Pink could hear Violet asking him where the fuck he had been all night. Smiling to himself, he fired up a single skinner, banged on Led Zep Two to do away with any chance of conversation and strolled into the kitchen to make a cup of coffee.

He was ready for the off when side one finished playing. Picking up Towser's sausages, he headed for the door, stopped to leave the radio on and turned to see Violet on Eight Ball's favourite wall. The cat was curled up in a ball in front of her, knocking out the zeds.

"Ok." She said. "You were right, but I can't help worrying, just like I can't help worrying about you on that building site. You will be careful, won't you?"

"See you later, Kitten," was all he said, and was gone.

Quickfire promotions

Pink was almost at the top of the track to the allotments before realising he hadn't bought a paper. It was too late to turn back. He blamed the Cate brothers for causing the distraction, occupying the space between his ears and blotting out all thoughts other than what was going on with the music. Towser was barking his head off, he thought they had taken themselves beyond all that until he sussed it was the fault of the bike. The animal would have to become accustomed to that now. Pink reckoned it wouldn't take him too long, not when there was food involved. He stopped creating when Pink spoke to him, and followed the bike the length of the fence. Five sausages sailed over one at a time, each of them expertly fielded before they hit the ground.

It was trying to rain when he parked his bike inside the storeroom. Barry, the wages clerk/timekeeper asked what was playing on his Walkman and Pink handed it over, he liked nothing better than to turn people on to good music.

Just as he was about to mount the single step to the canteen, a huge rat bolted from underneath. All the portacabins were raised about two feet from the ground and it hadn't taken the rat long to find which was his favourite. Mac was holding court, the sun was trying its best, peeking through the clouds and offering the chance of some work being achieved. Pink put his wellingtons on and was teamed up with Tanzi, a weathered old Irishman; they were to dig out holes for boundary fence posts. The old man was a grafter. Five foot nothing, sixty two years of age, had been travelling the building sites for forty five years and, because there were so many of his countrymen in the trade, had never felt the need to lose his heavy brogue. He gave off the impression he slept with his spade. Pink could hardly keep pace with him, the holes were seven feet apart and Tanzi seemed to be digging two to his one. He was glad when they were called in for the first break of the day, hitching a ride to the canteen on a tractor and trailer.

Barry was in the breakfast queue when Pink entered. He gave up his place near the front and joined him to discuss the Cate brothers, another satisfied customer. While they were eating, Mac asked Pink to jump on one of the new dumper trucks and deliver the concrete for the fence posts. He had never driven a dumper before, but he wasn't about to admit that to anyone. Patsy saw his hesitation and showed him how to use the starting handle. That done, he ran through the gear system and Pink was a dumper driver, easier than digging holes in clay by a long, long margin.

Mostly, the job entailed sitting astride the machine and tipping the bucket from time to time. This gave Pink the chance to pick the brains of other workmen in the vicinity; he had plenty of questions, the answers to which would go towards helping him fit in with the environment.

In the couple of hours between morning brew time and lunch, he picked up the basics of JCB driving, learned to reverse the tractor and trailer, quite expertly, and discovered the dumper couldn't be easily steered through the heavy mud, that's why the heavier plant machinery had caterpillar tracks. His dumper had to be assisted on more than one occasion by the long reaching arm of the JCB. He also discovered what the sections of rail were for, a tower crane; which was due to be erected next week. Mounted on rails, it would run the length of the site. Already, the earth moving equipment was levelling out what appeared to be a road from one end of the site to the other. Engineers had a theodolite set up and were taking readings to ensure the crane would be sited in the correct place.

Lunchtime came reasonably quickly, there seemed to be more workmen today. Abby asked Mac could Pink assist again. Pink was happy to help, knowing there would be a free meal in it for him when the queue died down. He had only just sat down to his meal when Mac entered to scare the men back out to work. The foreman ordered a cup of tea and joined him, closely followed by Abby. He asked had anyone seen Tanzi during the lunch break. No one could remember seeing him so Pink volunteered to look for him when he had eaten.

Borrowing the tractor, he followed the line of the post holes as far as the snake bend in the canal. This was where the site ended, but there was no sign of the little Irishman. Looking across the canal, Pink could just about make out a figure in the distance. Tanzi was still digging, but in a farmer's field. Luckily, there was no crop on the go. There was a flock of sheep, however, huddled in the far corner and keeping a wary eye on Tanzi and wondering what the fuck to do when he reached where they were.

Pink found the bridge where Tanzi had crossed, left the tractor where it was, leapt the fence which kept the sheep on their own side of the canal and managed to stop him in mid dig. At a conservative estimate they were about half a mile from the canteen. The old man had no idea of the time, merely following orders and digging holes in a straight line at seven feet apart. No one stopped him so he followed his line. Pink couldn't swear to it he had even used the bridge, there was every possibility holes for fence posts would be found if ever the canal was drained.

Mac appeared from the office door when the tractor rolled up. Pink told him Tanzi had become bogged down in the mud, a little white lie to spare his blushes. The old man was ordered to the canteen for a late lunch. Over a mug of tea he told Abby the full tale, big mistake, by afternoon brew time the entire workforce would know.

Pink kept charge of the tractor for another half hour and was happy to do so, the last thing he wanted was to be demoted back to the spadework. Mac asked him to run two men to the top of the lane, a couple of tipper trucks had been dropped off there, the drivers of the low loaders which had brought them couldn't see a way to turn their vehicles and get out if they went down to the site. When they reached the top of the lane they found three tippers, not two. Pink parked the tractor up and added another string to his bow. There was less to driving the huge trucks than there was to driving a dumper; more comfortable, too.

He spent the next hour ferrying ballast to the channel that had been gouged out for the tower crane's railway track. Things seemed to be moving pretty fast. Very little had been done yesterday, but today, the site was a hive of activity. This was when Pink had one of his bright ideas. He would make himself indispensable by mastering all vehicles; that way, he could fill in for anyone, do a different job every day with not much chance of being bored.

Raised voices from the canteen caused him to hesitate at the door, Mac was giving a few men short shrift for taking the piss out of Tanzi. Whoever was being told off were advised the old man was worth ten of them, they should be ashamed.

Pink entered and sat with Tanzi and it didn't take him long to find out who had spread the story. He would have to be heedful of what he said when Abby was around because she couldn't hold her own water. She was handy when it came to feeding Towser, he would keep her onside for that, that and the odd rumour he might want to put out himself for mischief.

After the break, he jumped into the cab of his tipper again and drove off for another load of stone. There was a hold up, the loading shovel, known as the Cat, had shed one of its caterpillar tracks so all three tippers were waiting to be loaded. Pink jumped out to see if he could lend a hand. The fitter had sent the Cat driver to the stores for a part, but in the meantime he had improvised and was ready to refit the track. He showed Pink how to operate the machine, not the shovel, just the forward and reverse movement. On the fitter's command, he was to roll forward to test the repair. That done, he was shown how to put the machine through several twists and turns. The fitter was happy with his work, gave Pink the thumbs up and wandered off in the direction of the cabins. No sign of the Cat driver so Pink had a play around with the controls, quickly finding what everything did. He didn't attempt to load any of the wagons, merely experimented with the hydraulics system, raising and lowering the huge shovel and spinning the machine in every possible direction. When the driver returned, Pink sat behind him in the cab and observed. When it came time for his own truck to be loaded, he felt confident enough to do it for himself. He saw the rest of the day out ferrying stone and loading his own truck, yet another string to his bow and the Cat driver said he was a natural.

The stone ballast was kept in a clearing close to the caravans of the travelling workmen. The woman who had directed Pink to the whereabouts of the foreman stopped him on one of his trips to complain about the dust being kicked up from the fast drying dirt road, she had a washing hanging out to dry and it was dirtier now than before she washed it. Pink promised to have a word with Mac for her. She had a good figure for her age and he spent longer than he should have delivering his promise and drinking in the view. She was wearing tight jeans and he let her turn back towards the caravans before carrying on with his work. He knew she knew why he did that.

Mac told him she was the wife of one of the bosses, always complaining about something or other. He would have a word.

Barry handed over his Walkman, complete with fresh batteries, could he have a copy of the tape if he brought a blank cassette in the morning? When Pink changed his shoes, Abby gave him the doggy bag. Towser was in for a treat tonight.

He waited until he was off site before sparking up his spliff, Towser wagged his tail off at the sight of him and even more so when presented with his supper. Pink spent five minutes with him, finishing his smoke and chatting away before donning his headphones and allowing the Cate Brothers to accompany him home. It was dark, the bike had no lights, but he knew the lane like the back of his hand.

Sira saw him passing the shop window and met him at the bike shed. She appeared undecided as to whether she should laugh or cry so Pink played it by ear, coaxing the story from her gently. The girls had apprised Moraji of his plan and she was all for it, so no problem there. That was the happy side of her countenance, now came the sad side. Johan had been in earlier, asking for time off. He had to go to India on family business and would be gone for ten days. It was all so sudden, she would miss him terribly. Mira poked her head out of the door and told them her father had just pulled up. Sira made her way back in and Pink went round to the front of the shop.

Mr Rapati called him in and asked could he do a few evenings as cover for Johan, Eight 'til twelve, if it wasn't too much trouble. Otherwise, he couldn't afford to let Johan go. Pink was only too willing to oblige, he knew where his friend was going and why. Of course he would cover for him, especially when told he would be working with one or other of the girls. Life just didn't get any better than this.

"How was your day, Honey?" Violet wanted to know before he was properly through the door.

"I'm starving hungry, me. Is my dinner ready, Kitten?"

"I wish I could cook for you, Pink. C'mon, tell me about your day."

"Not much to tell. I started off digging holes, lost an old Irishman, found him in the next county, graduated to the dumper, then the tractor, then the tipper truck, had a mess around on a JCB then ended up on the tipper again."

"Wait! Did you just say you lost an old man?"

Pink explained about Tanzi and his theory regarding post holes on the canal bed. Violet was in stitches. Eight Ball looked from one to the other before deciding to stay out of it, settling down for a nap at Violet's feet.

"What do you have to do about the dole if you're working full time now?"

"Shit. Good job you mentioned that. I'll write a letter and post it through their door tomorrow. They should send me a double giro because I don't get paid for a fortnight."

"Why's that?"

"I have to work a week in hand. That's the way of the building trade."

While they were chatting, Pink put his curry on a low light and set some rice to boil. Next, he put some decent sounds on since the DJ was driving him nuts with his incessant babble. He wondered how Violet coped with it all day long. Soon, he was in the shower and singing along to Joe Cocker. Violet joined him in the bathroom and harmonised, making sure he washed behind his ears.

The girls were outside the back door of the bakery, clapping their hands in time with the song and giggling when it was over.

Curry, cider, a large spliff, ten minutes with the dishes and he was ready for his nap. Violet asked for and was granted a listen to Tom Petty and the Heartbreakers. Pink's hair was still wet so he wrapped it in a towel, maybe Mira could plait it for him later.

He woke to complete silence. Rolling off the couch, he consulted the clock in the bedroom. Two hours worth of a nap had him well rested. If he was to manage both jobs he would probably need that rest every day. Violet invited him to choose the music when he asked did she have any preferences. Boz Scaggs was given the nod and the room filled with his efforts on 'Silk Degrees'. Violet squealed with delight and added her voice as Pink built a couple of joints. Searching out pen and paper, he wrote his resignation from the dole, at the same time asking for an allowance towards workboots and protective clothing for his new job.

Eight Ball scrambled through his window to let him know it wasn't raining, bringing the decision to deliver the letter there and then, otherwise he would be at the other end of town in the morning and unable to feed Towser; something he wasn't prepared to consider, being delighted at the change he had brought about in the animal's demeanour from savage brute to hand fed and docile.

Telling Violet he would be back before side two of 'Silk Degrees' was over, he wrapped himself against the elements and went for a ride on his bike.

His letter deposited in the dole office's post box, he was about to ride home when he heard a commotion, raised voices coming from just around the corner. Sure he recognised the female voice, he changed direction, turned the corner and came across Louise, wrestling with a couple of drunks. She didn't particularly want to arrest them, moving them away from the town centre being uppermost in her mind. Pink didn't know either of the men, but if he did it wouldn't have prevented him from intervening on Louise's behalf. Jumping from his bike, he tripped the tallest of the two from behind and stood on his wrist as he sprawled face down, rendering him immobile. Louise had the other's arm halfway up his back, forcing him into submission. Thus immobilised, both men gave assurances as to their future conduct and promised to make their way home in an orderly manner. Just for insurance, Louise took the wallet from her charge's pocket, found his address inside and read it aloud to Pink. Between them, they would remember it.

She thanked Pink for his assistance, then complained he hadn't called on her. To put matters right, she offered to cook him a meal on her day off, which just happened to be the following day. Pink was all for it, although it would very much depend on when Johan was going abroad. He explained he was now working two jobs and didn't wish to let anyone down. He promised faithfully to call her at lunchtime tomorrow, saying he would know how he was fixed by then. Louise looked at her watch, her shift was over, the main reason she didn't wish to arrest the drunks; the paperwork it would have created going in the men's favour.

They hit on the idea at the same time, maybe a quickie, if they could find somewhere to go. Pink stashed his bike in a back alley and jumped in the police car. Keeping his head down, he directed

Louise to the allotments and to an isolated spot between two plots. It was cramped in the car, but they managed in the end, one for his memoirs; no one would ever believe him, but at least he himself knew it to be true. A policewoman in full uniform, and in her very own police car.

Louise dropped him off where he left the bike, making him repeat his promise to call her. This he did and was soon on his way back to the High Chaparral.

Violet was on her favourite wall, arms folded like a housewife talking over the fence.

"You said you wouldn't be long. I hardly see you now you're working full time."

"I had to assist the police," he explained, going on to tell her what had transpired.

"That was very public spirited of you, Honey. I hope you were suitably rewarded for your trouble."

"The smile on the policewoman's face was reward enough for me, Kitten."

Needless to say, he didn't relate the full extent of his reward.

The girls had gone home by the time he went downstairs, he would have to tie his hair in a pony tail tomorrow and tuck it into the back of his shirt for work.

Johan planned to leave on the Thursday. Himself, Ash and Pink would share his travelling expenses and chip in an equal amount each towards the purchase of the merchandise. They shared a joint and chewed the fat for an hour or so. Since the goods were to be delivered to the restaurant, Johan would let Ash know they had been dispatched, and more importantly, when they could expect delivery.

Pink talked about his new job and Johan was suitably impressed with his rise through the ranks. Knowing his friend as he did, he expected nothing less. As for Pink's plan to gain Johan favour with Mr Rapati? From discussion with Ash, the waiters and his uncle, it was deemed to be feasible and they were all keen to play a part in it. Alongside that, Moraji had been approached by both girls; she wanted a word with Johan and Pink, but she too thought it to be a wonderful idea. Her daughter's happiness was her top priority and Johan had an audience with her arranged for the following day.

The couple of joints they smoked had worked their magic. Pink's eyes were closing so he wouldn't need any rocking tonight.

Violet was chatty. He made a cup of tea and listened to her talk about what Eight Ball had been up to all day, a little more of her argument with her sister, songs she had heard on the radio and even some snippets of news from the various bulletins broadcast over the day. This caused him to realise just how much time she indeed spent on her own. He made a silent promise to himself, he would spend all day Saturday with her, he would probably be in need of a rest by then.

Bedtime at last. Violet reminded him, as always, to wind his clock up and as predicted, he didn't need any rocking.

CHAPTER 21

Raise and raise again

Pink could almost taste the lavender, he knew he wasn't dreaming. Violet had definitely crept into bed with him and no doubt about it. Yet, he knew if he were to open his eyes, she would be on the ceiling, watching over him. So, he did the only thing he could do in the circumstances, kept his eyes tight shut, snuggled up and went back to sleep.

The alarm went off and had him naked in the middle of the floor, wondering what the fuck was going on. Violet squealed with laughter and Eight Ball claimed the warm spot he had vacated on the bed.

He put the radio on for the news, catching the seven o'clock bulletin, as soon as it was over he put the stylus to the Doobie Brothers. If the DJs came out with a lot of shit during the day, they came out with even more shit in the early mornings, not an ideal way to start the day.

He doubled up on his porridge intake. If he had to use a spade at work he wanted plenty of fuel inside him.

"On or off, Violet?"

"On or off, what?"

"The radio, do you want it left on?"

"Oh .... no .... thank you, no. I'm getting more like you every day, I much prefer quality as opposed to quantity."

"Good girl. See you later."

"Take care out there, Pink. Bye bye."

He only managed to get halfway downstairs, Barry wanted a copy of the Cate Brothers tape, he could have Pink's, he could do another copy at the weekend.

Towser had to make do with a couple of bread rolls for breakfast. Pink inserted a lump of old cheese into each of them, the dog wouldn't complain.

The heavens opened as he was clocking on. He made his way to Barry's office, gave him the tape, accepted a blank in return and made arrangements to use the phone at lunchtime.

There were two card schools on the go when he entered the canteen. Pink sat with Patsy, he liked his patter, the guy never shut up and most of what he had to say was amusing. When Mac called for drivers only, Pink was about to rise. Patsy tugged at his sleeve to stop him, whispering he wasn't being paid as a driver. He was to give it five minutes, Mac would be sure to return for him, he was then to renegotiate his salary.

Right call. Mac came back and gave him a shout, asking him to spend the day on the tipper again. Before Pink could open his mouth, Mac informed him his wages would be those of a tipper driver, backdated from Monday. No argument there.

The morning passed by quickly. Running between the ballast and the layout for the tower crane, the only person getting wet was the clerk of works, who had to inspect everything was just so. Pink gave him a lift to the canteen at brew time and asked was he having fun. He actually managed a smile at that, but for the most part he was as miserable as sin.

Pink thanked Patsy for the earlier advice, good advice as it turned out and discovered Barry had nominated him for Patsy's pub pool team. The new league kicked off soon, was he interested?

He couldn't see why not, it was time he started going out and about a bit more. Yes, put his name down.

The loading shovel driver slipped and broke his ankle while climbing into his cab. Pink was on hand to assist him to the office and Mac sorted out a lift to the hospital for him. Now, he was short of a shovel driver. Pink mentioned he had experience on said machine and his wages were adjusted for the second time that day; again, backdated from Monday.

The nature of the loading job meant he had almost twenty minutes between activities. There were only two wagons to load now, the distance they had to travel to dump the ballast affording him time to listen to a few tracks on the Walkman.

In one of these idle moments he switched the engine off since the cab was red hot. The outside temperature was pretty low, but he had more skins on than an onion. The shovel was parked up facing the caravan site. Pink let Jackson Browne fill his ears, tilted the seat back to the rest position and was about to recline when he realised he could see into the living room of the nearest caravan. The woman he had been admiring yesterday appeared in the middle of the room dressed only in a towel. He willed her to get rid of it and she duly obliged, parading in the altogether, obviously ignorant of the fact she could be seen, or was she? It seemed to Pink she was actually flaunting her nudity, posing in the mirror and putting her body through all manner of contortions. Unfortunately, one of the tipper trucks interrupted his matinee just as it was getting steamy, he would be sure to park up in exactly the same position in future and hope for a repeat performance. What an out and out turn on that was. He had a feeling it was for his benefit alone, this train of thought being galvanised when the woman closed the curtains as the tipper arrived.

Now he was horny. Louise didn't exactly help matters by letting him know, via his promised phone call, of her plans for later that evening.

He wasn't hungry and gave the canteen a miss. Instead, he wandered to his proposed garden patch and dug it over again, let the elements at it. The brambles were already trying to encroach on his land, he would set his mind to thwarting them; after all, he worked on a building site, there should be all manner of materials lying around to suit the project.

On his way back to his machine he called in on Mac to let him know they were running low on stone. An hour later, Mac stopped by, accompanied by the boss whose wife had provided the floor show. The stone was on order, due in an hour or so. A Range Rover pulled up, Mac and the boss jumped in, joining another boss who was driving. Mac winked at him and simulated drinking a pint, making it obvious where they were going. They were no sooner out of earshot than the caravan door opened, she was in her dressing gown, tugging at it above the belt line and revealing her pert breasts. Pink killed the engine and made a beeline for the caravan, uppermost in his mind was that he didn't want her to catch cold. She all but dragged him in, saying she had noticed how he looked at her, did he like what he saw? Could he help her out, please? Her husband was a useless pisspot. Please could he help her out?

To say she was gagging for it would be something of an understatement, almost ripping the clothes from his back. She led him by the cock to in front of the mirror, dropped to her knees and helped herself to as much of him as she could possibly cram into her mouth. That was for starters. He had to cover her mouth when he entered her from behind, her screams of ecstasy shattering the relative silence of before. He remembered thinking the whole site would be aware of what was going on. Still, he stuck to his task, determined to get as much out of it as she obviously was. Twenty minutes later he escaped her clutches, she wanted him to promise he would service her regularly. Enjoyable as it was, he told her it would have to be a one off, it was his first week in the job and he didn't want to rock the boat. That was when she turned nasty, telling him her husband would find out if he didn't comply with her wishes. Pink stood his ground, told her to fuck off, told her he didn't succumb to threats and wondered aloud just how much damage his shovel could do to a caravan if he were ever to lose control of the thing.

The stone hadn't arrived by the afternoon break. Pink went to the office to chase it up and came upon Patsy and Barry. With a flash of inspiration, he swore them to secrecy and told them the boss's wife had been flashing her tits and giving him the come on, shame he didn't fancy her, maybe if she was ten years younger? The three men had a good laugh about it and he had some insurance; yes, good move that, slotting his retaliation in first.

Still no stone when he returned to his machine. He didn't fancy sitting around where he was and decided to put the Cat through its paces, enjoying the horrified look on the woman's face as he flashed past, bucket raised to window height and only inches from the caravan. She would think twice about trying to drop him in it.

Splashing through the mud, he suddenly slammed his foot down on one of the brake pedals. This was how the huge vehicle manoeuvred; stop, or slow one side of the tracks and the other turned to change direction. A broken section of concrete pipe lay discarded by the side of the makeshift road. Split exactly down the seam, it would be an ideal solution to his bramble problem. He scooped both halves into the bucket and headed towards his plot. Stopping at the steel bending plant, he scrounged four rods of similar length and the short term loan of a lump hammer.

It didn't take him long to hammer the rods into the soft ground and prop the sections of pipe wrong way round, so that the bramble creepers would run round the concave shape of the pipe and double back on themselves; a fine piece of engineering, even if he did say so himself.

Mrs boss was standing in her porchway when he gunned the Cat back up the hill. The stone had arrived and one of the delivery drivers wanted to know where to get rid of his load. If Pink hadn't shown up, the bloke might not have been given the answer he was expecting. Mrs boss disappeared when she heard him approaching, leaving him to sort the driver out.

It was almost home time. Pink tidied up his work area, signed the delivery sheet and called it a day. By the time he handed the sheet in to the office it would be pointless going back up the hill again.

Towser didn't bark at the bike, he looked a lot healthier than when Pink first laid eyes on him. A regular feast of sausages and bacon will do that for a dog.

Mira joined him at the back of the bakery as he stowed his bike, she was going home, but she wanted him to know Moraji had arranged for her to meet her intended at the weekend. Chaperoned, of course

Pink told her he wouldn't be available to act as chaperone and was rewarded with that warm, throaty laugh of hers. She recovered enough to tell him Moraji had already volunteered, then kissed him full on the mouth.

"Music please, Pink. I think maybe you could leave the radio on for me in future. The silence is almost deafening."

Pink obliged and headed straight for the shower, no nap today, he had a date with Louise No strings attached, good food and good sex. What more could a man ask?

"You off out again, Honey?"

"Got to go and see that policewoman from last night, Kitten," he explained. "Give a statement."

"Then you going straight to the bakery?"

"I might have a couple of pints while I'm down that way, I'll leave the radio on for you."

"Thank you, Honey. I've really missed you today."

"Me too, Kitten. Me too."

Louise picked him up at the shops as arranged; thankfully, in an unmarked car. She looked good enough to eat, showing her legs off in a little short skirt. Her top half was equally delicious, clad in a tight fitting shirt flapping open almost to her navel to let him see she wasn't wearing a bra. Taking his hand, she placed it between her legs and he rewarded her with a huge grin. The little minx was also knickerless.

What Louise wanted first was a joint. Pink asked her did she know it was illegal before producing a large, ready rolled spliff. Whatever was cooking smelled delicious, but it would have to wait, his afternoon romp had only served as an appetizer to the main course. Louise played with herself while it was his turn to toke on the joint, this was one horny young lady and when she tasted her fingers, it was more than he could bear. His head between her legs, he dug his hands under backside and force fed her pussy into his eager mouth, delicious. Louise squealed and moaned in equal measure, begging him not to stop, not to dare fucking stop.

Over dinner, he asked did she have any like minded policewoman friends, remembering the one he followed down the road. Yes, there was this one who definitely fancied her, made it only too obvious, in fact. Pink was interested, until Louise told him she was a desk sergeant, having found it absolutely necessary to pass her sergeant exams since she could no longer fit in the patrol cars; she was twenty stone if she was an ounce. Pink shivered, he would stick with what he had, thank you. Although he'd had a shower earlier, he couldn't pass up the chance to share a bath with Louise, allowing her to plait his hair before sucking his cock dry. They relaxed in the bubbles then, scented candles adding to the ambience along with a portable radio, which surprisingly held on to the pirate station without wandering all over the place.

All too soon, the interlude was over. Louise made him promise, hand on heart, to call her and not be a stranger. After tonight, how could he possibly refuse? Now she was apologetic, not that she wanted to be rid of him, but her next shift was six o'clock in the morning and she really did need her beauty sleep. Pink could have argued on that point, but this was what he liked about her. No mushy sentiment, just honest to goodness down to earth lust. A girl after his own heart.

He left her a lump of hash and a packet of skins, a small price to pay for some quite excellent entertainment

Louise dropped him off at the shops again, reminding him of his promise to call her before gunning the car down the empty road in the direction of home.

Pink went to the bike shed to make a withdrawal from his cash stash before entering the bakery, Johan was off on business tomorrow and would require Pink's stake before he left.

Johan was alone in the bakery. Pink could see he was itching to divulge something and told him to spit it out. Further discussion with Ash and company had brought about a slight change to the imminent revelation of his nobility. What did Pink think of it taking place while he was away? Ash and the waiters could turn up looking for him, bearing the necessary gifts and fawning attitudes, all of which would really give Mr Rapati something to scratch his head about. In truth, Johan felt a little embarrassed about the whole thing, desperate enough to get together with Sira to try anything, but he didn't consider himself to be that good of an actor to carry it off. The sheer relief on his face when Pink smiled and confessed to liking the the alteration to his plan was a picture to behold. He stressed Johan would still be required to put on a bit of an act on his return, but by then he would have been made aware of Mr Rapati's reaction and could fashion his act to suit.

Mr Rapati dropped by to wish him bon voyage and to Johan's delight, Sira had tagged along for the ride. Pink took Mr Rapati into the shop proper to discuss his contract for the coming ten days, easily reaching a mutual understanding. He kept him chatting for about half an hour, giving the lovebirds some valuable time alone.

When they left, Pink handed over his stake, shook his friend warmly by the hand and told him to be careful, not to take any unnecessary risks and God speed. "Who plaited your hair, Honey?"

"Oh, one of the girls downstairs. Has she made a good job of it? They do their own you know, I don't know how they manage it. Must be double jointed or something."

"Is Johan looking forward to his trip?"

"It's hard to tell, really. He'll be happy to see his relatives, but I think there's an illness or some other issue with one of them."

"Are you tired, Pinkee?"

"Not really, why?"

"Roll a joint and tell me about your day, will you?"

"Anything for you Kitten….anything."

"You're so sweet. Have I ever told you that?"

"Probably."

Her laugh had him almost aroused again, maybe she would lie with him later? He relaxed with his smoke and Eight Ball wrapped himself around the back of his neck like in the old days. Violet giggled softly as he recounted the events of his day; some of them at least. All was well with the world.

Sure enough, Violet slipped between the sheets with him. He sensed she was about to before he felt the bed move slightly under her weight, the scent of lavender gave her away. They went at it like knives and in the dark recesses of his mind he chalked up yet another hat-trick, but mostly he concentrated on making love to the beautiful Violet Hiccup. Later, she massaged his neck. He wondered how she had known it was aching, then he remembered. Eight Ball, perceptive as ever, had given it away.

CHAPTER 22

Back to the drawing board

Pink dreamt he was high again. Not stoned high, but way up high, high. He could see for miles, clouds permitting. The alarm brought him down to earth with a bump and he was quite relieved to find he could put both feet firmly on the bedroom floor.

"Good morning, Honey. Did you sleep well?"

"I did and I didn't." He answered with a huge yawn.

"Explain, please?"

"It's the lavender. I know you're close when I catch a whiff of it. Don't get me wrong, it doesn't disturb me, only makes me acutely aware of your presence."

"Is that a bad thing? Please say it isn't?"

"I'm not complaining, far from it. I like it that you seem to be so close to me, maybe a little frustrating sometimes."

"Good answer. You can be very tactful when you want to be. I think I love you, Pink."

"Me too, kitten," he told her without a moment's hesitation; not a word he would ever consider bandying about, but within the context of their relationship, he felt totally at ease with the admission.

"Ooh, I've come out in goose bumps. See what you do to me, Pinkee? I imagine you've had that effect on all the women you've known?"

"I wouldn't go so far as to say that," he stalled, edging ever closer to the stereo, alarm bells sounding off in his brain. He wasn't too keen on the direction the conversation was taking.

Violet let it go when Lynyrd Skynyrd cut in. They both sang along as Pink dished up his porridge, a sly smile on his face at the neat sidestep he had executed. No doubt Violet would pick up on the same tack at some point, but it wouldn't be today.

He gave her the choice of having the radio on or off before leaving for work. She elected to have it playing, but only because it was such a long day without him. Eight Ball was company, sure, but he tended to sleep for most of the day.

Eight Ball actually tried to bar his way to the door, he wasn't stupid, demanding to know why Pink had half a tin of cat food concealed under his jacket. Was he feeding another cat? Violet was left with the task of explaining, and surprisingly he accepted it without fuss; a little miffed Pink couldn't broach the subject himself, but, being philosophical, as long as he was well fed, why should he bother to complain?

Towser had no complaints, either, following the bike to the far end of the fence and sitting up to beg for his food. In a blindfold test, a cat would be able to discern between dog and cat food. A dog would eat both in the order they were served up, and would probably eat the cat too if it stood still long enough.

Mac had him in the office as soon as he clocked on, Mrs boss had been complaining about the close proximity of his driving. Pink explained he was only making way for the stone wagons to drop their delivery, both she and her caravan were never in any danger. Then again, hadn't Mac mentioned she was always complaining about something? Mac let it go, he was to consider himself suitably admonished.

At the rate they were going, the foundation road for the tower crane would be in place by lunchtime; he was to assist the engineer, it would then be time to lay the railway tracks.

Borrowing Barry's newspaper, he made his way up the hill to the shovel. If there was to be no floor show, at least he would have something to read. Mrs boss kept her curtains closed, either that or she was still in bed. One hour into the day, Pink had the engine switched off and was poring over the sports pages. Looking up, he spied the fitter furtively sneaking from behind Mrs boss's caravan and darting for the front door. He didn't knock, just kicked his muddy boots off in the porch and marched straight in. Maybe she had a leaky tap or something? Pink didn't wear a watch, at a guess the fitter spent twenty five minutes in the caravan and still the curtains remained closed. When he finally exited, he employed the same stealthy manner as he had used for his entrance. Highly suspicious.

Brew time. Pink sat with Tanzi and Patsy. He thought about telling Patsy of the fitter's visit, but decided not to, he wasn't one for spreading idle gossip; maybe he would mention it to the fitter when he caught him on his own, check out his reaction? Then again, maybe not.

After the break, Mac told him they had enough stone for the rail track, but he was to sit at the top of the hill for an hour or so until the foreman was absolutely sure. Pink settled in and picked up where he left off with the paper. Then, he closed his eyes and was asleep within seconds, waking with a jolt when the boss roared past in his range rover. He stayed where he was, snug as a bug. Five minutes later, another shadowy figure crept from behind the caravan. Mac, it seemed he too was dipping his wick, this woman was something else. Pink resolved to have a word with her, he had a friend in town who would gladly fit her a revolving door and save her a lot of time. She would certainly know how to go about paying him, too.

While Mac was busy, he made his way to the office and returned the newspaper to its rightful owner. Barry told him another sixteen men would be starting in the morning, a squad of steel-fixers and a concreting gang. Pink re-thought his plans for Mrs boss, maybe they could work together? He would offer to install a red light as well as the revolving door; he would be her pimp and they could share the proceeds. Knowing her as he did, she would probably give it away. Not much profit there.

Abby came into the office to report rodent droppings in the canteen and Barry told her he would inform the boss as soon as he returned. Then Abby asked Pink could he help out, she was well behind with the lunches. He had nothing better to do with himself, and besides, he could murder a coffee. The rats were making their way in through a hole under the sink. Pink nipped to the stores, borrowed a screwdriver and unscrewed the lid from a metal drill case; it wasn't heavy, but with a two gallon container of washing up liquid on top of it, the rats would need to find another point of entry.

His half hour lunch break turned into an hour and three quarters. He assisted Abby over the busy period and had his free meal with a couple of cups of coffee. The engineer stuck his head round the canteen door and asked was he ready to help with his measurements. All he had to do was carry a large pole bearing red and black numbers and position it in various places for a reading. Being as it was a lovely spring day and he wasn't operating any machinery, he fired up a spliff and made the most of it. The engineer involved himself in an argument with the clerk of works and he edged closer to catch what it was all about. The clerk of works wasn't at all happy with the depth of the ballast, he wanted at least another two feet of stone beneath the sleepers. The engineer had taken several level readings from these sleepers, threequarters of which had already been laid. Mac and the site boss joined the fray, this would knock them back two or three days, but the clerk of works stood his ground. It was all to do with the load spread of the tower crane. Built above old mine shafts, any subsidence would buckle the track and cause an accident. Deep concrete piles had been sunk throughout the entire area of the site, but he wasn't for taking any chances with such an elevated structure.

The argument became heated to the point where blows were about to be exchanged. Pink had perched himself on the tractor trailer along with a few others who had stopped to watch the show.

The engineer stormed off in disgust, closely followed by the boss. Everyone went back to work while Mac begged the clerk to pass the base as it stood. Still, he wouldn't give way, he was quite adamant, the crane would need a more solid base to work from.

Pink had been surveying the problem from a half stoned point of view, coming up with a suggestion which was immediately ridiculed by Mac, but was seriously considered by the clerk of works. Since the sleepers had all but been laid, why not put a double row of twelve by twelves atop each side of them, then a single row on top of that, this would help to spread the load more evenly. When Mac saw the clerk's interest, he took the suggestion on board himself, dragging the clerk and Pink back towards the office and the drawing board, see if they could make it work.

The engineer knocked out a few diagrams on being told of Pink's suggestion and agreed they had found the solution. Pink took the pencil from him and added further sections of twelve by twelves, spaced at regular intervals and spanning the gauge of the tracks as added insurance. The clerk of works gave it the thumbs up and everyone was on speaking terms again.

Pink wandered off, only to be called back by the boss, inviting him to join himself, Mac, the fitter and the engineer for a drink.

Throwing Pink the keys to the Range Rover, the boss jumped into the passenger seat while the others squeezed into the back. Deciding the ex-servicemen's would be full of the usual reprobates, he drove them to the Canine Dog Club, marvelling at the vehicle's suspension on the way; he wouldn't mind one of these for himself. As he had suspected, the club was almost empty. Pink kicked his muddy boots off at the door and invited the others to follow suit. He wasn't allowed to put his hand in his pocket for the next two hours and that gave him just enough time to skin them at poker. They were all on good money and fancied themselves as high rollers. Pink brought them down to earth with a thump. To a man, they were as readable as a children's comic; his luck was still holding out admirably. Long may it last.

His feet were well and truly under the table now. Not exactly how he wanted it, but easily better than having to keep looking over his shoulder every five minutes. On the drive back to the site, the boss told him there would be a bonus in his first wage packet next week. Pink persuaded him to hand it over as cash to save him being taxed on it. The vehicle handled like a dream, especially on the rough terrain approaching the site. They arrived just in time for Pink to clock off. Patsy was envious of the fact he had been drinking all afternoon and getting paid for it while he had been working his balls off. When Pink told him he had also turned them over at the card table, the air turned blue, all good natured. Patsy shook his hand and told him well done, then hinted he wouldn't mind an invite next time. Pink promised to see what he could do for him.

Abby had left Towser's doggy bag in the cupboard where he kept his boots. There was far too much for one sitting so he split it between two bags; the other would do for the dog's breakfast.

Moraji was in the shop when he passed by on his bike. With Johan away, she was filling in on days while her husband copped for night shift. She joked it would keep him from getting under her feet. Pink came up with another cunning plan when she told him this, he would volunteer to do the Saturday night shift, give Mr Rapati a night off then arrange for Ash and his crew to go into their routine on the Sunday. Moraji promised to make sure her husband would be in the bakery to meet them, she wanted to be there herself to witness the show.

"Sounds like you've had a good day, Honey," said Violet when he entered whistling.

"I earned my corn today, Violet, and didn't strain any muscles while I was about it."

He had her giggling as he explained how he had used his head to great effect, and wangled a couple of hours in the club into the bargain. The radio was still playing and Violet cleared her throat when he walked past her naked without thinking of playing some decent music. She chose the Cate Brothers and he was happy to oblige. As far as he could see earlier, there was only Moraji and one of the girls' cousins downstairs, but they made more noise than he had heard up to yet in appreciation of his vocal talents.

All his headwork had made him tired. He was about to sort something out for his evening meal when he heard a knock at the front door. It was Moraji. Mira had phoned the bakery, she would be bringing him some food at eight o'clock and working with him until midnight. He wound the alarm clock, set it for half past seven, rolled two joints, set up the Frankie Miller tape and collapsed on the couch. The last thing he remembered was Violet softly singing him to sleep. Wonderful.

He woke before the alarm and realised someone was sharing the couch with him, managing to hide his disappointment when he saw it was Eight Ball and not Violet. There was a faint hint of lavender, though, and he sniffed at the cat's fur, making Violet giggle. Nothing better than a happy and contented ghost. The tape had finished so he put the stylus to Lynyrd Skynyrd and limbered up for a thrash at his air guitar, mesmerising both Violet and Eight Ball with his skills. Two songs into the album he remembered he had a couple of joints to go at and left the guitar work to the experts.

Mira told him Moraji loved his singing, she had often heard the girls talk of it, but this was her first concert in the flesh, so to speak. He tucked into spicy chicken casserole, pausing only to ask if Mira herself had made it and asking her to marry him when the bowl had been wiped clean with two chunks of freshly baked bread. This earned him her gorgeous smile, closely followed by a sad frown, she was to meet her fiance this coming Tuesday and was more nervous than she cared to admit to anyone, anyone bar Pink it would seem. He told her not to worry, if it didn't work out he would look after her, if she was so good in the kitchen, surely she must be equally as good in other rooms? She was smiling again and chattered non stop until her father came to relieve them at ten to midnight.

Pink was asked to drive her home and bring the car back for Mr Rapati. Mira chose that very moment to remind her dad he had promised her a car of her own, maybe Pink could help her to choose one? He suggested a Range Rover and had Mr Rapati choking on the glass of water he was drinking.

Mira grabbed him up for a lingering kiss when he dropped her off, telling him he was very special before running up the drive to the house. He was about to pull away, then spotted her running back towards him, Sira would be working with him tomorrow and would prepare his evening meal. Another peck and she was gone.

On his return with the car keys, he invited Mr Rapati to have a night off on Saturday. This was instantly and gratefully accepted. They had five minutes together then said their goodnights. Eight Ball poked his head over the low bakery roof to let him know he was there. Unless Johan had told him he was going away, the cat would be in for a shock when he saw Mr Rapati on night shift.

"I think you should go straight to bed. You look really tired, Pinkee."

"Only if you'll join me. I am tired as it happens, must be all that brain activity."

"He-he. You should pass the joints round at work, then they could all do their own thinking."

"That's not a bad idea, Violet. Knowing my luck they'll come up with a few bright ideas and be too stoned to do anything about them. C'mon, let's go to bed."

"Ok, Honey. Right behind you."

Something was nagging at him as he lay awake in the dark, but it couldn't have been important. He was asleep within minutes, dreaming in colour, a field of lavender. He knew Violet was somewhere close by. He could smell her.

With no knowledge of how long he had slept, he was sitting bolt upright in bed. Now, he knew what was missing, the clock. Before he could throw his legs over the side, Violet slipped into the lounge and back to the bedroom in an instant.

"It's ok, go back to sleep. You've another three hours left, Honey. Eight Ball's home. I'll have a chat with him and keep an eye on the clock for you."

Pink grunted his thanks and collapsed into the pillow again. Soon, Violet was in the field with him, dressed all in lavender; hat, dress and shoes. If she was wearing nail polish, it too was lavender. She kissed him full on the lips, her breath smelled of lavender. He only blinked for a second and she was gone. Not much chance of finding her in a field of lavender.

Big boys' meccano set

Pink woke to the call to prayers, coinciding with Violet's wake up method of singing out his name and giggling at the same time. He closed his eyes in a vain attempt to resume his dream and she set Eight Ball onto him. That was that, no rest for the wicked, he had no option but to face the day.

With the porridge simmering away and two joints safely tucked into his hat, Pink fed Eight Ball then looked into the freezer compartment to see what was for his evening meal before remembering Sira would be feeding him.

Between mouthfuls of his breakfast, he asked, "do you dream?"

"Huh?"

"Do ghosts dream?"

"What a strange question, Honey. I suppose if I did they would surely have to be daydreams, reason being I don't sleep."

He was prepared to let it go at that, but not Violet, her curiosity kicking in and taking a firm hold.

"Why do you ask?"

Pink told her about the field of lavender, her outfit of lavender and the smell of lavender.

"Sounds idyllic, beautiful. Did it disturb you in any way?"

"Not at all. In fact, it was very enjoyable, it meant I was with you. I think I could put up with that."

"Oh, that's so sweet, Pinkee. I could listen to you talk like that all day, but sadly, I can't."

"Why not."

"Because .... you'll be late for work."

She giggled as he wrestled with his boots, then again when he became entangled in the wires for his Walkman.

Something had been trying in vain to get to Towser's breakfast. Pink had tied it high on the fence to prevent scavengers from helping themselves. He was no wildlife expert, but at a guess had foxes in mind as the most likely culprits. The dog wagged his tail off as usual and followed him to the bottom of the allotment, safe in the knowledge he was about to be fed.

The two new gangs were congregated by the clock when he arrived. Directing them to the canteen, he told them he'd let Mac know of their whereabouts. Mac asked him to jump on the shovel straight away, the tower crane was coming today. He was to get hold of the tipper drivers and between them they were to fashion a makeshift road to as near the rail track as they could possibly make it so the low loaders could drive on and off without being bogged down.

Mrs boss was at her window. Looked like she was smiling at him, but he ignored her. No way was he about to go there again, and besides, he was pretty sure she was getting quite enough of what she liked without any further input from his good self. The fitter stopped him for a word, how would he like to be his mate? He would need some help with the assembly of the tower crane. The riggers would do most of the work on it, but he would have to fix up the pulleys and electrics. Pink already had enough work on so he suggested Patsy for the job, remembering he had said something about being an electrician's mate in the past.

Five minutes later the fitter was in with Mrs boss, perhaps he was considering offering her first refusal for the position in question, and several other positions besides.

Down by the track, Mac was shouting at the ganger in charge of laying the rails; the poor guy didn't know where to look as the foreman gave him both barrels. Apparently, there were four, fifteen foot lengths of rail with a raised motif, these were to be lain at either end of the track to warn the crane driver he was almost to the end of his road. The ganger had laid plain rail instead and had to endure an ear bashing for his oversight.

Brew time and the queue in the canteen was to the door. Pink squeezed in, headed for the hatch and lent Abby a hand. When everyone was in it was standing room only and some were still queuing when the fifteen minute break was over. Mac seemed to be looking to Pink for a solution to the problem, either that or there would be chaos at lunchtime.

When the queue finally died down, Pink poured himself a cup of coffee and repaired to the corner of the room. Mac wasn't long in joining him, what did Pink think of a shift system, so many to take a break at nine thirty, the rest at nine forty five and so on and so forth for the rest of the day? Pink knocked the idea on the head as totally impractical almost as soon as Mac had finished suggesting it. Say the concrete gang were in the middle of a pour, or the shuttering joiners were waiting for the steel-fixers to finish a job? The result would be absolute pandemonium. The only way round it as far as Pink could see was expansion. Bring in another portacabin and marry it up to the one they were sitting in, add some new tables and stools and there would be adequate room for all. Of course, Abby would need more help than her daughter could provide, maybe Mac should contact the labour exchange, unless …. did he want to leave it with Pink?

So it was he found himself at the wheel of the Range Rover once again. Lily, Dave Thom's mother, answered the door and invited him in. Dave was still in bed. Not that he was lazy as such, more that he had nothing to be up and dressed for. Lily made a pot of tea and Pink took a cup upstairs, pushing Dave's bedroom door open with his stockinged foot. He wasn't asleep, wide awake and sitting up reading. Pink told him about the job and his eyes lit up, now he had something to get out of bed for. Pink had a cup of tea and chatted with Lily while Dave put some clothes on. She said not to be a stranger as they left and Pink asked Dave which of them was she talking to. He knew Dave was a dab hand in the kitchen, as long as the recipe involved cheese. He wouldn't be doing much in the way of cooking, just serving the food and pearl diving. Seeing the puzzled look on his friend's face, he explained. Pearl diving meant washing dishes.

Dave was introduced to Mac in the office. Barry greeted him with the familiarity of an old friend, they had gone to school together. Abby also knew him, she was a friend of Lily's.

Pink left them to it, the tower crane was arriving, a giant, part built Meccano set. Bright yellow in colour and needing all of five low loaders to transport it.

Patsy shook his hand, thanking him for pointing the fitter in his direction. Pink told him, as locals, they had a duty to look out for each other; besides, Patsy had helped him out.

The sections of crane were laid out neatly by the side of the track. The fitter made a show of checking each component over before signing for delivery, then asked Pink would he take the paperwork to the office. Since he had nothing better to do he obliged, it was about half an hour 'til lunchtime. He really wanted to observe the construction of the tower crane, but that would be later than planned; the rail wasn't in place yet.

The new portacabin was on its way down the hill as he approached the office so he gave Mac a shout and was landed with the job of assistant to the foreman in operation new canteen. The job turned out to be simple enough. With a door at either end of each structure, it was simply a matter of setting the levels of the short stilts to much of a sameness and shoving the two units together.

No matter how hard they tried there was still a bit of a gap, but not enough to be of any danger to anyone. Pink suggested running a timber seal around it, followed by plastic sheeting and finished off with roofing felt. Mac decided they would have their lunch first to avoid the rush. Until the furniture arrived for the extension, there still wouldn't be enough room for everyone. Being the foreman, Mac didn't eat with the hoi polloi; instead, he took his meal into the office.

Dave had been thrown in at the deep end. Given an instant start, he was to be paid cash in hand for today and start afresh on Monday. He wanted to buy Pink a drink later as thanks for the job. Pink had to decline, he had something else on tonight; besides, he reminded his friend, trouble always seemed to find them when they went drinking together. Dave saw the sense in what he was saying and laughed his head off, he would catch Pink again.

The fitter overruled his idea of using wood to seal the gap between the units, opting instead for some resin putty, he would let that go off then cover it with waterproof tape. Pink left him to it. He didn't mention there might be some movement between the portacabins, thus dislodging the putty, he would wait until it rained in before pointing that one out.

Crisis, the concrete batcher had ground to a halt. A big pour had been scheduled for the afternoon. The fitter and his new mate were all over it, no good, they would have to send out for a part. The boss was running around like a headless chicken, he really wanted that pour to go ahead. Pink calmed him down, there were three ready mix plants not far from the site, why not buy from one of them?

The boss asked Barry for the telephone directory, but Pink urged him to use the personal touch, the batcher might break down again over the course of the job. If he showed up in person, explained the situation and offered to use the same firm in time of need, he might well be given a discount, saving the company a lot of money. Settled, the boss was calm now, Pink could drive him there and let him do the talking. When he went looking for the keys to the Range Rover, Pink told Barry to call a mutual friend, tell him to expect them, but he wasn't to let on he knew Pink when they arrived.

The Range Rover was beginning to feel like his own personal property and he enjoyed tooting the horn at acquaintances as they headed out of town. The plant was about fifteen minutes drive away via the scenic route. The boss might be in a hurry, but Pink certainly wasn't.

Groover tried his level best to keep a straight face when he ushered them into his office. Pink took a back seat after the introductory handshakes, listening to the boss go all round the houses instead of going straight to the point. Ten minutes later he felt the need to cut in, asking Groover about prices and discount for future patronage. Thankfully, the boss kept his gaze on Groover while Pink signalled ten percent for the boss and five percent for himself. Done deal, more handshakes and talk of looking forward to doing business with each other.

Halfway between the office and the car, Pink realised he had left his tobacco tin behind. Telling the boss he wouldn't be a minute, he returned to the office to be greeted by Groover's toothy grin, the invoice to the firm would show a ten percent discount, but would show as a fifteen percent discount on Groover's books, the difference would be split between Pink and Groover; everyone a winner.

The boss asked him to turn into a pub car park on the way back to the site, he wanted to buy Pink a drink for his part in the negotiations. On the third pint, he got round to what he really had on his mind. How would Pink like to be a chargehand with the view to becoming foreman in the future? Pink wasn't ready for that one, thinking the conversation would concern Mrs boss. Nonetheless, he didn't want the position offered, he was quite happy with where he was in the scheme of things. The boss shrugged and didn't pursue the matter, merely expressing his regret and telling Pink he had been impressed with his input. One more for the road and they headed back to the site, just in time to see the convoy of ready mix concrete wagons make their way to the pour.

The furniture for the canteen had arrived in his absence and Mac asked him to give Dave a hand to install it. By the time they were done, it was the afternoon break. Pink helped at the service hatch, chuckling to himself as he observed the men marking out their territory within the new layout.

Mac joined him for a coffee when the men went back to work, expressing his disappointment at Pink's refusal to take on the chargehand job. Pink repeated he was happy as things stood, he really didn't want the responsibility. Like the boss before him, Mac didn't try to force his hand, happy enough to accept his reasons.

The riggers arrived to erect the tower crane. Pink and Mac led them to the job, the rail had been set in place and the engineer was happy with it. He joined them on the tractor trailer and watched as they made a start. First, the wheelbase, much smaller than a train's wheels. Chocks were placed under each of them, then the giant Meccano set began to take shape. Pink wandered off to where the crane's cab rested on the ground and had a look inside. There were only two levers, clearly marked with their functions; first chance he was presented with he would be having a go. The riggers knew what they were about and within an hour, all that remained to be put in place were the huge concrete ballast blocks. These would counterbalance whatever weight was lifted by the crane. By this stage, all four mobile cranes were employed and no one else was working; the entire compliment of men being held spellbound by this feat of engineering.

When the show was over, Patsy walked with Pink towards the office to clock off. If he was pleased earlier with his new job, he was doubly pleased now. The fitter had asked him to clock on early in the morning and do a bit of overtime. Not only that, there was a fair possibility of a double time Sunday to boot. Pink was happy for him and told him as much. A lot had happened in his first week on the job, so much so that the time had simply flown by.

For the exact same reasons as Pink, Dave wanted to keep his new job quiet. He didn't want the local deadbeats descending on site and letting the side down by doing a couple of days at most then giving it up when they lost interest.

Towser was treated to double rations, it would probably be Monday morning before Pink was down this way again.

Fifty yards on from where he left the dog, he could see the front end of a car sticking out from the bushes. Closer inspection revealed it to be a police car. Thinking he was about to find a couple of coppers up to no good in the back seat, he dumped the bike and approached stealthily. It was Louise; head back, eyes closed and fingers at play under her skirt. He stood and observed for over a minute before she sensed she had an audience. Her face was a picture, caught red handed, flicking away at her bean. Pink mimed rolling the window down and asked did she want any help. He unbuttoned his overalls to show her how pleased he was to see her. Louise, in turn, worked her way out of her knickers, stepped out of the car and spread herself over the bonnet. He mentioned he had been thinking about her as he fucked her hard from behind and Louise grunted she had been fantasising about him while she was masturbating. She insisted on him splashing her tonsils. Being halfway through a twelve hour shift, she didn't wish to spend the rest of it squelching around and seeping their combined juices. Afterwards, they spent ten minutes together, long enough to share a joint and arrange a get together for Sunday lunch at Louise's.

A call on the radio had her scrambling back into the car and racing off to wherever the emergency was, siren wailing.

"Quick, quick, Pinkee. Play some decent music, please. This guy's driving me up the wall with his nonsense."

Pink laughed. "That's quite appropriate, Violet, considering you spend most of your time on one wall or another."

"Oh yes, very funny, I'm sure. Could I have some Led Zeppelin, please, but before you play it, how's your day been, Honey?"

Pink rummaged through his collection for her choice and told of the good day he'd had, conveniently forgetting to mention his fumble in the allotments; no point in rocking the boat.

"Remind me never to play that when I'm in the shower again, will you?"

"Why, don't you like it?"

"No, it's not that. I was doing ok with the vocals, but when I tried to keep up with Jimmy Page on my air guitar I slipped and almost ripped the shower-head from the wall.

"Hehe. You are silly, but that's dangerous. I knew I should have come in there with you. Are you ok?"

"Only just, but what could you have done if I'd fallen, Violet?"

"I could have had a good laugh, he-he."

"Charming, that. Nice to know who your friends are. Do you want to hear side two."

"Are you having a nap?"

"Yes."

"Steve Miller band then, please."

When he woke, Violet demanded he should play it again from the start, his snoring had drowned out every single note. By the time the tape rewound he had two joints made and another almost complete. Eight Ball sat on the arm of the chair and watched him, he seemed to get a kick out of that.

"Aren't you eating again?"

"I get fed downstairs. It's written into my contract."

"Shame that, I just love to watch you eating. You go at it like you're expecting someone to come and take it from you."

"That's my jungle training kicking in. Eat or be eaten."

"You say a lot of things like that. I never know when you're being serious, but this time I really think I believe you."

"So you should, Violet. So you should."

He jammed with the Steve Miller band, smoked a joint, rested in the chair for twenty minutes, splashed his face and went downstairs to work, leaving the radio tuned to the pirate station for Violet.

Whatever Sira had concocted for him smelled delicious, he hadn't realised quite how hungry he was until he caught a whiff of it. Sira had already filled the ovens so all he had to do was sit and eat. If Mira was good in the kitchen, her sister was her equal, baked fish with lashings of curried vegetables, fresh baked bread for mops and a chilled bottle of cider to wash it all down. It didn't last long. He told

Sira he would be a regular visitor when she and Johan set up home together.

Over the course of their shift, he ran through his plan for Sunday. Moraji and Mira were up to speed, Sira told him she too had been prepped, but she wanted to hear it from the horse's mouth. She was nervous, but excited at the same time. If she had been unsure of her feelings for Johan before, his absence galvanised the realisation he was definitely the man for her. Pink gave her his best look of disappointment and dejection, there didn't seem to be much hope for him, then? Sira's smile lit up the entire room, a joy to behold. Pink could only hope and pray things went according to plan.

The conversation came back round to culinary skills. With four women in the house, they all took turns in the kitchen. Tomorrow, it was Kira's domain. Sira claimed her younger sister was the best cook from all four and this surprised Pink, she was so young. He was further surprised to learn she had already mapped out her own career path, setting her sights on having her own restaurant as a target.

He mentioned he was on night shift tomorrow, Saturday, maybe Sira could mention it to her sister? If he could sample her cooking, he would then be in a position to offer his critique. Sira laughed, she would make sure she made enough for him. Second thoughts, going by the way he went at it, maybe a double helping would be in order? Pink couldn't find it within himself to argue with her logic, that would only be rude of him.

Mr Rapati rolled up at a quarter to twelve and asked Pink to take Sira home. This he did with pleasure, being rewarded at the end of his trip with a hug and a smacker on the lips. Payment enough.

Mr Rapati was scratching his head when he returned, a phone call when Pink was out. Someone claiming to be the local football club chairman wanted eighty of the baker's pies for a function tomorrow afternoon, could he manage that? To be fair, it wouldn't be a problem, Mr Rapati's only concern being it could be a hoax call. Pink knew the club to be notorious for after hours drinking, chances were the call had been made from there. Snatching up the car keys, he resolved to find out if the order was genuine or not.

Sure enough, the order was for real; their usual caterers had let them down. Pink singled out the most compos mentis member of the committee, made him repeat the order, talked him into adding a batch of Mr Rapati's world famous pastries and quoted a quite outrageous price for the immediacy and urgency of the request. A deposit and a handshake sealed the deal, with a free pint of beer thrown in for good measure.

A normally calm Mr Rapati was in a flap now, delighted at Pink's initiative, but in a panic as to how he would cope with the extra output. Pink helped out with another three hours of batching and preparation, somehow getting his boss in front of himself. He had somewhere he needed to be at lunchtime tomorrow, but if he could have the car he would gladly deliver the order to the football club. Done deal and goodnight.

Eight Ball chose that very moment to amble in. Ignoring both men, he stretched out on the pile of flour sacks between the ovens, washed his paws and settled down to sleep. Before Pink could say something in his defence, Mr Rapati explained he kept the vermin down.

"That cat's well in with the boss downstairs."

"What d'you mean, Honey?"

Pink explained what has just occurred, a fair amount of disbelief in his voice.

"Well, he's so loveable. Isn't he?"

"If you say so," admitted Pink, somewhat reluctantly, lighting either his first joint of the day or his last joint of the night, he couldn't make his mind up which. The music centre had held on to radio Caroline, a station which specialised in mostly album tracks, providing a valuable source of information to Pink and other like minded souls. The presenter announced Savoy Brown's 'Hellbound Train'. Violet let out a yelp and Pink cranked up the volume.

Four in the morning seemed like a good time to be going to bed, he had been nodding in his chair. Remembering he had things to do in the morning, he set the clock for ten and was asleep before he hit the pillow. He knew Violet and her lavender had joined him. He also knew Eight Ball had managed to squeeze himself between them.

Banquet for one

Pink had his high dream again, and this time he worked it out. What he was seeing was the view from the tower crane, like he was meant to be there. What had given it away was the spinning effect. Not fast like a waltzer at the funfair, more measured and deliberate. He heard the call to prayers, ignored it knowing it was Saturday and made it back to sleep, minus the dream this time.

"What's on today, Honey?"

"I'll be out for a couple of hours, then it's a lazy day in lounging around with you; watching the sport on the telly and getting stoned, but not too much. I've to work a night shift later."

"Sounds good, at least the staying in with me part does. You play music while you're watching the sport, don't you?"

"All except for the Rugby League, that's a must listen to commentary."

"I remember that from the last time. Isn't that where you throw things at the telly?"

"I didn't know you were hovering around then, Kitten, but I'll probably still throw things, yes."

The lady in the bric-a-brac shop had nothing for him when he stuck his head round the door. Dropping his washing off, he bought a paper, a pint of milk, some tobacco and three packets of skins. He had it in mind to visit the butcher, then remembered he had been invited out to Sunday dinner. Louise called it lunch, but she wasn't brought up on the wrong side of the tracks. The middle meal of the day would always be dinner to him..

No food for breakfast, just a cup of coffee and a joint of home grown. He was counting on being fed shortly after dropping the pies and pastries off.

With Violet's request 'Late for the sky', playing, he flicked through the sports pages. One of his horses, 'Keep on the grass', was highlighted as a potential winner in a big handicap at Haydock Park. This spurred him into scanning the rest of the televised races, looking for horses with connections to his drug of choice.

Scratching around for a piece of paper, he scribbled the names and times of his three selections. Acapulco Gold, Keep on the grass and One for the pot. He would have a modest wager, sort of an interest bet while he could watch them on the telly. A quick flick through the news pages, which didn't take long, then a glance at what sport he had to look forward to. Further down the schedule the name of John Martyn leapt to his attention, in concert at seven o'clock. He wouldn't mention it to his wallflower, save it as a surprise.

Violet asked him to leave the tv on, she liked the cartoons on a Saturday morning.

Mr Rapati wanted a lift home so Pink took him to the football club with the goodies, made sure he was paid then took him home; he didn't fancy driving around with money that wasn't his. Kira came out to say hello and asked was he going through town, could he drop her off, she needed some ingredients for her day in the kitchen. Pink went out of his way to oblige her and immediately wished he hadn't. The girl knew something was going on and set about trying to pick his brains, her mother and sisters were plotting something and she was determined to find out what. Every time she went anywhere near them they clammed up. Pink asked when her birthday was. No, it couldn't be that, that was six months away. Then, a bright idea came to her, she would ask her dad if he could shed any light on what all the secrecy was about. Why hadn't she thought of that before?

Pink couldn't be sure, but he had the feeling he was being manipulated. If Kira probed too deeply, the game would be up. She had him between a rock and a hard place; but if she knew it, her innocent, doe eyed expression gave nothing away.

He had no choice, was she in any hurry? No? Ok, all would be revealed within the next hour or so. Turning back the way they had come, Pink headed for Ash's restaurant. Kira fired all manner of questions at him, but he wouldn't give anything away, not yet. If she wanted to play games, he would give her a quick lesson on how he too could play. When he told her to stay in the car while he put his bet on, she looked like she was about to have kittens.

Ash greeted him with a bear hug, had he eaten, was everything ok? Pink introduced Kira and watched her eyes bulge as he unfolded his plan for tomorrow. Now, she had a fair idea as to what had been going on. Pink stressed the need for secrecy, she was to express real surprise when it all unfolded. Now, she was firing questions at Ash. One day she would have her own restaurant, how did this, that and the other work? Ash rustled up a meal for Pink, a veritable banquet for one. Kira had already eaten, but that didn't stop her from sampling everything on the table. When she went to the rest room to freshen up, Ash handed Pink a note written on one of the waiter's pads, 'goods expected Thursday', then he passed a bag of grass. Pink stuck his nose in and inhaled deeply, he had been stretching his stash out to make it last, this would tide him over nicely. On her return, Kira mentioned she needed certain spices and Ash pointed her in the direction of the local market. Then he told her to call round when the mood took her, he would give her a few pointers on how to run a restaurant.

Pink thanked him for the meal and was gathered up in another bear hug, they would see each other tomorrow, although they would be strangers then.

The market smelled wonderful. Luckily, Pink had only just eaten or he would have been tempted to partake of some of the produce available. Colourful too, with roll upon roll of bright fabrics on show. They attracted some strange looks as Kira linked his arm and steered him to wherever she wanted to go. She impressed him with her bartering skills, never paying what she was first quoted. The girl had a bright future to look forward to.

Moraji met them at the end of the drive, she was to drive Pink home. Kira kissed him and thanked him, she would send his supper round when it was ready.

He had to let Moraji know Kira was aware of their plan and she seemed relieved, like a weight had been taken from her shoulders. She had been worried about how to broach the subject, knowing Kira would want to be involved and pleased it was Pink, who had himself stressed the need to keep it simple, had found it necessary to let the cat out of the bag. Pink in turn aired the view Kira had been playing with him, like a kitten plays with a ball of wool. Moraji smiled that knowing smile of a mother who knows her child only too well.

He followed Moraji into the shop and asked Mira for a couple of pies and a small loaf, a larger loaf was what he really needed, but he had to have an excuse to call down in the morning at the appointed time. The girls had arranged it so Sira would be on late shift tonight and therefore off in the morning, allowing the others to surprise her with news of Johan's elevated status. Pink warned her Kira would most likely make up the numbers, just a theory.

"Is that you in for the day, Honey?"

"Until ten o'clock, yes."

"What's that you've got there?"

"A nice little bag of grass, can't wait to try it."

J J Cale strummed away while he picked the seeds from the weed and settled down to watch his first race, chuckling to himself when One for the pot romped home comfortably. Between races, he made a cup of coffee, flipped J J Cale over, built a joint and settled down to see if the tipster in the paper had called it right. Sadly not.

Keep on the grass was narrowly beaten in what looked like a rough ridden race, so, only each way money left to play for; maybe his luck was deserting him? One bright spot, the grass was excellent; top notch in fact.

With J J about to go into his last song, Pink cracked open a bottle of cider and let it breathe a little before the match kicked off. A quick tidy up, which had Violet chuckling, then, stripping to his underwear, which brought about an hilarious attempt at a wolf whistle. He turned the volume up on the telly for the commentary on the last race. No win necessary for this one, somewhere in the first three would guarantee a reasonable profit from his stake. Acapulco Gold carried the race from pillar to post at big odds of twenty five to one, giving him an estimated return of seventeen pounds. He wasn't greedy, the sum was totally acceptable.

"Whose playing, Honey?"

"Another local derby. Widnes versus Warrington, fifth and fourth in the league. Should be a decent match."

"And who are we supporting?"

"Don't know about you, Kitten, but I'm a neutral unless Wigan are playing. Just hoping for a good, hard game."

Eight Ball watched with them, losing interest towards the end of the first half when Widnes racked up what Eddie Waring declared to be an unassailable lead. Pink wasn't so sure, there were still forty minutes to play, anything could happen in this game.

Half time, Pink fed the cat and helped himself to another bottle of cider. He thought of playing some music, but decided against it, building a joint instead. Warrington pulled it back to within four points, rousing Eight Ball from his nap to witness an exciting final five minutes. Having said he was a neutral, Pink was on the edge of his seat, throwing ping-pong balls at the screen and shouting his head off. Widnes survived the onslaught, both sides having served up a veritable feast of football.

An attack of the munchies was fended off with a large cheese, tomato and onion sandwich. He thought he would be tired by now after a late night and an early start, but no, the adrenalin built up from the match keeping him buoyant. He had a night shift later; not hard work as such, but a certain amount of vigilance would be required. It was five o'clock, he would time his evening meal for six thirty, watch and record John Martyn, rewind the tape and crash out for an hour or so before work.

In the meantime, there was music to be listened to. Violet startled him by appearing on the wall above his record collection as he riffled through it.

"SHIT! you freaked me out. Have you been watching Eight Ball?"

"What d'you mean, Honey?"

"He likes to creep around and startle me."

"I'm sorry, Pinkee. I only wanted to see what you were playing."

"It's ok. What did you want to listen to?"

"Something I haven't heard. What's that one with the shoes on the front?"

Pink flicked back a couple of records and picked out 'Bumpers', a compilation sampler. Why not? He hadn't heard it himself in quite a while. All the artists were household names; up and coming stars when it was released, but most of them pretty well known now. He put his pies in the oven on a low light, sparked another joint up and blew smoke rings for Eight Ball. Violet was swaying in time to the music. To Pink's semi-stoned eye, she resembled a beautiful curtain billowing in a breeze.

He hit the shower just as his favourite track from the double disc set came on, Jimmy Cliff singing 'Going back west'. An infectious little Reggae song about how he was ripped off by big business. Of course he sang along, the bathroom lending just the right acoustics to bring the best out of his voice. Generous applause from downstairs told him he had hit a few decent notes.

Violet loved it, wanted to hear it again and suggested he should make a compilation tape, something he had been thinking of himself. He let her think it was her idea, and a good one at that. Trouble was, he had run out of blank tapes, the last one being set up to record the concert. What he could do, she advised, was write down which tracks he intended to record, making it easier when he acquired some tapes. The girl had brains as well as beauty.

John Martyn, who incidentally had a track on the aforementioned Bumpers compilation along with his wife Beverley, didn't let them down. All three sat enthralled as he wrung the neck of his guitar, squeezing the most unbelievable noises from it. Violet recognised the tracks he played from 'Solid Air' and let out a series of appreciative squeals when he launched into them. All at once, Pink wished he could take her to a live gig; even to see a pub band, that would have tickled her no end.

"That was amazing, Pink. I've never seen anything quite like it."

"I had an idea you were enjoying it," he said, rewinding the tape for another listen. Eight Ball said nothing, probably too stunned by the performance.

Pink smoked the half joint he had nipped in the ashtray, flopped onto the couch, closed his eyes and drifted off to the repeat performance.

When he woke, Eight Ball hadn't moved. Violet was singing softly, unaccompanied, the clock said quarter to ten.

"I've had the best day ever, thank you, Honey. I love it when you're at home like this."

"Me too, Violet. We'll do it again soon."

"Promise?"

"Promise."

"Tomorrow?"

"No, not tomorrow, not quite so soon. Some shit to deal with tomorrow. I'll be around until about one o'clock, but I'll be asleep for most of that time. You're perfectly welcome to join me."

"I might just do that. Thank you, Honey."

"Don't mention it, my pleasure entirely, Kitten. I'll see you later."

"Not if I see you first, he-he."

Sira was locking the back door when he turned up for work, Pink was to drive her home then pick Mira up at five thirty in the morning. Although the shop didn't open on a Sunday, it was cleaned from top to bottom along with the bakery. The ovens would be shut down for about four hours. Some trade would be conducted from the back door for those in the know. Being a shrewd businessman, Mr Rapati wouldn't turn customers away. Mainly small hoteliers and restauranteurs, there was always a demand for freshly baked bread.

Kira met him when he dropped her sister off, his meal was back at the bakery, he was instructed to put it in the bottom of the oven for half an hour before he was ready to eat. Sira remarked she herself had partaken earlier, he was in for a real treat. Both girls kissed him and said goodnight. Moraji appeared in the doorway, put her hands together as if in prayer then gave him a wave. He reckoned the prayer would be for tomorrow.

The snow came from nowhere. Well, it came from the sky, obviously, but without warning. He had heard a couple of forecasts, neither of them making any mention of snow. So heavy, the wipers on the car were working at full speed. On the short drive to the bakery, a young girl stepped into the road in front of him, she wasn't dressed to suit the weather. It took him a few moments to recognise her. Sara, from the Boulder, her hair matted to her head by the downpour. She didn't seem to know where she was or indeed who Pink was when he stepped out of the car to help her. Pouring her into the passenger seat, he told her he would make sure she got home.

With the interior light on, there was evidence of bruising around her right eye. Sara pleaded with him not to take her home, slurring her words through drink and filling up with tears. He stopped the car and coaxed the story from her, finding she had been on a date. The guy had tried it on a bit too heavily, she protested, he gave her a backhander and threw her out of the car to face the elements. She wouldn't give his name, sensing Pink was none too happy with what she had told him. What she needed was to clean up a bit, sleep for a couple of hours and to sneak home in the early hours. Her parents were under the impression she was staying over with a girlfriend.

Pink had no choice but to take her to the bakery. In the brighter light, he could see she would have a black eye in the morning. The heat was appreciated. He made her relax in one of the chairs, covered her over with a large towel and his coat, put the radio on low and attended to his work. She was asleep within minutes. Pink sparked up one of his ready rolled joints, set the oven timers and settled into the other chair to do his crossword.

Sara mumbled in her sleep, but he didn't pay much attention to her until she became agitated. Still asleep, she repeated a name several times, followed by the word 'no'. Pink shivered, one of the younger Blunts, Chubby, following in the family tradition. Sara became even more upset so he put his hand on her arm. She woke with a start, saw she was with Pink, half smiled and went back to sleep.

Eight Ball padded in just as he was about to tuck into his meal, curry, not hot like Johan liked to cook it, but mild. Tender chicken with a strong hint of coconut and sweet with lumps of apple and a sprinkling of sultanas. The girls were right, Kira was a better cook than them. There wasn't a lot in it, but the proof of the pudding, as they say. Eight Ball had a sniff at Sara then curled up in a ball on his flour sacks.

By four o'clock Sara was drinking a cup of coffee and toking on a joint. Pink asked her again what had happened and again she wouldn't tell. If her father found out, he would put the Blunt boy in hospital at the very least, this in turn would antagonise tribe Blunt; who would probably then transform the Boulder into a pile of rubble, or a smouldering ruin. Pink was angry enough himself, he liked Sara, but he felt his hands were tied. If she wouldn't come right out and say who had given her the shiner, there didn't seem to be a whole lot he could do, only save what he knew to memory.

Sara tidied herself up as best she could and let him drive her home. He told her not to mention where he worked and she understood, thanked him for his help, gave him a kiss and let herself into the pub by the side door. The snow was heavier if anything, no other vehicles on the road except for a snowplough. Pink rolled his window down as he came alongside it, killed the car's engine, brought out his last spliff from the rim of his bob cap and spent a quiet ten minutes with his good friend Jimmy Clayton from the Albatross. Jimmy had been located in the disco by his boss and offered treble time to go to work, otherwise many of the local roads would have become impassable. He negotiated quadruple pay and a day off in lieu, splashed his face to wake himself up and went to work. Pink asked him to clear the road between the bakery and Ash's restaurant, he was expecting visitors tomorrow. Jimmy obliged, said goodnight and carried on with his duties.

Mira couldn't believe the weather when she came to the door, turning back for a heavier coat and a change of footwear. On the way to the shop she asked Pink would Ash and his friends be able to make it later. He reassured her, everything possible had been done to make sure it would go according to plan. He kissed her goodnight, it had been an eventful shift, not boring as he had expected; so much so it had flown in. Now, he was tired. Big day tomorrow, or later today to be more exact. He spent half an hour with Violet before she suggested he should retire and no argument was offered.

Five minutes later he was high again, spinning slowly, his nostrils full of lavender and something else, something different, not pleasant, what was it? Ah, yes, that was it. Damp cat fur.

CHAPTER 25

Kira nails it

Pink rubbed the sleep from his eyes and fumbled for the clock. Half past eleven, he could hear traffic on the move and was happy the roads seemed to be clear. Maybe another half hour's kip? Not a chance.

"Morning, Honey. Did you sleep well?"

"I slept well, but maybe not enough."

"Go back then. I'll just twiddle my thumbs."

He returned the sarcasm with, "No, no. I'm wide awake now, but thanks for your kind offer."

"Maybe we'd better have some music?" She invited, catching his drift.

"Anything in particular?"

"Play the John Martyn concert again, please. I really enjoyed that."

Pink did as she asked then gave himself a quick wash, knowing he would probably end up in the bubbles with Louise later.

Violet joined him in the kitchen during the applause between tracks.

"What you having for breakfast, Honey?"

"Crunchy scrambled eggs."

"Crunchy? …. How do you make those?"

"Simple …. I leave the shells in."

"You're in a funny mood today, Pink."

"You started it."

John Martyn interrupted them, possibly preventing a full blown row and they both sang along. Pink changed the menu to porridge, inviting further comment, but none came.

Eight Ball curled up at the feet of his mistress while Pink built half a dozen joints, sparking up the first of them before continuing with the task. It looked to Pink the cat was being protective towards Violet, especially when he totally ignored the smoke rings.

At five minutes to one he put his jacket on, picked up the basket and blew Violet a kiss. She returned the kiss and carried on singing. Eight Ball took it easy.

The snow had all but melted except for where Jimmy had banked it at the side of the road. Half a dozen kids tried in vain to build a snowman, the stuff being so wet they couldn't compact it sufficiently.

Ash cruised past with a car full of Kadamba worshippers. Pink gave him the thumbs up and waited for a couple of minutes while they went into their act. The kids had given up on the snowman and were attempting a snowball fight, but it just wasn't that type of snow. With a clear sky and rising temperature, it would be running down the drains within an hour.

Mr Rapati looked puzzled when he approached the back door of the bakery. Surrounded by seven inquisitive Goanese and with most of his family looking on, he appeared to be at a loss for words.

Pink dived into the middle of it, all bluff and bluster and asked Mr Rapati did he require any assistance. The little man tried to explain what all the fuss was about while Ash made a big effort to fill in the blanks. Pink let Mr Rapati see the realisation something which was secret had been revealed cross his face. Turning to Ash and his party, he explained Johan would never accept all this commotion. Didn't they know he wished to lead a quiet, private life? All the Goans started talking at once and Pink hoped they were saying the right things because he couldn't understand a word of it; he was sure Mr Rapati could, though. His face was a picture, first of bewilderment, then slowly, realisation, and last but not least, the deeply furrowed brow of concentrated thought.

Mira was horrified when Kira stepped into the circle and addressed Ash. Did someone mention Kadamba? The same Kadamba who had ruled parts of India for centuries? She had been reading about them at school. Was Johan, their Johan, related to that same Kadamba? Ash assured her he was and apologised to Mr Rapati and his family for springing this on them. Could he please leave his address, or beseech Mr Rapati to allow them a visit when Johan returned? The baker didn't know whether he was coming or going. Moraji sent Kira into the shop for a pen and paper, but Mira invited everyone in for a cup of tea, seeing as they had come so far and it was rather cold to be standing around outside.

Pink kept the game going by quizzing Ash on how he had discovered Johan's secret. Ash was vague, although he did manage to drop Johan's uncle into the conversation.

When the worshippers left, Mr Rapati apologised to Pink and spoke to his family in his native language, he knew it was going well when Kira winked at him and cheekily stuck out her tongue; out of her father's sight, of course.

He picked up a couple of loaves, one for himself and the other for Louise. Putting his hand on Mr Rapati's shoulder, he told him he'd be round at eight o'clock for work then said goodbye to Moraji and the girls. The man was obviously still trying to come to terms with what had been sprung on him, but still found the manners to thank Pink for his help. Pink almost forgot his own manners, turning back to thank Kira for last night's delicious meal. Mira followed him to the back door and saw him out, telling him Sira would have been proud of him, she was proud of him, Moraji was proud of him, Kira was proud of him. Pink told her to stop before he got a big head. She kissed him, then again, and promised him his supper later.

Halfway upstairs, there was a knock on the door. Kira, could he drive her mum and dad home? She was grinning from ear to ear, but her dad couldn't get his head round the fact he had a real live Prince in his employ. Moraji was having fun playing along with it.

For the sake of the plot, Moraji quizzed him as he drove. How long had he known of Johan's elevated status, why was it such a secret, surely he was proud of his ancestry? Pink played it cagey, he had been sworn to secrecy, Johan had his reasons, he should be the one to divulge if he so wished. One thing Pink knew for sure, Johan would be horrified his secret was out. Maybe they would be wise to play it down a bit? Mr Rapati spoke for the first time in a while, saying he had always liked the boy. He could perhaps understand why he would wish to keep quiet about this. Many others wouldn't hesitate in using it to further their own ends. Moraji smiled at Pink and mouthed the words 'thank you' to him.

Sira met them on the drive, she wanted to go to her sisters, Mr Rapati was in a daze and hardly noticed her. Jumping in beside Pink, she bent his ear all the way to the bakery. He managed to tell her all that had transpired, all except for what was said in Indian. The girls would have to advise her on that. What he could say without shadow of a doubt, she had Kira to thank for swinging the tide in her favour. The tears flowed freely when all three girls sorted out who said what and who did what. Pink was embraced and kissed on more occasions than he felt he deserved, but he didn't once complain. Mira rounded on him for involving Kira, then told him it had been a stroke of genius. She had been a star, putting their father in no doubt as to the authenticity of the worshippers' visit. Hadn't they been convincing? Especially Ash. She had ended up believing their story herself. How could they ever repay Pink? Again, he played it down, their obvious happiness was payment enough; oh, and if they could keep on feeding him, that would do it. He left to the sound of their laughter and excited chatter, ready for a joint, a feed and a fuck, in whatever order they presented themselves.

"You're looking pleased with yourself, Honey."

"I've had a good result with the matchmaking, there's every chance Johan and his young lady will be allowed to step out together with her father's blessing."

"You've such a quaint way of putting things. Step out, indeed."

Pink gave her a blow by blow account of the proceedings, impressing her with his cunning and determination. She was still giggling when he made his exit at five to three, all thought of their earlier minor skirmish a dim and distant memory.

Louise wore a catsuit which fitted where it touched. The term, figure hugging, had been coined for such an item of clothing. In leopard print, it left nothing to the imagination. Sparking up a joint, he slipped it between her bee stung lips and told her she looked good enough to eat. On leaving the car, he followed her up the path, knowing full well she had no knickers on again; they would have shown through the flimsy material of the catsuit.

Determined to take his time, he let Louise fetch a beer from the fridge, fired up another joint and produced his camera. She could have been a model. Pink, to prove his point, had her posing and pouting to order. Halfway through the shoot, he paused to regret not keeping hold of one of the Polaroid cameras from the catalogue job, Louise would have been up for a much more adventurous photo session.

Her cooking wasn't anywhere near as accomplished as that of the Rapati girls; edible all the same, but lacking in the various spices he had recently become accustomed to. A liberal sprinkling of pepper helped it go down easier. The flat was smaller than his own, so much so he could sit in the chair by the window and watch Louise dance around the kitchen in her skin tight outfit while she washed the dishes. Over her shoulder, she asked did he want a sweet. He had her giggling when he replied he could see his pudding from where he was sitting.

Another joint while their dinner settled, Pink could feel himself sinking into the large, comfortable armchair. Louise helped him smoke the joint, reached beyond him to close the curtains and treated him to a somewhat ungainly striptease; the catsuit not lending itself to the finesse required for such eroticism. He had known she was naked beneath the garment, but delighted just the same to feast his eyes on what she had to offer. Then she undressed him slowly, remarking his hair could do with a good wash, but not yet, that would have to wait. They took their time, exploring each other, kissing, nibbling, sucking, licking, probing, massaging and caressing; culminating in a triumphal, mutual exchange of bodily fluids.

Louise practised her joint rolling skills while Pink raided the fridge for another beer. They sat around smoking, drinking and talking; or rather Louise talked and Pink listened. She had become disillusioned with the police force, in particular her own role within it. The other night with the two drunks was only one of many recent ugly instances. If one of her male colleagues had come upon them, the two louts would have sobered up considerably and complied with his wishes. Louise, on the other hand, was treated as a figure of ridicule. Lack of respect was how she put it. Pink sympathised, he had no doubt she was a capable and quite excellent copper, but he did express doubts as to whether it was a suitable occupation for a young lady. The question was, what else could she turn her hand to? He had already suggested modelling, she would probably find plenty of work in that field. Saying that, Louise was a down to earth, say it as you see it sort of girl so maybe the self centred, egotistical, pretentious, stuck up world of modelling wouldn't exactly be to her liking? Unwittingly, he had said enough on the subject to put her off the idea. What she wanted to do was travel. Some friends had disappeared to follow the hippy trail. Since meeting Pink and finding how relaxing and thought inducing the hash could be, her mind had taken to wandering in the direction her friends had taken.

The alarm bells were ringing now, fuck, was she about to ask him to go travelling with her? Neatly changing the subject by sticking his tongue down her throat, he squeezed her bare bum and sent her to run their bath. His neat bodyswerve saved the day and the topic didn't arise for the remainder of his visit.

Louise washed his hair in the bath then made love to him, slowly and sensually, forcing him to think. Maybe it wouldn't be a bad thing having a year off with Louise? There were plenty of worse fates could befall a man.

Another spliff while she made a rope of his hair and it was almost time for work. On the way to the bakery, he thanked her for a lovely day, good food and good company.

All three girls greeted him by the back door, still chattering excitedly about earlier events. Pink was soon on their case, asking why not one of them had bothered to check on Mr Rapati's reaction once he'd had time to take it in. Mira said she would phone home, but what could she say if her dad answered? Pink told her to ask which of them should have the tedious task of working with him until midnight, and was thrown a disdainful look from Kira when he discounted her from the job by explaining tomorrow was a school day. Her education was important. Kira remarked he sounded just like her dad and her sisters agreed.

Silence while Mira used the phone. It was Moraji, but she couldn't talk, Mr Rapati was in the same room. She did say Pink was to call for his supper, the girls were to sort it between them who should stay behind. Since Sira had been last to arrive, it was decided she would stay; even though she would probably be keener than her sisters to know of their father's reactions. Pink suggested they should lock up and he would drive all three home. Moraji would be sure to meet them at the door with his supper and that would give her an idea of what to expect.

The girls were excited again, running round checking everything was in order and hustling Pink from the premises. Sure enough, Moraji heard the car pulling in and opened the front door. She put her finger to her lips, Mr Rapati had gone to bed for a couple of hours before his night shift started. Whispering, she let them know he was still in a state of shock, but slowly coming round to the realisation he had a real life descendant of Indian royalty in his employ. He had even joked with his wife as to how he should address Johan on his return. Pink found himself surrounded by the four Rapati females, all trying to kiss him at once. In the delightful melee, at least one of them had a grope at his backside. Mira promised to relay what she found out to Sira, who collected their supper and climbed back into the car. Pink had an idea he wouldn't get much work out of her tonight.

With the ovens running at full capacity, they settled down to eat. Sira wanted to know what Pink's plans were to bring herself and Johan together as a couple, complete with her father's approval? Pink gave her his best look of absolute shock, it was now out of his hands, down to Sira, Johan, Moraji and the girls. He had set the ball rolling, quite successfully by the sounds of it. No, his involvement was over.

Sira couldn't hide her disappointment. He thought she was about to burst into tears; certainly her bottom lip was trembling, but the phone snapped her to attention. Moraji, cleverly telling her three daughters the tale simultaneously. Pink could see where the girls had inherited their brains from.

Sira's mood had lightened considerably by the time the conversation ended.

Having caught only the odd word while he carried on with his work, Pink sat down to listen to the details. Mr Rapati, for the most part, was overjoyed at the revelations. Johan had always been special to him. Hadn't he trusted the boy almost instantly with his business, and most importantly, with his daughters? Yes, he could quite understand why he would wish to keep such a thing quiet, if only for the sake of his own privacy, his own sanity. If today's proceedings were anything to go by, he was very wise to keep his own counsel on the matter. What Mr Rapati couldn't understand, admittedly, a little selfishly, was why couldn't Johan have trusted him with the information? Now his secret was out, maybe he would find it within himself to address the situation. Granted, he hadn't exactly lied, but he hadn't exactly told the truth, either. Hopefully, nothing would change, but realistically, that would all depend on how Johan saw things on finding he had been rumbled.

Pink was smiling now, another cunning plan surfacing while Sira spoke. He made her wait as he attended to the ovens, fine tuning what he had in mind while he did so.

With everything running smoothly, he sat Sira down and outlined what he had come up with. Mr Rapati's adherence to the caste system had so far put any possible union between the two far beyond the realms of possibility, but what if the shoe was now firmly on the other foot? Only a suggestion, but if Sira were to approach her parents, confess to a long standing fondness for Johan; coming more to the fore since the discovery of her intended's predilection for people of his own sex. Now, alas and alack, with Johan's recent elevation, wouldn't he have suddenly become too good for her? Or, put another way, could she ever be considered good enough for him?

Sira had the look of someone who should have been taking notes, there were tears combined with the realisation of what Pink had set before her. Yes, it was like challenging her father to do everything within his capabilities to make it happen. It wasn't brilliant, it was pure genius. She would huddle the girls and her mother together first, see what they thought. Pink had gone from leaving her in the lurch, abandoning her, to once more saving the day. How on earth could she ever thank him? He suggested she might empty the ovens for starters and was rewarded with her dazzling, best smile; the one she always seemed to save for him and him alone. Thanks enough, he told her.

Eight Ball chose that very moment to inform them it was snowing again, one huge flake managing to last until he was almost settled on his flour sacks. Before they knew it, the clock had lurched forward to a quarter to midnight and the end of their shift. Sira had regained most of her composure, with only the odd sniffle betraying the fact she had been upset. With the ovens set to run for another forty minutes, they locked Eight Ball in while Pink drove Sira home.

With Mr Rapati replacing his daughter in the passenger seat, it was twenty question time. How long had Pink known? Did anyone else know? Why should Johan keep it from his boss? How would it affect him when he discovered his secret was no longer a secret, and the classic; proof if indeed proof were needed that Mr Rapati had swallowed the bait hook, line and sinker, should his behaviour, his demeanour towards Johan alter in any way as a result of this earth shattering revelation?

Pink did very well to keep a straight face and hide both his pleasure and relief, telling Mr Rapati he hadn't known for long, that Johan felt guilty about keeping it from his boss, had shown relief at having shared it with Pink, knowing it would go no further. Now, Pink was sorely afraid Johan might believe he had given it out and sincerely hoped his friend could cope with it and not take flight as a result. This caused the little man to take on a deeply worried countenance, which in turn prompted Pink into playing his trump card. Johan often spoke of his great love and admiration for Mr Rapati and his family. If they all pulled together and showed their support, it shouldn't come to that. Pink promised to do all he *could* to help, he didn't want to lose a friend, plus, he too harboured a great deal of affection for the Rapatis. Mr Rapati shook him warmly by the hand, thanking him for his kind words and for jumping in earlier when he thought there was trouble afoot. He was sure between them they could convince Johan they would protect his secret. Pink spoke of his intention to go and see Ash and friends, try to convince them to keep it low key, for Johan's sake at the very least. He left the baker feeling a whole lot better about the situation, reaching his front door before remembering he had left Towser's pies in the shop. Approaching the back door, he overheard Mr Rapati pouring his heart out to Eight Ball. He decided to pick up the dog's breakfast in the morning, safe in the knowledge Eight Ball would provide his own brand of reassurance.

"Had a good day, Honey?"

"Oh, so-so."

"Are you tired or can you play me some Boz Scaggs before we go to bed?"

"Can do. Did you say before *WE* go to bed?"

"He-he. You know what I mean, Pinkee."

Mercifully, Boz killed the conversation. It would have taken him all night to tell her about his so-so day.

Money for old rope

P ink wrestled with Violet all night long and woke to find her
gone. When he slipped out of bed to go for a piss, his legs
couldn't, or wouldn't support his weight. What the fuck was going
on? He used the bed to baby himself to the door and stubbed his
toe when he made a grab for the handle. The pain shooting up his
leg came as something of a relief, he could strike paralysis from the
list of horrible ailments he had conjured up in his brain. Slowly, he
managed to stand unaided, but not before Violet noticed something
was amiss.

"I thought all that thrashing around would wake you up. What's
the matter, Honey?"

"I couldn't feel my legs. I couldn't stand up."

"You're standing now, you were kicking like someone demented.
Must've tired yourself out. That's why I was in here, you punted
Eight Ball to the other side of the bedroom. I've been calming him
down, telling him you didn't mean it."

"What time is it? Never mind. I'll look when I go back to bed,
feels like I've gone twelve rounds with Henry Cooper."

"He's a boxer, isn't he?"

"Yes, why?"

"Just .... boxers aren't allowed to kick, are they?"

"Violet, it's fuck knows what time in the middle of the night and you want me to run through the Marquis of Queensbury rules with you?"

"Well, you were kicking. Boxers don't kick so you couldn't have been fighting Henry whatsisname."

"Goodnight, Violet."

"He-he. Night night, Pinkee."

Back in the bedroom, the clock said half past five. He crawled into bed, put his head on the pillow then sat bolt upright again. He muttered to himself on the way to the bathroom, the distraction had taken the fact he needed to piss from his mind. Violet and Eight Ball had a good laugh at his expense.

Seven o'clock came round without another wink of sleep. Pink was up before the call to prayers, radio on for the news, porridge on for the breakfast and his cycling gloves on for the boxing. Violet squealed with laughter. He caught himself in the mirror and decided he looked ridiculous wearing nothing but a pair of gloves. Eight Ball cast him a glance which would have turned a lesser man to stone, then curled up at Violet's feet.

His laundry was done, but it was still at the launderette so no work overalls, he rooted for the jeans Mira had patched for him, they would do for today.

Mr Rapati was all smiles when he called for Towser's pies and remarked on how good a listener Eight Ball was. Pink told him it was all an act to curry favour and the baker's smiles turned to laughter. Maybe Pink was right?

Towser didn't want to wait until they reached the bottom of the allotment, but Pink was in no mood for his games, asking if no one had fed him all weekend. The answer to that one came when the pies didn't touch the sides. Those bastard Blunts shouldn't be allowed to keep a dog if they weren't prepared to look after it.

He had completely forgotten about the tower crane over the weekend. Now, it stood tall and lean and bright yellow, dwarfing everything else on site. Patsy introduced him to the driver, Keg, a huge barrel of a man. Pink wondered how the fuck he managed to climb the narrow ladder to the cab. He would have some fun watching.

Dave told him Reg had heard from Mad Frank. He passed on his regards, he was doing alright for himself, wasn't missing anyone and had promised to send some dope at his first opportunity. Pink was just relieved his friend had managed to get himself sorted out.

Mac chased everyone from the canteen, all except for Pink. He was to go to the office and pick up the keys to the Range Rover, take it to the car wash then pick up three big bosses at the station. They were due at eleven o'clock, he could suit himself what he did until then as long as the vehicle was cleaned.

He would be afforded another chance to watch Keg ascend the ladder, meantime, he had almost three hours to play with. This wasn't work, it was money for old rope, the hardest thing about it was climbing out of bed in the morning. The boss gave him the keys and asked why his hand was still outstretched. Pink told him he didn't mind doing all the running around, but the money for the car wash sure as shit wasn't coming from his own pocket. A pound note was handed over, easily enough for the car wash; and a large breakfast at the Greek café besides.

His first port of call was the launderette, take his washing home, change into his overalls, nab some cash from the stash and hit the supermarket while he had some transport. No need to disturb his stash, a quite generous Giro cheque having landed behind the door. Pink reflected. Not too long ago when he was poor, he would have been crouched behind the letter box like a wicket keeper, waiting for his dole money to arrive.

"Pinkee .... Did you get rained off again, Honey?"

"Nah, I've to pick up some big wigs at the station, but I don't like wearing my favourite jeans for work."

"You helped yourself to more than one pair of overalls. Why didn't you wear another pair this morning?"

"Have I? Where are they? Did you see me putting them away?"

"Bottom drawer in the bedroom, remember? It came off its runners and you almost trapped Eight Ball behind it?"

"I could say I remember, but I honestly don't, must've been in orbit. Thank you, Kitten."

"That's ok. If you've time to smoke that joint could we have some music, please?"

Pink gave Steely Dan an airing then suddenly remembered the winning betting slip from Saturday. Trouble was, he had put it somewhere for safe keeping, typically. For the life of him he couldn't remember where. He would ask Violet between tracks since she seemed to know where everything was.

The grass was tinder dry and it took the back of his throat out on the first toke. Rushing to the kitchen, he ran the tap and reached into the cupboard for a glass. Bingo, the betting slip turned up of its own accord.

The supermarket was a nightmare. The sneaky bastards had rearranged all the shelves so he had to go hunting for the items on his list. His mood lightened when he bumped into Jenny and her friend, Elise, a workmate. Not only that, Elise was also her room-mate; since Bea's defection to the seaside there was room for a lodger. He asked after Bea's health and was told her mother, the old witch, would be paying her a visit at the weekend. Why didn't he drop round with some of his dope on Saturday? They could have some fun. Elise unashamedly gave him the once over and he returned the compliment. He would check his diary, if Jenny didn't hear anything to the contrary she was to expect him around lunchtime.

Nine thirty, time for that breakfast. He had dropped off his shopping and put the radio on for Violet, his time was his own now.

Clem was suspicious about the Range Rover, how the fuck could he afford such a vehicle? Pink explained about his new job and Clem shook his hand in congratulation. The waitress was as miserable as sin with a face like a slapped arse. Nice body and quite pretty really, but even the Pink charm couldn't coax a smile from her. She wouldn't need to bother looking for a tip.

Ash was still in bed when he hammered on the restaurant door. The key to the side door was dropped from the upstairs window, along with the order to put the kettle on. A bear hug greeting then Pink told what he knew. He had promised Mr Rapati he would have a word, perhaps if Ash were to commence using Johan's place of work as his source for baked goods, he might then be granted the occasional audience with the young Prince. Ash was having almost as much fun as Pink with the game. Yes, if that was ok with the baker, it was just fine with him. Food was offered, but he had only just eaten, a cup of coffee would do. While it was cooling, he nipped to the betting shop, managing with great difficulty to conceal his surprise when seven hundred and forty four pounds and eleven pence was counted out in front of him. A quick exit before the dude had time to realise his mistake, he was re-counting it on the back kitchen table in front of Ash. There was a rolled up Sunday newspaper on the sill of the Range Rover's dashboard, Pink brought it in and turned to the results page. Of course, he'd had the sound turned down and the music on. An amended result following a steward's enquiry had given the race to Keep on the grass. Maybe his luck was holding out after all?

One of the waiters stumbled in, straight from a night out by the looks of him. Pink peeled thirty five pounds from his wad and handed it over, the waiter was to share it with his mates. They had given up part of their day yesterday for the cause, it was much appreciated. He jabbered at Ash in his native tongue then turned to shake Pink by the hand, offering up a thousand thanks and grinning from ear to ear. He told Ash it would probably be evening time on Thursday before he could pick up the imported goodies, he would see him then. Another bear hug and he was gone, a quick run through the car wash then heading for the station to meet his charges.

Pink could have picked them out of a crowd, two of them at least, expensive suits and the look of men walking to the gallows; not happy to have been wrested from their comfortable office chairs. The other, older, weather beaten; not scruffy, but not at home in his suit.

He was like a kid with a new toy, a broad smile on his face as Pink held the passenger door open for him.

One of the two men in the back seat whined he'd had nothing to eat through having to come to this God forsaken place. The old man told him to shut up then asked Pink to drive them to the nearest eatery. Pink told him the site canteen was as good a place as any to eat and he was invited to take them there.

The site boss was almost on his knees, bowing and scraping; he had deferential down to a fine art. When Pink steered the party towards the canteen, the look of horror on his face was a picture to behold. He then went into his headless chicken routine when the concrete batcher was reported broken again. Pink ushered him away from the visiting dignitaries and offered to make arrangements for however much ready mix was needed. He was sent to find Mac and the clerk of works, make a note of the amount and consistency required then go in person to the same place as before and order it. He didn't want the job to fall behind on the very day the main man was in attendance. As luck would have it, the duo in question walked into the office before Pink could go to the canteen for his work-boots. The clerk of works wrote down the specifications for the concrete and Pink jumped into the Range Rover again. Before he could set off, the old man, the main man, flagged him down and climbed in beside him; he wanted to go along for the ride..

Luckily, Barry saw this. He ducked back into the office and made a quick phone call, warning Groover to expect them.

On the way, the old man introduced himself as Sandy. He had built the company up from scratch, not boasting about it, but by way of explanation. He hated the business side of it and would rather be getting his hands dirty than sit in an office all day. His sons, the two in the back seat earlier, were the exact opposite, which was why he dragged them along on his site visits. He was in his element on these days out and liked nothing better than to watch a project taking shape. Sandy then surprised Pink by telling him he had heard good things about him. Pink, modest as ever, played it down, explaining his input as simple common sense.

He introduced Sandy before Groover could open his mouth, unaware of the fact Barry had forewarned him. Pink handed over his shopping list, Groover phoned it through to his chargehand, produced a bottle of single malt whisky and three glasses and offered drinks. Pink refused, but Sandy was only too happy to join him. He thanked Groover for the discount and found out Pink had been instrumental in negotiating it. His remark about having a good idea it couldn't have been his site boss told its own story.

Sandy had the taste now, would Pink take him to the best pub in town, did they do food? He wouldn't be embarrassed, would he?

The Boulder was practically empty, too early for the roofers. With fine weather they would be plying their trade somewhere out of town. Black eyed Sara was behind the bar. Pink introduced Sandy as his boss, ordered two pints and sat at the nearest table. Sara brought the drinks to them and refused payment. Sandy raised an eyebrow, said nothing, let Sara wander back to her post then asked Pink what all that was about. Pink explained about the other night and asked the old man what he would like to eat. He settled for a sandwich and ordered up another round of drinks, telling Pink it was only to see if he too could get them for free.

By the third pint, Pink was feeling peckish himself and Sandy ordered a sandwich for him on his way to the toilet. Sara took her chance while he was alone to thank him again for looking after her, she owed him one. One what, he could only guess at.

Sandy saw him peeling a note from his wad to pay for the sandwich and remarked he must be paying him too much. Pink explained about his win on the horses and had the old man beseeching a tip from him. As hard as he tried to play it down as a lucky bet, that he wasn't a regular gambler, Sandy was having none of it, Pink should humour him. Sara brought the paper. Sandy opened it at the racing page, looked at his watch and asked Pink to pick a horse from the one thirty at Ludlow. Nothing took his fancy, but in the one forty five at Uttoxeter, Chauffeur Driven seemed the obvious choice. Sandy didn't even look at the horse's form, the odds, the going or the connections. He gave the paper back to Sara, fished a wallet from his suit pocket, handed Pink a twenty pound note and asked him to bang it on the nose. The betting shop was two minutes away, when he returned his sandwich was ready and another two frothing pints had been served up.

Sandy's sons were seething mad when the Range Rover glided back on site; they kept their mouths tight shut, though. Pink was asked to put his wellingtons on and to find a pair for Sandy, it was time for the grand tour, no one but Pink would be allowed to conduct it. He had to stop Tanzi in mid dig, laughing as he snatched his cap off, wiped his hand on the front of his shirt then surprised everyone by throwing an arm round Sandy's neck and hugging him; they were old friends from way back when. After the tour it was back to the canteen for a coffee. Sandy excused himself and disappeared to the office, the site boss would be upset if he didn't spend some time with him. Winking at Pink, he asked if he could he bring the car round in about fifteen minutes, rescue him and take the trio back to the station?

As soon as they were in the car the two sons had a good moan at their father, spending the day on a shithole of a building site just wasn't their cup of tea. Sandy rounded on them, told them to stop whining, a good day's work would see the pair of them off. At the station he handed Pink an envelope and thanked him for a good day, he would be back in a month or so and would be obliged if Pink could look after him again. A firm handshake and he was gone. Pink watched the train leave, stuffed the envelope into his overalls pocket and hightailed it back to the site. It was almost clocking off time and he didn't need the overtime. He would be paid for eight hours. At a rough estimate he had spent an hour and threequarters on site without dirtying his hands; not bad going that.

Towser, as always, was happy to see him and even happier when he tipped a bagful of leftovers up for his evening repast.

If anything, Sira was more pleased to see him than Towser was, gathering him into an embrace before he could lock the bike away and thanking him repeatedly. Apparently, the Rapati womenfolk had put their collective pretty heads together and had come up with the unanimous decision, stage two was a goer. Moraji had this very day been down to the local library and laid claim to two tomes on Indian dynasties. Her husband was by now well aware of the high regard still felt for the Kadamba name, that, and its fine traditions of having ruled with kindness and benevolence. Sira wasn't finished there, dragging him into the bakery and throwing the fridge door open to reveal a case of his favourite cider.

The giddiness left her suddenly. She was happy, ecstatic, that was Pink's doing. Now, all thoughts were for Mira, tomorrow was a big day for her. Somewhat surprisingly, Mr Rapati seemed to have softened his approach concerning the arranged marriage, make that arranged marriages in general, telling his eldest daughter he would trust her judgement and stand by her if she felt it wasn't right. Sira suspected that had something to do with Pink's influence as well.

"You're looking pleased with yourself, Honey. Had a good day?"

"Oh, you know, so-so."

"By the spring in your step I'd say it was more than so-so. C'mon, Pinkee, spill. I'm really interested. You know that, don't you?"

Violet squealed with delight as he recounted the events of his day, positioning herself so she could look over his shoulder as he opened Sandy's envelope. It contained the betting slip he had written out earlier and a handwritten note. Apparently, Sandy had listened to the results service on the radio while in the office. Chauffeur Driven had won and Pink was to pocket the winnings, with thanks.

All Sandy wanted in return was for Pink to call him on the number provided and tip one horse per day, with assurances there would be no comebacks on him if they lost.

"How much was the horse?"

"Huh? .... Oh, you mean what price was it? Four to one in the paper."

"So, how much have you won?"

"If it came in at those odds, just short of a hundred quid."

"Wow, Pink. He did take a shine to you, didn't he?"

"I suppose he did. One thing I do know, driving him around beats working for a living."

"You can roll a joint and have your nap now, Honey."

"Why, thank you, Violet. Don't mind if I do."

The John Martyn concert scored top marks in the what to play debate. Pink reasoned he shouldn't have been tired, he hadn't exactly been overworked; then, he remembered all that beer and was asleep before he could even think of sparking up his joint.

Violet woke him at quarter past seven, calling his name until he emerged from his slumbers. At one point she almost gave up and was about to ask Eight Ball to do the honours. Before the cat could oblige, Pink was alert, sitting up and toking on his spliff.

Violet chose 'Cry Tough', but quickly changed her mind when she realised Pink was heading for the shower, now she wanted the Jimmy Cliff song from the 'Bumpers' album She just loved to hear her man singing that one.

The girls downstairs seemed to enjoy it as much as she did. Judging by the applause, it had been one of Pink's better recitals.

Mira was to be his beautiful assistant, he gleaned this knowledge from Kira, who leapt on him as soon as he walked through the door. Pink freed himself from her embrace and asked had she done her homework, bringing Sira's delightful laugh into play.

For all his teasing, Kira still insisted on claiming the passenger seat when he drove them home, nattering on about how her father couldn't shut up about him. He had become something of a celebrity as far as the Rapati family were concerned. Pink, modest as ever, advised her to curtsey next time she saw him. Kira, not to be outdone, advised him to kiss her arse, inadvertently providing him with more fantasy material.

Maybe the girl was right, when he arrived at the front door and dropped them off the entire household was on the front step. Pink rolled his window down and thanked Mr Rapati for the cider. The baker gave him a dismissive shrug and told him to think nothing of it.

For the first time in full sight of their father, the girls he had dropped off stuck their heads, one at a time of course, through the window and gave him a smacker on the lips. Mira slipped into the passenger seat and proceeded to bend his ear all the way back to the bakery; her one and only topic, tomorrow's meeting with Sanjeev, her intended.

Pink set about the batching and the baking. Mira invented and voiced several possible scenarios, asking his opinion on each of them. Mercifully, Eight Ball padded in and settled himself on her knee, breaking her concentration and affording Pink some blessed relief.

With everything ticking over nicely, he sat in the opposite chair and told her to stop worrying, to be herself and, echoing her father's words, not to let herself be rushed into anything.

Eight Ball crept onto his makeshift bed. Mira, who had all but talked herself out, did the first useful thing she had done all evening and opened a bottle of cider for the worker; then she put the curry, made by her own fair hand into the bottom of one of the ovens.

When she returned to her seat a frown tortured her beautiful features and Pink realised she didn't know whether to be excited, or scared, or a combination of both. He took her hands in his, stood her up and looked deep into her big brown eyes. She was to act natural, that's what had made him fall for her the first time he laid eyes on her. She was beautiful, highly intelligent and had a wicked sense of humour. If anyone should be apprehensive it was Sanjeev, she would knock him sideways or his name wasn't Pink Lynt. That brought a smile and a more relaxed Mira actually got round to doing a bit of work while Pink sorted out the food.

The phone rang, Ash, Johan had called. Ash had given him the state of play to let him know what he was walking into when he returned. Johan was delighted with how things had gone, he had a lot to thank his friends for, especially Pink.

With Mr Rapati now in the passenger seat, Mira stuck her head through Pink's window and landed one on his lips. All he told her was good luck and to be herself.

He let the little man know of his visit to Ash and of his suggestion for Ash to use the bakery as his main source for bread to the restaurant, thus bringing about the odd audience with Johan. Mr Rapati couldn't thank him enough, thought it to be a marvellous idea, especially since it brought more business in. The conversation came round to his family, did Pink think he was a good father to his daughters? He was forever worrying whether or not he was raising them properly. Pink reassured him it was obvious he was a good father, his finest attribute being the ability to listen to them and realising his own upbringing was far removed from that of his kids. Many customs and ideals didn't travel well. Mr Rapati seemed able to work out which did and which didn't, thus keeping everyone in harmony.

He left the baker to ponder that one, shook his hand, picked up the dog's breakfast and headed for the hills.

He realised he hadn't smoked a joint for several hours and sat down to rectify that fact. Violet asked for Steely Dan and serenaded him as he relaxed with his spliff. All in all, it hadn't been a bad old day. Long may it last.

CHAPTER 27

You can see our house from up there......almost

Pink froze. Someone was tickling the sole of his foot, then he heard Violet.

"His toes, Eight Ball. Do it to his toes. It's time for him to get up for work, anyway."

He grinned at the strange wake up technique she had devised and told her she wasn't right in the head.

"Do you still love me, Pinkee?"

"As much as anyone can love a ghost. Why do you ask?"

"You didn't ask me was I coming to bed last night."

"You shouldn't need to be asked, Kitten. You can do pretty much as you please, invite all your friends round for a party if you like."

"You're my only friends, Pinkee. Eight Ball and you."

"Well, since everyone's here, let the party commence."

"He-he. You're funny, Pink. I think that's why I love you so much."

"Good girl. Now, sort my breakfast out, will you?"

"You know I'd love nothing more. I hope and pray you know that?"

Pink gave the stylus to Steely Dan before she came over all maudlin. He hoped and prayed for the same things, but common sense told him it wasn't possible; he, at least, could live with that. Violet couldn't, in more ways than one.

The money from the betting shop was still in his overalls pocket. He thought of stashing it in the flat, but no, he was about to visit the bike shed, might as well tuck it up safe with all of its friends.

He bought a paper on the way to work, for Sandy's sake more than his own. Before mounting the bike, he turned to the racing page. Chauffeur Driven had indeed won at four to one, more money for the coffers; as soon as he had the chance to redeem his winning ticket that was.

Now, he was running late. Towser still managed to catch his food before it hit the ground, even though it was served up on the run, so to speak. He didn't appear to be too upset when Pink didn't stop to exchange pleasantries.

There was rain in the air when he clocked on, but it didn't stop Mac from shooing everyone from the canteen on the stroke of eight o'clock, all except for Pink. He was to study the diagram on the canteen wall, then go to work with Keg.

The diagram was a series of hand signals by which the crane driver and the banksman, his assistant at ground level, communicated. Pink accepted a cup of coffee from Dave and did as he was asked. Along with the hand signals there were instructions on how to hook up certain loads safely, all pretty straightforward. He changed his footwear and made his way to the base of the tower crane before signalling to Keg and letting him know he was banksman. The heavens opened and everyone either took shelter or headed for the canteen. Keg opened the cab window and motioned for Pink to join him. It was a straight climb for about one hundred and ten feet, then, depending on where the ladder was situated on the rotating part of the machine, it could be a leap of faith to access it. Keg was a big man, but he managed to vacate the seat and let Pink squeeze through so he was face to face with the view and the controls. Nothing to it, although he wouldn't like to be afraid of heights. By break time he could have landed the chains, the business end, on a sixpence. With there being only two levers, joy sticks, he could slew left or right, run along the railway track and either raise or lower the hook as it ran the length of the long jib, easy. Keg told him he had a real talent for it. Although the site was in a bit of a valley, he could see parts of the town. He could even see Towser if he was at the bottom end of the allotment near the shed, and had a fair idea of where his flat was from his vantage point..

After the break, he was taken off the job. Most of the men were rained off, sitting in the canteen and playing cards or exchanging banter. Pink had the keys to the Range Rover again, he was to pick up a part for the batcher. Did he go past the ready mix yard on his way? Yes? He was to order the next pour, ask for it to be delivered after lunch. It wasn't a big job, the concrete gang would work in the rain for an hour or so, then they could go home; job and finish, no complaints. Since Pink had advised the personal touch the first time they ordered concrete, the boss had it in his head it must always have to be that way. Pink wouldn't be the person to put him right on that one. It meant escape for him and a chance to ride around in the Range Rover.

A familiar figure walked in front of him as he sat at the traffic lights, he couldn't believe it. His best friend from schooldays and now a priest, complete with dog collar and black suit. Pink let him walk directly in front of the vehicle and gave a loud blast on the horn, laughing loudly when Father Mysoll made a mad dash for the kerb. When he saw it was Pink, he shook his fist, grinned a mile wide and hopped into the passenger seat. Since he wasn't in any particular hurry, Pink decided to take him on his rounds, catching up as they went. It was calculated they hadn't clapped eyes on each other for six years, Father Mysoll having been involved in missionary work for most of that time. His name was Peter, but Pink hadn't called him that since before secondary school. Peter had always shown a leaning towards religion and the clergy, so Pink nicknamed him Pon. He was no saint, always involved in all manner of scrapes with Pink. In the end, everyone called him Pon and no one was surprised when he entered the priesthood. Now, Pon was about to take on his own Parish not five miles from where they were; Pink would have to call round for a drink, catch up on old times. Maybe he could bring a few spliffs with him?

Groover knew Pon, since they were all much the same age. Pink ordered the concrete, took charge of a sealed envelope from Groover, shook hands and drove off with Pon to his next port of call.

The part for the batcher was ready for pick up. Pink reversed the Range Rover to the large foundry doors and watched as two men carefully deposited it just inside the rear door. He wasn't happy with how it was sitting and asked for some form of packing. As well sprung as the vehicle was, he didn't want the part to bounce around in the back.

As far as Pink was concerned, it was lunch time; so, he treated Pon to an all day breakfast at the Greek café. There wasn't a roofer in sight. With the rain lashing down they would be watching the clock for pub opening time. Pink told his friend of recent events, about being well in with the Rapatis, his business with Johan, his scheming and plotting regarding the girls, his fun get-togethers with Louise and the rest of his ladies; but stopping short when it came to Violet, it just didn't seem right to mention her. Pon borrowed the surly waitress's pad and wrote his number down for Pink. With Easter looming, it might be best to leave it for a couple of weeks. He was being thrown in at the deep end and at one of the busiest times in the church calendar.

When Pon left, Pink settled the bill. He could tell the waitress was warming to him since she didn't snatch the money from his hand this time. She hadn't warmed enough yet to merit a tip, though.

He could kick himself, Pon would have been the ideal foil to pick up his winnings at the betting shop, save prying eyes latching on to the fact he was flush. Nothing else for it, he would have to collect for himself.

The betting shop was quiet, only Chubby Blunt and a couple of his hangers on in the far corner. Pink balled his fists when he saw him, but did no more than that, remembering Sara's reluctance to speak up. He made a pretence of studying the form, then realised he should be looking for a horse to pass on to Sandy. Five minutes later he was writing a bet out for himself. Not over confident at such long odds, he put three pounds each way on Bossa Nova in the two fifteen at Market Rasen; currently trading at sixteen to one so he took it at that price. One or two punters saw the large amount of money change hands and no doubt they also saw which pocket it was crammed into. If he was on foot he might be a little worried, but the Range Rover was parked about twenty feet away, they would have to be quick if they wanted a handout.

He made it to the car before they exited the shop, their puzzled faces a picture as they scratched their heads and wondered where the fuck he had disappeared to so swiftly.

The office was empty when he reported back so he helped himself to the phone. Sandy's secretary put him straight through and the two men exchanged pleasantries for a couple of minutes, Pink taking the time to thank Sandy for the bonus. He advised the main man to place an each way bet on Bossa Nova and to take an early price.

The canteen was ram jam full although the concrete gang were showing signs of making a move. There were nine huge holes, or tanks, as they were known, each at a different stage of development. One section of a tank was to have the majority of the concrete delivery; another, still surrounded by driven sheet piles, was to have what was left to shore up the corners. One of the shuttering joiners complained to Tony, the labourers' chargehand, that there was clay between the shuttering and the piles. Tony didn't want to know, he seemed keen to make an impression, dismissing the joiner with a shrug of his shoulders to give of the impression he knew what he was doing.

The joiner had a word with Mac and he too told him not to bother himself with it. If the chargehand said it was ok to pour, it was ok to pour.

Pink headed for the canteen and had a coffee with Dave, he was having another dinner break. He had been on the road all morning if anyone complained. Mac joined them, would Pink man the Cat, make sure none of the concrete wagons came to a standstill in the mud? That suited him, he had his newspaper and some music to keep him occupied, and a probable early finish if he wasn't very much mistaken.

The wagons made it to the pour fully laden, but for some reason became bogged down on the way out. Pink towed them to safe ground, read the paper from cover to cover, did the crossword and listened to John Martyn in concert; it was still money for old rope.

By half past two the concrete gang were in the toilets, wringing out their clothes and preparing for the off. Mac let them disappear then called it a day, telling everyone to say nothing to the concreters, let them believe they had stolen a march on the rest of them.

Pink had to whistle for Towser's attention. With the rain still hammering down the dog had wisely taken up residence in his makeshift kennel. Again, no time for pleasantries. The food was poured over the high fence and Pink jumped back onto his bike. Towser demolished his meal and hightailed it back to his shelter.

Sira didn't know how Mira had fared, she hadn't returned, or if she had, no word had reached the bakery. Mr Rapati called him in, opened a bottle of his cider for him and offered to phone home. Actually, he had been looking for an excuse to do so. Pink's interest gave him good reason to call.

No answer, they could only assume things were going well, otherwise they would have returned by now. Pink relaxed in the chair, sipping at his beer. Sira sat in the other chair and let her father look after the shop while they chatted. She had told both parents of her fondness for Johan and had met no resistance thus far.

A commotion in the shop put an end to their chat, Moraji and Mira, both talking at the same time in a strange mixture of tongues. Luckily, Sira managed to follow it and translated for Pink. Mira had been bowled over by Sanjeev. They had so much in common it was unreal. What had impressed her most was his support for his younger sister, a fledgling reporter on her local newspaper, an occupation which would have been frowned upon not many years ago for a young lady of her upbringing. Sanjeev had talked his parents into allowing her free rein in her chosen field. Also, he had many cross cultural friends and couldn't wait to meet Pink, both Moraji and Mira having spoken very highly of him.

Mr Rapati couldn't conceal his delight. After the shock of Sira's intended marriage going south, he was happy to be able to celebrate at least one upcoming wedding; tentatively, of course, best not to tempt fate. He was fast learning his daughters had minds and tempers of their own.

When the hubbub died down, Mira cornered Pink and thanked him for all he had done, not only for her, but for her sisters; in fact, for her entire family. She knew Sanjeev was quite taken with her, he had put her at ease instantly and had shown the utmost respect for Moraji, all genuine and mirrored by the respect he afforded his own parents. If she had to pick a husband, she would be hard pressed to do better, present company excluded, of course. Pink kissed her, wrapped her in his arms and told her he was genuinely delighted for her, she would always have his friendship to count on, that was a promise. Moraji broke it up, but only so she could kiss Pink for herself, telling him he was the bees knees and having to explain the phrase to her beaming husband. Mira demanded one more date with Sanjeev, solo this time; her parents bowed to her request without hesitation. Things were moving apace.

He almost had to shoehorn his way out of the back door, not that he minded being surrounded by grateful Rapatis, but shouldn't someone be at home to greet Kira from school? That did the trick, the real boss of the household barked a few orders and the huddle broke up. She smiled at Pink and mimed her thanks.

"Good or bad, Honey?

"Que?"

"He-he. Your day, good or bad?"

"Oh, you know, so-so."

"You don't give much away, do you?"

"Sorry, Kitten. Not much of a talker me, more a man of action. Now, where did I stash my hash?"

She laughed again, that delightful, throaty sound then steered him in the direction of what he was looking for.

He told her about his day without mentioning Pon. He had already decided to invite his friend round for a drink and a smoke, check out Violet's reaction to a man of the cloth getting wasted on drugs and alcohol, just a bit of sport.

"Weren't you scared all the way up there in that tower crane? They never looked safe to me those things. You must have been scared?"

"It was unbelievable, just like in my dream, like Deja Vu. You know, you can see our house from up there almost."

"Oooh, Pinkee. I like how you said that. Is that how you see it, our house?"

"Yes, Kitten. That's how I see it from up there almost."

Thursday couldn't come quick enough, he was running low on dope; no real panic, but it would be touch and go on whether he could make what he had stretch. There were places he could score, but for now he was quite happy to be out of circulation.

Violet asked for the John Martyn concert and, although he had been listening to it on and off all day, he obliged, it was nap time. Violet would hear more of it than he would, guaranteed.

It must have been talk of the tower crane as that's where he found himself. With the cab window open, he was nipping buds from a huge marijuana bush. Not that he could possibly expect his own plants to flower or bud, the local climate wouldn't tolerate it, but fuck it; he was having fun, he didn't want to wake up.

The scent of lavender changed his mind for him, he couldn't remember undressing, but he was naked, perched precariously on the edge of the couch, an indent and the scent of lavender alongside him.

He gave 'Reelin' in the years' the full treatment in the shower, Violet squealed her approval and those in the cheap seats down below applauded loudly when he was done.

Sira looked tired, she had been either in the bakery or the shop all day and it showed, her useless cousin's shift finished when he was in the shower; she did so little work it was a waste of time her being there. Pink tended to agree, he wasn't overkeen on her himself.

He had gone down half an hour early to add to his cash stash. More and more he was considering opening a bank account now that he was relatively flush. The funds were never there before to merit such a notion.

He locked up and took Sira home first, she was missing Johan, missing out on sleep too from worrying how things might turn out. Pink told her to trust him, had he ever let her down?

She kissed him softly on the lips when he dropped her off and promised to take his advice, have a good night's sleep.

Kira came bouncing out when she heard the car, she had cooked his supper, but mostly she had missed out on all the hugging and kissing earlier and wanted her share, almost dragging her sister away from the car window to get to Pink

Of course Mira had to give him chapter and verse on her big day out. Moraji left them to it after the greetings. Sanjeev turned out to be quite the young businessman, confident, amusing, intelligent and attentive. Pink had heard most of it earlier, albeit interpreted by Sira, but he let her chatter on excitedly, delighting in her animation and satisfied this relationship was destined to run and run. For the four hours they were together that evening, he was hardly allowed to squeeze a word in edgeways. Again, he did most of the work, willingly, using hand signals to indicate he was ready for his supper.

She was still in full flow when he drove her home and almost up to the part where it was all his doing. He had timed it just right, there were only so many ways to say it was his pleasure, that she should think nothing of it, they were friends and what were friends for? Mr Rapati laughed when he heard the topic of conversation. Apparently, Moraji had talked of nothing else, either.

Eight Ball weaved between the baker's legs, purring loudly. Pink left them to it, picking up Towser's pies and making a quiet exit.

"Have you seen Eight Ball, Honey?"

"He's downstairs with Mr Rapati. Getting on famously the pair of them."

"Oh, as long as he's ok. You having a spliff before beddy byes?"

"Don't mind if I do, Violet, don't mind if I do. Have you rolled me one?"

"He-he. You know I'd love to. I think I could. I've watched you do it often enough. Can we listen to something quiet, please, maybe Leonard Cohen?"

Pink obliged, he could think of nothing better to relax him. He was confident now he had enough drugs to last him until Thursday, realising there wasn't much need for it while he was holding down two jobs, his time really didn't seem to be his own at the moment. Not that you would hear him complaining since he was having too much fun.

The now familiar smell of lavender filled his nostrils as sleep overtook him. There were caresses and fumbles, but all in all, a very peaceful night's rest.

CHAPTER 28

A bad day at the office

P ink could feel the sweat trickling down between the cheeks of
his arse, the change in the weather had brought with it a sharp
rise in temperature. Put simply, he had too many clothes on. The
cycling felt like hard work and the perspiration proved his point.
Towser was positively basking in the far corner where the sun had
reached, summer was definitely on the way, the clocks went forward
at the weekend. Easter followed on the next weekend, the days would
be longer, the crops would be sown; if there was a plan it was coming
together nicely.

Five minutes early clocking on so he took rest in the canteen and
opened his paper at the racing page. Bossa Nova scraped fourth place
in a seventeen runner handicap at odds of fourteen to one, he had
it at sixteens, which meant five times his place money, the bookies
paid fourth place in a handicap field of sixteen or more runners. This
meant he was still in credit, Sandy too, if he'd followed instructions.
This also meant they were playing with the bookies' money. He
scanned the day's meetings as the canteen filled up, filtering his
selections down to two horses, he couldn't decide between them. Sky
Pilot, a double reference to the tower crane and his meeting with
Pon, and Head Honcho, an obvious reference to Sandy. Both had
excellent credentials, he would invest half his profit on a double and

suggest the same to Sandy. With his mind made up, it was time to go to work.

The banksman's job would have him as fit as a butcher's dog. Within the first half hour he had covered the entire site on foot, hooking on, hooking off and running all over the place. He still found time to stop for a chat with Patsy, whose duties as fitter's mate involved filling the pumps with diesel and maintaining them. The pumps ran all day every day. With so much concrete being poured, the less water around the better.

At morning break, Keg slipped off the tower crane's ladder and knocked three teeth out. Luckily, he was on the bottom rung when he slipped, otherwise it could have been a whole lot nastier. A timely reminder if any were needed, building sites could be dangerous places. Mac was in a flat spin, he had some work set out which only the tower crane could reach, the mobiles were busy elsewhere. Pink had been asked to take Keg to hospital and was already in the Range Rover waiting. Keg, mumbling through his damaged mouth insisted Pink could operate the crane, bringing about a change of plan with Mac now in the Range Rover and Pink left in charge of the tower crane.

He was quite excited, this would be his first solo flight. He was no sooner in the driver's seat than he spotted Tony, the chargehand, signalling to him. He wanted a compressor picked up and dropped off outside the tank his crew were working on. Easy peasy. That done, he was at the far end of the site and unloading steel from a couple of wagons. Between lifts, he scanned the paper and tuned Keg's radio to a station he could listen to. Suddenly, a shout went up behind him. Looking back, he could see a couple of labourers running around like headless chickens. At first he thought it was horse play until one of them signalled for him to travel along the rail and drop his chains. The other ran through the mud towards the office and Pink knew then something wasn't right. Now, he had a bird's eye view of the spectacle, but he couldn't make out what the problem was. A crowd had gathered in one corner of the tank, all looking worried, even scared. It looked like bad news, an accident of some sort.

Tony's leg was trapped. He had ordered the removal of the shuttering from the corners then set his men to breaking up the bored concrete piles with jack-hammers. The vibration had freed one large block of concrete and it had fallen on Tony. Pink dropped the chains to just above head height, thinking he might lift the block and allow the men to drag the chargehand free, but he was waved away. There was much wringing of hands and opinions being exchanged, but no decision making.

An ambulance careered to where it foundered in the mud; its occupants, to their credit, ignored the conditions, leapt from the vehicle and started to plough their way towards the tank. With the equipment they had to carry and the distance they had to cover, Pink could see they would be a while. Looking around the site, he spotted a safety cradle which was used to fit the pile driver to the tops of the sheet piles. Patsy was attending to a pump close by. Within seconds he had slewed round and dropped his chains to the cradle. Patsy saw what he was up to and hooked him on. Next minute, the cradle was dropped in front of the struggling ambulance crew. Without hesitation, they loaded their gear and climbed aboard. Pink lifted the cradle and transferred them to the side of the tank where the ladder was. Mac arrived at the same time and did his best to clear the area, let the dog see the rabbit so to speak.

Full fifteen minutes passed. One of Tony's gang, a confirmed ex smoker, climbed from the tank and bummed a cigarette from Patsy, who had made his way over to see what the fuss was all about. Mac signalled for Pink to drop his chains into the hole and took on the banksman's role. Inching the concrete higher, Pink could see one of the ambulancemen trying to stem the flow of blood from Tony's upper leg. Five minutes later, Mac covered the chargehand's head with his jacket and blessed himself, there was nothing more the ambulance crew could do.

A doctor had been sent for. Pink had the unenviable task of lifting Tony from the hole in a covered stretcher and dropping him by the ambulance doors. The doctor then confirmed he was dead.

The job was suspended for the day. Pink was thanked by the ambulancemen for his quick thinking, telling him every second counted in moments like these. Little consolation, but he appreciated their thanks all the same.

The day had started with a promise of summer in the air and was dampened with a tragic death. Mac gathered everyone in the canteen and sent them home. Pink noticed Tanzi was missing and pointed it out. Mac asked him to go and find the old man and tell him he was done for the day. Pink jumped on the tractor and headed for where he had last seen Tanzi working, but there was no no sign of him. When he came alongside the hole he could see the old man having a rest, unusual, trusty spade by his side. He climbed the ladder to the hole and shouted over the wall. Tanzi didn't move. Pink presumed him to be asleep and approached to give him a nudge, watching in horror as Tanzi toppled forward; not resting, but stone dead. Racing on the tractor to catch the doctor before he left the site, he sounded the horn and managed to swerve in front of his car. With the doctor on the trailer he swung by the office to let Mac know what he had discovered. Most of the men had disappeared, Dave and Patsy were roped into finding something in which to wrap the old man in order to bring him out of the tank and onto dry land so to speak.

The doctor pronounced him dead. Pink climbed the crane once more and, for the second time that day, carried a dead man to the edge of the site. He stayed with Mac until another ambulance arrived, using the office phone to let Sandy know of his old friend's demise. Sandy had been informed of Tony's death and thought Pink was providing more detail on that, the shock was evident in his voice, he had lost a loyal and trusted employee and a good friend. He thanked Pink for letting him know personally, for realising he would want to hear of it from someone who knew of his relationship with the old man.

If Towser had owned a watch he would have been thinking it had gained a couple of hours, Pink was far too early with his evening meal. He didn't exactly complain, but he did seem to be somewhat puzzled.

Violet too was puzzled, soon realising something had happened. Pink told her the tale while he built a large spliff.

"Poor Pinkee. Had you ever seen a dead body before today?"

"Only you."

"You know what I mean, Honey. Trust you to come out with the gallows humour. Did you ever see a dead man before? There, I've re- phrased it."

"No, never, and now I've seen two in one day. Just how lucky can one dude be?"

"Did it upset you? Is that why you're treating it like that, with the humour?"

"It did and it didn't …. and yes …. about the humour."

"What d'you mean, it did and it didn't?"

"My first thought, both times, was that I was glad it wasn't me. Sort of relieved I suppose."

"That's completely natural. I'd guess more than a few of those there would have thought the exact same as you."

"I need something to cheer me up, any suggestions?"

"Cry Tough. I'd say that's pretty uplifting. Wouldn't you agree, Honey?"

"Only one way to find out, it'll be your fault if it doesn't work. Are you prepared to take that chance?"

"He-he. Yes, I think so. Yes, let's do it. I'll take the blame."

Nils had them singing along halfway through the first song, Violet's medicine was doing the trick. Pink thanked her between tracks and treated her to a slow striptease in time to the music, mesmerising her with the fluidity of his movement. The discarded underpants landed squarely on Eight Ball's head, causing Violet to scream with laughter, then again when the cat refused to acknowledge their presence, keeping his composure and remaining exactly where he was. He didn't seem to mind how ridiculous he looked.

With the forced early finish he found he had time on his hands. An executive decision had him on the train and hurtling towards Gwynneth's place of work with business on his mind.

He should have phoned. Gwynneth was on evening shift, but not to worry, he knew which bus to catch. The girl was overjoyed to see him, had he brought any hash with him? Someone had let her down on a score, word was filtering through of a big bust and she feared her shipment was involved.

Pink split what he had down the middle, it wasn't much, Gwynneth's plight could turn out to be a blessing in disguise. He had agreed with Johan and Ash it would be his task to shift the incoming goods and he could think of no one more trustworthy than her to act as middleman. To seal the deal, Gwynneth shed her clothes and helped him out of his. Both knew this would have come about whether or not they had business to talk of. Taking their time, they explored and tasted each other, saving the act of union until they were both absolutely gagging for it and then going at it like rabbits. The warm weather played a big part, causing them to slip and slide all over each over, laughing and losing the plot, exploding in unison, totally at ease with the situation.

A relaxed spliff, taking a few moments to thrash out the finer points of their business dealings. A quick shower together, with Gwynneth plaiting his hair before accompanying him on the bus into town for her shift. Although the pub would be closed, she had offered to go in early and set up for the evening, let her friend take off early.

On leaving the bus, Gwynneth was apprehend by a couple of drug squad officers. Not sure of whether or not she was carrying, Pink told them to leave her alone, he had just informed her of the death of a close friend, how heartless were they prepared to be? Surprisingly, they walked. Gwynneth kissed the face off him. Yes, she was carrying. Only the small amount he had given her, but enough to be busted. Pink had saved the day again, she could quite easily get used to that.

Barry was on the platform when he alighted the train and was headed for the Flat Iron to score. Pink told him not to bother, the drought was pretty much widespread, and besides, the squad were on the prowl. Instead, they went for a pint and a game of snooker in the ex-servicemen's club, deathly quiet, the black economy workers were taking advantage of the decent weather.

Barry went to the bar and returned ashen faced, the barman had just taken a phone call. Clem, a good friend to both had fallen from a roof and was in intensive care, he wasn't expected to live. Pink ordered double whiskies to take the sting out of the day. Barry claimed to have had the worst day ever, a bad day at the office.

Pink had the taste, but knew he had a shift later. Another phone call, Clem was gone. Pink made sure Barry had company before slipping away, the early morning sunshine a dim and distant memory.

Nils Lofgren couldn't lift his spirits now. Probably no one could. He let the inane chatter of the radio DJ persist, rolled a joint and smoked it, told Violet of his fresh news then collapsed onto the couch.

He didn't feel rested when he woke, plus, his neck was hanging off, he must have been lying funny, Barry had it spot on, a bad day at the office.

Sira, on the other hand had been having a good day. Pink let her exuberance envelop him, take his mind from his own negative thoughts and involved himself in her account of how Moraji had been reading extracts from 'A history of Goa'. Mr Rapati could have no doubt now, Johan was of royal blood and could be considered suitable husband material for one of his girls.

She sensed he was upset and coaxed it out of him as he drove her home, apologising for her own upbeat state. Of the three deaths, Clem's had saddened him the most.

Sira suggested he should have the night off, but he insisted he would much rather work, no point in moping around at home. Mira bounced out to greet him, carrying supper for two. Pink rallied a little. If anyone could bring him round it would probably be Mira.

Five minutes into their shift the phone rang, Ash, the package had arrived a day early. He had opened it, more compressed hash than he had ever seen in his life, but something else. Pink let a huge grin cover his face when Ash described it. He wouldn't tell Ash what it was over the phone, not with Mira listening in, he would see Ash as arranged tomorrow and all would be explained.

Now, suddenly his mood had altered to the good. Mira looked relieved, she had been struggling for words of comfort. She went over what Sira had already told him. Moraji had followed her dad all around the house, reading aloud from the library book, funny wasn't in it. Kira had joined in when she came home from school, Mr Rapati was slowly letting the message seep in, Johan had a lot to live up to when he returned from his travels.

Eight Ball padded in and made a fuss of Pink. He suspected Violet had sent him, but didn't complain. Sensing his master was ok, the cat made his way on to Mira's lap and settled in for the long haul. Pink didn't mind doing all the work, he was used to that lately what with the girls being more rapt in their love lives than having their eye on the ball.

He scanned his newspaper and did the crossword while Mira and Eight Ball dozed. His selections from the racing page remained unbacked, events had sort of overtaken him, putting them out of his mind.

By the end of the shift he wasn't tired, all manner of thoughts keeping his brain on the go. His supper had woke him up somewhat, usually he was ready for a kip when he dined so late. When he dropped Mira off he took Mr Rapati to the bakery and asked could he borrow the car for an hour. The baker had no objection, he wouldn't need it until seven in the morning, by the way, his wife had been educating him on the Kadamba family. Fascinating people, fascinating.

Pink smiled to himself on the way to Jenny's, he wouldn't knock if there was no light on, but he would check the sill for the key. There was a light, the flickering light of the television, he knocked on the window and Elise poked her head through the curtains. The front door opened, she put her finger to her lips and motioned him inside. Having someone different to talk to or whisper to made him feel better somehow. Elise was a good looking girl, even without the make-up she had been wearing when they first met. He told her as much and she blushed shyly. Pink had a feeling she wasn't so shy, but he didn't push his luck, just happy to have an ear to bend. Half an hour later he was on his way, knowing she was there for the asking and that suited him for now. He told her he would bring some dope at the weekend and she needn't wear any make-up, not on his account. Their lips brushed lightly and he thought of staying, then decided it was bedtime, he could wait until the weekend. Similarly, he had the notion of visiting Ash, but he would end up staying there for hours, sampling. No, call it bedtime.

"How you feeling, Honey? You look tired. Why don't you go straight to bed?"

"What, no cocoa?"

"He-he. I think you can manage without cocoa tonight, don't you?"

"Ok, you can tuck me in and tell me a story then."

Painting with matchsticks

Pink picked up the consignment from the restaurant, flour sacks, packed to the rafters with grass. He looked around for his transport and found himself in the tower crane, surrounded by the aforementioned sacks. Sticking his nose in one to check on the quality, he discovered they were full of fresh cut lavender. No way was he smoking that, but maybe Violet could find a use for it? Trouble was, how on earth could he transport it such a distance without the lavender squad seeing him? A question which remained unanswered, the alarm clock biting into his senses and jolting him awake.

"What do you expect to happen today, Honey?"

"If I knew that, I probably wouldn't bother going in. It's a new situation for me, Violet. I couldn't hazard a guess, truly."

"Just be careful. I know I say that every day, but I do worry about you."

"I know, Kitten. I'll be careful, promise."

"Be sure you do."

Mira was at the back door when he went for his bike, her oddball cousin had phoned in sick and she had fallen for the extra shift. Pink told her to check her wage slip at the weekend, make sure she was paid for it. Mr Rapati overheard him and laughed his head off. Mira made the wages up so not much chance of her being shortchanged.

Four of yesterday's pies sailed over the fence, expertly fielded by Towser. Pink took the time to chat, he didn't feel in any hurry to clock in for work.

The canteen was a sombre place to be as most of the men were only just finding out about Tanzi. Barry stuck his head through the door and called Pink over, more bad news. The mens' wages wouldn't be ready, could Pink break it to them gently; if they could wait until lunchtime tomorrow?

No one seemed particularly bothered by the news, still numb with the shock of the two deaths. No one was allowed on site until the health and safety officer had inspected it and he was taking his time in getting there.

Ten minutes later, Barry came in again, phone call for Pink. Sandy, could he pick him up at the station. He wanted to show his face. He also wanted to arrange Tanzi's funeral. The old man had no known relatives and Sandy wanted to be sure he had a proper send off.

Pink let Mac know and was sent to have the Range Rover cleaned again, take his time and do a good job of it. He knew Sandy didn't stand on ceremony so he went for a paper, didn't bother to clean the vehicle and headed for the Greek café, see if he could put a time and date to Clem's funeral.

There was quite a gathering, as sombre as the canteen had been. Clem was popular and as careful as anyone in the roofing trade. No decision had been made on his funeral, but his offsider, Malky, promised to let Pink know of the arrangements.

A cup of coffee and he was on his way to the station. With ten minutes to spare, he made a start on his paper, both horses he had picked yesterday failed to make headlines. Sad to say it, but circumstances had worked in his favour there. He picked one for the day just in case Sandy asked. Ace of spades, for Tanzi.

Sandy shook his hand as he held the car door open, could Pink take him round to the site first, and did he have a horse for him?

Pink passed the paper and told Sandy to select one from the one forty five at Carlisle. He came up with the same horse as Pink had, a wry smile passing over his face. Sandy would be a couple of hours on site being briefed on what had brought about Tony's death, would Pink pick him up at twelve and take him to the undertaker's. Before that, would he put fifty quid on that nag's nose?

That was all the encouragement he needed, managing to drop Sandy off and make a quick exit without being spotted. An hour and a half would be ample time to inspect the goods at Ash's, he was looking forward to this, his first attempt at drug smuggling already successful now that it was safely stored.

Ash was expecting him, the parcel had been left in the packaging. Ash had checked the contents, but he wanted Pink to see how clever Johan had been in concealing the drugs. Surrounded on all sides by shallow trays of herbs and spices and neatly packed, it was a true work of art. From the core of the parcel, Ash produced a bottle containing a thick, green, foul smelling liquid; the same puzzled tone to his voice as had been in evidence last night. Pink grinned a mile wide, took the bottle and placed it near a bubbling pan on the stove. Next, he selected a match from a nearby box and chewed at the non sulphured end. Ash's face was a picture as he watched Pink select a single skin from the packet and lay it on the table before drying the match end with a napkin and beating it with a knife handle. Dipping the crudely formed brush into the liquid, he painted the skin, stuck three more skins together, sneaked a cigarette from Ash's packet and built a joint. He didn't light it, giving Ash that pleasure, explaining it was hash oil, the jar was worth a small fortune.

Dealers didn't much like it, too messy to work with. Some did as Pink had and painted hundreds of skins with it, selling it off in packs of ten. Trouble was, everyone who then came into contact with it found themselves covered in the sticky goo. The tidiest method was to heat it slightly and syphon it off into pop bottle caps using an ear drops dropper, seal it round with cling film and let someone else deal with the mess.

With Ash having the licensed restaurant, he would have plenty of caps to go at. Pink popped to the nearby chemist's shop and purchased the ear drops, washing the dropper thoroughly on his return and demonstrating how it should be done. Ash was smiling, Pink presumed in understanding, but it turned out to be the oil; he was mightily impressed with it, no question.

With a little patience, Pink taught Ash how to apportion the stuff, taking the first ten caps for himself to try out the market. The solid blocks were carefully weighed on the kitchen scales. Pink ran an expert nose over one of them, closed his eyes and made big plans for the Easter weekend; the sky was the limit, or perhaps even beyond. All business now. One block would remain in Ash's custody to be split between the three of them, the rest would be delivered to Gwynneth, he had time to do that before picking Sandy up. All they had to do now was sit back and watch the money rolling in. He left Ash to his industry and drove straight to Gwynneth's place, where she inspected the goods, then started tugging at his clothes. Sadly, he had to run, but he would see her soon, that was a promise. As an afterthought, he handed her a cap of oil and threw her a wink. He stopped at a betting shop on his way back to town and placed Sandy's wager before heading for the site and, hopefully, his lunch.

Sandy sat with him while he ate. Health and safety had cleared the firm of any blame for Tony's demise, a tragic accident being given as the cause of death. Pink told him of his friend Clem's fall and subsequent death and Sandy sympathised. Now, he had to sort Tanzi out, not something he was looking forward to.

Pink followed him into the undertaker's office, ready to offer any assistance he could. Sandy dealt with it well, telling the clerk where both Tanzi and his death certificate could be located and instructing him to select a plot in the local graveyard. He then chose a coffin for his old friend, at the same time showing the first signs of the torment he was experiencing. Pink comforted him, supplied the clerk with Sandy's phone number, to be contacted when all the arrangements were in place.

As luck would have it, the undertaker's was only half a block away from the Boulder. It seemed the logical place to take the edge off Sandy's grief and he didn't put up anything of a fight when Pink led him there.

Pink went for a piss while Sandy headed for the bar. Sara recognised him from before and peered over his shoulder, expecting to see Pink. This tickled Sandy and brought him out of his dark mood. He told the girl Pink wouldn't be long and she blushed an attractive crimson, embarrassed to be so obvious.

Pink had half expected the pub to be full of roofers, but the weather was fine, they wouldn't want to dwell on one of their number taking a tumble for sure. No matter what the weather was on the day, they would all attend the funeral.

Sandy glugged down what was left of his pint when Pink motioned for him to follow, it was almost time for the race and the betting shop was close by. Not the shop he had placed the bet in, he had learned his lesson there; the walls had eyes in that particular establishment. Sure enough, the usual suspects were gathered in a corner. Pink ignored them and watched the one forty five from Carlisle, whispering to Sandy to show no emotion when Ace of spades obliged with a narrow victory. Sandy was four hundred pounds better off for his outlay, toasted, along with Tanzi's life, five doors away at the Boulder. Pink was offered ten percent, plus, ten percent of the winnings from earlier in the week. He asked Sandy to put it towards Tanzi's internment and was knocked sideways when Sandy told him he could claim the funeral expenses against his taxes as part of the business. Still, he was overwhelmed with Pink's gesture, knowing he wasn't exactly the highest paid of employees and insisting he should take his cut when he picked up the winnings. As an afterthought, he invited Pink to attend Tanzi's funeral with him, providing it didn't clash with that of his good friend. Pink had no problem with that, he had come to like Tanzi's company in the short time he had known him and thanked Sandy for the invite.

They found themselves locked in the Boulder for the second time in a week. Sara flitted around them like a butterfly, topping up their drinks and laying on a tray of sandwiches, gratis, although Sandy insisted on paying for them at the end of the session along with a handsome tip for the girl. Pink thanked his lucky stars he hadn't taken any of the oil on board, it had blown Ash's head off earlier, mixed with the drink he would have been incapable of driving Sandy to the station. Truth be told, he shouldn't have been driving, anyway.

The site boss wanted to know where he had been all fucking day. Pink was offhand with him, saying he should ask Sandy. In a quiet corner of the canteen, he laid a cap each on Dave and Barry, they could pay him later, he would defer Dave's payment for seven days due to him working a week in hand. Barry would be expected to cough up on the morrow.

Once again, he would be paid eight hours for sitting in the pub; oh, and for sorting out a few little bits of business on the firm's time. Plus, his kickback bonus from Sandy, money for old rope.

He pushed the bike as far as Towser's allotment, a doggy bag on each handlebar, one for now and the other perched high on the fence for the morning. The dog listened to his drunken slur while he dined, wagging his tail all the while in appreciation of the food.

"God. You've had a good day, haven't you?"

"How can you tell?"

"You've got a thirty bob sway on and your eyes are rolling."

"I haven't heard that for years."

"What .... your eyes are rolling?"

"No .... the other one, thirty bob sway .... we've gone decimaliserational, you know .... decimational"

"You mean decimalisation."

"That's what I said, isn't it? …. Isn't it? Is it?"

"Good job I know what you meant. Maybe you should have your nap, Pinkee? You can tell me about your day later .... Pinkee …. Pink? Oh, you took my advice. Good."

When he woke his arm was still fast asleep and his neck was hanging off. Violet showed no sympathy as he tried to restore the bloodflow to both. Pink played it cool, knowing full well she would come round when she wanted a particular album on the stereo. He stumbled into the bedroom to check the time, an hour and a half before he had to make a move for work. The thought came to him, he'd had the oil in his possession for over nine hours without sampling it, some sort of world record. Now, he was ready, cautious, but ready; trouble being, he couldn't roll a single skinner, not with oil. In the dim and distant past he had mixed the stuff with tobacco, very messy and not recommended. Three skins it was then. He saw Violet edging around the walls, but focused on making a matchstick brush. She followed him to the kitchen, fascinated as he mashed the end of the match with a knife handle; she wouldn't ask and he wouldn't tell. He placed the cap carefully on the spout of the kettle as it came to the boil then gingerly removed it to the table top and proceeded to paint a single skin. Next, he filled the joint with tobacco and skinned up as normal.

It felt strange toking on a spliff with no music playing, but he held out, knowing Violet couldn't wait for much longer. After all, she was a woman, wasn't she?

Sure enough, she cracked.

"Why are you sitting in silence? .... Sore head?"

Pink dragged deeply on the joint and inhaled loudly.

"Please, Pink. Will you play Dan Fogelberg for me? Not too loud if your head's nipping."

"Sure, I can do that. Just as loud as you like, Kitten."

"What's that you're smoking? It's different isn't it?"

"Full marks for observation, Kitten. Hash oil, a by product of the compression process. To think it was once discarded as non profitable."

"Is it strong?"

"You get a good hit from it, but it wears off too soon, sooner than the block stuff or good grass."

He had intended to smoke only half, but found he couldn't put it down, especially when Dan Fogelberg cleared his throat to sing.

The shower felt good, the acoustics seemed to be better than usual, he put that down to the new dope, no other explanation for it; but only half hearted applause from the gallery. They didn't deserve him.

"So, will you tell me all about your day, Honey?"

"I was about to play the other side."

"Oh, ok. Maybe just a brief synopsis, the highlights. Please, Pinkee. You know I like to hear what you've been up to?"

Pink took a deep breath and rattled away without coming up for air.

"I didn't do a hand's turn as regards work. The boss phoned for me to pick him up and I managed to go for the dope while he was on site. Then I dropped it off to the dealer before picking the boss up again and taking him to arrange Tanzi's funeral. He got a bit upset so I took him to the pub and the rest, as they say, is history."

"He-he. There, that wasn't so hard, was it?"

Side two kicked in, the oil kicked in another notch, Eight Ball padded in, Violet closed her eyes and swayed to the music. Pink thought about another joint, but decided against it, he didn't know who his offsider was tonight. If it was Mira he would be busy, the girl would be preoccupied, in fact both girls would be preoccupied.

Mira was in the bakery when he rolled in, an odd looking smile on her face like she was up to no good. Pink didn't pursue it, he knew something was in the air, but was laid back enough with the oil to just let whatever it was happen. They locked up and he drove her home, her animation giving it away, she had something up her sleeve. He found out when he dropped her off and Moraji jumped into the passenger seat, where Sira carefully sat a pan on her lap. This would be different; with all the respect he had for Moraji, they had never before spent more than ten minutes in each other's company. Mira kissed him through the window, followed by Sira. Kira waved and blew him a kiss and Mr Rapati grinned a mile wide.

Moraji knew the bakery inside out, but still had time to marvel at the little improvisations Pink had installed to make the job run that little bit easier. Her husband and the girls had apprised her of such, but this was the first chance she'd had to witness them for herself. They nattered away like they'd known each other for years and Pink could see where the girls acquired their easy going natures. He learned from their conversation that she liked Mira's future husband, such a handsome young man, intelligent and with a good business head on his shoulders. Also, Mr Rapati had never been so relaxed. Having spent so many years building up his business, he was now so contented he was almost like a different man, taking more interest in his daughters and his wife than for a long time. Happy to spend less time at the shop now knowing he had a good, reliable team to depend on. Moraji claimed it had a lot to do with Pink, but he played it down as usual. Eight Ball strolled in and sat at her feet while they talked through supper, something else Moraji had wished to experience.

They couldn't believe how quickly the evening had passed, good company does that sometimes. There were many more topics they could have touched on, but those would just have to wait. Moraji was a bit sceptical about leaving Eight Ball in the bakery. Pink reassured her he would probably be there now until Mr Rapati was ready to go home as they were big pals. Moraji repeated herself, her husband was definitely a different man lately.

Pink filled his basket before leaving the baker to his nightshift. No pies tonight, Towser's breakfast was safe unless that fox had learned to scale an eight foot fence.

"What would you like to hear, Violet? I'm for another joint of that oil, me."

"You choose, Pinkee. I seem to be monopolising the music lately."

"J J Cale it is then .... You know, Kitten. I'm going to write to him, ask him to write a song about lavender just for you."

"Ooh, Pink. You can be such a romantic sometimes. I love you so much."

"Me too. Now shut up and listen."

The room reeked of lavender when he woke up for a piss. With Eight Ball still out on the tiles, the presence he had felt in the bed could only have been Violet. Strange how she managed to disappear when he woke. He didn't really mind, feeling rested and oddly satisfied as if he had just recently romped and emptied his sac somewhere warm and inviting. Maybe he should ask her if she was on the pill?

CHAPTER 30

A domestic interlude. (Sideshow)

Pink hoovered up his breakfast, running late for work. To say he felt rested earlier, he had managed to sleep again after switching the alarm off. Violet roused him and had him running around at a hundred miles an hour in an effort to get his shit together. He was ready for the off when Eight Ball scrambled through the kitchen window and demanded food.

Towser didn't much care for the shower of leftovers, until he realised just what had been launched in his direction.

Keg, minus his front teeth, had managed to drag himself in to work, unaware of the drama which had unfolded in his absence. Pink filled him in on the details as they walked to the base of the tower crane, to which Keg came over all jittery, claiming a sense of foreboding had passed through him that very day, a sense something bad was about to happen. Pink reminded him about losing his teeth, which had a calming effect on the big man. Pink was banksman for the time being, another day of running all over the site in prospect so the last thing he needed was a nervous crane driver.

Half an hour into the day, Mac approached with a youth in tow, Roddy, the son of one of the concrete gang. Roddy was fresh out of school and Pink had the task of training him up to be banksman. The kid was intelligent, obviously not intelligent enough to carry on at school, but enthusiastic, quick on the uptake if you discounted the half hour he spent in the stores waiting for a long stand. By break time he was as proficient as Pink could make him, bearing in mind he would be required to work with the boy at some point when Keg wasn't available to drive the crane.

Dave made approving noises about the oil when Pink went to the canteen to borrow his paper. Being on the last minute earlier, he hadn't had time to buy one.

'One more hole', in the two fifteen race at Beverley, another reference to Tanzi, shorter odds than his usual pick with every chance of showing its competitors a clean pair of heels. In the office, Barry had a grin a mile wide courtesy of the oil, if Pink could spare another cap he had the cash ready to purchase it. Speaking of cash, it was payday, Barry had all the wage packets arranged in a box and was about to tour the site in order to dish them out. Pink's were handed over, two envelopes, one containing his bonus. Sandy called and arranged to be picked up at the station at one thirty on Tuesday. Tanzi's funeral was scheduled for two thirty.

Mac told him to jump on the Cat, the health and safety had griped about the poor access afforded to the ambulance so a decent road of sorts was needed as a matter of priority. The stone had been ordered, if Pink could sign for it when it came and load the tippers, then level it off when the tippers had done their stuff.

He borrowed Dave's paper again to stave off the boredom while waiting for the delivery. He parked opposite the caravans, switched the engine off and settled down with the Cate Brothers for a read.

Five minutes later he saw the site boss enter his mobile home, a split second after that a piercing scream ripped through the tranquility. Pink was unaware Mrs boss had company, as was the boss, until now. Now, they both knew, and soon the entire site knew. The caravan was rocking and obscenities were traded along with punches until the show spilled out onto the playground. Pink was impressed with the boss's tenacity and appetite for the fight, getting the better of the much bigger concrete ganger. His wife was screaming her head off, wrapped only in a towel, and Pink couldn't quite make out who she was barracking for. He had learned a long time ago not to get involved in a domestic, a hard lesson having come between a married couple of his acquaintance. The female of the pair turned on him and almost had one of his eyes out with her talons. Never again. Nothing for it but to sit back and enjoy the show from the grandstand. When the boss picked up half a brick, the ganger thought it prudent to get the fuck out of there. Barefoot and still trying to buckle his belt, the half brick struck him squarely between the shoulderblades, hastening his retreat as opposed to hampering it. The boss then rounded on his woman, ripped the towel from her and gave her a mighty kick in the arse. Pink had seen all she had to show before, but delighted in the spectacle all the same as she tried to hide her ample charms, realising she had nowhere near enough hands to do so. The couple disappeared into the caravan, but he suspected the show was far from over.

The sound of the arriving stone delivery drowned out any chance of hearing what was being said, although, as he was signing the sheet a suitcase came flying from the door of the caravan, a pink suitcase. He presumed it didn't belong to the boss. Sure enough, the ex Mrs boss followed it out five minutes later, immediately demonstrating her way with men by cadging a lift from one of the delivery drivers to the top of the lane, or beyond. Pink caught her eye and blew her a kiss for good luck, or maybe good riddance.

He busied himself with the stone and had a decent road into the heart of the site furnished before the lunch break. As far as he could tell, the boss hadn't shown his face since the fracas died down. However, the concrete ganger had picked his wages up and left the site without shoes or shirt, he wouldn't be back.

More problems with the batcher meant he was on the road again after lunch. With the boss keeping a low profile, Mac was running the show, it was he who had to go for the keys to the Range Rover while Pink ate, returning with not only the keys, but the ganger's clothes to boot.

Groover was pleased to see him, it meant more work for his men. Pink didn't stay long. With other fish to fry, he wanted to sort out his business and get the hell out of there quicksmart. Groover gave him his bonus, invested in a cap of oil then told him not to be a stranger.

His next stop was the betting shop to pick up yesterday's winnings for Sandy and to have a modest wager on No more holes. After all, he was still playing with the bookie's money.

Ash beamed when he entered the back door of the restaurant, he had been busy. As luck would have it, today was pop delivery day. He had taken the caps from all of the empties, washed them and dropped a measure of oil into each one. Thirty five caps sat waiting for him in the fridge. The oil set like soap when cooled, easy to transport, no spills. Ash had also divided the remaining lump of black into three equal parts, warning Pink to be very, very careful with it; prime hashish. He took the lot home and stashed it in the bike shed. If he had gone to the flat, Violet would have him chatting and he wanted to be back on site. This concrete run suited him, an escape, no point in spoiling it.

The boss was staggering around outside his caravan when he returned. Raising both hands above his head, he stood squarely in the path of the oncoming vehicle. Pink braked and rolled the window down, smelling the booze before the man could breath anywhere near him. Rather unpleasantly, he asked where the fuck Pink had been and demanded the vehicle from him. Pink didn't argue, he wouldn't have said a word, but the drunk grabbed his shirt front and attempted to drag him from the driver's seat. Pink helped him out. Using the momentum, he landed with both knees in the man's chest and explained he didn't know his own strength. He then demonstrated this strength, picking the boss up by his lapels and dusting him down rather roughly; he seemed to get the message. The drunk jumped into the driver's seat and revved the bollocks off the

Range Rover before tearing up the dirt lane. Ten seconds later, Pink heard an almighty crash, followed by the continuous blaring of a car horn. He took his time, following the lane and turning the corner in the direction of the sound to see the boss half hanging out of the windscreen. He was alive, blood pouring from a wound in his head, conscious and rambling. Pink told him to stay where he was and walked to the office to call an ambulance, and to let Mac know what was going on. Mac rode on the tractor with him to the scene, they could hear the ambulance approach; the man was still conscious, still ranting incoherently. It turned out to be the same crew who had attended before and when they caught a whiff of the alcohol, they suggested the police should be involved. Mac looked to Pink for help. Pink whispered it was private land, the police probably couldn't do anything about it. Mac relayed this to the ambulancemen and they agreed, not right away, but after a short discussion between them. They poured the boss into their vehicle, made him comfortable and advised Mac to get rid of the Range Rover, the police would still want to know what had caused him to leave the road and would probably interview him at the hospital.

Of course Pink just happened to know the proprietor of a local garage and arranged for a breakdown truck to tow the wreck away. Mac asked him to sort it out and accompanied the boss to the accident and emergency.

Pink inspected the damage for himself, the Range Rover was built like a tank. The front end hardly had a dent in it, he would work something out with Tonka at the garage, have him declare it to be a write off then ask Sandy would it be ok for him to attempt a salvage job on it. Sandy could then claim the insurance, or use the wreck as a tax loss and Pink could have his wheels.

Tonka told him he'd be there in forty minutes, just time for a coffee and a chat with Dave. No such luck, Sandy was on the phone for him. Pink filled him in on the state of play. He left out the fight and the inebriated condition of the boss, confirming he'd had no problems with the vehicle earlier in the day and would let him have the mechanic's verdict as soon as it became available. Sandy insisted he would need a replacement almost immediately, he would phone around and be in touch before close of play.

Tonka had no problem calling the Range Rover a write off, and no problem doing a little cosmetic work to make it look brand new.

Now, he had time for that drink. Dave served it up and sat down for a chat, telling him the oil was strong, good stuff. There wasn't a lot of smoke around. If a dude had any amount of anything he could name his own price what with the long Easter weekend coming up. Just then Barry called Pink to the phone, Sandy again; could he take a taxi to the local car dealership, pick up the new vehicle, take it home for the weekend and drop it off at work on Monday morning?

He looked at Barry's watch, four thirty. With no foreman or boss around, he collected Towser's food, jumped on the bike and rode to the allotment. Towser wagged his tail off and gratefully accepted the leftovers. Pink spent five minutes chatting to him then rode back to the site to lock the bike in the stores.

His taxi arrived with Mac inside, Pink asked how much to the dealership and Barry handed over the fare from the petty cash. While the driver wrote out a receipt, Pink explained about the Range Rover and got the script on the boss from Mac. He would live, the police had turned up, but stopped short of charging him with drink driving since he had been on private land. Pink had called it right.

Another Range Rover, Pink would have sworn it was new before he slipped into the driver's seat. Borrowing a pen from the salesman, he made a point of noting down the seven hundred and fifty miles it had done before signing the documents. He didn't mind making a few quid on Sandy, but for some strange reason he did mind anyone else doing so, or attempting to.

The traffic was too heavy for him to put the new vehicle through its paces, so he went straight home with half a mind to try the black. Ash's warning changed his mind for him, best to sort out some business instead, start bringing in a return for their collective outlay.

"How was your day, Honey?"

"Oh, so-so. You know?"

"Grrrrrrr. One of these days you'll just come out with it. I know you're teasing me, Pinkee. C'mon, what you been up to today?"

Pink tut tutted, his makeshift brush had solidified. Violet followed him to the kitchen while he fashioned another.

"I witnessed a marvellous domestic, picked up some more caps, drew my wages and two bonuses, called an ambulance to take the boss to hospital"

".... Which boss, not Mr Rapati?"

"If you'll let me finish, the site boss. He wrapped the car round a tree after catching his wife shagging a bloke from the site"

".... He-he. Don't you mean he was shagging her?"

"You don't know her. I think I got it right first time. Anyway, where was I? Oh yes. He caught them in the act, kicked the shit out of the bloke, poured fuck knows how much whisky down his neck, jumped in the Range Rover and pointed it at the tree."

"Two bonuses?"

"One for my ideas about the tower crane and one from Groover, my percentage of the concrete deal."

"Jackson Browne?"

"What about him? He's got enough money .... Is he here?"

"He-he. Sorry. You've rolled your joint. Play Jackson Browne for me, please."

"You should be a DJ."

"I only know what I like through you, Honey. Maybe you should be a radio DJ, then I could listen to you when you're out? Mmmmmn, that would be perfect."

Jackson Browne interrupted her, silenced her; still, Pink would give her idea some serious consideration. After all, it wouldn't be hard to better the drivel coming from at least seventy five percent of music radio.

Something Dave said earlier came back to him, something about naming his own price for the only drugs in town. He left Violet with Jackson Browne and jogged along the road to the telephone box.

Gwynneth was at home. They exchanged pleasantries and then he told her to sit on the black until next weekend and increase the price in accordance with demand. Gwynneth was ahead of him on that one, clever girl that she was; the hash was well and truly stashed, and by the way, it was the best shit to hit these shores in a long, long time. She also wanted more of the oil. Pink promised fifteen caps for when she started work later, kissed her down the phone lines and headed for his own stash.

He left ten caps on his shelf in the bike shed, called in at the shop to tell Mira he would be ten minutes late for work then took the rest upstairs.

Side two of 'Late for the sky' played as he had a quick shower. No time for a nap, but it was Friday, he could lie in bed all day tomorrow if he so desired.

Gwynneth let him in the side door of the Flat Iron, kissed the face off him, poured him a pint and thrashed out how much the caps should be sold for. He assured her there was more oil to go at, but with a slight increase in cost for next weekend.

Since it was fifteen minutes 'til opening time, they made the most of it. Gwynneth was given the opportunity to examine the nap of the pool table from close quarters as Pink rammed her urgently from behind, the best ever way to seal a dope deal in his humble opinion.

Next stop was Louise's. She opened the door in her uniform, night shift beckoned, he rolled her a joint of the oil on the kitchen table, told her to be careful out there, kissed the face off her and promised they would have a session soon; she knew what he meant.

He helped Brat unload the van and set out his stall for the evening, the Albatross would be wall to wall with punters looking for dope tonight. Pink wouldn't be staying, but Brat could distribute ten caps without anyone knowing where they had come from. Whatever he cared to charge over and above what Pink had quoted was his. The men shook hands, time to go to work for both of them. Brat called him back and loaned him Fleetwood Mac's 'Rumours', for one night only; if Pink could let him have it back tomorrow.

Last port of call was to Jenny's; he wanted to prime her for tomorrow, the old witch was well on her way to the coast for her visit. Jenny answered the door in her dressing gown and led him into the kitchen. He rolled a couple of joints for her, fumbled under the gown to make sure everything was where it should be, kissed the face off her and drove off into the night. He didn't ask the whereabouts of her roommate. He wanted to, but he didn't wish to appear over keen.

In the end up he was only five minutes late for work. He called it work, but in reality it was even easier than the building site; plus, it paid his rent.

Mira was in no hurry, obviously, she had news for him, important news. Sanjeev would be coming to town on Sunday. Trouble was, where could they go? She didn't want to sit at home all day with the Rapati tribe looking on, she wanted some privacy. Pink suggested that with the weather on the improve, she should pack a picnic, show off her culinary skills, drive into the country to a little secluded spot he knew and they could have all the privacy in the world. Her arms gathered him in, a wonderful idea. Sanjeev would be coming by train, she would ask her dad for the car and disappear for the day. Pink made it easier for her, he had the Range Rover, any other Rapatis needed a lift, he would oblige.

To prove his point, he took Mira home in the Range Rover. Sira was suitably impressed when she saw it, telling her dad she wanted one for her birthday. Mr Rapati had a good look round it, inside and out, obviously wondering how Pink could afford such a fine vehicle. Pink let him wonder for the sport of it.

He guessed it was Kira's turn to cook as soon as he smelled the curry, his belly was rumbling and thinking his throat had been cut. Fortunately, Sira was hungry too, it would take half an hour to warm. They forged ahead with the batching so they would be in front of themselves, then they could relax with their meal.

Sira was counting down the hours, Johan would be back on Monday; she hadn't realised it was possible to miss someone so much, the time seemed to be dragging. Pink told her to be sure to curtsey when she next saw him.

Sira picked at her food while Pink all but poured his down his neck. This is how she had been for the last few days, she told him, thinking she could eat like a horse one minute then pecking like a sparrow when the food was set before her. Pink told her she was in love, had it bad, then helped her out with the curry, no point in letting it go to waste. He thought the meal would have made him drowsy, especially since he hadn't taken his nap. It had the opposite effect on him, so much so that he slipped out to his stash and sliced a piece from the block of black. He had been hanging to try it since both Ash and Gwynneth had recommended it so highly.

Sira yawned her head off as he drove her home, she obviously hadn't been sleeping either through missing her man. Pink told her to try her best to get some sleep, Johan wouldn't like the idea of her wasting away to nothing. She promised she would, what he said made sense, what he said always seemed to make sense. She stuck her head through the window and kissed him as her dad climbed into the front seat. Pink stepped out and let him drive to the bakery, almost having him off the road when he told him Sira had specified she would like a pink one for her birthday.

Ferreting the 'Rumours' album from under the front seat, he wondered how he could sneak it in without Violet seeing it. As luck would have it, she was in conference with Eight Ball, and only smiled in acknowledgement when he strolled in. He managed to slip the record onto the turntable before the conference finished, but he didn't play it, leaving the radio on until he had a spliff together.

"Eight Ball's not happy."

"How so?"

"He likes Johan, but he hasn't seen him for over a week."

"I told you he was on holiday, surely you've let the cat know? Anyway, tell him Johan's back on Monday and see if that cheers him up."

"He's gone out."

"Good, maybe I can have my joint in peace then."

"You went to work early."

"Just putting the Range Rover through its paces and running a few errands. Anything you want to hear?"

"Anything but that radio. It's been abysmal tonight."

Pink put the stylus to 'Rumours', sat back, and delighted at the puzzled look on Violet's face. She wouldn't dare ask while the music played, itching to as she was, the first song would have to finish before she opened her mouth.

"Who is it?"

"You asked me to get it for you."

Track two kicked in, stalling the conversation again. Pink kept her going until side one was over, but the black had floored him. She wanted to hear more and had to accept he was incapable of both speech and movement for the foreseeable future. Furthermore, she wanted to know who the fuck was playing. Clever girl that she was, she glided round to the music centre and read for herself, letting out a scream which would have awakened the dead. The same scream almost spurred Pink to action. Almost, but not quite.

He managed to crawl into bed without playing side two, without undressing and without saying goodnight to Violet; all three of which upset her to varying degrees, but what could she do? She loved him to bits. Plus, he tolerated her, didn't he?

A domestic interlude.
(Showtime)

Pink had a feeling the flaps had malfunctioned as he came in to land. Luckily, the bed cushioned his fall, or was it a field of lavender? Going by the indent in the other pillow, someone else had landed before him. Violet was speaking softly, one of her monologues directed at Eight Ball. The cat absorbed every word, tilting his head this way and that as the tone of her voice altered. Pink yawned, stretched and scratched his balls in one fluid movement to let them know he had surfaced. If he had dreamt in the night, the landing was all he could remember.

Eight Ball appeared in front of him, stuck his nose to within a centimetre of his face and purred loudly.

"That's so good to see, Pinkee. He hasn't exactly been your best friend for a while."

"He stinks of fish. I think I preferred it when he was keeping his distance."

"I know you're joking, Eight Ball knows you're joking, but sometimes it's hard to tell with you. That's what confuses him. Shit, that's what confuses me, too."

"If you're both confused, how do you think I feel? The states I get myself into I deserve to be more confused than anyone."

"He-he. Hurry and put your clothes on. I want to hear the other side of that new record. Please, please, please."

Violet squealed as he continued to scratch while walking to the music centre, the thing was still switched on from last night.

The testers had been spot on with their verdict, that black was serious shit, the best in a long time. Selfishly, he regretted laying so much on Gwynneth. Maybe the triumvirate should have saved more of their stock for future consumption?

'Rumours' turned out to be a compelling piece of listening, wreaking every possible emotion from its music and lyrics. Pink taped it as usual on the second play.

"Why do you play it once before you record it, Honey? I'm really curious about that."

"I'm making sure it doesn't jump anywhere, some scratches aren't always visible."

"What if it jumps?"

"That's easy. Balance a coin, or a couple of coins on the arm of the stylus and try it again. If it plays ok then, it's ok to tape."

"Clever."

"I know, it's been said I'm too clever for my own good sometimes."

"He-he. I wish I had said that."

"You will, Kitten. Of that I have no doubt."

While side two was recording, he went to the shops for a paper and a pint of milk, dropping his laundry off at the same time. The lady in the bric-a-brac shop called him in to inspect a pile of records she had taken delivery of. He came away with two of them. Jackson Browne's 'For Everyman', of which he had only heard the title track, and Jim Capaldi's 'Short cut draw blood'. Brat played a track from that one regularly.

Kira appeared from nowhere and linked his arm, wanting to know when he would be going to the restaurant again. Pink opened his paper at the racing page and told her to be ready in half an hour, 'No more holes' had obliged at two and a half to one.

"You going out today, Honey?"

"To the restaurant, then maybe a couple of hours in the pub, see what the arrangements are for Clem's send off."

"Where's the restaurant? I've heard you talk of it, but I don't know where it is."

Pink explained the geography, telling her it was part of a converted school.

Violet squealed. "My sister and I used to go to a youth club in that building. There was a disco every Friday night, but they never played anything like the music you play. Not that I paid much attention to the music, we were more concerned with what talent was on show."

"So, you weren't into music then? Surely everyone's into some sort of music, even pop stuff?"

"I must have been like you on that without even knowing it. In one ear and out the other like when you have the radio on."

"You seem to be a bit of a music lover now, though; a bit of a connoisseur, even. What brought that on?"

"It's only since you came to live with me, Pinkee. I liked the way you really seemed to listen to your records and must have started to do the same. My sister was more into music than I ever was, but I couldn't tell you who for the life of me."

Pink laughed at that last utterance and Violet laughed along when she realised what she had just said.

"So, it's all my fault, is it?"

"Isn't it always?"

"I can't argue with you there."

"He-he. Anyway, I was saying, we were brought up not far from there, that's how I know the area."

"It's posh round that way, you must have come from money?"

"What makes you say that? I would never have called it posh. C'mon, Honey, why would you say it was posh?"

"They've got lids on their dustbins."

During the conversation Pink had been busy, eating his breakfast and rolling four joints, two of oil and two of best black. If Jenny wanted to get stoned, Jenny would get well and truly stoned.

Kira loved the Range Rover, saying she felt like royalty being perched so high above the smaller cars. Pink told her to try waving like the queen did, not expecting her to do so. It must have sounded more like a dare than a joke to Kira and her laughter as some waved back was a pure delight to hear.

Ash made a fuss of her, treating her to the same bear hug as he greeted Pink with. The girl was all business after that, firing questions from all angles and soaking up the answers like a sponge.

Pink almost had to drag her away when he'd finished his coffee, Ash's ears were ringing with her persistence. He wanted to pick up his winnings and he wanted a smoke. Kira talked his head off until he dropped her at the shop. He checked to see he hadn't gone deaf when she disappeared inside.

Planning ahead, he followed her in and asked Mira for three pies, the munchies would be sure to strike before long.

Armed with Pon's number, he stopped at the phone box and gave him a call, arranging to pick him up on his day off, Wednesday. They would have a drink and a smoke, but Pon would have to get the train back home.

Midday, and Elise was still in her dressing gown. Jenny had been to the shop so she had clothes on, after a fashion. The skirt would have made a good belt for someone else, not that it didn't look good on her. A tie-dyed t-shirt completed her attire, no bra, highlighted by the fact her nipples were protruding like coat pegs. Elise noticed them and gave one a playful tweak, confirming Pink's suspicions they were as much into each other as he was into them.

He laid the four joints on the kitchen table and spread his newspaper out while the girls washed the dishes. The more they frolicked and touched each other, the less interest he took in the paper, giving it up as a lost cause when Jenny moved in behind Elise and cupped a breast in each hand. In turn, Elise put one hand behind her back and up Jenny's short skirt; the mercury was rising, fast.

Casually, he selected a joint of oil and made his way to the lounge, his hard on restricting his gait. He tuned the radio to a half decent station, knowing Jenny didn't have much in the way of a record collection. When he turned, both girls were sitting on the couch and inviting him to join them. While Jenny toked on the joint he ran his hands under Elise's dressing gown, delighted to feel she was naked underneath, naked and moist. When the joint was passed he concentrated his efforts on Jenny, finding her equally receptive to his touch.

With the joint finished, both girls tugged at his clothes until all three were more or less naked. Pink didn't know where to look for the best, there was flesh in abundance and he only had the one pair of hands. The room was warm before the frivolities began, and now, it was a furnace. Pink slipped easily in and out of every orifice the girls surrendered to him, the perspiration almost turning to steam as they sucked and fucked with abandon, the girls quite happy to sample each others charms as well as Pink's.

They ended it breathless and in a heap on the floor, Pink being first to recover and lighting a joint of the black, being careful to have just the odd toke to himself and allowing his naked companions to go at it greedily. They wouldn't know the difference for five minutes or so, this was turning out to be more fun than he could have ever imagined.

Elise sat on the floor between his legs while Jenny did her best to share herself evenly. The black kicked in, leaving only the radio capable of functioning with any conviction. Jenny managed to ask if it was different dope, but apart from that, the music drew them into themselves.

Pink must have closed his eyes momentarily. When he opened them, he burst into laughter, couldn't help himself as framed in the living room doorway stood the evil witch. The girls followed his lead, they couldn't move, but they could laugh hysterically. When the witch moved towards them, the laughter suddenly stopped. Bea entered the room behind her, eyes swollen with tears. Someone sniggered and the laughter kicked off again, they couldn't help themselves; it was so contagious, infectious. Bea and her mother stormed upstairs and still the laughter continued, three naked bodies, helpless, hapless, thoughtless and so high they couldn't care less.

Pink, having smoked less than the girls, was first to break the deadlock, dragging his clothes on, kissing both girls where he could reach and leaving them to their fate. The scene had been self explanatory and nothing he could say or do would be able to rectify it for a long, long time.

He managed to steer the Range Rover to a car park near the Boulder, it was Saturday afternoon and packed to the rafters. He bellied up to the bar and caught Sara's eye, her beaming smile letting him know the spark was still there. The pint came at no cost to his good self, but she accepted the joint of oil he slipped to her and threw him a cheeky wink. The wink disappeared when half a dozen Blunts shoved their way towards the bar. Pink blew her a kiss and headed for the pool room, otherwise he would have been tempted to stand on a few toes. As mellow as the black had rendered him, the hackles still rose when he thought of the stress the young girl had endured.

A sea of long faces greeted him in the pool room. Of course, no dope around. One or two would have oil courtesy of Brat, but were wisely keeping it to themselves. The drought forced that upon them, usually it was share and share alike.

He followed Light Waite to the toilet, handed him the joint of black, asked for news on Clem's funeral and warned the dope hadn't come from him. Light understood.

Light and Heavy left the pub for five minutes, circled the block and returned all smiles. As loud as you please, Light asked Pink for a light, he had bumped into an old friend outside and scored himself a joint of black, best black according to his friend. Pink stood back and looked on as the masses crowded round, necked what was left of his pint and made himself scarce, his good deed done for the day.

He decided to take lunch at the Greek while he was in town. The surly waitress greeted him like an old friend, wiping the table as soon as he sat down and enquiring after his health, a huge change in her manner. Pink turned on the old charm, had her eating out of his hand; smiling, laughing at his humour and charging him for a cup of tea only instead of the pie chips and beans he had demolished. He hoped Jenny and Elise were making good use of the pies from the bakery, he sure as shit wasn't thinking of returning to lay claim to them. The waitress touched his arm as he gazed into her eyes, wrote her name and number on the pad and handed it over. Pink glanced and fell about laughing, apologising immediately when the surly frown reappeared on her face, now he had another Jenny to contend with. She smiled again, she looked a different girl when she did that. Pink gave her bum a squeeze on his way out and promised to check his diary.

The market was busy, he scored a pack of five tapes then joined with Bob the busker for a rendition of 'Honky Tonk woman'. More people wandered off than listened, so he threw fifty pence into Bob's open guitar case and left him to it.

Telling Kira he'd be ten minutes late again, he went home to listen to his new records, and to spend some time with Violet before she complained he didn't spend any time with her.

"Hi, Pinkee …. Rumours, please."

"I haven't heard any rumours lately."

"No, no, no. You know what I mean. Play Rumours for me …. please."

"I've got a couple more to listen to. I like Rumours as much as you do, but I think we should give these a spin; do you know what I mean?"

"Yes"

"Do you see where I'm coming from?"

"Yes."

"Are you with me?"

"Yes."

"Do you get the picture?"

"Yes."

"Are we on the same page?"

"Yes."

"Do you follow?"

"Yes."

"Am I making myself clear?"

"Yes."

"Do you understand what I'm saying?"

"Yes."

"Capishe?"

"Yes."

"Do you catch my drift?"

"YES, YES, YES. JUST PLAY SOME FUCKING MUSIC, PINK .... PLEASE."

"Violet Hiccup. Wash your mouth out with soap. Wherever did you hear that language? Certainly not from me."

"He-he. Stop it now. Play some music. What have you brought me?"

Pink played the Jim Capaldi LP, made a new matchstick brush and rolled a joint of oil. No more black today, his belly was sore from laughing and he had a shift to work.

No singing in the shower, either. He wasn't sure of the lyrics, although 'Johnny too bad' sounded familiar. Someone else had recorded it, but for the life of him he couldn't remember who.

Sleep came almost instantly. He'd had visions of the black playing games with his thought process and keeping him awake. Mercifully, it left him alone.

Violet wanted the Rumours tape played when he left for work with the album tucked under his arm. It didn't matter to her if she was left in silence until he returned; that's how desperate she was to hear it.

Brat handed over a wad of banknotes, telling him they had both profited from the oil. If there was any more of it around they could probably ask for and be given double. Pink promised some for next weekend, Easter, there would be even higher demand. Brat let him know he would be absent on Friday, a prearranged gig at the Flat Iron. In his place would be a very good pub rock band by the name of Quarantine. The Albatross crowd were very lucky to have them play there being that they were prevented from leaving the country to perform at a big festival in Holland. With their van emblazoned with their title, the customs officers suggested a name change, otherwise they would be confined to these shores indefinitely. Quarantined, in fact.

He arranged to meet up with Brat on Good Friday then the landlord of the Albatross asked Brat could he do Thursday night, easier for Pink, less running around. Yes, Thursday suited him just fine.

Sira and Kira stood in the middle of the bakery floor, arms folded across their chests and eyeing the clock on the wall. Just joking, but too bad if they weren't. Pink promised to make up the lost time tomorrow, which seemed to appease them. He then told them to make their own way home as he had a lot of work on. Finding himself sandwiched between two young ladies brought his earlier romp flooding back, wondering how Jenny and Elise had coped with the witch, and of course, Bea. What was the story with Bea and those puffy red eyes?

The girls were tickling him, they knew he wouldn't let them walk home. Between them, they locked the bakery. Kira claimed the front seat beside him although both of them could have fitted on quite comfortably.

It was Sira's turn to scan the time, wondering where they had got to, she couldn't shoo the girls out of the Range Rover quickly enough. Mr Rapati came out and asked was Pink ok to do all the running about tomorrow so Mira could have the car. He pretended to know nothing about such a proposition. Kira and Sira laughed, but Mira wasn't too sure.

Sira was as excited as ever, her man was another day closer. Yes, she had slept, but she hadn't stopped worrying about what the future had in store for them. Pink did his best to reassure her, subtly changing the subject and asking what was for his supper. The Rapati women were such fine cooks, he couldn't care less if he didn't eat another of Johan's curries.

Eight Ball made a beeline for Sira as soon as they entered the bakery, he had sneaked in unnoticed when her sisters were carrying on. The cat took her mind off her worries, curling up in a ball on her knee and allowing her to pet him. Pink, as usual, did all the work. He even had to sort the food out since Eight Ball showed no signs of moving. Sira managed to eat this time, claiming it was because she had cooked the meal herself, but Pink knew better; his little pep talk had brought her round to his way of thinking. That's how he perceived it, anyway.

A phone call from the football club with a large order of pies, saw Pink liaising with Mr Rapati and having the big clean put on hold until the order was filled. Pink would be on hand to deliver them and collect payment on Sunday afternoon.

Sira placed Eight Ball on the flour sacks when her shift was over, but he wouldn't settle. Realising she was going home, he headed for the door, deciding it was time for his prowl.

Pink wasn't tired when he dropped her off so he gunned the vehicle towards the restaurant. He still had the oil money in his pocket. Not wishing to confuse it with his own, he gave it to Ash for safe keeping. A joint of oil in the back kitchen and a chat with a couple of Ash's staff, he was ready to hit the road again. Ash gave him twenty more caps and told him the bottle was now on the half way mark. A quick flurry of mental arithmetic brought a smile as he drove. The bottle of oil, when sold, would recoup one half of their original outlay and they hadn't scratched the surface of the block stuff yet; how cool was that?

"Thank you, Pinkee."

"For what?"

"For 'Rumours'. It's beautiful, wonderful, thank you."

He wanted another joint of the black, but he also wanted to listen to all of his new Jackson Browne LP. If he smoked a joint of black, he would be incapable of flipping the disc for a while. Decisions decisions. He opted for the oil, easier to work with. Halfway through side two, he changed his mind, rolled a single skinner of black, let the record finish, flipped it back to side one, set the tape and sank into the couch. Violet appeared to have tears in her eyes, she didn't speak when his music played, but in the intervals between tracks, she enthused about the man's way with words. Pink had to agree, it had probably been said a billion times before, but the dude was a genius, no doubt about it.

He woke up on the couch again, this was becoming a bit of a habit. His mouth was dry, he had somehow managed to tuck one foot under his body and could no longer feel it. That didn't stop him from standing up to go for a piss, nor laughing uncontrollably when the numb leg wouldn't support his weight, causing him to topple like a felled tree. Luckily, he rolled with it and managed to escape without injury.

"You ok, Honey?"

"Eight Ball tripped me, I think it was deliberate. Did you see that?"

"Don't be silly, Eight Ball's out. You've only yourself to blame for that one."

"If it wasn't him it must have been you. Why did you do that, Violet?"

"Go to bed, Honey. You must have banged your head when you fell. You're confused."

"Ok .... but I want answers in the morning. You wont let me forget, will you?"

"No, honey, You get some rest. You'll feel a lot better for it. Can you manage ok?"

"Maybe if you could turn the blankets down for me, then jump in and warm the bed while I have a piss?"

"He-he. C'mon. You're tired, Honey."

Funnily enough, when he entered the bedroom the blankets were indeed turned down. Violet giggled from her perch on the wall, perhaps she would join him later?

CHAPTER 32

Where did the day go?

Pink filled the spliff with lavender leaves. He knew he wouldn't get high off it, but he loved the smell, had become accustomed to the smell. The sheer horror of what he was doing had him sitting bolt upright in bed and sweating like a stuck pig. He had smoked many strange things in an effort to get high; tea leaves, dried banana skins and hemp to name but a few. Lavender, he knew where it fitted, where the notion had come from, but he didn't fancy smoking it. He would leave that to some other experimentalists, his guinea pig days were well and truly over.

The overpowering scent of the stuff filled his nostrils as he came to, evidence Violet had been there, or thereabouts.

"Ah, what kind of temper are we in this morning?"

"I don't know about you, but I feel hot to trot."

"I hope that means you feel good, Honey."

"Let me have a joint and I can let you know for definite."

"A joint before breakfast?"

"Before, during and after."

"It'll be that funny oil then, not best black?"

"Clever girl."

"That would mean we can have some music, you left the tape running last night, do you remember?"

"I've slept since then. Good job you remembered."

"So, you've still got side two of that Jackson Browne record to tape, am I right?"

"Like I said, I've slept since then, but if you say it is so, I reckon you'll be right."

"Goody, goody goody."

Pink took the hint, rewound the tape to the end of side one, flipped the disc and began recording. Violet hummed along. Like Pink, she wasn't too sure of the words yet; again like Pink, she would have them all before long or her name wasn't Violet Hiccup.

The fridge held most of the ingredients necessary for a huge fry up, a couple of rounds of toast being all he would need to add. Violet left him to it, preferring Jackson Browne's company. She had come a long way musically in a few short weeks and Pink gave himself a pat on the back for that. Now, if he could only manage to talk her into doing some housework his life would be complete.

Moraji and Kira were on bakery duty, running the big order of pies for the football club. Pink's services weren't required until two o'clock; he was to help with the delayed big clean after delivery, so he drove out to see if his favourite police constable had anything on, in every sense of the word. As luck would have it, her shift began at four o'clock, which meant she had time to play. She was naked and had made a start on her own before Pink could build a joint; mind you, all she had been wearing was a flimsy dressing gown. Pink undressed while she toked greedily on the joint, he had inadvertently forgotten to mention it was space travel strength. Not to worry, she would find out soon enough. He found a half decent radio station and smiled as Louise ran the joint under her nose, the realisation spreading across her face; that's what made her a good copper.

Their lovemaking had to be a good deal less frantic than was the norm. Louise tried her best to co-operate, but the fast acting black rendered her almost limp. Pink, with a slightly higher tolerance, helped himself to her charms. All she could do was moan appreciatively; that, and bear his full weight for a full forty minutes when they were done. When she could finally speak, Louise asked for a couple of joints worth to help her relax at the end of her shift. Pink obliged and warned her to be careful with it, the stuff was absolute dynamite.

A light lunch an hour and a half later, followed by another romp and this time both participants were better equipped to go at it, treating the neighbours to a torrent of encouraging obscenities before collapsing in a heap of arms and legs and breathlessness once more.

With an hour to kill, Pink decided to call on Dave to find out the full extent of the drought. Good news, the shortage was county wide, possibly nationwide. Pink and his fellow smugglers were sitting on a goldmine. He knew Gwynneth would be aware of the situation and would act accordingly, sure in the knowledge she could charge like a wounded buffalo without fear of recrimination. Lily made him a cup of tea and he chewed the fat with Dave and his dad, Frank, having to say no to joining them at Frank's club for a few drinks; he had business elsewhere.

He took Kira and Moraji home, both ladies using him as a sounding board to the extent he found it difficult to keep up with the conversation. Luckily, it was a short trip. The two main talking points, as usual, were Mira's date with Sanjeev and Johan's imminent return. He wondered aloud how they managed to conceal their excitement from Mr Rapati, especially on the latter subject. Moraji explained, they had a built in mechanism for such occasions. Not to be outdone, Kira ventured that her father was thick, anyway. Pink and Moraji howled with laughter. In all probability, Kira was the only person who could get away with such a statement.

Of course Sira wanted to know what all the merriment was about, but with her father admiring the lines of the Range Rover again, she would just have to wait for an explanation.

Since the Rapati car wasn't in the drive, Pink assumed Sanjeev would be enjoying his picnic by now. Sira confirmed this in as far as Mira had set off to meet him at the station and so far hadn't returned.

She asked Pink would he keep her company as she would be on her own for six hours. Sadly, he had to decline, a visit to the restaurant was on the cards, followed by a good nap. He did, however, roll up his sleeves and get stuck into the cleaning.

Ash and three of his staff were totally wasted in the kitchen. From the look of it they had set about the black as soon as work was over for the night and topped themselves up whenever one of them could manage to put a joint together. Pink had let himself in, only to be met by four fits of the giggles, very similar to the fits he himself had fallen foul of at Jenny's house.

At a guess, Ash hadn't made any effort to transfer what was left of the oil to caps. Pink put the kettle on for a coffee and built a large spliff for the gigglers, his nap would be sooner than planned. He reminded Ash to pick Johan up at the airport tomorrow, drank his coffee, passed the joint across the room to one helpless soul and made good his escape. The kitchen's inmates were on an entirely different planet so it didn't make sense to hang around.

"If you put 'Late for the sky' on the other side of the tape from 'The Pretender', we can listen to both LPs without interruption. What do you think, Honey?"

"You're not just a pretty face, are you?"

"So, will you do it for me? Huh? Will you do it for me, Pink?"

"Anything for you, Kitten. I'll have a joint and listen to side one with you, then it's nap time for me, Sira's on her own downstairs and I promised I'd help her out."

"Thank you, Honey. You look after your friends, don't you?"

"I try my best."

Eight Ball must have heard the conversation and rose from his slumbers, stretching as he walked between them. When Pink settled down after setting side two on to record, the cat curled up by his head and purred contentedly; they both nodded off at more or less the same second.

On waking, he had one of Eight Ball's paws on his forehead. Violet laughed quietly, happy to witness the closeness of her two favourite males.

Pink was allowed to choose the music for a change, plumping for J J Cale. It was shower time and 'Crazy Mama' was given the full treatment.

Clearly, Sira was no longer on her own, too much applause for that. Pink dressed, put Jackson Browne on for Violet and went to investigate. The Rapati car stood outside the shop, which would suggest Mira's date was over and suddenly he was curious to find out how she had fared.

He didn't have to wait long to find out. Mira had brought Sanjeev to meet her sister and he had made himself comfortable in one of the chairs. When Pink entered, he immediately rose to his feet and offered his hand while Mira made the introductions. He had heard a lot about Pink, all of it good. Of course, Pink couldn't reveal what he knew about Sanjeev, or where he had learned it from.

Seeing them together had him all of a quandary, unsure of his feelings, happy of course for Mira, and for himself for finding the decency to stand back having once harboured thoughts of debauchery where she was concerned. Sanjeev was friendly, open and obviously besotted with the girl; Pink couldn't fault him there. The concern had disappeared from Mira's face to be replaced with the serene calm she tended to display when all was well. He could tell Sira approved of the young man, she didn't have to say a word, her own worries had taken a back seat as she rejoiced in her sister's happiness.

When Pink set about emptying the ovens, Mira instinctively cleared a space on the large table, gently steering Sanjeev out of the way and causing him to grin widely; she was so relaxed she had forgotten it was her day off.

If further proof of Sanjeev's suitability were needed, it came when Mira announced it was almost time for his train. Sanjeeev pumped Pink's hand, saying how pleased he was to finally put a face to the name; he then gently shook Sira's hand. Mira threw her arms around Pink and kissed him on the cheek while Sanjeev grinned even wider than before, showing no animosity towards their friendship. Pink knew they would get along just fine.

Sira couldn't contain herself when they left, so happy for her sister. Once again, Pink did all the work while she gushed about the forthcoming nuptials with no mention of her own problems.

Mira reappeared half an hour later and the two girls nattered excitedly. Pink interrupted, asking which of them was responsible for his evening meal, or would he have to go to the Chinese takeaway. Sira looked at the clock, her shift was almost over. Mira offered to take her home and bring Pink's food, she would then work with him until midnight, Moraji could wait for her report on the big date. Before they left, Pink reminded Sira to make sure she rested, Johan would rather see her bright eyed and bushy tailed than jaded from lack of sleep. He was rewarded with a hug and a kiss for his concern, along with her sworn promise to comply.

Mira talked non stop about her day with Sanjeev. She had taken him into the countryside as Pink suggested, found a quiet spot for the picnic and spent a wonderful afternoon with him. Pink stopped her before she reached the sports pages and delighted in her laughter at that.

The leading headline from their time together, Mira insisted Pink was to be the first to know which was why she decided to share his shift, was that the wedding now couldn't come quickly enough for both of them. The correct observations of tradition, protocol and a slightly more modern approach bringing the couple to this mutual understanding. Sanjeev wasn't totally aware of the fact it was mostly down to Pink, but this was only the smallest of secrets to keep from her future husband.

The phone interrupted them. Pink, being closest, answered and heard Sanjeev at the other end. Mira made a play for the handset, but Pink held tight, offering his warmest congratulations to the young man and chatting away like an old acquaintance. Sanjeev carried the joke, going higher by the second in Pink's esteem. When he finally passed the phone to Mira, he pulled faces, embraced himself and blew kisses to put her off. Leaving them to it, he headed towards his stash to make sure everything was as it should be.

They were still whispering sweet nothings when he returned to empty the ovens, at that stage where neither wanted to hang up nor say goodbye. Again, Pink helped them out, taking the phone from Mira and telling Sanjeev he was highly embarrassed listening to them cooing. Sanjeev laughed heartily and asked Pink to say goodnight to his sweetheart for him. Pink's turn to laugh now and to delight in replacing the handset without returning it to Mira. She feigned horror at his actions, but kissed him on the cheek anyway, admitting she had been running out of things to say. Not to Pink, though, following him around while he filled the ovens and talking non stop of her plans for the future. Having met her intended, he felt much better about how things had worked out for her.

What with all the excitement, supper was late. They tucked in, Pink's ears being afforded respite while they dined. Eight Ball honoured them with a visit and listened politely as Mira ran through her day for him. Pink had heard it all before so involved himself with the baking.

Eight Ball snuggled into his makeshift bed when he realised it was time for Mira to go home and Pink's left ear took the brunt of her chatter for the duration of the short trip.

Mr Rapati was disappointed to see it was his own car and not the Range Rover come to take him to work. He had five minutes with Mira while Moraji had a chat with Pink. All he could safely tell her was her eldest daughter seemed to be content and happy.

The little baker was still a little apprehensive about Johan's imminent return. Pink reminded him he would still be the same person, if perhaps slightly miffed to discover his secret was out. As long as people didn't make a fuss, everything would be back to normal soon enough. Mr Rapati then revealed his middle daughter appeared to be interested in Johan. Pink feigned mild surprise, suggesting she could do much worse for herself, he was sure Johan had the utmost respect for the entire Rapati family.

As he climbed the stairs to the flat, he asked himself, where did the day go? A so called day off, apart from helping out in the bakery, had positively flown by. A quick joint was called for, listen to some sounds then hit the hay.

"Have you seen Eight Ball, Honey?"

"A big black cat with a white circle on top of his head?"

"Yes."

"No."

"He-he. Is he in the bakery? He's been out for quite a while."

"Mr Rapati's bending his ear. I think he'll be a while yet."

The radio seemed to be doing a good job of entertaining them so he rolled an oil joint and told Violet about most of his day. She was glad of the company, Pink's busy lifestyle had put her nose out of joint a bit lately. He finished his spliff, sorted out his work clothes, gave Violet another ten minutes worth of chat and fell into bed exhausted.

Violet joined him almost immediately, massaging his neck and shoulders before slipping her hands beneath his body and massaging where he needed it most; they made love slowly for what seemed like hours. When he got up for a piss, the clock told him he had been in bed for fifty minutes only, the omnipresent scent of lavender lending credence to the reality of their activities, or the dream thereof.

CHAPTER 33

Return of the Prince

Pink called for a newspaper and steered the Range Rover down the narrow lane between the allotments. By the look of him, Towser hadn't been fed since Friday. He wondered if reporting the Blunts to the R.S.P.C.A. would inconvenience them in any way and decided against it. Guard dogs were ten a penny in that the Blunts wouldn't find it hard to replace Towser if he was taken from them.

Three stale bread rolls with a lump of cheese in each would keep the wolf from the door, in a manner of speaking. Those, and a five minute pep talk went towards improving the animal's mood.

He handed the keys to Mac and was told to hold on to them, the batcher was still under repair and a lot of concrete had to be poured. Mac was trying to get in front of the game since most of the workforce would be at Tony's funeral tomorrow.

A low loader blocked his exit from the site and a word with the driver gave him at least half an hour to play with. Luckily, the first pour was timed for nine o'clock so he would hide in the canteen and have a chat with Dave, maybe a cup of coffee too.

He was shocked to learn the low loader had come for the site boss's huge caravan, which would suggest Sandy had heard the full story of events leading up to the crash. Dave assured him that was the case. With working in the canteen, he picked up on a lot of things he perhaps shouldn't have been privy to. The same applied to Barry in the office, the old adage of the walls having ears ringing true.

Pink followed the low loader up the lane, happy to see it turn into the main road in the opposite direction to where he wanted to go.

Groover rubbed his hands in anticipation at the sight of Pink walking towards him, letting out a low whistle when the size of the order was revealed. Since the boss had been removed, a new boss probably wouldn't appreciate the need for the personal touch in ordering concrete so Pink assured Groover he would ask Barry to ring the order through, keeping both the work and the rake off going.

The first wagons were ready to roll as he headed back to the site. With fair weather and a steady supply, Mac would be well in front by the end of the day.

Barry called him to the office. Sandy had called and wanted a lift from the station at twelve o'clock. Mac asked him to jump on the tractor and ferry some steel around the site, the tower crane would be involved with the concreting all day. With the promise of an early summer still very much in evidence, it was a pleasure to do so. Finding himself down close to his own little allotment, he turned the soil over, scooped a couple of shovels full of raw sewage from a bed of the existing plant and spread them over his patch. Looking around, he realised he couldn't be observed from anywhere on the site, even from the tower crane. Hopefully, that would keep his crop from prying eyes.

After the morning break, Mac left the site in his car. Pink gave him five minutes to clear the area and gunned the Range Rover up the lane. Johan would be at the restaurant, be best if he could prime him before he met up with his boss. A slight detour and he was on the road out of town, windows open in the warm spring sunshine and the radio blaring at full volume.

Johan looked dog tired. After the hellos and good to see yous, Pink offered to stand in for him later, but he was keen to see his girl and refused the offer point blank; with thanks, of course. Ash had filled him in on the mass visit to meet the Prince. Pink gave him chapter and verse on subsequent events, reminding him to play it cool, surprised but cool. Johan was delighted at the popularity of the oil and with Pink's packaging ideas for its sale, looking on in amazement as Ash furnished a matchstick brush and built a joint.

Pink couldn't hang around, but promised to drop in on Johan at ten o'clock, help him out with his reception and interrogation.

Sandy wanted to see the wreck. Luckily, Tonka had it nose to the wall with all manner of unrelated junk surrounding it. Sandy took his word for it being a write off, but it could be made roadworthy with a new engine and a fair bit of body work. Pink asked how much to fix it then asked Sandy would he mind if he had the work done. Sandy had no qualms about that, even offering Pink some help with payment for the work. Pink refused, his winnings from the horses would just about cover the costs. He thanked his boss, winked at Tonka and told him to make a start on his vehicle.

Mac was still missing when they reached the site. Sandy asked Barry where he had gone, but he couldn't help. Taking pen and paper, Sandy wrote a brief note, stuck it in an envelope and told Barry to make sure Mac read it on his return.

With that, they were back in the Range Rover, heading first for the betting shop, then the Boulder for refreshments. Pink's tip for the day was 'Wellington boot', the only reference he could find to the building trade that looked like it might chase a place. Before he could advise Sandy should back it each way, he had gambled one hundred quid on the nose. Pink shuddered and refused to put a single penny on it for himself, certain his tipster days were drawing to a close, fast.

Sara was as pleased to see Sandy as she was Pink. The old man told her she looked so much prettier without the black eye, making her blush vivid pink. Pink tended to agree with his comments, but then he had always thought along those lines.

Lunch turned out to be the usual boozy affair, during which Pink wangled the following day off work, he wanted to attend Clem's funeral as well as Tanzi's. Sandy was happy with that, as long as Pink picked him up at one o'clock. He would make sure he was paid for the day, very generous. How could anyone ever have a bad word to say about working on a building site?

Also during lunch, he was afforded an insight into the nature of the new foreman, a no nonsense fellow who had worked his way through the ranks. If Sandy could vouch for him, who was he to argue? The introductions would be made after the Easter break.

After pouring Sandy onto his train and asking the guard to make sure he didn't miss his stop, he steered the Range Rover in the direction of the site, making it just in time to clock off and pick Towser's supper up. There was enough for two meals, but he threw the lot over the fence, remembering he had a day off tomorrow. Next week, it would be daylight at this time, with the clocks going forward for summer. He managed to drive home without incident considering he had devoured copious amounts of beer. Now, he was looking forward to his nap.

"God, look at you. You must really love your work?"

"Getsssh better every day, Kitten."

"He-he. Play some music for me and have your nap. You need to bake later."

"No more baking. Jo .... Jo .... Johan's back tonight."

"So, you don't have to go?"

"No .... yes .... yes. Just for an hour or so at ten."

"Oh, ok. I'll wake you up. If you play Jackson Browne for me."

"Done deal, Violet. Done deal."

For the first time he could remember, Sara was in his dream. She too wore lavender and strangely, she could massage his feet and his shoulders at the same time, what a girl.

Accompanying the Doobie brothers in the shower, he heard what sounded like an audience of hundreds applauding him from below. Curious, he dressed quickly and ran downstairs to see what the fuss was all about. All five Rapatis were there, dressed in their Sunday best, or the Indian equivalent of same. Johan would probably turn and run from such a reception, but it was too late to do anything about that. They would just have to wing it.

Cowboy time, ten to ten to ten to ten to ten. Johan entered the back door to the bakery and into a riot of colour. The surprise and puzzlement on his face was a good start, no need to fake it and quickly followed by the humour, telling all present it wasn't his birthday. The party spilled into the shop, the bakery being unable to accommodate the throng. The Rapatis talked almost as one, how was his trip, it was good to have him back, they had missed him, he was one of the family.

Johan continued in humorous vein, assuring them he had brought them all a little something back with him. With a little more room to breath, he dug in his bag and produced wrapped gifts for everyone. Mr Rapati was pumping his hand affectionately, the womenfolk smiled adoringly, Pink yawned loudly and started filling the mixer. Someone had to attend to the work.

Eight Ball came to investigate, saw Johan and ignored everyone else to get to him; he too had missed his friend.

Ten minutes later, the Rapatis piled into their car, but before they could leave, Pink asked Sira if she would sew a pair of work jeans for him. If she could stay behind, he would run upstairs for them and drive her home himself. Moraji encouraged her daughter to do as she was asked and instructed her husband to take the rest of them home. Mira and Kira blew kisses as they disappeared from view.

It took him all of the Jim Capaldi album to find the jeans and unpick Mira's work on them. He unwrapped his present and found a new bob cap, more in the way of a skull cap, multicoloured and a perfect fit. It was so comfortable he kept it on. The lover's appreciated the time together, Violet appreciated the bonus of some good music and Pink's company, offering up her thanks as he left the flat.

Sira looked so happy he didn't like to call time on the couple, but call time he did. Using his usual diplomacy, he stepped between them before they could go into another clinch.

Asking Johan would he be safe on his own, he drove Sira home. He even managed to slip a word in edgeways, which surprised him. All the kidology was about to begin now. Mr Rapati wouldn't know if he was coming or going, his womenfolk would see to that. Pink wasn't prepared to rest until his mission was complete; he wouldn't let everyone involved rest, either.

He told Sira to let her sister sew his jeans. Not that he couldn't trust Sira to do a good job, but he had witnessed Mira's skills with the needle at close quarters, better the devil you know. Sira kissed him, thanked him for arranging the extra time with her man and asked would it be ok if she didn't sleep tonight.

Johan had a joint of oil ready and waiting for his return. They talked at length about his trip and how easy it had been to export the goods from Goa. Masking the smell of the dope with spices was inspired thinking. A couple more trips like that and they would be rich men. Pink suggested, if his plans for Johan and Sira went according to plan, he should maybe show her his birthplace by honeymooning there. The smile on his friend's face told him he had hit on a good idea, but then, hadn't all of his ideas been good of late?

They talked well into the night. Pink was in no hurry to retire since his nap had refreshed him. He remembered telling Violet he would only spend an hour or so with Johan, but they had so much catching up to do. Since Violet no longer had any real sense of time, he reckoned she wouldn't be too bothered. Either way, he would soon talk her round.

Johan was enthralled to hear of Pink's exploits, saddened by the three deaths in one day and very keen to hear his new music.

Eight Ball hadn't left Johan's side, weaving under his feet as he worked. However, he must have had a hot date at three o'clock, disappearing into the night at five minutes to the hour.

Pink decided to call it a night. With two funerals to attend, he would be in need of a few hours sleep.

He smoked a joint and listened to the radio with Violet, telling her about the return of the prodigal and she didn't once complain about the length of his absence. Where oh where could he ever find a woman like that?

Sleep came instantly, instantly followed by the dream; he was at the graveside and surrounded by strangers. The only person he recognised was Violet, but Violet's name was spelled out in flowers on top of the coffin. He didn't know much about flowers, somehow he just knew they were violets. Violet's name was spelled out in violets. Try as he might, he couldn't snap out of it, he wanted to ask Violet about her funeral. He didn't care much if it upset her because now it had upset him. He tried to converse with Violet by the open grave, but she wouldn't even look his way. Someone tapped him on the shoulder, dead Tony, on one leg and using crutches. Tony hopped to one side to reveal Tanzi, spade at the ready to fill in the grave. Face to face with Pink, Tanzi pointed to his right. Pink followed the indicator and saw Clem, resplendent in bow tie and waistcoat, chalking his pool cue and laughing his head off. When he turned away, half of his face was missing.

That woke him up in a sweat, eyes wide open looking for the crowd, breathing a sigh of relief when it dawned on him he was alone; alone with Violet, the now reassuring aroma of lavender filling his nostrils.

"You ok, Honey? You were mumbling incoherently. I've been trying to wake you. Bad dream?"

"Where are you buried?"

"Why?"

"Tell me, I might want to put flowers on your grave."

"Something to do with the dream? Or was it a nightmare?"

"Where, Violet?"

"Hyndburn road cemetery."

"I'm going there tomorrow, twice. I'll keep an eye out for you."

"Twice? You said you were going once, and to the crematorium once for Tanzi."

"I have to attend Tony's funeral now. I wasn't going to bother. He'll be well represented, but I've decided to go."

"Must have been some dream."

"Trust me, it was."

"Ok, tell me about it when you're ready. Are you up now? Play some music if you are please."

Pink looked at the clock, that couldn't be the time, ten to seven, it would appear the dream hadn't been quite so instant as he had initially thought. He wouldn't sleep now so might as well do as he'd been asked, something loud. He didn't particularly wish to hear the call to prayers, not today.

CHAPTER 34

An unenviable hat trick

Pink left Violet with Alex Harvey and bounced downstairs to find Johan, still in the bakery and looking for an exit from the polite probing from Mr Rapati. The relief on his face when Pink interrupted and told him to go home to bed was priceless. Mr Rapati took it on the chin, accepting Johan would be jetlagged and ready for a good sleep; his questions could wait. Behaving completely out of character, he hugged Johan before sending him home, then asked Pink to drive him. Pink obliged, his intention had been to pick up a couple of leftover pies for Towser, but that could wait.

Johan seemed calm enough about his boss's questions. So far, they were easy enough to deal with, Pink had prepped him admirably and his obvious reticence to speak about his ancestry tended to limit the extent of the gentle probing. One thing, his wages had been almost doubled as a result of a suggestion from Moraji, apparently. Pink nodded knowingly. They both understood who wore the trousers in that family.

Dropping the keys off at the bakery, he remarked, speaking as a comparative outsider and really being none of his business, but he had noticed how close Sira and Johan had suddenly become. He hoped he wasn't speaking out of turn, but they seemed to enjoy each other's company. Mr Rapati remained silent for a moment, taking in what Pink had laid on him. He then shrugged his shoulders, telling Pink he would see what his wife made of it. Result, nothing wrong with a gentle nudge now and again.

Already the sun was warming the air and Towser wagged his tail as Pink approached on foot. He spent ten minutes with the dog, his parting words being it was a lovely day to be buried; not in humour, more a statement of fact. People, mourners looking back on the day would remember how warm it had been.

"You look a bit more at peace with yourself, Pinkee."

"I'm not looking forward to the day ahead of me."

"You'll be ok. Just don't get morbid about it. Promise me."

"I won't. I'll end up in the Boulder, there'll be humour aplenty at Clem's send off."

"That's the spirit, Honey."

"Was that humour?"

"Oh, spirit? I see what you mean, yes. Coming from me it would have to be, he-he."

Even though Nils Lofgren was playing full pelt, Pink didn't sing along in the shower. He wandered the flat with a towel round his waist, forced himself to eat something; fully dreading the thought of putting on the restrictive clothing he would be required to wear for the day. Dress trousers, sensible shoes and a white Ben Sherman shirt, all free gratis from the catalogue warehouse.

Four joints of oil fitted snugly into the pocket of the shirt, he couldn't see himself coping with the day ahead without a crutch of some sort.

"Do I look ridiculous in this get up, Violet?"

"You look very smart, Honey, but maybe you should find someone to tie your hair back?"

"I'll see if any of the girls are downstairs yet. You're right, it should be tidy."

"See you later, Pinkee. I'll be thinking about you."

"Don't wait up, Kitten. I may be some time."

Moraji dragged a chair outside, dug in her bag for a hairbrush and tied the best plait he had ever worn, at the same time telling him how clever he had been. Her husband had mentioned the earlier conversation concerning Johan and Sira. Moraji had considered it for all of five minutes before telling Mr Rapati she would monitor the situation, stressing it wouldn't be a bad thing if they became serious.

He couldn't avoid it. While sitting at the traffic lights, Jenny and Elise banged on his window. Thankfully, it was only to kiss him and have a laugh about their recent romp. Bea had forgiven them after her initial shock, but the old witch was still banging on about their outrageous behaviour. Bea had moved back in and the girls were on the lookout for a flat to share. Pink promised to keep an eye out for them.

Feeling a little happier now about life in general, he parked the Range Rover near the church and crept in to the back pews, finding Mac and a few others from the site in attendance.

The service was mercifully short and Pink's attention kept being drawn towards the widow, wondering how she would cope. A good looking woman with no kids on show, he reckoned someone would be sniffing round before long; after a reasonable bout of grieving of course. Funny what runs through ones brain at funerals.

They were all invited back to Tony's local pub after the internment. Pink declined, but most of his workmates went along, no point in wasting a day off.

He didn't go to the graveside, preferring to sit in the nearby park and offer up a spliff in memory of Tony. He had only known him for a couple of weeks. If there really was a God up there, then God bless him.

He sat in the vehicle for half an hour with the radio on. The church for Clem's send off was five minutes walk away and he knew he would have to get there in plenty of time. Clem was popular, no one had a bad word to say about him, alive or dead. The church would be full and standing.

Dressed as he was in his finery, he attracted a few double takes from people of his ken, but no more than he afforded them in turn. To a man, they had all made the effort.

As predicted, the church was ram jam. He stood in the aisle with Reg, Cowboy and the Waites. This time he knew the widow, having felt the sharp edge of her tongue on more than one occasion, being held responsible for Clem missing meals or appointments through being in his company. This was the reason he hadn't been round to offer his condolences, but he would do so at the send off in the pub. Surely she wouldn't shout at him there?

He couldn't make it stretch that far. Sally, Clem's wife, dragged him from the safety of his friends, walked him as far as the pulpit and insisted he should deliver a eulogy to his friend.

Totally unprepared, half stoned and aware all eyes were upon him, he cleared his throat and recounted Clem's prowess as a drinking partner, as a pool partner, as a loving and faithful partner to Sally, a loving, doting father to his son and daughter. His passing was a sad loss to everyone present and he would be greatly missed.

Sally was sobbing, others joined in, she clasped Pink to her, covering his shirt in liquidised make up and tears. Clem's kids hugged him, thanked him for his words, then Sally asked him to help carry Clem to the hearse; he would have liked that.

At the graveside, Clem's sister sang 'Amazing Grace'. If there were any dry eyes after Pink's speech, they were wet with tears now.

He made his excuses to Sally, he had yet another funeral to attend, but he would make it to the Boulder later.

Seven acquaintances squeezed into the Range Rover beside him, it was the least he could do to drop them off at the pub. He had a call to make in town anyway, then change his shirt before picking Sandy up at the station.

"How's it going so far, Honey?"

"Not good. I had a speech forced on me. I was a bag of nerves, but I don't think anyone really noticed."

"Poor you, but I'd say you're over the worst of it?"

"I wouldn't swear to it, I've a feeeling Sandy's going to come over all emotional about Tanzi. Does this shirt look ok?"

"Yes, I like the colour. I could really go for you in that."

"What …. with a knife?"

"He-he. Trust you. Have a nice joint to calm you down."

"Ok, Violet. See you later."

He put what was left of the cap of oil in his pocket, the Waites had bemoaned the fact there was no smoke around, he would slip it to them quietly at the Boulder. Same script, they would be sworn to secrecy as to its origin.

Sandy's train was bang on time. He looked much older than his years, but brightened when he saw Pink. Could they drop by the bookie's, his horse had dead heated first place with another outsider and he had a lot of money to pick up. At least half of Pink's luck seemed to be still riding high. To think he had wanted to suggest an each way bet. Of course he was asked to select another while they were there and, determined to test his no lose streak to the limit, he chose a rank outsider 'Digger's lament', from a field of eighteen. Sandy put fifty quid each way on it, handed Pink a wad of notes and told him he was ready for the crematorium.

Pink had a word with the non-denominational dude in charge of the place while Sandy went on inside. When the curtain opened on Tanzi's coffin, his wildflower bedecked spade lay squarely on the top, courtesy of Pink. The service was short and sweet, only the dude, Sandy and Pink attended. Sandy collected the urn and asked Pink to drive him to the site, where he scattered the ashes to the winds. Tanzi would have liked that.

Of course Sandy wanted to see his old friend off with a drink in the Boulder, but Pink explained there was already a send off in full swing there. Seeing Sandy's disappointment at this, he decided they should go, his friend had buried a friend same as everyone else that day, no reason why he shouldn't be allowed to drink there.

With that, he ended up in the Boulder earlier than planned, finding it packed to the rafters, just like the church earlier. Many handshakes were exchanged as he fought his way to the bar. He caught Sara's eye and was supplied with two pints right away. He introduced Sandy around when they managed to move anywhere, slipped Heavy the part cap of oil when he was sure no one was watching and ended up sharing some floorspace with Dave and Barry. When Sandy braved a trip to the bar, he lit a spliff and shared it with them before anyone else cottoned on to the fact it was burning. Sally and the kids appeared from nowhere and thanked him again for his words. She was about to unveil the buffet in the pool room so Pink followed her, thinking it was about time he ate something.

He filled a plate for Sandy as well as himself. With no spare hands, he asked Groover to slip the offered envelope into his back pocket, knowing there would be no need to count it.

Sandy was telling a group, including Barry and Dave, about Pink's floral tribute to Tanzi with the spade. They, in turn spoke of his eulogy to Clem. He did his best to play it down, going so far as to refuse offers of alcohol. He did intend getting hammered, but later, after he saw Sandy safely to his train and dumped the vehicle at home. Sandy already had a sway on. Pink had caught sight of the hip flask over the course of the day and reckoned that would be the old man's way of getting through it.

Since buying the first round, he hadn't put his hand in his pocket. With the intention of rectifying the oversight, he headed for the bar, taking note of the fact two Blunts and an associate were giving him the evil eye. For some reason he noted the time, six thirty, then thought of asking them if they had a problem. Realising it was neither the time nor the place, he put it on the back burner, but he knew they were talking about him. They would keep.

He had to half carry Sandy from the pub, even more so when he hit the fresh air. The old man sang his praises all the way to the station. Pink could do no wrong in his eyes.

Making sure the guard knew where to deposit him, he saw the train out and headed home for a spliff and to change into his jeans for comfort.

Why was the bottom door open? Closer inspection showed it to have been forced. Creeping upstairs, he saw the top door was also open, but he had never ever locked that one. Quietly, he ascended the stairs, if whoever had broken in was still hanging about, he was in for a surprise.

"Oh, Pink. It was horrible. They knew you had drugs and maybe money. They looked everywhere."

He put two and two together while surveying the damage. The settee was upside down, the backs were off all four speakers, records were out of sleeves and the carpet had been uprooted from the far corner where there was no furniture. The bedroom had been well and truly turned over, mattresses separated, drawers emptied with clothes strewn all over the floor. The same in the kitchen with cupboard contents everywhere. The stench hit him as he entered the bathroom. Again, nothing in its rightful place, plus, something which definitely didn't belong. Someone had taken a shit in the shower tray.

Holding his composure admirably, he confronted Violet.

"Three of them? Right?"

"Yes."

"Describe them. No, wait. I'll describe them. One ugly fat bastard wearing a garish yellow shirt, one skinny runt with missing teeth and the other, red hair, long, with trousers at half mast. Am I right?"

"Yes, the fat one was called Chubby, or Tubby."

"Who shit in the shower?"

"The fat one."

"Did they take anything?"

"Two bottles of cider."

"Nothing else?"

"Not that I could see, they were very disappointed."

"Me too, Violet. Me too."

"What do you mean, Honey? You seem very calm about it?"

"What did you do?"

"What could I do?"

"You're a ghost for fuck's sake. Why didn't you do some poltergeisting? I mean, that would be the natural thing to do in a situation like that."

"I …. I …. didn't think. Please don't be angry with me, Pink. I was scared. Really scared."

"Scared? A fucking ghost? Scared? I've got a resident ghost and she's scared. I've a good mind to have you exorcised."

"I've said I'm sorry. I didn't know what to do. Please, Pink. Don't talk like that."

"Where's Eight Ball. Was he in when they came?"

"No …. but he's been in since. He's ok."

Pink set about correcting the furniture, gingerly picking the shit up with the aid of a plastic bag, flushing it down the toilet and scrubbing the shower tray clean. That done, he left the rest as it was, didn't bother to get changed, locked the top door, jumped into the Range Rover and headed towards the Boulder with murder in mind. Maybe not murder, exactly, but something very, very close to it.

Calm as you like, he rejoined the wake, accepted a pint from Dave and scanned the room. Chubby and his pals were by now three sheets to the wind, staggering around and being their abusive, obnoxious selves. Pink excused himself when Chubby lurched towards the toilet, followed him in as the door closed and rabbit punched him on the back of the neck, forcing him forward and causing him to topple and crack his head on the thin end of the cubicle door. He landed with his head above the toilet bowl and shortly thereafter had Pink standing on his back, forcing him down the pan; again and again and again. Someone entered, Barry, saw what was going on, said nothing and turned back into the room. Pink continued with the business at hand, or to be more precise, at foot, booting the shit out of the offensive lout. Mostly for himself, but sparing a thought for his friend Sara.

Luckily, he tired, or he would surely have killed the fucker. He slipped back into the room to find Barry and Dave by the door, keeping an eye out. They shepherded him to the middle of the room where the Waites stood and joined in conversation with them. Two minutes later, Chubby crawled on his hands and knees from the toilets, tried to stand and fell into another group, some of them women; who screamed at the sight of him covered in blood and wet through, his yellow shirt resembling more of a tie dyed ensemble.

Light Waite laughed under his breath, saying it couldn't have happened to a nicer chap. No one argued with his reasoning.

Pink decided he had a date and would leave as soon as he finished his pint. Dave and Barry looked at each other knowingly.

Timing his exit, he reached the door ahead of Chubby and his assistants. He remarked some people couldn't hold their drink and let the door swing back on the crown of Chubby's forward leaning head.

Still seething and stone cold sober, he drove to Doc's, jump started the van, Doc's wife was at the Boulder, and headed for the building site.

He soon found what he was looking for, bolt croppers. Next stop was the allotments, one allotment in particular.

Towser didn't seem to mind the fact he was trespassing, not when he recognised him. Nor did he mind when Pink began emptying the shed box by box. He didn't know what was in the boxes and he didn't much care. If the Blunt's found it necessary to store them here they had value of some sort.

Towser followed him around like a lost puppy, wagging his tail and getting underfoot. Pink decided he couldn't leave him there to face the music, the Blunt's would probably kick the shit out of him for allowing this to happen. He introduced the dog to the passenger seat of the still running van and told him to stay. Returning to the shed, he found some newspaper, piled it against an old sofa and set it alight.

He could see the flames spreading in the rear view mirror as he drove away, but he still wasn't satisfied, not by a long way.

Stopping a safe distance from the allotments, he investigated the boxes. Cutlery, silver cutlery, not stainless steel. Sets of thirty six pieces in presentation boxes, nice, but not nearly enough by way of compensation. Forty boxes, he would stash five in the bike shed and take the rest to Fester; one set would serve as a decent wedding gift to Mira.

He stuck his head inside the bakery door. Johan was fast asleep so he left him to it, closed the door quietly, jumped in the van and headed out of town.

Braking suddenly, he turned back towards the Blunt household, an idea taking shape, a fiendish plan of retribution and havoc.

Pulling up a street away, he armed himself with a screwdriver, sneaked to the front of the Blunts' house and punctured one rear and one front tyre on their van. Assuring Towser he would come to no harm, he tied a piece of cord to his collar and fastened it to the Blunts' letterbox, then stepped into the shadows to observe.

Towser's activity alerted the household and Pink counted them out one by one. They sussed immediately something was wrong at the allotment, no one could call them fools. Ignoring Towser, they piled into the van and managed to drive all of ten feet before realising there was also something wrong with their transport. With no van, they had no choice but to set off for the allotment on foot, already arguing among themselves as to who was to blame.

Very kindly, they left the door open, saving Pink the trouble of breaking in. He led the dog inside, looked at the clock on the mantle and gave himself twenty minutes to conduct his business. The Blunts being the Blunts, there would be all manner of pickings to be had before he finally torched the place.

Bedrooms first. He flipped the mattresses, rummaged through the drawers and lifted the beds clean up from the floor. Nothing much in the way of valuables, but all combustible. In the bathroom, he resisted the urge to shit in the sink. No, he would save that for the kettle downstairs. If they salvaged it after the fire, they would be sure to enjoy their cuppa. He had a piss though in the proper place. Looking down, he noticed one of the bath panels had come away slightly. With fingers in the gap, he managed to take it off completely, revealing a treasure trove of jewellery, baubles of every description, masses of the stuff.

After a few minutes of contemplation, all bets were off. He hand picked several items, replaced the panel, straightened the bedrooms, gathered up Towser and headed for the door. There would be no fire, no shit in the kettle, no one would know of his intrusion, no one but Louise. The Blunts had given her a dog's life in the past, she would enjoy finding red hot jewellery in their possession.

He pulled the front door closed, hoping they had all forgotten their keys in their haste, a little added bonus.

With Towser occupying the front seat in the van again, they set off once more in the direction of Fester's. A box of cutlery under his arm, he banged on the door. Twenty minutes later, Towser had a new home, Fester had been on the look out for a decent guard dog. With Pink's glowing reference he was awarded the gig and assured of a more comfortable lifestyle than he was used to of late. Still, he fretted when Pink said goodbye. A few words in his ear had him sitting at his new master's feet and wagging his tail contentedly.

The van's engine stalled as he attempted to get going again. When he knocked on Fester's door for help, Towser barked loudly, showing off his credentials. Fester hooked up the jump leads, gave Pink a wave then went inside to make a fuss of his new partner.

Pink killed the engine as he turned into Doc's street, allowing the van's momentum to take it up the drive; still no lights on in the house, no one would know he had ever been near the place.

Louise was none too pleased about being rudely awakened by the phone, even when she realised it was Pink; a five o'c;ock start will do that to a person. However, what he had to convey had her sitting up in bed and reaching for her notebook. If she had to be knocking about at five, a dawn raid would be the ideal way to start the day. Making Pink promise to visit soon, she dived back under the blankets; but she wouldn't sleep, not now.

"I'm really sorry, Honey. I was frightened. I couldn't think straight. I've never tried to move anything. My God, they really put the wind up me; please tell me you didn't mean what you said?"

"What did I say?"

"About exorcism. Tell me you didn't mean it? I couldn't bear it if you did that to me."

"It was definitely an option at the time, Violet, believe me. I mean, all you had to do was show your face and the fuckers would still be running."

"It wont happen again Pink, promise."

"We'll see. I'm for bed. You coming?"

"He-he. That's my Pinkee. I'll be there shortly."

No dreams and no smell of lavender. Eight Ball landed beside him in the night soaking wet, but Violet stayed away.

CHAPTER 35

Scare tactics

Pink covered his ears at the sound of the alarm, then, recalling last night's events, leapt out of bed. The flat was upside down. It wouldn't take long to fix, but he wanted it done before he went to work. He burned lavender scented joss sticks in every room, for no other reason than to rid his mind of the realisation he'd had visitors, unwelcome visitors.

Violet held her position on the wall, Eight Ball at her feet like in the old days. She wasn't sure of what to say so said nothing; not to Pink, although she kept up a whispered conversation with the cat.

For the first time since he started at the site, he left the house without breakfast, the clean up process had taken longer than expected. At ten to eight, he said a curt goodbye to Violet, jumped in the Range Rover, called for a paper; stopped himself from going down the lane to the allotments and headed for work.

He made a beeline for the tradesmens' table in the canteen, finding one who was a time served carpenter and arranging for him to fix his door; put a deadbolt in to fend off any future invasion.

The workforce was no sooner out on site than the heavens opened, making everyone scurry back to the canteen. The join between the two portocabins had finally given way, with water seeping down the walls and forming puddles on the floor. Mac asked

Pink to collect some of the roofing felt he had advised some time ago, and he in turn asked could he take Chocolate to fix his door while they were rained off. Chocolate, so named by his mates because he loved himself; thinking it an offence to walk past a mirror without checking his hair was just so, dived into the passenger seat and asked to be taken to a hardware shop for the lock after first inspecting the damage. Pink left him to it and drove to the Greek café. He had no intention of buying the felt, plenty owed him favours, there would be no problem acquiring the right amount. Word had spread about Chubby Blunt, someone had put him in hospital, and not only that, the Blunts had all been arrested in a dawn raid. According to Stef Johnson, who was to supply the felt, they were still in the cells, but no one knew why. Pink made out it was all news to him, inwardly smiling at the good result, but he wasn't finished with the Blunts, not by a long way. They had picked on the wrong dude this time.

Jenny scowled at everyone bar Pink. Stef noticed and shook his head in disbelief; he, among others, had been trying their best with her. He went to his van and passed Pink half a roll of felt, he wouldn't need it today, not if the rain persisted.

Chocolate had made a good job of the lock. Pink ran upstairs and brought down a bottle of cold cider, which they shared along with a joint of oil. He wouldn't accept payment for his work, simply glad to be away from the site for an hour, drinking cider and toking on a spliff. Pink told him he was alright, even if he did have a daft name.

Back on site, Pink had a coffee and an early, or late breakfast while the felt was applied. Dave and Barry joined him to ask what the problem had been with Chubby last night. He couldn't say he'd been burgled without quoting Violet as proof, so he told them Chubby had had it coming for some time, last night had presented the opportunity and it seemed a shame to waste it. Barry and Dave nodded knowingly. How many people could say that about any one of the Blunt family?

Pink further entertained them with news of their incarceration, the result of a dawn raid. Sadly, no further information was available at this time, but they could bank on it being true.

Mac wanted him in the office, Sandy was on the phone, he was to pick him up at twelve and take him to another site about six miles away; and by the way,' Digger's lament' ran in fourth. They had money back at a quarter of the odds.

Pink put the phone down and smiled. '*They*' had money back. Sounded good to him.

Another coffee while the rain hammered down. Patsy joined him for a quiet word, did he have any plans for Saturday morning? Pink had a good think, nothing that couldn't be put off. In that case, how would he like to earn a few quid?

Patsy had his attention now. The site would be closed as of end of play Thursday, closed until the following Tuesday. Patsy had earmarked at least one wagon load of scrap metal, some of which would have to be cut down in size. If Pink could man the tower crane, bring it all together and load it into Patsy's mate's wagon, the Easter weekend could turn out to be very profitable. Agreed, done deal. No hesitation, Saturday morning it was, ten o'clock on the dot.

Now he was restless. The others seemed happy to be doing nothing while it rained, but they were tied to the site. Pink, on the other hand, had become accustomed to the freedom afforded him through being in charge of the Range Rover. Eleven o'clock and he was looking for an escape clause, he would suggest to Mac the Range Rover needed a good wash. Hold the phone, cancel that thought, the vehicle would be clean enough in the rain, a goddess stood framed in the doorway. Of course, Abby's daughter, home from her studies and ready to start work after Easter.

Ever the gentleman, Pink escorted her through the canteen to the service hatch, aware all eyes were on stalks. It wasn't every day the site was graced with such a vision. He hung around waiting for an introduction, but upon laying eyes on each other the two women kicked off with the verbals. Apparently, they didn't see eye to eye about something or other. Pink didn't fancy hanging around to find out what, he had a boss to pick up.

Sandy looked refreshed considering he had been legless last night, he fancied the hair of the dog, but Pink convinced him to get his site visit out of the way before imbibing. A suggestion Sandy bowed to as common sense.

The other site was smaller than that local to Pink, a pipeline connecting two existing water treatment plants. Pink accompanied Sandy on the tour, being introduced as his right hand man; maybe he was at that. Whatever, he was afforded every courtesy by the foreman and site boss.

They had a cup of tea in the office and Pink studied the form while Sandy conducted his business.

With the site boss doing his utmost to impress and Sandy gagging for decent refreshment, Pink wrote 'Pipe and slippers' on a piece of paper and passed it to him. Sandy smiled, thanked Pink for reminding him and made his excuses to the fawning boss, laughing aloud as they made good their escape.

At the betting shop, Sandy split the winnings down the middle. Pink didn't argue, but put a fair wedge on the horse du jour while his luck seemed to be holding out.

The Boulder was theirs and theirs alone. Pink had expected the rained off roofers to be present, but Sara hadn't seen hide nor hair of them. Still, she was happy to have Pink and Sandy to herself, being so very fond of Pink and a big fan of Sandy's old fashioned good manners. Whispering, she asked Pink if he knew anything about Chubby's altercation in the toilets last night. All Pink could do was wink, giving nothing away.

Sandy persuaded her to run to the chip shop for three portions of fish and chips, then invited her to join them. This she happily did, providing half a loaf of buttered bread as accompaniment. Half an hour later, Sandy nodded off where he sat. Sara locked the front door and asked Pink for some assistance in the cellar, a request he couldn't refuse.

They only made it as far as the bottom of the stairs, ripping at each other's clothes like people possessed, no time for finesse or foreplay. He had to cover her mouth to stop her from waking Sandy and from alerting either or both of her parents. She dropped to her knees as he was about to unload and he was quite happy to refrain from covering her mouth then.

Sandy rallied and ordered another round, making sure to include Sara as thanks for the lock in. The rain continued to hammer down as they vacated the Boulder. Sandy asked to visit the site, just to show his face. The place was deserted, Mac had sent everyone home, giving the day up as lost to production.

Pink headed for the railway station by the scenic route, checking out the ashes of the Blunts' shed as he drove through the allotments. Sandy thought they were taking a shortcut and Pink smiled serenely to himself.

He spent an hour with Ash, working out his visit to the bakery to see the Prince and to order his bread products. A lot of acting would still be required. Ash knew of flats for rent local to the restaurant and wrote down the phone number. Pink would relay it to Jenny and Elise, the least he could do.

The sound of the deadbolt when he turned the key gave him reassurance. Anyone wishing to break in now would have to make a hell of a noise to do so, perhaps he should get Chocolate to fit one to the bike shed? He turned the key again to lock the door, thinking it might be advisable to let Mr Rapati know he'd had visitors. He told Mira instead, assuring her the door had been fixed with a new lock. Mira had news for him, a date had been set for the wedding. She laughed at the surprised look on his face when she revealed it would be two weeks from Saturday, one hundred miles away and close to where Sanjeev lived. Pink wiped the smile from her face immediately by asking was she pregnant. His turn to laugh, but she wasn't long in joining in. He made a mental note to buy some expensive wrapping paper for her present, gave her a kiss and returned to the flat, feeling a nap coming on.

For badness, he played Comus, 'First utterance', knowing Violet wasn't over keen on it. No matter, he was asleep within seconds.

Something woke him, someone pounding at the door. Still half asleep, he stumbled downstairs to find Pon standing there, resplendent in frock coat and dog collar. Shit, with the excitement of the last couple of days he'd completely forgotten about his friend, but surely he was earlier than arranged? Pon explained he had been in the area administering last rites and couldn't be bothered going home to get changed.

With mischief in mind, Pink showed him in, remembering his last words to Violet were a threat to have her exorcised. He touched on the subject right away as soon as Pon sat down. Violet wouldn't show her face, he knew that, and managed to stay on the topic for ten minutes before producing a joint of black and playing his 'Cry Tough' tape. Five minutes later Violet would have realised the situation. Pon sat on the settee, swilling cider, toking on a nasty joint of best black and swearing like a trooper, but it was fun while it lasted. The two men caught up; smoked, listened to some old soul music, Pon's favourite, and put the world to rights.

After the initial dumbing down effect of the black, the two men reminisced, recounting old exploits and different scrapes they had jointly been involved in. The evening flew by. Pink offered to drive his friend home, but Pon insisted a lift to the station would suit him fine. If Pink could bite off a couple of joints worth of that black for him, he would be a happy man.

Pink left the tape running for Violet, Frankie Miller to be exact, Pon asked why and he explained it was for Eight Ball. Eight Ball had shown his face briefly, sniffed at Pon's outstretched hand and disappeared into the bedroom, presumably to sit with Violet.

Pink took Pon round to the bakery to introduce him to Johan and found Mr Rapati in residence. Quick as a flash, he introduced Pon as the celebrant Mira had asked him to provide for the forthcoming nuptials. Mr Rapati knew his humour by now and collapsed laughing into one of the chairs, eventually managing to rise and shake Pon's hand. Pink asked where Johan was and was surprised to learn he was walking out with Sira. Moraji had worked her magic on the baker; he had no qualms, not now, now he knew of Johan's ancestry. Result.

Halfway down the road, they came upon the young lovers and Sira almost dragged him out of the window before realising he had a passenger. The introductions were made, rather hurriedly, Pon was about to miss his train if they didn't get a wriggle on.

Johan was walking on air, going about his job like a man possessed, dancing between the ovens and the table, unable to contain his delight at his acceptance to the fold. If he was happy with his lot before, he was ecstatic now, all down to Pink and no mistake. Pink played it down, inwardly patting himself on the back; that's what friends were for.

They had a joint, mainly to calm Johan down, it would take some time for it to sink in, but already Mr Rapati had changed his address from 'my boy' to 'my son'.

"Bastard, you fucking bastard, Pink. I could kill you. I might just take up poltergeisting now. Maybe you should put a lock on the knife drawer? I thought you had brought that priest in to get rid of me. I really did."

"Whatever gave you that idea? I sometimes wonder what goes through that head of yours, Violet."

"You knew what you were doing even if you won't admit it, you knew the effect it would have on me."

"I'm not sure I follow your drift. That meeting with Pon had been arranged for some time, so long ago I had completely forgotten about it."

"Pon? .... What sort of a name is that for a priest?"

"His full title is Father Pon Mysoll. He was destined to become a man of the cloth with a name like that, wouldn't you agree?"

"I never know when to believe you. Will you play 'Rumours' for me please, now that you've calmed down a bit?"

"I'm always calm, me. When am I not calm?"

"Last night. You had murder in your eyes last night."

"That was an exception to the rule. I managed to dispel all of the anger, quite satisfactorily as it turned out."

"I won't dare to ask how you did it. I'm just so relieved you did because I was frightened, frightened for you."

"Rumours it is. I think I'll have a spliff before bed, just for a change, and some toast, I haven't eaten for a while."

"He-he. That's what I like to hear, back to normal. I love you, Pinkee. I truly do."

Eight Ball joined them, looked from one to the other and shook his head. Raising his eyes heavenward, only Violet heard him muttering to himself. 'Humans'.

CHAPTER

36

One more notch on the bedpost, and a narrow escape

Pink tossed and turned. He should have been content. All was well within his world with money coming in from here, there and everywhere, and his recent annoyance at Violet's failure to put the fear of God into Chubby and co subdued. Still, something was gnawing at him, preventing sleep, something he couldn't quite put his finger on.

He must have nodded off, Violet was in beside him and groping with some urgency. He didn't struggle, simply turning to face her and granting easier access to what she was after. They made love slowly at first, lavender filling his nostrils and blood filling his cock until he felt he was about to explode. Violet slowed the pace, rolled on top and rode him rhythmically, whispering all manner of pleasantries in his ear. The thought struck him, if she could touch him like this, surely she could move inanimate objects as a deterrent to intruders? He had been through all that, time now to concentrate on what she was doing to him.

Violet's turn to play it cagey, he put the question to her.

"If you can touch me physically, why couldn't you throw things at the burglars?"

"Where do you get it from I can touch you, Honey?"

"You mean last night didn't happen? It was all a dream? A figment of my imagination?"

"What happened last night, then?"

"We fucked each other's brains out. I don't have time to go into detail, but I know and you know it happened."

"You seem so sure, it sounds divine. Crudely put, but I don't mind that, not from you. Tell me more, Pinkee."

"Like I said, I don't have the time. What I can tell you is I know every contour of your body, right down to the birth mark under your arm."

"I do have a birthmark, I didn't know you knew, though."

"See you later, Violet. We'll talk about this again."

"Bye bye, Honey. I'll be waiting."

But for the fact he still had the Range Rover, he would have gone to the bakery and called in sick. The rain continued to fall mercilessly, offering no respite. Unless Sandy called for his services it would be a long, long day.

He stopped for a paper, no doubt he would have a chance to read it cover to cover. Maybe he could find a quiet corner and snooze the day away?

Nine o'clock and Patsy appeared in the canteen doorway, could Pink help him with the pumps? He'd been promised an early finish and wanted to make it even earlier. Another reason for asking, he wanted to point out the extent of Saturday's business, give Pink an idea of what was involved. They worked through the morning break. Pink climbed into the cab of a JCB and smoked a spliff while Patsy finished fuelling the pumps. The cab was snug and warm, no one would miss him if he got his head down for a couple of hours.

Same thing, sleep wouldn't come, neither would Violet, not way out here. After twenty minutes of trying, he ploughed his way through the mud to the canteen.

Barry appeared with the wages and announced an early dart for everyone, everyone bar Pink, he was to hang around and ferry Mac and a few others to the station. The Easter weekend officially started here.

Noon, and Mac was last to leave the site and Pink asked could he use the Range Rover for the weekend. Mac shrugged his shoulders, he couldn't care less. Come Tuesday, he was being sent to another site, and not local. Pink would now have to train up a new foreman as well as a new site boss.

He drove to the Boulder. Mac wasn't in any particular hurry; he deserved a decent send off, the two men had understood each other from the word go. End of an era.

Sara was delighted to see him again, serving up the first round on the house as proof of such. She sat with them since they were her only customers, picking up on Mac's sadness at having to leave and sympathising. Pink sent her to the chip shop again, same script, plus a meal for herself. Before she left she buttered half a loaf, replenished the drinks and provided all the necessary condiments.

Mac appeared to be heading for a session of melancholia so Pink winked at Sara, made an excuse he had to be somewhere else and took the foreman to the station. He didn't hang around to put him on the train, Mac was big enough and ugly enough to do that for himself. They shook hands warmly. If Pink didn't see him on Tuesday for whatever reason, maybe they would meet again?

Sara responded to the knock on the window immediately, it was now past closing time for the afternoon. Pink wasn't too concerned about having another drink, Sara's warm and welcoming embrace would do nicely.

Since her parents were upstairs, the cellar was nominated once more as the place to be. Pink stepped out of his overalls this time, they tended to hamper his seventeen jewel movement. Sara wore a short skirt which he asked her to keep on, the knickers would have to go, though. They would come in handy when she started with the screaming. Sara bit him playfully when he tried to gag her, then, realising his reasoning, allowed him to cram the underwear into her mouth. The trouble with that was, he couldn't remove it quickly enough when he was coming and presented her with a pearl necklace.

They narrowly missed being caught out by Sara's mum, Pink quickly making a show of changing a barrel as she descended the cellar steps. If she had glanced at her daughter's neck, half the evidence was still clearly on show and glistening in the cellar's bright light. Mercifully, she turned on her heel, happy everything was in hand. She was aware the fittings could be stiff from time to time and thanked Pink for helping out.

Outside in the rain, Mick Blunt approached, he and his clan had been allowed out on bail. No surprise there since the police wouldn't want the cells cluttered over the Easter holiday. He was asking everyone, not only Pink, he stressed, did anyone see or know who had beaten his brother up? Pink couldn't help him, he had problems of his own, someone had turned his flat over. If he found the culprit he would surely kill him.

With caps to pick up at the restaurant, he pointed the Range Rover in that direction and hit the first set of lights. The police car opposite flashed its headlights at him, Louise stuck her head out of the window and indicated he should turn left and wait for her. A few moments later, she pulled up behind him and, aware they were more or less in the town centre, pulled out her notebook and approached on foot. Pink rolled down his window, winked and listened to what Louise had to say. The cache of jewellery had been connected to several burglaries, and, although the Blunts had been bailed, she was sure they would all be allocated jail time. Her sergeant was curious as to her source, but accepted her anonymous phone call claim. Anyone in the police station could have taken it. She was just happy they had secured a result from it. On a lighter note, she was off on Sunday, how would Pink like a cooked dinner and all the extras he could handle? A time was set, Louise ripped the sheet from her notepad and passed it through the window. Pink drove off with his weekend filling out quite nicely.

He read the note outside the restaurant, laughing out loud and attracting funny looks from passers by. In her best policewoman's handwriting, Louise said 'Be prepared for a fun filled feast of fucking, feeding, smoking and drinking. Consider yourself warned, you will not be let off lightly. Signed .... Lou .... 999'.

Ash had the caps ready, telling Pink he and two of his staff had tried hash oil and best black cocktails to great effect. Pink had been prepared to let all the caps go for sale, but now his mind had been changed for him. Why hadn't he thought of cocktails?

A small bowl of Ash's vegetable curry accompanied by a joint of oil and he was set up for the rest of the day. One more call to make then he could have a shower and perhaps try one of those cocktails.

He only closed his eyes for a moment and was rudely awakened by Bea, it was safe to come in, the wicked witch wouldn't cast a spell on him. A new addition to the household put the shits up him, a black cat, like Eight Ball, but without the white circle on his head. Pink felt the urge to rummage through the kitchen cupboards for a cauldron and the ingredients necessary for witchcraft.

Bea made him a cup of tea. The witch merely acknowledged his presence and disappeared to another part of the house. Soon, Elise joined them, poured herself a cup of tea and pulled up a chair. Pink told her about the flat, he could arrange a viewing around two-ish tomorrow if the girls were interested? Elise expressed her delight by launching herself at him, landing on his knee, throwing her arms around his neck and planting a smacker on his mouth. Then, remembering where she was, looked sheepishly at Bea to check for a reaction. To her credit, Bea smiled sweetly and said she'd be glad to see the back of them, both Elise and her sister. Pink wasn't at all sure she meant it, but Elise seemed to be in no doubt. He arranged to pick them up tomorrow. Jenny made her entrance as he left and he managed a quick feel of her backside as they squeezed past each other in the front doorway.

"I expected you home earlier, Honey. Eight Ball says it's been raining all day."

"Been the ferryman, me. The site's deserted until Tuesday. I've delivered all the campers to the station."

"Campers?"

"Those who live on site. They're all away for Easter."

"I only found out the other night from the radio it was Easter this weekend. I've no sense of time at all. I mean, I know when it's day or night through you, but the calendar is a mystery now."

"No point me asking you to remind me to put the clocks forward on Sunday morning then?"

"He-he. Trust you. I don't think you'll be too bothered about that, Honey."

"Music?"

"I thought you'd never ask .... Lynyrd Skynyrd, if you will. I want to see you air guitaring and dancing."

Pink obliged, casting his overalls aside for the second time that day and putting a cocktail together. He wasn't in for the night, but he was in for long enough to put Ash's recommendation to the test.

Since they were derived from the same plant source, both forms of the drug complimented each other perfectly; the smoothness of the oil somehow tempering the intensity of the block stuff and making it possible to actually move about; albeit with limitations, but what a buzz. Why oh why hadn't he thought of it before? Now, he couldn't wait to dose Louise with cocktails; sex would be out of this world after such a joint, sex in orbit, bring it on.

The mellow feeling lasted for a couple of hours without needing to top up. He even dispensed with his need for a nap, managing to change the record when required, dance like a loony and play his air guitar as Violet had wished.

Sure he had the words to at least the title track, he played 'For Everyman' and jumped into the shower as the last track was about to start, regaling anyone who cared to listen with his vocal skills. No applause from downstairs, but it was raining, he could forgive that. Violet praised him in the absence of an audience, then asked him to play it again.

Three Rapati sisters surrounded him as he entered the bakery, all talking at once. He tried to leave and soon realised he had nowhere to go. The gist of the conversation was that Sira and Johan were now official, had the approval of everyone who mattered. Pink held his hands up for silence, had no one considered asking him did he approve? After all, he might be interested in Sira himself.

Kira and Mira asked why they shouldn't be included in the mix, causing Pink to quickly change the subject. Talk of the wedding would get him out of a hole.

The girls all chimed in at once again, what they would wear, explaining the service to Pink, all the rituals still strictly observed, suitable gifts, of which folding money seemed to take prominence. He already had a suitable gift, but was in a position to back it up with a few quid if necessary.

He had only called in to leave word for Johan, let him know it would be after midnight when he dropped by; provisionally, that was. He was off to the Albatross so anything could happen. He kissed the girls one by one and returned to the flat. Five cocktails were thrown together quick smart, the rain had relented, the walk would do him good.

He passed a bag of caps to Brat at the door and had a peek inside. Dave occupied a corner table, half slumped, it looked like he hadn't been home; the combination of an early finish, the long weekend and pay day proving too much for him. He managed to sit up straight when Pink brought him a fresh pint, but they both knew he wouldn't last the night. Pink also knew the cocktails would be wasted on him and kept quiet about them.

The place filled up slowly as the men talked, or rather Pink talked and Dave mumbled. Someone squeezed into the seat beside him while he chatted, someone who smelled delicious. Turning to see who it was, he came face to face with Gloria, looking good in the half light and smelling wonderful. Pink was civil, Gloria was pleasant, he sent her to the bar for drinks and shared his time between her and

Dave. The old spark was still there and he fondly remembered their romps.

Dave slumped in the corner again as Pink sparked up a joint and shared it with Gloria, passing the last third or so to Brat. On his return, Dave rose to his feet and promptly fell over two tables, spilling drinks and people all over the place. Pink helped him to his feet, told Gloria he'd be back in ten and led Dave across the busy road. He lived two minutes away, but with two steps forward and one back it took all of fifteen minutes to reach the front door. Frank took over, thanking Pink for looking after him and for seeing him home.

The prize had her tongue down someone else's throat on his return, a narrow escape, which immediately suited Pink since he'd caught sight of Jenny, the waitress from the café. Her smile was for him and him alone and not only that, she insisted on buying him a drink. They shared a joint, well, three ways with Brat who had conveniently rid himself of the caps and handed over a wad of folding. Pink secreted the money about his person and turned his full attention to Jenny, complimenting her on her attire and charming his way slowly into her frillies. The hash had her eating out of his hand, her own hands straying to touch his knee, his upper arm; then, casually, one arm round his neck and playing with his ear. He too was busy, letting her sit on his hand when she returned from the ladies and slipping between the buttons of her shirt under cover of the half light. He let her spark up the third joint of the evening and stashed the last of them in her handbag. It hadn't been mentioned, but he would be taking her home, home to her place. She had already let it be known her flatmate had disappeared for the weekend.

She lived fifteen minutes walk away, which would have been fine on a clear night, but the rain was back with a vengeance. Pink showed his style by insisting Brat should go out of his way and drop them off, in return, he would help load the gear into the van. Jenny chipped in and soon they were on their way. Brat even stopped at How Long's while Pink scored all three suppers as payment for the inconvenience.

Jenny's flat was twice the size of Pink's. Spacious and well furnished, her music collection was nothing to write home about, but, with good reception on the radio, all was not lost.

Since both parties knew why they were there, any awkwardness was quickly banished. Jenny disappeared while Pink tuned the radio, then sashayed into view in a flimsy see through negligee. If her charms weren't obvious before, they certainly were now.

Pink took his time, savouring her delightful contours, running his hands everywhere without a word of objection. Jenny moaned and purred like a contented cat while helping Pink out of his clothes. She asked what the dope was, letting him know it was easily the best she had ever smoked, although to be fair, she wasn't all that experienced in such matters. Pink covered her mouth with his to shush her, talking could come later; right now, there were other sensations to enjoy. No argument from Jenny, a most willing partner and they went at it like dogs in heat, working up quite a lather before finishing together and collapsing in a heap. Pink wasn't sure whether it was the dope or his ministrations which had glazed her eyes. When she regained her breath, Jenny let him know she'd had boyfriends in the past, but not one of them could hold a candle to Pink.

Their supper was stone cold and had to be reheated in the oven. Pink recovered in time to slip her another length while they waited. Jenny trembled throughout, loving every thrust and almost deafening him with her orgasm. The last joint followed the supper. The beast with two backs loomed once more before Pink took his leave, thanking Jenny for having him, in more ways than one. Her smile said it all, he would be made welcome again.

He had to pass the Blunt residence on the way home, the place was in darkness. Full of mischief and just for badness, he crashed an Accrington brick through the biggest pane of glass on view then jogged the rest of the way to the bakery.

Ash hadn't told Johan about the cocktails, he wanted to build one there and then, but Pink was ready for bed. He congratulated his friend on becoming 'official' and took his leave, planning to lie in his scratcher until he peed it.

Upstairs, the radio sounded so good he rolled a single skinner of oil, folded himself into his chair and invited comment from either Violet or Eight Ball.

"Have you had a good night, Honey?"

That was Violet, although Eight Ball did manage to look interested for a change.

"Oh .... you know so-so."

"Cat got your tongue?"

He looked at Eight Ball, who in turn looked directly at Violet, a puzzled look on his fizzer.

"You know what I mean, Pinkee. Why so quiet?"

"Stoned as a rat, Kitten. Been on cocktails all night and I intend spending the weekend as high as I can possibly manage to ascend. Would you care to join me?"

"There's nothing I'd like better, Honey. You can take that to the bank and cash it in."

"That's my girl. I'll let you sleep with me tonight, how does that sound?"

"Just try to stop me. You're so convinced it's possible for me to do that I might as well believe it myself."

"Good answer, Violet Hiccup, and goodnight."

"Hehe. Night night, Pinkee. I love you so much it almost hurts .... almost".

CHAPTER 37

A roomful of lovers

Pink somehow knew Violet would be as good as her word, the lavender warning him of her impending arrival. She didn't let him down, creeping in beside him and curling up in a ball so as not to disturb his rest.

The call to prayers woke him half an hour later than he would normally rise, these guys didn't celebrate Easter, more was the pity. Try as he might, he couldn't fall back. Nothing for it but to pull his shorts on and have a nice cocktail.

"Good sleep, Honey? You're up early."

"I asked whatshisname up the road there to give me a shout. I don't want to miss the mosque."

"You didn't, did you? I never know when to believe you."

"I did, but I made it for lunchtime."

"He-he. Can I listen to Frankie Miller, please?"

"I was thinking more along the lines of Steely Dan, ease us into the day, but Frankie's a good choice, Kitten."

"You're so sweet."

"Don't I just know it."

"He-he. You can choose the next one .... if I don't think of something else."

Eight Ball chased smoke rings, Frankie crooned, Pink became one with his chair and Violet sang gentle backing vocals. Eight o'clock in the morning and it could have been Martini time; anytime, any place, anywhere.

The mood was set, a slow day in prospect. Nothing to do until two-ish and all morning to do it.

Still very much surprised at how much movement he was allowed from the cocktails, Pink stripped the bed, cleaned the bathroom from top to bottom, washed all the windows on the inside, rolled another joint, smoked it, rearranged the contents of the fridge and changed over to Nils Lofgren for Violet, all before breakfast time. His air guitar was in evidence the whole time. He had unlocked the key to maintaining a constant buzz and being able to operate on it, more than able if truth be told.

He walked to the shop with his laundry and spent twenty minutes browsing the bric-a-brac, his prize, a good condition copy of 'Dark side of the moon', which he first checked didn't have his mark on the disc. Someone had made off with his copy from the old place. Al Stewart's 'Modern Times' was also snatched up. Violet was in for a treat. He knew every note of the Pink Floyd album, who didn't? 'Modern Times' was a bit of a mystery to him.

Kira emerged from the post office and linked his arm, demanding to know when his next visit to Ash's would be and further demanding to be taken along, putting the idea into his head he should go immediately. Giving her ten minutes to let her dad know where she would be, or at least who she was going with, he took his new records upstairs, put his cash in the bike shed stash and drew the Range Rover up outside the shop. Mr Rapati came to chat as Kira jumped in beside him. Pink informed him, now that Mira and Sira were fixed up, he would be glad to take Kira off his hands. Kira squealed and laughed out loud, drowning out whatever it was Mr Rapati had to say on the matter, perhaps just as well.

Kira nattered non stop for the ten minutes it took them to drive to the restaurant. He heard her plans for the holiday weekend, how

Moraji wanted her to stay on at school, how many boys were after her and that she didn't fancy any of them. Pink was relieved to park up and shoo her from the vehicle. Her sisters could talk, but Kira never seemed to come up for air.

Ash made a fuss of her as usual, then baulked at her demand she should work in the restaurant at weekends for work experience, agreeing only when Pink suggested she should get permission from her dad first. While the men chatted, Kira busied herself in the kitchen having been given free rein by Ash. She came up with a lunch of spicy fried chicken and a side salad. Ash was impressed, Pink said nothing, not until he'd cleared his plate; but then, he was well aware of her culinary skills.

That killed a good hour. Kira wanted to stay, but Pink reminded her one of her sisters would probably be on her own in the shop. Taking the address for the keys to the flat from Ash, he manhandled her back towards the Range Rover and endured another ten minutes of non stop chatter.

Sira wasn't alone, Johan turned up with the excuse he had left the book he was reading and couldn't sleep without first having read a couple of chapters. Pink and Kira believed him, but thousands wouldn't.

"Time for another spliff, Honey?"

"Always."

"He-he. And music?"

"Always, we can listen to this Al Stewart album."

"Is it new? Have you heard it before?"

"Not new, and no, I haven't heard it before. Heard of Al Stewart, yes, but not this LP."

Like 'For Everyman', the title track had been saved 'til last. Both Violet and Pink had already given the album their seal of approval before 'Modern Times' kicked in, knocking them sideways with its content. Violet, in particular, showed signs of over involvement in the lyrics. Pink swore blind there were tears there, but he didn't mention it..

He built two cocktails and listened to side one of 'Dark side of the moon'. It had been a while, but every single note had been committed to memory.

The witch twitched the curtains when he sounded the horn. Bea trooped out with the girls and cadged a lift to town, she didn't fancy spending an afternoon alone with her mother. They all knew what she meant. The thought crossed his mind, maybe Bea would like to look the flat over? Then again, he would have enough on his plate with the other two.

With Bea safely out of the way, the mood lightened. Pink pointed the Range Rover out of town and they sang along with the radio. He commented on the fact both girls were showing their legs off and was treated to more than a flash of inner thigh and spider's legs, enough to leave him slavering in anticipation.

They fell in love with the flat even before entering. Situated in a quiet little cul-de sac; like Pink, one floor up, but above a little corner shop, convenient. Inside, the girls oohed and aahed, discussed what would go where and screamed when they saw the bathroom, complete with deep enamel bath.

Pink sparked a joint up and passed it to Elise, Jenny kissed the face off him and rubbed herself suggestively against him. Elise took over like a reverse relay racer, passing the baton then getting stuck in to the task at hand. In the forty minutes they were inside, every room was christened. The people in the shop downstairs must have wondered what the fuck was going on. They would have had a fair idea when three dishevelled people exited the building, laughing and kissing for all they were worth. Without hesitation, the deposit changed hands and Pink was roped into helping with the flit. The girls wanted to take immediate possession. Mental lists were made, timetables drawn up, his weekend off looked less likely by the minute, but the rewards far outweighed any misgivings he might have on the matter.

Elise insisted on buying him a drink for his kindness, Jenny decided she would like to do the same. Pink parked up in a quiet back street and fired up the second joint.

The Boulder was noisy and busy with everyone making an early start on the weekend, well after closing time, a secret knock was required to gain entry. Word had spread about the presence of best black in the parish and Pink was asked did he know anything four times before he could take a sip of his pint. He told the Waites to take a drive out to the Flat Iron and to mention his name to Gwynneth, she would be there or thereabouts, preparing for her evening shift. Also, they were to keep quiet about it.

Bea joined them. Pink looked around and realised four of his favourite ladies were within the same four walls, and without one word of animosity exchanged between them, amazing. Bea listened intently as Jenny and Elise spoke of their new flat, she was pleased for them, at least that's what she told them. Pink sensed a little green eyedness about her manner, but kept it to himself.

Sara joined them. Pink introduced the girls as friends he had sorted out with a flat; she in turn sensed there was a bit more to their relationship, but she too kept it to herself, clever girl.

Two pints miraculously turned to five. The Waites reappeared, grinning from ear to ear, their weekend had taken a turn for the better. Pink was offered another pint, but felt a nap coming on, he didn't want to miss Quarantine at the Albatross. Wisely, he didn't mention this to the girls as he took his leave. No point in complicating matters.

"It's nap time. Isn't it, Honey?"

"For me and Eight Ball, yes."

"That's ok. I like to watch you sleep. So peaceful."

"I'll tape side one of Al Stewart, then side two when I wake, how does that sound, Kitten?"

"Sounds about right."

"Done deal."

He set the tape up, discarded his clothes and was asleep within seconds. Eight Ball joined him and Violet watched over them, concentrating on the music at the same time.

Eight Ball was swimming out to Violet, who was floating out to sea on an air bed. When he reached her, he tried to clamber aboard and punctured four sets of holes in the thing. All Pink could do was laugh helplessly, until the pair disappeared from view, then he started to worry. He knew he should jump in after them, but he didn't want to get his new pyjamas wet. Chubby Blunt appeared with his sore face and Pink immediately forgot about his missing friends, breaking into uncontrollable laughter again.

"You ok, Pinkee? You've been laughing in your sleep."

Pink told her about the dream, but she couldn't shed any light on it. Eight Ball couldn't, or wouldn't help either.

Another silent shower as side two of 'Modern Times' recorded. Violet listened intently, eyes closed, swaying in time to the music and Eight Ball scrambled out of his window since no one was taking him on. While the recording finished, he rolled half a dozen cocktails and a single skinner to smoke there and then.

Johan turned up for work at eight o'clock just as Pink was leaving for the Albatross, he said it was so Mr Rapati could have an early night. Neither Mr Rapati nor Pink believed a word of it, both knew it was so he could have a couple of hours with the middle Rapati girl. Still, the baker took full advantage of his kind offer and had an early night. Pink cadged a lift to the pub. It wasn't on the baker's way, but it wasn't too far out of his way, either.

A large bald dude barred his way at the door, said he was with the band and there was a cover charge.

Thinking on his feet, Pink told the guy he worked behind the bar and was granted admission; there would be plenty of suckers who would stump up the fifty pence, though. Whoever heard tell of a door charge at the Albatross?

The band had set up opposite the door and not in the corner Brat played from. This made the room bigger somehow, which was just as well, the band's entourage took up almost half of the seating area.

Pink followed the singer to the toilet and sparked a joint up, he knew he was the singer since he was doing fuck all regarding the setting up. Toking greedily on the spliff, he informed Pink the drummer was a copper, drug squad. Not in this area, but they all pissed in the same pot, didn't they? Thanking Pink for the smoke, he went back for the sound check. The dope had taken immediate effect since the fucker couldn't count beyond two.

As people drifted in, Pink told those he thought should know about the drummer's day job. When the two scrotes who had turned his place over with Chubby walked in, he didn't let on to them; instead, he sent his good friend Katy J after one of them when he went to the bar, providing her with two joints to sell him and telling her to get the drinks with the proceeds.

The scrote couldn't have timed it better. As the drummer took to his stool the joint was fired up, sending a plume of thick smoke in his direction. Without even looking at the scrote, he left his stool and walked to the public phone in the foyer; then it was game on. Three well executed cover songs into the set, the local drug squad stopped the gig momentarily, took the wink from the drummer and frogmarched both scrotes out of the building and into their car.

Pink had taken precautions in case of his own arrest. Katy J was asked to secrete his spliffs about her person. One thing he had learned over the years, they didn't ever bring a female officer with them so the best place to stash anything was on a woman. He and Katy J listened to the next two songs from outside the open window. It was dark, but still warm from the sunny day. Mischievously, Pink blew the smoke from his last toke through the open window in the hope the drummer would catch a whiff of it.

Katy J had been out of circulation for a while. Pink discovered her long term boyfriend had thrown her over for her best friend. Of course he sympathised, but the more he did so, the closer they became. There had always been a chemistry, looked like tonight would be the litmus test. He plied her with drink, they sneaked out for another spliff and the live music loosened them up considerably.

They were standing by now, having lost their seats when they went outside, their bodies moving ever closer; no doubt in either mind as to what was on the menu later.

Fifteen minutes before chucking out time the band made a mess of one of Pink's favourite songs. Katy J didn't put up a fight as he led her away from the place and in the general direction of her place.

Halfway there, she stopped and asked where they were going. It turned out she had vacated the flat when her boyfriend shit up her back and moved in with her parents again. They had walked in the opposite direction to Pink's place, besides, he didn't want to take anyone back there yet, any females at least. They dragged each other into a playground, got the roundabout spinning as fast as they could in the dark and smoked another spliff as they went round and round and round and round and round. The kids' playground turned into an adventure playground for half an hour as they utilised the equipment to their best advantage, quite sure the see-saw had never borne witness to such debauchery. Since he was a gentleman, he walked Katy J the rest of the way home and was glad he did. She dragged him round the back and they sorted each other out once more. A good night was had by all.

It took him forty minutes to walk home, arriving just in time to share a joint with Johan. He didn't know if he was tired or not so spent an hour with his friend, listening to a progress report on his wooing of Sira and how he was to be left in charge of the bakery for four days before Mira's wedding. Protocol dictated the ceremony would last for three or four days, Mr Rapati's presence would be required for a big part of that. Pink promised to help out in the bakery.

Upstairs, he cracked open a bottle of cider and let Violet do her DJ routine, spinning discs to her command and enjoying a couple of spliffs. Bedtime was four thirty. He remembered to set the clock; he had to be at work by ten, there was money to be made.

Patsy takes an unexpected drop in wages

Pink drank two pints of water when he woke for a piss, then couldn't sleep, then almost nodded off when the call to prayers came. Next thing he knew the alarm was mashing his brain, causing him to complain he'd had no sleep.

Violet laughed. "That means you snore when you're awake, Pinkee."

"So, I did sleep then?"

"Yes, but you were restless."

He felt like having the hair of the dog, but decided to roll a cocktail instead, that would do him more good than a drink; besides, he was now on the last minute for work.

With no time for breakfast and feeling as rough as a bear's arse, he clambered into the Range Rover and headed for the site. He waited at the top of the lane for Patsy to show and needn't have bothered. Patsy rolled up in the passenger seat of the scrapman's wagon so he followed them down the lane. It turned out Pink knew the scrapman, which seemed to upset Patsy somewhat. Pink sensed the amount of coinage quoted would have to be amended. If Patsy thought he was cute, he wasn't anywhere near cute enough.

Pink climbed to the top of the tower crane and had to descend as soon as he sat in the chair, someone had turned the power off. If they couldn't find the isolating switch they would be as well calling it a day. Half an hour later, they managed to make a start. Pink found the switch by retracing the sunken cable leading to the crane, then drove the cutting gear to where Patsy wanted it in the bucket of a dumper. A quick word with Andy the scrapman verified his earlier suspicions, the split was to be twenty, thirty, fifty. Pink with the thin end and Patsy with the lion's share. Andy explained he hadn't known of Pink's involvement, but he would make sure it was split three ways, that was a promise. Pink knew him well enough to trust his word, but Patsy had gone down in his estimation.

From his vantage point on high, he found even more scrap than Patsy had at first realised and ran the legs off the little Irishman for fun, and for his cheek. He sparked his joint up as Andy burned the steel and Patsy took a moment to gather his thoughts, then, Patsy jumped on to the back of the wagon and unhooked as Andy hooked on. Twice, for a bit more fun, Pink almost took his head off with some rather accurate loading. With a little room left, Pink dropped the chains onto a compressor. Andy didn't hesitate; Patsy protested, but unhooked it all the same. Someone would be sure to pay a good price for it, after a lick of paint of course.

Leaving the site as they had found it, and remembering to switch the electricity off, Pink followed the struggling wagon up the lane and along the road to the scrapyard for the divi. Patsy wanted a lift back to the site to do his pumps, but Pink was late for an appointment in the opposite direction, he would see him on Tuesday. Anyway, it was only a forty minute walk, Patsy would have that long to reflect on the error of his ways.

Pink's appointment was with two rather attractive young ladies. He wasn't late at all, but he wanted time to stash his cash, roll a couple of joints and borrow Doc's van.

Mr Rapati stopped him for a chat, flapping about the wedding. Pink told him to relax and follow Moraji's instructions to the letter, that way he couldn't be blamed for any mishaps, if indeed there were any, fingers crossed. The baker calmed down considerably, insisting Pink should attend the actual ceremony to witness him giving his eldest daughter away. Pink wasn't too sure about that, causing another worry line to etch itself onto Mr Rapati's face. Wasn't it up to the bride, or groom, or both to invite him?

Upstairs, he opened a bottle of cider and sat down to build his cocktails. No time to play his choice of music, but the radio was entertaining enough on a Saturday.

"You say you've got another job to do, Honey?"

"Flitting some friends to their new flat. Maybe I should take another bottle with me? Sounds like thirsty work."

"Good thinking, Honey. Can't have you dying of thirst, he-he."

He drove to Doc's place and was about to park up in the street when Doc himself appeared in his rear view mirror and walked towards his front door. Rizla met him halfway along the path and was immediately sorry he did. Doc butted him square on the nose and followed it up with a sharp knee to the groin; he then proceeded to kick seven colours of shite out of his so called best mate. Pink's policy of never involving himself in a domestic stood firm. He started his engine and went looking for another van, he didn't wish to let the girls down. After half an hour of driving around racking his brains, he headed for the garage. He remembered seeing a trailer when he took Sandy to view the damage to the original Range Rover. The garage was closed, but the trailer stood outside. Seconds later, he was on his way, hoping the police wouldn't pull him for having no signal lights on the trailer.

The girls were hyper, anxious to be away from the witch; it took twenty five minutes to load the trailer with their stuff from the house. Mainly clothes and a couple of sticks of furniture, including a bed Pink recognised as belonging to Jenny. Bea joined them for the first run, she wanted to view the flat, maybe Pink could drop her off in town before he picked up some more furniture from various addresses?

They had been busy. Curtains, bathroom fittings, lampshades, radio and a television for Pink to watch while they gave Bea the grand tour. Elise brought him a cup of tea after his exertions in emptying the trailer almost single handedly. The girls cleaned windows and sinks along with other female pastimes and prepared themselves for the second run.

They dropped Bea off in town then picked up more furniture and fittings from relatives and newspaper adverts.

By five thirty all the running about was done with. Pink sparked a joint up, Jenny opened a bottle of wine, Elise found a decent radio station and ran a bath for the workers. He asked her to make sure the door was locked, he didn't fancy another intrusion by you know who.

He did an admirable job of ensuring both girls were clean, then got down and dirty with them, all part of the service. Another bottle of wine, his bottle of cider and another cocktail helped the party go with a swing. The girls were reluctant to let him leave. To be fair, he was just as reluctant, but he wanted to be rid of the trailer. Plus, there was no drink left and he had his drinking head on.

The police car pulled him as he turned in towards the garage, but his luck was holding out. Louise shone the torch in his face, asked him if the vehicle belonged to him, stuck her head in the rolled down window and kissed the face off him. An update on the plight of the Blunts regarding the stolen jewellery. The tribe hadn't seen the sense in only one of them taking the rap, resulting in every single one of them being charged, including Chubby from his hospital bed; a fair enough result. Also, the two scrotes' evening had been well and truly spoiled by a night in the cells and a thorough inspection of their accommodations. Louise questioned his connection to their initial arrest and Pink told her he was merely being a good citizen. They arranged to meet at her place when her extra shift finished on Easter Sunday; he was to bring some booze and some good hash. Done deal.

"That was a long job, Honey."

"Complications, then a run in with the cops."

"Trouble?"

"Nothing I couldn't talk my way out of. Actually, I blamed it all on you, the police are looking for you right this minute."

"He-he. They'll never find me."

"I told them they'd never take you alive."

"He-he. That's great. I'm a desperado, me. Thank you, Pinkee. I've always wanted to be wanted."

"Anything to make you happy, Violet Hiccup."

"How long you in for?"

"Long enough to drink this bottle of cider, have a shower and roll a few spliffs. You want some music or are you happy with the radio?"

"Tom Petty, please."

"A splendid choice, madam. Excellent."

"He-he."

Pink immersed himself in the music, had a spliff and listened to the entire first half, jumping into the shower when he flipped the disc and singing along at the top of his voice.

Warm applause from downstairs put the idea in his mind he should visit, see if the girls were sticking to the plan; and if not, why not?

A quick stop off at his stash and he was in the bakery where Mira and Kira welcomed him with open arms. Mira, in particular, looked radiant. Pink asked how things were going and was reassured by the younger girl. With preparations for the wedding in full flow and filling everyone's minds, Sira and Johan were seemingly allowed free rein in order to become better acquainted.

Mira locked up for ten minutes and drove him to the Albatross. Kira wanted to go in with him and Pink asked her how long she wanted him to live. If her father ever got wind she was in a pub his life wouldn't be worth living. Kira backed down, but he just knew she would ask again. That was a safe bet.

Brat had news from Gwynneth, she wanted a word with him. Nothing serious, but could he give her a bell?

Pink dialled the Flat Iron, dropped ten pence in the slot just as Carlos Santana let rip and arranged to see Gwynneth at her place on the morrow; at least he hoped it was Gwynneth, the loud music left him unsure of who he had actually been talking to.

He shared a joint with Brat and the brothers Waite then sat on the stool Katy J had saved for him. He had no intention of sitting with her all night, but stashed his ready rolled in her bag just the same; an old habit, but a good one.

Some of his imported black, dealt by Gwynneth, had filtered through so the room quickly filled with the familiar aroma. Pink advised Katy J to steer clear of the early offerings of joints and she soon found out why, its sheer potency rendering everyone who partook incapable of anything but eye movement. Brat stirred the pot by playing all manner of psychadelia, slipping in a sly track from the Comus album while they were helpless. It worked, many of them freaked out, but were unable to ask what the fuck they were listening to, giving both Pink and Brat reason to split their sides laughing. Between them, Katy J and Pink smoked his ready rolled cocktails and poured a healthy amount of beer down their necks. They decided on a repeat of last night's manoeuvres, said goodnight to Brat and headed for the door. Katy J excused herself to powder her nose seconds before Pink found both arms up his back. Drug squad, he was the first person they landed on, fair cop.

They didn't search him there and then, simply cuffed him and fed him into the back of the car, one of the officer's sliding in alongside to keep an eye on him. At the cop shop they gave him the full treatment, strip search, rubber glove probe, filtered his tobacco and demanded to know where he now lived. Pink was having none of it, inviting them to either charge him or set him free. Since they found nothing on him they couldn't very well press charges so they locked him in a cell, citing abusive behaviour and obstruction. Five minutes later he was fast asleep, no point arguing with the bastards. The cot wasn't very comfortable, but it had often been said he could kip on a clothes rope.

With no idea of how long he had been there, he woke to the sound of the key turning. He opened his eyes and grinned widely at the vision in the cell doorway. Louise, in full uniform. She was to kick him at the end of her shift without charge, but she had other ideas. To Pink's delight, she closed the door behind her and set about unbuttoning her tunic, telling Pink they were alone apart from a couple of drunks sleeping it off in another cell, and that she had her own form of punishment to administer.

He didn't argue, not with a police officer, taking his medicine like a man and giving the cot the strictest of examinations in durability. Yet another feather in his cap, although one he couldn't crow about; at least not for a long, long time.

Louise made him a cup of tea in the little messroom behind the sergeant's desk. She wanted to drive him home as soon as some other officer showed up, but he told her he would rather walk. However, he was in no hurry now and would sit with her for an hour, have another cup of tea and run his eye over the log book.

It made interesting reading. The two scrotes he had burned last night had only gone and given his name up as their source, even though they too hadn't been charged. As luck would have it, they were unsure of his address, citing somewhere in the Asian neighbourhood, hence his horrendous ordeal of earlier. Steps would have to be taken.

Reading back, he smiled at the arrest of the Blunts and their ineptitude and infighting during questioning. They deserved all they had coming to them, and more if Pink could arrange it; but right now, their associates were at the top of his 'to do' list. He borrowed a pen from Louise and noted their addresses; they just happened to be on his way home, and next door to each other at that.

Kissing Louise, he collected his effects and slipped out into the cool morning air, promising to see her later as planned and thanking her for her hospitality.

With no one around, he could have put any number of windows in, but that wouldn't be enough of an inconvenience to satisfy him. In dire need of a piss, he made his way round the back of the houses, letting out a long sigh of relief as he relieved himself. On a hunch he tried the back gate of the first scrote's house. Open. He recognised the motor bike and cursed himself; a tank full of piss would have provided an ideal first step to his revenge campaign.

His mind went back to when he put a match to the Blunts' allotment shed. He wasn't an arsonist, he knew that, having no desire to watch anything burn or to wait for the fire engines to turn up. However, fire could be his friend. He crept over to the dustbin, opened the lid and selected an old duster from the various items of rubbish therein. Unscrewing the petrol cap on the bike, he fed one third of the duster into it, made sure his escape route was clear and lit the fuse. He was two streets away and being ushered through Donny Boot's back door when he heard the explosion. Donny's woman also heard it and Pink managed to look as shocked and as puzzled as she did, there was his alibi if it ever came to that. Donny's kitchen light had been on, which was why he took the chance of giving the secret knock. He was handed the makings and made welcome. There was no black for sale, they only had enough for themselves, Pink managed to look suitably disappointed. It was heartwarming to know one of the town's main dealers knew nothing of his import business.

The straight black knocked him out, but not so much he didn't remember to refuse a hot drink; then, Donny's woman moved higher in his estimation by offering an ice cold bottle of cider. Conversation became stilted on account of the drug's potency. Once again, Donny came up trumps with the music, using sign language to tell his woman to let Pink have a squint at the album sleeve pertaining to what was playing. He knew the voice, but couldn't put a name to it, the style had him confused. Realisation spread through his brain as the sleeve told him it was Captain Beefheart, an album he wouldn't have guessed at, intriguing and different from him and a few years old at that. One track on side two, "Further than we've gone', had him floating on air with its prominent piano breaks and air guitar opportunities. Needless to say he left Donny's an hour later with it safely tucked under his arm; that, and a generously donated joint's worth of best black. It would have been rude to refuse either.

Johan had a good laugh at the state of him, then at his recent exploits, sending him home to bed before he collapsed.

"I was getting worried, Honey."

"More police trouble, but most informative, Violet. Most informative indeed."

"You should go to bed."

"Thanks for waiting up for me."

"Not a problem. C'mon, let's get you into bed. You can tell me about the police in the morning."

"Done deal."

"He-he. Eight Ball's been keeping it warm for you. He wont admit it, but he's been worried about you too."

Lightning strikes twice

Pink felt he should have been far more tired than he actually was, then remembered he'd slept in his cell; the call to prayers woke him. Johan had been fifteen minutes from the end of his shift when he saw him, which meant he'd had not much more than an hour's sleep. With a raging thirst water couldn't quench, he made it to the fridge and stuck his head inside, his eyes resting on a bottle of cold cider. Maybe that would do the trick. He sat by the open fridge door and glugged noisily on the bottle, lovely stuff, one more of these and surely he would find his rightful place in the land of nod.

Eight Ball was having trouble clawing his way into a wrapped lump of cheese when he regained consciousness, having helped himself from the open fridge. Pink thought it was another of his strange dreams until his hand settled on the cold puddle of cider by his side.

"I've been trying to wake you. It's like you went into a faint."

"I've a faint idea of what you mean .... I think."

"I think you should lay off for a day or so."

"So that's what you think. Is it, Violet? Don't you know I'm on holiday?"

"Holiday or not, you can't tell me you're doing yourself any good."

"Good grief, is that the time? I'm running late."

"Late like me if you keep burning the candle at both ends. How would you like that?"

"That isn't an option at the moment, much too busy to consider such a notion. Things to do, people to see."

"See you take a rest at some point."

"Point is, I'm a very busy man. What I will promise, is that I'll make some time for play."

"Play some music, there's no point in arguing with you."

"You give in too easily. What would you like to hear, light or heavy, or what?"

"What did you bring home with you?"

"You don't miss a trick, do you Kitten? Ok, here we go."

"Go and have a shower now, you must stink from lying in that cider for so long."

She wasn't too sure about the Beefheart album, although she did recognise the J J Cale song. Pink reckoned a couple of plays and she'd be as keen as he was on it.

After cleaning the kitchen floor, he drove to the supermarket to re- stock; mainly cider since he was under orders to supply the drinks for Sunday. Cider and two half pound blocks of lard.

He let Violet hear side two of 'Bluejeans and Moonbeams' while he threw a few cocktails together. He didn't really fancy driving out to Gwynneth's place, but he had given his word. Besides, his hair was all over the place, he had just washed it and couldn't do a thing with it. Gwynneth would sort it out for him.

Leaving Violet in charge of the radio and Eight Ball in charge of half of the lump of cheese, he said his goodbyes and see you laters.

Gwynneth welcomed him with open arms, then asked him to open a jar of marmalade she had been wrestling with. It freed itself easily. Gwynneth claimed she must have loosened it with her own efforts and Pink agreed, he was in an agreeable mood.

Down to business. She dug out a wad of cash and insisted he should count it; the black had flown off the shelves although she confessed to keeping some back. The figures added up, the money was as agreed with the handy bonus of half of what black she had retained, that would come in very handy. He sparked a joint up, but Gwynneth refused a smoke until he explained about the effect of the cocktails. She stared at him as though he was talking through his arse, not believing a word of what he was saying. Half an hour and some dexterous demonstrations later, he had her converted to his way of thinking, never again would she doubt his word.

They made love with familiar ease, throwing each other all over the place with abandon before toking hungrily at another spliff. Gwynneth offered to cook lunch and had to apologise when she found the cupboard to be bare. Stashing his cash and hash, Pink drove her into town and followed her round a few shops before ending up in the Flat Iron for a free pint. Food was forgotten about as they both found a taste for the cider. Gwynneth used all her guile and wangled a night off so Pink could take her to the Albatross, she fancied a good night out and could think of no better company.

Back at her place, they fell into bed and were asleep before either could interest the other in anything else.

He woke some hours later to the scent of lavender and thought he was at home with Violet. Instead, it was the aromatic bath Gwynneth had prepared in his honour. She washed his hair over the sink then joined him in the bath for a soak, which turned into a slap and tickle fuck fight, which in turn was declared a draw with both protagonists shaking hands on it.

By the time Gwynneth had tied his hair in a plait he had two more cocktails rolled and they were ready for the off. The Albatross would be in full swing now, but he didn't intend driving directly there, keeping Gwynneth in suspense until he steered her through the side door of the restaurant. Ash was all over him, bear hugging and handshaking as he liked to do. Gwynneth was a little bemused until she was introduced and afforded a similar greeting, taking to Ash straight away.

Pink handed over the wedge of cash without mentioning the hash stash at Gwynneth's place. Of course he would share it, but he would wait until everyone else had run out of the stuff. Ash sparked up a cocktail and they shared it before leaving, refusing a free meal as they were by now well behind time. Gwynneth was invited back anytime; any friend of Pink's and all that. Another bear hug each and they were out of there.

Pink parked the Range Rover a couple of streets away and led Gwynneth to the Albatross. The place was jumping, well, half jumping; it being patently obvious who had best black and who didn't. The only available seats were close to Katy J so he led Gwynneth there, introduced them, passed his ready rolled to Katy J and headed for the bar, giving Brat a wave as he did so.

Weaving in and out between swaying bodies, he made it back to the girls without spilling a drop, years of practise standing him in good stead. Gwynneth asked Katy J what the 'J' stood for, but Pink told her not to tell, he liked a bit of mystery. Gwynneth then wanted to know why he had concealed his joints on Katy J, giving a nod of understanding as he explained the drug squad knew her as something of a distributor and wouldn't hesitate to pull her in on sight if the mood took them. They made room for Dave and Reg, who had news of Mad Frank; he sent his regards, was doing ok and again, not missing anyone or anything. Good news indeed.

The beer flowed, the drugs flowed and the music flowed until the house lights flickered on and off, a warning the squad were either on their way or were already on the premises. Those in the know busied themselves in getting rid of their drugs. Sadly, those of them reduced to eye movement only were caught in the headlights. The squad had come prepared, with plenty of transport. One third of the Albatross's clientele were carted off in one of the worst raids in recent memory. Half an hour later the sly bastards raided again, this time catching Brat as he was about to spark up a joint and hauling him off with another half dozen or so. Pink managed to run some interference and take Brat's keys from him, promising to load his music into the van for safety. The decks could remain in the pub as Brat would be the entertainment for the following evening, Easter Sunday, he could pick his keys up at Gwynneth's place.

Show over, Gwynneth invited the table company back to hers for what was left of the evening and they trooped off in the direction of the Range Rover. Reg asked Pink to swing by his place and emerged with his woman. This suited everyone since she was carrying a case and a half of beer, party time. They followed Gwynneth, who was driving Brat's van, carefully sticking to the speed limit so as not to attract unwanted attention.

Gwynneth had no oil left and Katy J had one last cocktail in her bag, no matter, there was nothing spoiling. They would have to manage on straight black, beer and vodka. Pink tuned the radio, knowing no one would be capable of changing a record after a while. No point clearing a space for the air guitarists, either, they would be having a well deserved night off .... if they had any sense.

Katy J helped prepare snacks in the kitchen for later while Dave and Reg skinned up. Pink sparked the last cocktail up and passed it to Reg's woman, who had been home alone all night with no smoke, she joined the ladies in the kitchen to share it and see if she could help with the buffet. Pink did his barman act, spreading liquid refreshments where required before kicking his shoes off and marking out his crash space for later. With two joints of best black doing the rounds, conversation was minimal as the girls joined the men in the front room and announced the buffet to be officially open. No one moved a muscle, no one could move more than an eyeball in time with the music and even that seemed a strain on resources.

Pink was first to recover and immediately built another joint before serving the drinks. One by one the party stirred to action, gulping at their refreshments then toking on the joint before collapsing into the furniture. This was repeated God knows how many times. Pink even managed a quick fumble; first, with Gwynneth, who followed him to the fridge, then with Katy J who did the same. A clumsy fumble was all they could manage with the black rendering them incapable of anything else.

Shortly after one round of drinks and drugs, someone hammered on the front door and everyone froze like frightened rabbits. Pink looked at the time, half past four. He peeked through the curtains to see Brat shivering on the doorstep.

The DJ had been charged with possession and had been on the loose for an hour, weaving through the streets in his paranoid state to make sure he didn't lead the drug squad to the party.

He didn't want his keys, not yet. The women made a fuss of him, providing a cup of tea and a joint.

The next thing Pink knew it was nine o'clock. He could smell food and found Dave in the kitchen. The buffet sandwiches had curled up and died. Gwynneth had left the oven on with the door wide open, a trick Pink taught her, free gas heating for ice. Pink had noticed the curling buffet on his trips to the kitchen and paid it no attention.

Ever resourceful, Dave had toasted them and with his partner in crime, Katy J, necked every last one.

Brat seemed something like his old self, thanking Pink for looking after his gear and vowing not to let his drugs bust upset him too much. He would be in fine fettle for his Easter Sunday stint at the decks.

Pink nipped to the corner shop for no other reason than to buy Gwynneth an Easter egg, and ended up gulping down a pint of milk on the way back. Gwynneth was delighted with the gift, cracking the egg open and sharing it round. Pink returned from the toilet to find nothing more than the packaging left; he did, however, find half a bottle of beer behind a chair and made a show of throwing it down his neck.

With those wishing a lift home loaded into the Range Rover, he kissed Gwynneth and promised to visit soon. Reg's house was nearest, his woman mentioned there was more beer inside and Dave beat her up the path to the front door. Pink thought it would be rude of him not to join them, Katy J agreed and the party reconvened. Breakfast was offered, but Pink refused, preferring now to stick to his liquid diet. The others wisely made sure they ate before partaking of any more black. Pink headed for the living room, finding his spot and settling in for the long haul.

Long haul it turned out to be. Four hours later, Reg declared the bar to be closed, bringing no response from either Dave or Katy J, who were zonked to the point of being comatose.

Pink rose unsteadily, shook Reg by the hand, blew his woman a kiss by way of thanks for her hospitality and lurched down the path to his vehicle.

"Just look at the state of you. I've been worried sick, Eight Ball too. I hope you're going straight to bed? Don't look in the mirror, please, Pinkee."

"Be quiet, woman. Where's my clean shirts, have you seen them?"

"I don't believe you're thinking of going out again. You look like you haven't slept for a week."

"I'll find them myself if you don't want to help. I'm on holiday, me. Where's my shirts, Violet?"

"In the bottom drawer. I hope at least you'll have a shower."

"I can do that, yes, I can do that. Which drawer was it again?"

"Bottom. I can't persuade you to stay in?"

"This bottom, is this the drawer?"

"Have your shower. I give up, you're on another planet."

No one knew what he was singing in the shower. He preferred to think of it as a medley, but no one on Earth would have guessed.

With his booze in a carrier bag and five roughly rolled cocktails tucked safely in his shirt pocket, he put food down for Eight Ball and bade Violet good evening.

Louise's car wasn't there when he rolled up so he got his head down in the front seat and waited. The rattle on the window put the shits right up him. As wake up calls went, this was right up there with the freakiest of them.

Louise had to assist him to her flat then return for the booze, letting out a sigh of relief when she asked him did he want one and he refused. No, he didn't want one, he wanted two and he wanted them now. He was in better condition than she at first thought, making her relax and laugh with tales of his weekend. A short nap while she ate and he was as good as new.

He sat in the bathroom and watched her shower, feeling his urges return as he towelled her dry. The bed was comfortable, almost too comfortable. Snapping himself awake, he got down to business, making Louise squeal with delight as he ravaged her passionately before collapsing in a crumpled heap beside her.

He was on much better form a couple of hours later; still drunk, but strangely rested. He took his time, caressing Louise to the point of torment then making love slowly, methodically, until she let the neighbours know of her absolute joy.

She lit him a joint and fetched him a bottle of beer in bed since he seemed determined to continue on his liquid diet. No amount of persuasion on her part could coax him into eating.

Yet more sleep, punctured by the alarm clock. Louise had a midnight start, but told him he could stay where he was. He was tempted, but decided against it, asking instead if she would escort him towards home. She made him promise to call again, in a better state than his present visit. She in turn promised to find out what he could use against scrote number two.

He flashed his lights in her rear view mirror when she signalled to turn towards the cop shop, he could manage from here.

Noticing the Rapati family vehicle parked outside the bakery, he decided to investigate. Sira was saying goodnight to Johan and commented she could get drunk on his breath. Johan walked her to the car and found Pink asleep on one of the chairs on his return, Eight Ball perched precariously on his shoulder.

The wedding had reached the exchanging of the vows stage, or its Indian equivalent. Eight Ball padded along the carpet towards the betrothed, proudly carrying the rings on his howdah. One of the peacocks must have looked at him the wrong way because he changed course and leapt at the bird with his claws showing. Pink covered his eyes, not wishing to see his carefully choreographed arrangements go to absolute ruin. The applause surprised him into opening his eyes. Kira had the headless peacock in one hand and a bloodstained machete in the other. She passed the dead bird to Moraji who began plucking it furiously. Pink relaxed, presuming it to be part of the ceremony. Eight Ball rejoined the catwalk and made it as far as the feet of the happy couple. That's when Pink noticed the wellingtons, who the fuck got married in wellingtons? Allowing his gaze to rise, he was shocked to see Sira and her original intended facing each other; so where was Johan?

Searching frantically through the congregation, he spotted his friend crouching in a corner and gambling with dice, seemingly oblivious to the fact the love of his life was about to be married without him.

Mira appeared from nowhere, offered the couple a drink from a huge silver ladle then bounced it off both heads.

Mr Rapati shook him awake and told him to go to bed, advice he readily took on board. On his way home, he made sure to keep an eye out for machetes and silver ladles, extremely happy to make it in one piece.

Eight Ball didn't much care for the strange look cast in his direction and made himself scarce, hastily clambering through his window like someone had it in for him.

"He hasn't done anything wrong."

"You weren't there."

"Where?"

"In my dream."

"Tell me."

"Maybe later. I need a drink, care to join me?"

"If I could I wouldn't. You're still drunk from whenever."

"Suit yourself, all the more for me."

"Isn't it work today?"

"Now who's drunk? It's Easter Monday .... I think. How can I find out?"

"You're right, I forgot. Why don't you have a sleep, Pinkee?"

"I've just had about six hours downstairs. I'm still on holiday you know."

"Ok, I'm not your keeper. I just don't like to see you like this. It seems so out of character."

Pink was bitterly disappointed to see he only one bottle of cider in the fridge. Never mind, that and a joint of best black would knock him out until the shops opened. Settled into his chair, he played 'Rumours' on tape, glugged his drink down and managed to smoke half of the spliff before succumbing to its charms. He was aware of Violet chattering away; not remonstrating as such, but not exactly friendly, either. Either way, he was in no position to join the conversation. Luckily, Eight Ball came in and sat at her feet. Everybody happy.

He woke dead on twelve o'clock, parched to the core, but happy he hadn't dreamed this time.

Robin Trower's 'Bridge of Sighs' album eased the atmosphere while he showered, then sensibly laid his work clothes out for the morning. In the kitchen, he took the two packs of lard from the fridge, rummaged in the drawer for a box of matches and emptied them all over the work top. Next, he slipped two envelopes from a pack and placed his kitchen scissors on top of them, whistling along with the music as he worked.

"What's all that stuff for?"

"It's a gift for someone .... for two people."

"A gift, two packets of lard? What about the matches, what are they for?"

"Watch and learn."

With that, he changed the record and cranked up the volume, Jackson Browne would keep her quiet while he concentrated. Violet didn't move from the kitchen, she merely squealed when she heard the opening bars, but curiosity had a better grip.

Pink inserted a match into each pack with the sulphur end and half of the stick protruding. He then sparked another match and put it to the red heads, allowing them to burn for a moment before blowing them out and inserting matches at random into both blocks.

Sparking a cocktail up, he pocketed the scissors and envelopes, blew a puzzled Violet a kiss and bounced downstairs.

He took his time walking to the park, soaking up the sunshine and making a mental note to start his seeds off when he went home. Packing the envelopes with trimmed grass, he sealed them and sat on a bench to finish his smoke, chuckling away to himself all the while.

"Is it some kind of bomb, Pinkee?"

"Close. It's more of a warning than anything else."

"A warning for who?"

"The two scrotes who came here with that bastard Chubby Blunt."

"I knew you wouldn't let that lie. How does the warning work?"

"I post one through each of their letterboxes. The burnt match suggests a failed attempt to start a fire and should be enough to put the wind up them."

"Clever, Pink, but will they know it was you?"

"Doesn't matter. Besides, I want them to find these too."

What's in the envelopes?"

"Grass."

"You're giving them some of your dope …. why? …. I thought that's the last thing you'd do?"

"Grass from the park; to let them know someone knows they're grasses, stool pigeons, copper's narks. Know what I mean?"

"Yes."

"Do you see where I'm coming from?"

"Yes."

"Capiche?"

"Yes."

"Do you follow"?

"YES, YES, YES ..... STOP IT. I understand. Thanks for explaining it to me. They should get the message from that."

"Count on it, they'll be shitting from here to breakfast."

"He-he. It's very clever. You're very clever."

"More music?"

"Silly question. Side two, please."

"A breath ago I was clever, now I'm silly, make your mind up, Violet Hiccup."

"He-he. Music, maestro please."

Downstairs again, he asked Kira to bring him some blotting paper for his watercress from school and was told she had some at home. Mr Rapati shook his head in complaint about her attitude to hard work, but consented to her going with Pink to pick it up, they could bring Mira back with them to save him a trip. Pink told him he wasn't strict enough with his daughters and had him laughing all over his face.

Kira begged to go to the restaurant, just for the ride out, the holidays were so boring she would rather be back at school.

Ash and Johan were sharing a cocktail when they landed and quickly extinguished it when they saw Kira. If she noticed, she didn't let on, hugging both men before they could hug her. Johan passed Pink an envelope while she quizzed Ash about the business, then asked him if he was feeling better, not that he'd been worried at all, but he seemed to think Pink had stopped breathing in the night. He wasn't sure, though.

Pink assured him he was as right as rain. Just a little overindulgence with the drugs and booze.

He had to drag the girl from the premises, literally. She kicked and screamed in mock rage, threatening to tell her dad all she knew.

Moraji made a fuss of him as he waited for Mira, filling him in on the wedding preparations and telling her eldest daughter off for not formally inviting him. When she finally got round to it, he told her he would have to check his diary. He had a funny feeling the date clashed with a visit to the dentist, something he wouldn't want to put off.

Sira heard the laughter and came bouncing downstairs, inviting a telling off from Moraji for showing much too much flesh in her flimsy nightie, but not before Pink copped a good eyeful to store in his memory for ever.

Mira apologised again for her oversight in not inviting him, she had presumed he knew he would be welcome. Pink smiled to let her know he had been pulling her leg, then sent her back in for his blotting paper.

He spent half an hour with Mr Rapati, listening to his slant on the wedding plans. By all accounts there were no problems, but he still had his fingers crossed. Stashing his cash in the empty bike shed and checking his stock, he made a mental note, another mental note to open a bank account soon.

Violet watched again as he placed the seeds between two sheets of blotting paper and set them aside in a corner of the kitchen. This time, she didn't question his actions. Besides, Steely Dan were keeping her quiet.

With four fresh cocktails in his bob cap and the sight of a half naked Sira still fresh in his mind, he set off in pursuit of sexual adventure, pointing the Range Rover in the direction of Jenny and Elise and their new flat. Result, the girls dragged him in, stripped him naked and fell upon him like scavenging wolves. He offered little or no resistance, he was outnumbered and recognized the fact, managing to undress both ladies as they wrestled. Elise had been ill so they hadn't been over the door all weekend and Pink told them of his own holiday break while they had a rest and shared a joint. They listened intently, inserting oohs and aahs in all the right places before setting about him again. All loved up, they wanted to go to the Albatross for a drink. Pink told them it would be deserted, but they were determined to get out of the house for at least one evening before work resumed.; they knew he liked the juke-box in the Albatross. What the hell, he was still on his liquid diet, another night on the sauce would do him no harm at all.

The Albatross was packed out. Brat had secured an extra shift to round off the weekend and the good thing was, no one would have told the drug squad. Dave made room for them, he looked in worse shape than Pink and insisted he was having one last pint before trying for an early night. The canteen wasn't hard work, but he still had to struggle out of bed in the morning for it. Four pints and three cocktails later, Pink and Reg took an arm each and dumped him on his front step, ringing the doorbell before leaving him for his old man to sort out.

Katy J turned up with half an hour of drinking time left. She had been visiting a friend and, like Pink, had been unaware of the extra night's rock disco. On leaving her friend's place, she had found a joint in the bottom of her bag. Pink gave her a light and introduced her to the girls. She asked where Dave was and threw her head back in laughter when Reg told her about taking him home.

At chucking out time, Jenny asked for a lift home and Katy J invited herself along, leaving Pink unsure as to which party he should drop off first. Since he had enjoyed the flatmates' company almost all night, he came to the decision they could be left to their own devices. They hugged and kissed him outside their flat, making him promise to call midweek. Katy J started noshing on his cock before he turned out of their street. He didn't complain; he didn't pull over, either, although he did find it difficult to concentrate on his driving. She made him promise to see her soon and he made a mental note to invest in some sort of diary. He couldn't keep up with himself.

Remembering the two 'bombs' on the back seat, he drove to the scrote's street to post them. Both houses were in darkness. He thought of sneaking round the back to inspect the damage to the bike, but changed his mind, he was tired and it was work tomorrow. He fed an envelope and a 'bomb' into each letterbox and headed for the High Chapperal and bed.

"Don't forget the alarm, Honey."

"Thanks, Kitten. Keep me talking while I get undressed."

"He-he. Eight Ball's been in and out like a fiddler's elbow all night. He wont say what's on his mind."

"Probably woman troubles. Remind me to ask him in the morning."

"He-he. Night night, Pinkee. Sleep tight."

"Uh-huh."

CHAPTER 40

Two new brooms

Pink heard Eight Ball clatter in through his window. He had been pondering getting up for a piss, but was so comfortable he was trying his best to delay it. Then, Violet screamed, making his mind up for him in a hurry. Eight Ball had taken a battering, blood seeping from an open wound on his head. He let Pink wash it and have a good look. First impressions had been wide of the mark, it wasn't deep, but still bleeding quite badly. Pink bathed it until the bleeding stopped, poured him a saucer of milk and promised Violet he would take him to the vet in the morning if he didn't look the part.

Eight Ball slept, Pink didn't. He checked up on his friend every forty five minutes or so until it was time for work. Just before he left, Eight Ball came out of it, struggled to his feet and tottered weakly towards his food. Violet was happy with that, there would be no lasting damage, Pink could go to work safe in the knowledge his companion would make a full recovery, but maybe he should be confined to barracks for a couple of days?

Pink called for Dave on the way to work. Going by the state he had left him in, a lift wouldn't go amiss.

How right he was. Lily had roused him and made his cheese sandwiches, but Dave had fallen asleep with his head on the breakfast table. Pink knew how to wake him, creeping up and threatening to steal his sandwiches. Result.

Two new faces when they clocked on. The replacement foreman, a bluff Yorkshireman by the name of Jimmy Glover. Pink took an instant dislike to him while Dave hadn't yet formed an opinion. The other man was the new boss, hopefully an improvement on the old boss.

The introductions were made in the canteen, then came a no nonsense speech from Jimmy Glover about timekeeping, shirking, safe working practises and observing strict mealtimes. The boss stood beside him and nodded his head in agreement like one of the Thunderbirds puppets. Pink sussed right away which of them wore the trousers in that relationship, and it definitely wasn't the boss.

He followed them into the office to hand over the Range Rover keys to the boss and Jimmy Glover took charge of them. He was then ordered, not asked, but ordered to clear a channel to the canal and create a car park for the workforce. This was so the foreman could observe who was coming and going. Half an hour later, Keg attracted his attention by tooting on the tower crane horn and signalling it looked like he was wanted in the office. On the way, he came across Dave, who looked distinctly out of place. He was wielding a jackhammer and growling like a bear with a sore arse.

Abby's daughter had started work in the canteen full time, and guess who was sent out into the field to do a proper day's work.

Quarter to nine and some of the men were working shirtless in the warm sunshine, reminding Pink he should get on with planting his crops. Jimmy Glover met him at the office door, handed him the keys to the Range Rover and told him to lead the way to the ready mix plant. Barry tipped him the wink, Groover would be forewarned of their visit.

The foreman drove a white mini van, which struggled to keep pace with the more powerful vehicle. Pink was tempted to try to lose him, but left it at that, curious to know what his tack would be with Groover.

Groover shook hands with the man and showed them into his office. As usual, Pink took a back seat to the proceedings, smiling when the foreman suggested concrete was much cheaper in his native Yorkshire. Groover called his bluff with his own suggestion, maybe he should fuck off over to Yorkshire and purchase his ready mix. The meeting ended there with a handshake, both men understood each other. Groover managed a wink in Pink's direction as they were ushered out of the office, no flies on him.

Sandy had been on the phone in their absence, Pink was to pick him up at lunchtime and bring him to the site. Jimmy Glover said he'd tag along, after today, he would look after the main man personally. Pink's dislike for the foreman became more deep seated, not exactly hate, but hate wasn't far away.

He was ordered back to the coal face, but went straight to the canteen instead, he couldn't remember the last time he had eaten and reckoned now might be a good time to resume.

Back on solids and with Carol eating out of his hand, he was feeling a lot better than he had of late; the liquid diet had played havoc with his gut and with his memory. He was still trying to piece together some aspects of the Easter weekend, a few blanks remained and that worried him slightly.

The foreman interrupted his conversation just as he was about to charm his way into Carol's knickers. How fucking long did he want for his morning break? Pink didn't much care for his attitude and told him so, impressing Carol by back-chatting. Not wishing to rock the boat any further than that for now, he gave her a wink and brushed past the foreman, jumped into the Cat's cab and carried on where he left off with the car park.

Now, there was a real clash of personalities. Jimmy Glover sat in the passenger seat on the way to pick Sandy up, and insisted things would be done his way or not at all. He wasn't there to make friends, he was there to make sure everyone pulled their weight and did a good job. Pink told him his man management skills were non existent. His predecessor, Mac, had the men's respect and obtained results via a combination of tact and understanding. The conversation ended there, the puzzled frown on the foreman's face leading Pink to guess he would have to consult a dictionary before engaging in round two.

Sandy at least was pleased to see him, slipping the bonus envelope into his overalls pocket in full view of Jimmy Glover, who looked on in horror at the obvious familiarity between the two. His nose was further put out of joint when he was sent back to the site on his own, Sandy and Pink would dine at the Boulder and would phone when they wanted picking up. The foreman was directed to the pub and told to expect a call in a couple of hours when he dropped them off.

Lunch was a leisurely affair as they caught up since last seeing each other. Sarah ran to the chippy, ate with them then made a show of looking after their every need. Pink picked a horse, 'White van man' in the two fifteen at Perth and advised an each way flutter. Sandy overruled him and demanded thirty quid on the nose. He was the boss, no argument.

The interlude stretched 'til four o'clock. Sandy rang the foreman while Pink changed a barrel and had a grope at Sarah's assets, she hadn't clapped eyes on him all weekend and had missed him.

Jimmy Glover's face was a picture when he pulled up outside the pub and he then had to suffer the ignominy of being told to look after Pink at work as he drove to the station. The veins in his neck looked fit to burst when Pink was asked to walk Sandy to his train. That didn't go down at all well with him.

Maybe that's what brought on his next move when they returned to the site. One of the labourers was showing off his sunburned torso, both front and back were crimson red. Glover sacked him on the spot; if he had been doing what he was paid to do only his back should have been burnt.

The new boss backed the foreman's decision up, galvanising Pink's theory about him being a puppet.

Dave was in a bad way as they walked to the top of the lane. Pink no longer had the Range Rover, another of the foreman's initiatives, so he pushed his bike and walked along with his friend.

The poor guy was shattered, the jack-hammer having come as a shock to his system. He was debating whether or not he should throw in the towel, the deciding factor being he hadn't quite saved enough for his next sojourn abroad. Pink persuaded him to give it another few days, see if he couldn't get the hang of it. Both agreed Jimmy Glover was a bit of a shit, make that a lot of a shit. He asked Dave did he fancy a pint and wasn't too surprised at his negative response, he reckoned it was well past his bedtime.

Pink added yet more money to his stash, it was getting out of hand, a slight paranoia creeping into his thoughts. The bank would now be a priority, sooner rather than later.

Kira met him at the bike shed, he was to take her to the restaurant. Pink threw a leg over the bike and told her to hop on the crossbar. There were tears, tears of laughter, but she would make the same demand when he next had a vehicle.

"He's been ok, Pink. Slept most of the day, but he's been eating and drinking."

"Has he tried to mess with the cut?"

"Only to wash it, maybe you could take a good look."

It wasn't quite as bad as it had looked to the bleary eyed shell of a man he had been earlier. There would be a scar, but he assured Eight Ball that scars sometimes served to attract females.

"No need for the vet, thank God, but I think maybe he's used one of his nine lives."

"I agree. He gave us a fright, didn't he?"

"No. He gave you a fright, then you gave me a fright."

"He-he. You're right again, Honey. How was your first day back?"

"Don't ask. Two new brooms turned up and one of them seems determined to sweep clean."

"New brooms?"

"A new foreman and a new site boss. The foreman's a bit of a bastard."

"Is that a worry?"

"Not to me, I don't think. I mean, I reckon I can handle him."

"I'm sure you can. You look in better shape than you did this morning."

"It'll be an early night tonight for me, Violet, and I wont need any rocking."

"He-he. You will play some proper music first, wont you?"

"Let me guess …. Fleetwood Mac?"

"Bob Seger first, please. Haven't heard that in ages."

"Thought you had no sense of time?"

"He-he. You know what I mean."

Eight Ball followed him like a lost sheep, still feeling a little sorry for himself, but over the worst. He had to settle for sitting at Violet's feet when Pink went to the off licence for some cider. Some might say he'd had enough over the weekend, but he felt the need to wean himself off it slowly.

Kira must have been listening out for him descending the stairs, it couldn't be coincidence he found her pacing outside the front door. She linked his arm and tagged along regardless of where he was headed. Pink was sure she had a little crush on him and made a mental note to try not to encourage her. He did enjoy her company, though; intelligent beyond her years and as headstrong as they come. Before he knew it, he had promised to borrow the Rapati car tomorrow after work and escort her to the restaurant, all without slotting a word in edgeways; manipulative wasn't in it.

He worked it out he had an extra pair of hands and loaded her up with cider, that would save him a trip later in the week; so much for cutting back on the stuff.

Kira would have followed him upstairs if he hadn't instructed her to leave the bottles inside the bottom door. He explained it wouldn't look right. Her father was an easy enough going man, but that could easily rock the boat. She understood his logic, but made him promise to come down and sit with her for half an hour while one of his bottles chilled in the freezer compartment.

Ten minutes and a cocktail later, he put 'Rumours' on for Violet, picked up a bottle of cider and went back downstairs. He reasoned he wouldn't get away with a mere half hour and could chill his drink in the shop freezer. Kira was on the phone telling one of her sisters to cook a meal for him, they would be round for it in half an hour. Mr Rapati took a call from Ash, a large order of baked goods for the restaurant and enquiries after Johan's health. For all his intelligence, the poor man was none the wiser. Making an executive decision, he knocked off work and drove home, he would send Sira with his food.

More subterfuge as both Sira and Mira turned up. Five minutes later, Johan appeared. Ten minutes after that, he and Sira drove into the night. Mira wore a worried frown when she dished up his food, Kira saw it and asked point blank what was bothering her. All it turned out to be, something and nothing really; Pink would be the only white man in attendance at the wedding, would that bother him at all? She smiled wide at his answer, he was part of the family, how could he feel out of place? Besides, his presence would be sure to take some of the pressure from the bride's shoulders.

Kira looked at him adoringly, he had an answer for everything, would he like his beer now? Yet again he came up with the right answer.

He took his time with the drink and listened to what was new regarding the wedding. Johan and Sira returned. Mira herded her sisters together and took them home, but not before each of them had given Pink a kiss and a cuddle.

Johan was in buoyant mood, his relationship with Sira coming on in leaps and bounds, did Pink think it was too early to ask her to marry him? Pink thought for a moment, more for effect than anything else. Yes, he should ask Sira as soon as possible, or at least before he himself asked her.

They shared a joint of oil, congratulated themselves for making a shitload of money from their import business and vowed to do it again; perhaps on a grander scale.

"What happened to your early night, Honey?"

"This is it. You're looking right at it."

"No shower?"

"Not unless you want to join me."

"Don't, Pink. You know I'd love to."

He pulled Sandy's betting slip from his pocket, fuck, he had forgotten about that. Never mind, Sandy liked to visit. He would catch him again.

Eight Ball purred loudly for the ten minutes he spent with him, he was on the mend for definite.

CHAPTER 41

End of an era; a whole new slant on things

P ink knew he was dreaming this time, how else could he explain
the swords made from glass, the knitted balaclavas with no eye
holes, the paper longship and the talking potato pies? Forget that, his
bus was here, why it was shaped like a giant blackberry was another
question entirely and one best left to the experts. Mr Rapati had
all the answers, shame he gave them out in his native tongue. Kira
couldn't, or wouldn't translate, she had gone all shy on him or was
too busy sewing Eight Ball's tail to his ear.

The conductress wouldn't let him on the bus, not because he was
buck naked, more because he didn't have the correct fare. He could
see where he wanted to be, but it was too far to walk. Jimmy Glover's
van came hurtling towards him with no intention of stopping. One
of the talking pies spread itself across the windscreen, causing the van
to disappear up it's own exhaust. A result of sorts, although the pie's
mates were none too pleased, they had lost their goalkeeper so Pink
would have to stand in. Bread gloves, tasty, wait a minute, where the
fuck were his fingers?

"Nasty dream, Honey?"

"It's better you don't know, believe me, Violet. What time is it?"

"Breakfast time, quarter to seven, but you should have a shower first. You've been sweating like a stuck pig."

"Nice analogy, I like that. Let's have some music."

The shower felt good, refreshing, the dream spoiled his reverie by returning momentarily; not in its entirety, but fast forward and in reverse order, weird.

He dampened the blotting paper while eating his porridge. Already, tiny little shoots had appeared, a couple of days and they would be ready for planting out.

Eight Ball was under his feet, looking for food and gazing longingly at his exit window. Pink told him to give it another day or two and was backed up by Violet. The cat accepted without argument.

Dave was showing off his blistered hands to anyone who would look. Jimmy Glover opined maybe he wasn't suited to this type of work, then turned his back and walked away. Dave was stuck for words, it didn't happen very often. Pink sensed if his friend's hands hadn't been blistered he would have balled his fists and laid into the foreman for free.

Keg was a no show. Pink didn't volunteer himself for the tower crane, he wanted Glover to sweat for a while, knowing full well there was a lot of concrete to be poured.

Patsy walked with him to his vehicle, the foreman had been asking about the missing compressor. Pink shrugged his shoulders, indicating he couldn't care less. After all, he hadn't been left in charge of the site over the holidays. The compressor would be on another building site by now with a filed down identity number and a brand new coat of paint.

The wind whipped up from nowhere, raising a duststorm from the parched earth and reducing visibility to ten feet or less. Pink closed the cab window and put his feet up. If anyone wanted him they would have to come looking.

With no idea of how long he had slept, he pointed the Cat in the direction of the canteen and slowly crept through the dust.

Jimmy Glover was on him in a flash, an element of gloating to his manner, it seemed Sandy had suffered a massive stroke and wasn't expected to live. Either way, Pink had no back up now, reduced to just another number on the worksheet. He wouldn't let the foreman see the shock he was feeling, looking beyond him and ordering a coffee from Abby. Glover tried to ram home his advantage by telling him to man the tower crane when his break was over. Pink ignored him and sat with Dave and Barry, struggling hard to keep his emotions in check.

A heavy shower of rain served to settle the dust at least, but the wind kept on howling. Pink drove the Cat to the base of the crane, borrowed a paper from his banksman and ascended the ladder.

No sign of the wagons so he stuck his nose in the paper, the sun was out now and combining with the wind to dry the land again. He saw Jimmy Glover drive his van from the office to the new car park, remonstrate with Dave, then walk back to the office. Dave set his tobacco tin on the van's roof, rolled a cigarette and fired it up. He stood there leaning on the van for a few minutes and Pink couldn't work out why. Then, realisation of what he was actually up to as he backed away and did up his flies. The wind and sun would probably dry the seat before Glover climbed in, but the stink of piss would linger for weeks. Well done that man.

Back to the paper. He checked the racing results and whistled low and long, 'White van man' had won at odds of sixteen to one. Sandy was better off by four hundred and eighty pounds.

Of the three pours, two were direct feeds from wagon to pour. The other had to be decanted into a skip and carried by the tower crane. Pink had to fight the wind to reach the pour, an almighty struggle with three quarters of a ton at the end of the jib. On the third slew, the motor cut out on him, the wind taking hold, slewing him in the opposite direction and into the upright jib of a mobile crane. A glance at the windometer told him the gusts were above sixty miles per hour. Keg had once told him fifty five was the safety limit, so he made his way down to report what had happened. The driver of the crane he hit wasn't a happy bunny. Pink calmed him down by explaining how it had come about, but Jimmy Glover didn't want to listen and ordered Pink back to the job. Pink refused point blank, quoting the safety implications. The fitter backed him up, but Glover served the ultimatum, up the crane or up the road. Again, Pink kept his cool, turned on his heel and headed for the office.

Barry's face told him all he needed to know, Sandy hadn't made it, end of an era. Suddenly, he didn't want to work there any longer, happy to have been sacked before he could find a way of damaging the foreman. He told Barry he would call for what was due to him on Friday, said goodbye to one or two friends and went for his bike.

The clerk of works barred his way. Pink gave him chapter and verse on what had occurred and was handed a phone number, maybe he should report it to the health and safety? Better coming from him personally.

The bike took him to the Boulder, where Sarah burst into tears at the sad news. Sandy was a nice man and had been very generous, no one else had ever given her a tip made up of folding money. That wasn't the only reason she liked him, of course, but it was what sprung immediately to mind. She asked Pink when the funeral would be and could she attend with him. He used the pub phone, spoke to Sandy's distraught secretary and was told to call back on Thursday, she would provide details then.

Health and safety thanked him for his call and promised to carry out an immediate investigation, the man asked did he belong to the union. If so, and depending on their findings, he might just get his job back. Pink told him to forget it, there was no union on site and he couldn't care less about the job.

Sarah helped him drown his sorrows, matching him pint for pint and running to the chippy for his lunch. At half past one, Dave strolled in, the site had been closed down pending the investigation. No, he hadn't been sacked, but he sure as shit wouldn't be going back, even when Jimmy Glover's black eye had healed. Sarah laughed when Pink mentioned the car seat and Dave joined in, he would have told Pink, but now there was no need.

A few roofers filtered in. Those who had met Sandy at Clem's funeral bunfight expressed their sorrows at his passing, they too had taken to him, their condolences were sincere.

When Pink next bellied up to the bar, he found Sandy's betting slip in his pocket, the old man would have no use for it now, he could find no real argument to availing himself of it. Sandy would have insisted and would probably have a good laugh about it into the bargain.

Sarah ushered Pink and Dave into the back yard until she could get rid of the riff raff, they deserved a lock in to compensate for their stressful day. Dave was impressed, Pink was nonchalant, it was no more than he expected of her.

Sarah's father came downstairs and joined them for a beer. Pink could tell he had something on his mind and told him to spit it out. He was sorry to hear about Sandy and about Pink losing his job. The thing was, he wanted to take his missus to visit relatives in the morning and the brewery had altered his delivery time. Would it be at all possible for him to help Sarah with the delivery and look after the place until tea time? Pink hummed and hawed and Sarah could hardly keep a straight face. What the hell, he was accustomed to getting out of bed in the morning now. Yes, that would be ok.

Again Dave was impressed, another pint each on the house; Pink had always been a mate, now he was his best mate. He had been saving hard for his next trip abroad, but walking out on the job left him about twenty five quid short of his goal. Pink quickly resolved that by dispatching him to the betting shop with the winning slip, telling him to be careful of who saw him. On his return, Pink peeled off forty quid and told him to stay away for an extra fortnight, which tickled him no end.

Pink left the bike in the Boulder's back yard and walked part of the way with Dave. They arranged to have a drink on payday, in fact, they would go to the site together in a show of solidarity. It was doubtful Jimmy Glover had any friends to back him up, but better safe than sorry.

The wind still howled, he had been wise to leave the bike. Crossing the road behind a bus, someone hammered on a window. Looking up, he saw Pon, complete with dog collar. He was waving and smiling. Two old ladies who had crossed at the same time took a sharp intake of breath and tut- tutted when Pink gave the priest the fingers; all good clean fun.

Moraji stood in the shop doorway when he rolled up, just taking the night air, the heat of the bakery being a bit too much for her. Pink followed her inside and through to the back. She was worried preparations for the wedding were going too smoothly and feared something was about to leap up and bite her on the bum, one of Pink's sayings, but she laughed like music and visibly relaxed. He offered to throw a spanner in the works, put a ladder in the traditional material for the bride's outfit or hide Mr Rapati's Sunday best shoes, he even offered to run away with Mira on the eve of the wedding. Moraji doubled up in fits of laughter, maybe everything would be ok after all.

Speaking of the Devil, Mira turned up to let her mum go home, Mr Rapati was waiting outside in the car. Pink took Moraji's arm and linked it into his own before walking her through the front door. Two regular customers, little old Indian ladies, swivelled for a double take, but Mr Rapati didn't bat an eye. Nothing Pink did seemed to bother him. Before he could drive off, Kira showed up and reminded him Pink needed the car for an hour. Pink had forgotten what with all that had gone on earlier. No escape, he and Kira piled in and took charge of the car at the Rapati household.

Ash made a fuss of her, for a change he wasn't stoned and ran through a few recipes and techniques. Pink took an interest, amazed at Ash's knowledge of the various herbs and spices involved, two pinches of this and a pinch of that. They were treated to a free feed; by now Pink didn't care if all he ever ate was Indian grub, and not just because it came at no cost to his good self.

He had to drag the girl away again, this was becoming a bit of a habit, then, one of his brilliant ideas struck like a bolt of lightning. Why didn't Ash volunteer to provide a few dishes for the reception, that way he could swing an invite and pave the way to be a valid presence at the next wedding? He and his staff could be caterers to Prince Johan. Kira squealed and scribbled her home phone number on a napkin. Her father was at home now, but Moraji would answer the phone. Ash could put it to her and she would sway the old man, brilliant.

Now, Kira wanted to go straight home. Ash was to wait for half an hour before calling, she wanted to see the reaction it effected on her parents and see if Pink was as clever as he thought he was.

Mira was happy with his suggestion. The more people she knew on the big day, the less nervous she would be, she hoped. When she told Pink he was wonderful, he didn't argue with her. He treated her to his best smile, let her see what she was missing.

Violet didn't question him about his day so he stopped short of volunteering any information. Eight Ball was perkier, his wound healing nicely. Pink told him another twenty four hours should see him right, he would be allowed out then.

A shower and a joint with the Doors as accompaniment and time now to reflect on his friend's passing. With stopping the job on safety grounds, he guessed Sandy's sons wouldn't exactly welcome him at the funeral; but fuck them, he would be going and that was that.

The potato pies were talking again, all at once so he couldn't catch a word of what they were saying. This time he recognised his surroundings, the Canine Dog Club, the games room to be exact. Light Waite was sharpening his cue and challenging him to a frame of snooker, the prize, a potato pie with a bite out of it. He accepted the wager, the pies quietened down and jostled for a vantage point to watch, all except for the one with a bite out of it which edged towards the door. Light saw this and threw a bottle of ketchup at it, missing completely and splashing two of its mates. They didn't flinch, they liked to be different, until the girl with the see through head ate them. Then, they wished they hadn't been different.

"What do you know about dreams, Violet?"

"They're weird. They don't mean anything. They're just weird."

"That's a big help …. thanks."

"You're welcome, glad to be of assistance. What was the dream, Honey?"

Pink talked her through it with the sure knowledge she wouldn't be able to shed any light. She did, however, come up with a suggestion of sorts.

"Maybe you should mention it next time you see your analyst."

"Cheeky mare. I'll keep my own counsel, thank you."

"Dream on, he-he. Get it? Dream on."

"You and I are heading for a falling out, woman. How long did I sleep?"

"He-he. About an hour and a half."

"Must be time for a joint, then."

"Isn't it always?"

"You're a smart arse tonight, aren't you?"

"Makes a change from you."

"I'm off to see Johan. You want the radio on or proper music?"

"How long will you be?"

"An hour, tops."

"Boz Scaggs, please. The tape, if you will, and I'll be timing you."

"Like I said, cheeky mare."

Johan had a smile a mile wide, Ash had been on the phone, he would be providing a selection of tasty treats for Mira's wedding. He and his staff would transport the ingredients to the venue and cook for the masses on site. One condition, Johan would be there, they weren't to make a fuss, simply treat him as they would the other guests. Now, why hadn't Pink thought of that? It would appear Moraji had.

They shared a joint and had a good laugh about how things were going. Everyone had taken so well to playing their parts that it was second nature to them now. Johan was gearing himself up to propose to Sira, he was just waiting for the right moment, not nervous as such, but itching to get on with it. Pink wondered aloud about leaving it 'til the night of Mira's wedding. Let Mira in on it, of course, and suggest it might take a little more of the pressure from her.

Johan shook his head in wonder before shaking Pink's hand, what would he have ever done without him? He truly was a good friend. Pink shrugged then told him to shut up and skin up.

As good as his word, he was back upstairs within the hour. Boz Scaggs had disappeared into the night and Pink replaced him with Savoy Brown; he made an executive decision without consulting the lady of the house. He fancied a bit of the blues and by God he would have some. Violet voiced no objections and Eight Ball seemed to be ok with it.

CHAPTER 42

Nine ten jack, a pair of spikes and a shattered record

Pink stuck to his routine. No real reason for keeping Violet in the dark about his unemployed state, he would look forward to the debate when it came to light. The milk was off so he skipped breakfast and strolled in the direction of the Boulder, enjoying the early morning sunshine and a joint of oil as he walked.

He was early for the delivery so Sarah made him a huge breakfast with a large mug of tea to wash it down. He told her she looked good and watched her blush bright pink. Usually, the only compliments ever to come her way were from beer goggled punters at chucking out time. He rolled a joint after his breakfast, but the delivery landed before he could spark it up.

The cellar was harder work than the building site, maybe because it was confined to one relatively small space compared to the vast expanse of the site. It took them 'til opening time to straighten things out, by which time he had a real sweat on. Sarah sent him upstairs for a shower. He presumed she would open up on her own, but she stepped into the shower while he was in mid wash and demonstrated her thanks for all his help.

They opened up half an hour late, but no one was around to notice, the sun was shining so no roofers would be out for an early drink. Pink read the papers from cover to cover, had another fumble with Sarah, behind the bar this time, smoked his joint then had a go at the crosswords. This work wouldn't suit him at all, by now he was used to being occupied in one way or another, even if it was only working the head. What he did notice, not one drop of alcohol passed his lips while he was behind the bar, strange. He asked for a cup of tea when Sarah brought his meal from the chippy, determined to keep a clear head and plan the rest of his day.

By closing time they had only poured twelve pints between them, not even enough to cover his wages. He kissed Sarah, jumped on his bike and pedalled down to the garage to see if his Range Rover was ready.

Tonka threw him the keys and told him to take her for a test drive. Beautiful, better than ever. No one would ever know it had been wrapped around a tree. Tonka was stripping what he could salvage from a written off Jag when he returned. Pink asked how much he owed, looked inside at the Jag's dashboard and made a bid for the radio cassette. Tonka shook his head and promised to have it fitted before closing time, at no extra charge. All in all the Range Rover had cost him the sum total of seventy five quid, a snip.

Cycling through the park, he heard a psssst and thought he had a puncture. The bushes rustled as he dismounted to check and Doc showed his agitated face, stepping out of the undergrowth like the wild man of Borneo. He owned up to having absconded from the loony bin a few days earlier by giving his minder the slip, but was now considering giving himself up. The inmates were crying out for some decent drugs and he had picked up on a debt of several tabs of acid. Pink was immediately interested, not in Doc's plight as such, but in the acid. He hadn't taken a trip in over six months and felt it was nigh on time he resolved that.

Doc couldn't show his face. If Pink could help him out there would be a little something in it for him. Pink had an idea the cops would like to speak to Doc about the severe beating he had given Rizla. If he didn't hand himself in at the nuthouse, he would most likely end up in jail and Doc knew which establishment he preferred. Pink told him to make his way to the park gates, he would be there in ten minutes.

Time was of the essence. Pink rode back to the garage and demanded another test drive. Tonka scratched his head and nodded towards the office where he kept the keys, he could see Pink was in a hurry and didn't ask questions.

Doc's eyes were at the back of his head, his first trip in five months taking effect and bringing on his paranoia a treat. Pink made him crouch in the back seat and drove out to the house on the hill. Doc had mentioned part of the protective wall was lower and he found it almost right away. Doc was off his head by now, he didn't know Pink, but somehow knew he owed him. From the lining of his coat he produced two sheets of blotting paper and told Pink to help himself. Pink admired the little squares, depicting a window with tied back curtains, considered the risk he had taken, and helped himself to a third of a sheet; fair payment. Doc was in no condition to argue, he wouldn't allow Pink to conceal his booty back where it had come from and shoved it loosely down his sock. Pink made a step for him with his hands and lofted him over the wall, hearing him land with a thud. He could be heard scurrying through the bushes on the other side, making what sounded like duck calls. Pink could do no more for him and silently wished him well.

At the bike shed he stashed the acid and counted out enough cash to cover Tonka's payment, plus a few quid for his back pocket.

Tonka sent him into the office to make a cup of tea while he fitted the radio cassette. Doc's name came up in the conversation, but only through Tonka guessing he had somehow skipped the country and was living with Mad Frank. Pink liked the theory, but added nothing of his own; as far as he knew, Doc was still with the shrinks.

He left the bike at the garage, it would have fitted into the Range Rover, but he didn't want to risk damaging the upholstery.

Towser didn't want to let him in until he recognised his voice. Fester told him to go and lie down and he complied without a whimper. He wagged his tail at Pink, though, maybe a little disappointed there was no food for him. Fester handed over a wad of notes, the cutlery had flown off the shelves; in fact, he could have shifted twice as much again. Towser was an asset, good company and the best tenter he had ever had the pleasure of working with. No one, but no one would pass over his threshold without the dog's say so. He asked after Gwynneth's health and told Pink to pass on his regards.

Seeing Pink out, he was impressed with his wheels, even more impressed when Pink revealed how he had come about them.

Promising to do business again soon, Pink rode off in the direction of the setting sun and the High Chaperral.

He didn't get changed. On a whim, he took four tiny squares of the blotting paper and went in search of the brothers Waite, finding them at his first port of call, the Marlborough Club. Not only that, he also dropped on the other objects of his affections, the two scrotes.

Slipping the acid to Heavy, he outlined his cunning plan and sat back with a pint of cider to watch the fun. The Waites' sister, Feather, was the barmaid, which went a long way towards him carrying out his plan. The scrotes were drinkers, not known for using and abusing drugs other than hash. Feather was given the task of spiking their drinks when they next visited the bar. Let the good times roll.

Pink played snooker and paid no attention to them. Light tipped him the wink when the deed had been done.

Forty minutes later, the bewildered scrotes staggered towards an imaginary door and tried to exit, twice. Then, one of them fell to his knees and crawled under a table, stood up again, spilling drinks and accepting a sore face for doing so. His mate burst into tears and started flapping anxiously at a swarm of imaginary bees until someone suggested they might be wasps. That didn't help his cause much since he became even more animated, making machine gun noises while brandishing a pretend weapon and had the rest of the club's clientele in fits. Scrote one had problems of his own. His legs wouldn't go where he wanted them to and he complained the wallpaper was swallowing him whole.

Someone rang the cops, or told Feather to do so; which was maybe just as well since things were getting decidedly out of control. Scrote two took a wobbly run at Light Waite and felt the butt end of the snooker cue in his ribs.

Pink heard the siren on the approach. Scrote one seemed to think it was music and tried to dance with his mate

Two burly policemen soon had the situation under control, or so they thought. Handcuffed together and obviously terrified, the scrotes made a bold bid for freedom, following the light from the window and crashing through it like a scene from a cowboy film; great stuff.

Pink and the Waites had tears of laughter blinding them. They followed the show outside with the other punters, squealing with delight as one scrote dragged the other across the busy road and tried to hijack a car, a moving car. The driver swerved in an attempt to avoid them, but clipped a stray leg. The cops managed to stop the traffic and bring them under control. They were quiet for a few seconds, then tried to run in opposite directions; realised they were tied together and began kicking seven colours of shit out of each other. The ambulancemen refused to take them until they were sedated and one cop asked the other how the fuck they should write it up. His mate told him it probably wasn't over yet, maybe they should take a few statements?

With the show all but over, Pink repaired to the club, shook the Waites by the hand, bought Feather a drink for her trouble, downed what was left of his own drink and went home happy as a sandboy; happier than a pig in shit.

"I was just about to send out a search party for you."

"I wasn't lost, just busy."

"He-he. Well, now you're here, can we have some music, please."

"What's you're pleasure?"

"Watching you in the shower."

"That makes sense."

"He-he. Doobie brothers, Pink. Yes, the Doobie brothers, please."

Pink obliged, then, remembering his promise, opened Eight Ball's escape hatch. The cat almost ruptured himself in his haste, a sure symptom of cabin fever.

Where had the day gone? Almost eight o'clock. Looking back, it had been eventful to say the least. He couldn't talk openly about most of it, but it would certainly live on in his memory.

He was ready to tell Violet about losing his job and about Sandy, but the music stopped him, maybe later. Instead, he had a shower, tingling with a strange erotic thrill with the realisation she liked to watch him, probably was at this very moment. He came to the conclusion, if he could ever manage to hold her for real, he would give up his other women in a heartbeat; truth.

He drove to Dave's, waited 'til Lily made a pot of tea and left them alone in the kitchen, then told him about the scrotes. Dave was planning his itinerary, unsure as to his destination as yet and with maps and atlases all over the kitchen table. Pink promised him a couple of tabs of the acid on Friday and arranged a time to pick him up to collect their wages. Since Monday had been a holiday, they would be a day late.

Bea was waiting at the bus stop when he left Dave's house. He stopped to pick her up, discovered the witch wasn't at home and accepted her invite of a cup of tea. She looked good, he told her so. She smiled and thanked him. Five minutes later they were throwing each other around in time honoured fashion. Fuck the tea, he would rather fuck Bea. He passed the witch on his way out of the street, but she didn't see him. Good job or she might have cast one of her spells.

Realising he hadn't eaten for a while, he headed out of town towards the restaurant and found himself outside Jenny and Elise's new flat. What the hell, he had no drugs on him, but he could invite them out for a meal. As usual, the girls were delighted to see him and even more delighted at the prospect of a free feed.

Ash found them a quiet table in the corner, gave Pink his customary bear hug and told him his money was no good. The curry, the beer and the wine flowed until all three were fit to burst. Ash closed the door and locked it then handed Pink a large spliff, just what the doctor ordered. Joining them at the table and finding the girls lived locally, he invited them to call in anytime, bring their friends and enjoy a generous discount.

Pink stung him for a couple of joints of oil before taking the girls home, the night was still young, he hadn't thought of it before, but a four timer was on the cards. It had never been attempted before. History was about to be made or his name wasn't Pink Lynt.

Jenny impressed Elise with her skills at skinning up, Pink impressed them both with his skills at unhooking bras, managing two at the same time. The bedroom had been transformed since his last visit. It looked like something from a glossy magazine he had once skinned up on. No matter, the bed took a real pounding, passing the test with flying colours and leaving its occupants gasping for breath.

Half past three in the morning and Pink woke up with a girl on either side. He didn't know which way to turn for the best so sneaked out without disturbing them; they both had work later, he could see himself out. Before he left, he constructed the other joint and left it in plain view, switched the light off and closed the door quietly behind him.

Johan was fast asleep in one of the chairs with Eight Ball dozing on his knee. Pink checked the ovens, helped himself to some baked goods and closed yet another door quietly behind him.

"You'll be knackered when it's time for work, Honey."

"I very much doubt it, Violet."

"What do you mean? You'll only have about three hours."

"Not so, Kitten. They've dispensed with my services, I'm afraid."

"Huh? …. What did you do to deserve that?"

"More what I didn't do."

"You don't seem too bothered by it? Tell me what happened."

"It all began a long, long time ago in a faraway place......."

"Cut to the sports pages, Pink. I'm curious."

"You in a hurry? Would you rather be somewhere else?"

"You know better than that. C'mon, what happened? Don't make me swear, Honey."

"Ok. It was windy, no visibility so I had a kip in the digger."

"And you got caught, silly man."

"Who's telling this tale?"

"Sorry. Do carry on, he-he."

"At morning break or thereabouts, I went to the canteen and Jimmy Glover decided to throw his weight around, ordering me here there and everywhere"

".... Well, that's his job, isn't it?"

"Grrrrrr."

"He-he. Sorry, Honey"

"Then, he told me Sandy had taken a stroke. I'll swear he was smiling when he said it. Anyway, Keg, the crane driver, hadn't turned up so I had to cover for him. The wind was still howling, but it was dry. The tower crane is designed to work only under a certain wind speed, it cut out on me once and I shit myself. The windometer said"

".... Windometer?"

"There's a twirly thing on top of the crane, it spins round in the wind and informs you via a dial in the cab how high the wind is gusting. If it isn't called a windometer, it should be. So, the windometer said gusting over sixty miles per hour and the safety margin is fifty five. Like I said, it cut out once, the wind took me into another jib, another crane, and I was down that ladder as fast as I could go. Jimmy Glover sent me back up, I told him to fuck off and he sacked me. Oh, I forgot to mention, when I was up in the crane, Dave had a piss through the open window of Glover's van. When I went for my bike, Barry told me Sandy had died and I lost all interest in the place at that very moment."

"Did Dave get the sack, too?"

"Not exactly."

"Explain."

"He sacked himself. Gave the foreman a black eye and sacked himself."

"If Sandy hadn't died you would have been given your job back, is that right?"

"Probably, but I wouldn't have taken it. I would end up killing the Glover bastard, arrogant shit that he is."

"Poor Pinkee. What will you do now, for work I mean?"

"Concentrate on my import business probably; there's no rush, no rush at all."

"I like the sound of this Dave. Why don't you bring him round for a drink and a smoke? I'd like to see him."

"You mean you'd show yourself? Talk to him?"

"He-he. No, silly. I'd just like to put a face to the name. It's a woman thing."

"I would bring him, but Eight Ball won't let him in the house."

"Eight Ball?"

"It's a mutual feeling between them. Dave's scared of cats and Eight Ball plays on it, he can sense it."

"But he's such a sweetheart."

"Who, Dave?"

"He-he."

"Anyway, I'm determined not to bring anyone back you won't talk to. Pon put the shits up you, didn't he?"

"True, but only because of what you threatened to do beforehand."

"But when you realised he was a mate of mine, you still didn't show."

"I don't think he's quite so laid back as you are. If I had appeared and spoke to him, he would most probably have to go back to the drawing board and reconsider his religious beliefs."

"Fair point, Violet, but until you're ready to come out, so to speak, it's you, me and Eight Ball."

"And the music."

"That goes without saying."

"Well, thanks for sharing that with me. As long as you're not too bothered about losing your job. When's the funeral?"

"Dunno yet. I've to phone later today."

"C'mon. Let's go to bed."

"I thought you'd never ask."

"He-he."

CHAPTER 43

One and two thirds sheets to the wind

Pink roses, pink carnations, pink of every flower imaginable and all smelling of lavender. Sandy stood at his own graveside, his lopsided grin aimed at Pink. Tanzi leaned on his spade waiting for the word to back fill it, but Sandy didn't appear to be in any hurry to take up residence. Jimmy Glover walked past the open grave and Tanzi clipped him on the back of the head with the spade, causing him to fall in. Pink and Sandy helped Tanzi to shovel the loose earth over him, then danced a jig on top when they were done.

"You were smiling in your sleep, Pinkee. Nice dream?"

"Hard to say. The end result was nice enough."

"Don't forget you've a phone call to make."

Pink looked at the clock, just after nine, he would take the dirty laundry down and make his call from the nearby box.

Suzanne, Sandy's secretary, was under orders not to disclose the funeral details to him. The two sons didn't want him there because of his efforts in stopping production. Pink talked her round by pointing out Sandy would have wanted him to be there. What the hell, she was about to throw the job in anyway, she didn't get on with the brothers and had no desire to work for them.

The lady in the bric-a-brac shop gave him a wave and beckoned him in, she had two albums he might like. Bat out of Hell and Dire Straits, the one with Sultans of Swing on it; both in mint condition. He gave her a kiss and told her to keep up the good work.

He followed breakfast up with a joint, a cocktail. Eight Ball was back to his best, chasing smoke rings like a daft kitten and making Violet howl with laughter; music to his ears.

Dave had news of the scrotes. They had been charged with affray, violent conduct and assaulting a police officer. Pink was pleased to hear it, maybe they would be allowed to spend some time with their good friends, the Blunts.

Dave's travel plans were more or less finalised. He would look up Mad Frank, stay with him for a few days then head for India. Pink handed over four sections of the blotting paper, two for Dave and two for Frank.

Jimmy Glover wasn't at all pleased to see them. Pink admired his black eye and complimented Dave on his work, doubting very much if he could have done better himself. They were advised to pick up their wages and get the fuck off the site; advice they completely ignored, a cup of coffee in the canteen and a chat with the many friends they had made, throwing the foreman's words back in his face.

They had a pint in the Canine Dog Club then went their separate ways, arranging to meet up for a drink at the Albatross later

Pink drove home, bagged up all his money and took it upstairs to count. He was shocked to find he was worth over three thousand five hundred quid, how did that happen? Not that he was bothered, mind you. On a whim, he picked out twenty newish looking pound notes. He would ask Kira to iron them, then wrap them with Mira's present.

"What you doing with all that money, Honey? Hey, I'm a poet. Did you hear? Money Honey?"

"It's getting a bit out of hand, I'm going to stick it all in the bank. I don't like the places, but I can't leave all this lying around, can I?"

"Where did you get it from? Is it legal?"

"Mostly it's from gambling and drugs, sort of legal"

"Won't the bank be curious?"

"Maybe, but if they want to ask questions I'll take it somewhere else."

"That's the way to do it, Honey."

He left her with the radio. Later, he would let her hear the new records, keep her quiet for a while.

The carrier bag snagged on the inside of the Range Rover door, splitting down one side and almost depositing the contents on the pavement. Some fancy fingerwork had it wrapped up again before that could happen; the walls had eyes and no one knew that better than he did.

He asked to see someone in private and was shown into an office. A smartly dressed young lady joined him. He could tell she was dying to ask where the dosh had come from, but wouldn't come right out with it. He let her do all the paperwork before mentioning it was from gambling, he wanted to bank it in case he was tempted to try his hand at increasing it. This seemed to satisfy her curiosity and she asked him to sign the deposit slip. The bank books were kept in the bottom drawer and he admired her hind quarters as she bent in front of him, the tight uniform skirt leaving little to the imagination.

Half an hour later he was in a phone box dialling Louise's number, no answer; the bank clerk had started his juices flowing. Nothing for it but to see if Bea was available.

Indeed she was, available and ever so willing to accommodate him. No sign of the witch, either, not that he would have cared with his rampant state being in dire need of attention.

On a whim, he bundled Bea into the Range Rover and treated her to a meal in the countryside, closely followed by a roll in the hay, or what would be hay later in the year. The sun felt good on his back, reminding him to get on with planting his own crop. Summer was definitely on the way.

Bea spoiled the moment by asking if the interlude meant they were back on, back to where they were. Pink was non-committal, as always, ignoring the question and all but pushing her into the vehicle to take her home. He ended up dropping her off in the town centre with no promise to meet up later. He liked her, but he liked his freedom more.

Moraji saw him walk past the shop window and met him at the back door, he knew what the topic would be and she didn't disappoint him. An update on the wedding plans then an invitation to drive the bride and her sisters to the venue. It meant an early start, but yes, he would be honoured, only thing was he had promised Johan a lift. Not a problem, he was almost part of the family now and Sira would be tickled pink at the idea.

He propped his bike against the wall and ran upstairs to skin a couple of cocktails up. A brief chat with Violet and he gathered his shoots and the bottle of piss he had filled. He had read somewhere that something in the urine was good for plants and decided to feed his crop with nothing but the best.

It felt strange not to see Towser at what was left of the Blunts' allotment. He had only been away from the site for a few days, but the stench was almost overwhelming. While he had been working there he had become accustomed to it, or at least was able to ignore it.

He planted the shoots, covered them with a thin layer of sharp sand from a pile he had conveniently spilled in passing while driving the dumper, and gave them their first feed of piss.

He cycled to the old water treatment plant, found his plank and picked as many mushrooms as he could fit into the bag he had carried the bottle of piss in. At home, he laid half the bag's contents on Moraji, telling her to wash them thoroughly, locked the bike in the shed and drove out to the restaurant.

Ash couldn't believe the size and texture of the mushrooms, he could use all Pink could supply; in fact, he had a mate down on the market who would pay handsomely for such produce. Pink was back in business with a good reason to get out of bed in the mornings, he could pick mushrooms early on and feed his plants at the same time.

One of the waiters brought an early edition of the evening local paper as Pink and Ash shared a joint. Doc's crazy eyes were on the front page. He had barricaded himself into his room at the nuthouse when the cops came to interview him about a recent assault, taking a young care assistant as hostage. When the staff and cops breached his defences, he took his leave via the third floor window. Luckily, his hostage landed on top of him and sustained little or no injury. Doc, however, didn't fare so well. He landed on his head and died instantly. A search of his quarters failed to show any drugs, which had Pink thinking maybe he dropped them when he landed over the wall. Only one way to find out, and he would have to be quick before they searched the grounds.

At the low point in the wall, he parked up and listened for any movement from within. Silence. He used the Range Rover's rear bumper as a leg up and was over in a flash at the exact point Doc had used. The place was foreboding, creepy; knee high grass and huge trees, as silent as the grave. Pink shivered and wondered if he hadn't made a mistake, maybe he should have thought it through instead of acting on impulse? Still, he was here now, might as well have a look around. Five minutes later he saw a sheet and two thirds of acid fluttering in the light breeze. He pounced on them before they could flutter any further and stashed them safely under his bob cap after quickly checking for dampness.

That had been easy enough, but now he had a problem. The drop was higher from the inside, something he hadn't accounted for and something he would have to contend with in a bit of a hurry since he could hear voices not too far distant.

Hiding behind the nearest tree, he peeked round and saw a line of coppers approaching. They'd obviously had the same idea as himself and were searching the grounds.

The trees were all but bare what with it still being spring, plenty of buds on show, but he really needed foliage of some sort. Finding a large conifer, he climbed inside and upwards until he resembled the fairy on a Christmas tree. Fir cones and needles were shaking loose as he climbed, but he managed to steady the ship before the police reached his perch. One of them stopped for a piss and he reckoned he could have knocked his helmet off with a well aimed cone.

Danger over, he spied his escape route from his lofty position. A wheelbarrow, a wheel-less wheelbarrow, but one which could be propped against the wall, thus allowing him to reach the top.

Halfway down from the tree, his bob cap was whisked off by a recoiling branch. Without thinking, he used one hand to save the acid and the other to recover his cap. Big mistake, he had the presence of mind to keep quiet as he fell, but winded himself when he hit the ground. At the time he felt maybe one or two ribs had copped it, but he wasn't hanging about to find out.

Dragging the wheelbarrow to the lowest part of the wall, he propped it up, judged all the angles as if lining up a pool shot, took seven paces back and ran full pelt at it, shit or bust.

If anything, his efforts were over productive, he barely touched the top of the wall and grasped frantically at it as he sailed over. This time it felt like two or three ribs on the other side had given way, but he was over and dashing for the Range Rover, stopping in his tracks when he saw a large policeman giving it the once over. Time for the bluff as the copper spotted him. He made a show of pulling up his zip and explained he'd been caught short, at the same time asking directions to the airport. The copper didn't bat an eyelid, told him to turn back, go about half a mile, turn left then follow the signs. Pink thanked him, let him turn back the way he had come from and gingerly checked his ribs for damage.

Gwynneth poured him a free pint of cider and set about shooing the hangers on from the pub, it was closing time, she had a home to go to if they didn't.

Seeing the pain etched on his face, she checked him out for broken bones then told him what he needed was a warm, salty bath, no argument.

She ran the bath, told him to jump in and disappeared to roll a joint, laughing her head off when she returned to find him soaking and still wearing his bob cap. Her eyes lit up at the sight of the acid, should she make a bid to get the night off? They could take a trip together, try it out for themselves.

Again, Pink had no argument. He would go home, change his clothes and return with some booze, but not before he gave his body a work out, see if he was up to it.

No problems there. Maybe not quite so vigorous as he would have liked to be, but no complaints from Gwynneth, as always.

He took another third of a sheet with him, stockpiling as he had done with the black and the oil, one never knew when the next drought would hit and by all accounts it was going to be a long, hot summer. If no one else had drugs, he and his nearest and dearest would; he would make sure of that.

Mr Rapati caught him at the back door and pumped his hand, thanking him for making himself available to take the girls to the wedding. He and Moraji could then go down a couple of nights before and stay with the in-laws, safe in the knowledge the ladies were in good hands. Pink thanked him in turn for his trust and confidence, thinking to himself his feet were well and truly under the Rapati table.

Sultans of Swing was given the shower treatment. Violet reckoned she had heard it a couple of times on the radio, but was still mesmerised and impressed with Pink's rendition.

Armed with four bottles of cider, he was on the road again and heading for Gwynneth's place; but fate was against him in the shape of Gloria. She stood at the traffic lights waiting to cross the road and saw him. In a flash and without so much as a by your leave, she was in the passenger seat and puckering up for a kiss. Pink tested the waters, a few choice questions to determine her state of mind and he drove her home, they both knew why; they both knew there would be no strings attached.

His intention was to be in and out, wipe his dick on the curtains and make all speed to his earlier destination. Gloria had other plans. Not in a bunny boiling way, it seemed she was short on company. So, Pink took a little more time than he had at first envisaged doing, allowing her to dictate the pace by playing the tape he had done for her, then a slow striptease which he found himself enjoying more than he would ever care to admit to the woman.

He knew her body, had devoured it greedily; now it was on a plate in front of him, he decided to push the boundaries and came across no resistance whatsoever.

Gloria didn't object when he put his clothes back on, merely invited him back anytime he liked, she didn't ever want to scare him away again. Pink told her she was a good girl, he would be sure to return if her attitude remained the same. Again, she told him, anytime; anytime at all.

Feeling good with himself, he put his foot down to make up for lost time. Gwynneth saw him through the window and opened the front door, taking the cider from him and placing it in the fridge for later. Pink suggested a night out at the Albatross, have a few beers and drop the acid towards the end of the evening. Gwynneth didn't need much persuading, happy to go along with the plan, she didn't care as long as she had Pink on her arm.

They had a cocktail in the bedroom as he watched her change outfits over and over again. He called it right when she plumped for the first combination she had tried, but that didn't detract from his viewing pleasure.

He trimmed ten squares from a corner of the blotting paper for Brat, thus isolating himself from the source. It would be sure to sell.

The evening passed pleasantly until half a dozen speed freaks spoiled the mood. Most of the clientele preferred the slow motion ambience of the smokers' world and such an intrusion tended to upset the applecart. Pink and Gwynneth decided there and then to neck the acid, perhaps an hour and a half before the allotted time, if things were to become more agitated they might as well get a head start on it.

The speedsters talked and talked and talked, eyes like pissholes in the snow. What they had to say was all shite, just for the sake of talking and Pink could see those nearest to them were looking decidedly uncomfortable.

Brat played a Hendrix tune and one of them stood to show off his air guitar, almost taking a young lady's eye out with his elbow and displaying even more bad manners by refusing to acknowledge the fact, merely carrying on with his flailing.

Pink knew from past experience the importance of a smooth start to a trip and took it upon himself to sort the problem out before it could get out of hand. He strolled over to Brat and had a word in his ear, then sat back down with his lady. When Hendrix finished wringing the neck of his guitar, Brat segued into Leonard Cohen's 'Avalanche'. The speed freaks took one look in Brat's direction, eyeballed each other, downed their drinks as one and bounced out of the room to the relief of all present.

As soon as Brat knew they were clear of the place he replaced 'Avalanche' with ' Bat out of Hell', quite a contrast, but no words of objection from the floor.

Pink looked at Gwynneth's watch, forty five minutes and nothing. He knew the validity of the acid from recent observations, namely the scrotes and Doc, so why was it taking so long to kick in? A word with Brat found him with another square of blotting paper clasped in his hand. Gwynneth provided a pair of nail scissors and he cut it diagonally, gave her half and both necked it, impatient for the trip to start, now impatient for the trip and a half to start.

Dave lurched in and joined them. No, he didn't want a drink. The last pint he had looked big enough to drown in, he was off his head on the acid. Pink and Gwynneth could feel themselves about to join him.

In a rush they were there, the house lights were flashing. Either the drug squad had landed or it was the sign for last orders. Pink went to the bar anyway. Faces blended with wallpaper. Jazz, the barman, asked 'Same again?' This saved Pink from trying to talk, a nod being sufficient. He managed to return to his seat with most of the contents intact and set the drinks down in front of Dave; mistake, he now had two swimming pools to contend with and recoiled at the prospect.

Gwynneth laughed nervously. Pink took a drink from one of the pint glasses in an effort to pacify Dave, but the game was up, the seed had been planted in his brain and he stumbled towards the exit and the night.

Brat offered them a lift, but Pink felt ok enough to drive, it was only a couple of miles after all. Gwynneth clung to him as they set off in search of the Range Rover, up and down side streets which should have been familiar to him, but suddenly weren't; where the fuck did they leave it?

Down an unlit street, he wouldn't have parked here, not in the grand canyon, he could feel Gwynneth agreeing with him as she tugged at his sleeve in an effort to steer him away from there. They found the vehicle on the next corner, clambered in, took a few moments to acclimatise to the surroundings and drove off.

He wondered why he couldn't see very far in front and eventually found the switch for the headlights, giving himself a fright when the full beam reflected off a window. On the main road, he marvelled at the many different coloured lights, a cross between Christmas and a funfair. Headlights, tail lights, street lights, traffic lights and what was that pretty blue light in the rear view mirror? Fuck, the police, did they want him? Should he stop or make a run for it? Relief, they flashed past in pursuit of something or someone else, but his heart was pounding now. Gwynneth fiddled with the stereo, oblivious to what was going on. The Pink Floyd tape calmed things down a bit, but he was regretting not taking Brat up on his offer of a lift now.

The traffic lights confused him now, was it green for go? Fuck it, there was no one around; shit, he almost mowed an old couple down on the crossing; perhaps red means go?

Gwynneth asked why they had stopped, unable to recognise her own house. Pink had to help her out of the passenger seat and pat her down in search of the front door key and this brought on a fit of the giggles, which spread between them like wildfire.

Then, an almost sobering experience as they passed the front window. Gwynneth caught her mirror image, stopped to take a good look, took six or seven steps back and charged head first at her reflection. Thankfully, Pink was on hand and had enough about him to stop her in her tracks; that could have been nasty. Somehow, he worked it out, the acid squares depicted a window, the scrotes took a header out of the Marlborough Club window, Doc did the same at the house on the hill. Dave, maybe Dave saw his reflection in the glass or it's contents? There was definitely a connection between the acid and windows, or maybe the acid was doing his reasoning for him? Just to be on the safe side, he closed all the curtains when they eventually accessed the house; no point in taking unnecessary risks.

Gwynneth struck up a conversation with an imaginary friend, Pink couldn't squeeze a word in so busied himself with the radio and found what sounded like a decent station. When the music stopped, the announcer seemed to be having trouble with his diction. Pink tried to ignore it, where did this dude go to school for fuck's sake? Certainly not round this way. Still, he was playing good music so they would let it go at that.

He opened the bottle of cider at the third attempt, poured some in the only receptacle he could find, which turned out to be a flower vase, and handed it to Gwynneth. She didn't bat an eye, drank deeply from it and carried on with her chat, one sided though it was.

Pink flicked through a newspaper, only looking at the pictures since his eyes didn't want to focus on the print. Until he came to the crossword that was, but he didn't have a pen. A flash of inspiration saw him upset Gwynneth's bag and empty its contents onto the floor. The nail scissors gleamed invitingly and soon he was cutting letters from the paper and placing them on the squares of the puzzle, all the while trying to decipher what the bloke on the radio was jabbering about between songs; even the news sounded garbled.

Gwynneth was shivering. She had set the coal fire before going out, but was now too scared to light it. Pink obliged and they were instantly lost in the dancing of the flickering flames. She asked him if he spoke German and he told her no. She asked him why he was listening to a German radio station and he had no answer for her, stuck for words as the penny dropped. The fire took their attention again, all manner of shapes and beings in evidence, and heat, so warm. They sat stock still like a couple of old damp Labradors, unable, or unwilling to move.

Daylight came with a chink of light through a gap in the curtains. Pink followed Gwynneth's gaze and was startled to see three empty cider bottles nestling in the embers of the fire. With no knowledge of how they came to be there, and the realisation it was a stupid place to keep them. That could have been nasty. Gwynneth had a headache, probably from coming down off the acid. Pink seemed to be ok, it wasn't his favourite part of the trip, and usually he made sure he had a couple of downers to provide a soft landing. Not to worry, a joint of best black would do the trick.

They snuggled down on the couch and made themselves comfortable before sparking it up. No sooner had they smoked it than someone hammered on the door. Had it been the drug squad, they could have helped themselves, planted all manner of shit and busted them good and proper. But it was Brat and the door was off the latch, had been all night. All three burst into spontaneous laughter on sight. Brat only wanted an update on the acid.

Pink aired his observations regarding the windows and Gwynneth remembered charging at her reflection as he recounted the actions of Doc and the scrotes. Brat decided to leave it for a while, see if anyone else came up with the same connection, outrageous as it seemed.

They woke up in bed, Pink subconsciously trying to get his leg over and Gwynneth wondering who the fuck he was. It all ended amicably as they jockeyed for the best position, his bruised ribs a dim and distant memory.

Breakfast was a leisurely affair, going over events of their trip and vowing to do it again soon. Gwynneth's watch said half past two, but with the curtains still closed it could have been night or day. The German announcer wasn't much help, either.

CHAPTER 44

Funny how things turn out

"Pink! Oh, Pink. Someone came to the door in the middle of the night. I was worried something had happened to you."

"Who was it?"

"I don't know."

"What time?"

"Just after the four o'clock news, I think."

"How many times did they knock? How long did they try?"

"Twice, about three or four minutes."

"Well, if it's important they'll come back. Don't worry your pretty little head about it."

"Like I said, I WAS worried. You've been such a long time."

"Oh, I've been on a trip."

"Somewhere nice?"

"Out of this world."

"Music please, Honey. I need some decent music."

"Coming up, Violet. What would you like?"

"Joe Cocker, so I can play my air guitar."

"Where's Eight Ball?"

"On the bed. Johan fed him, then one of the girls fed him so he's content."

"He told you that?"

"He-he. Yes, he told me that."

Pink played Joe Cocker as requested, had a long piss in the empty milk bottle and rolled a cocktail. There hadn't been any rain, his plants would be crying out for a drink.

On a whim, he drove round by Dave's. All the window's seemed to be intact, which was a good sign. He rapped on the front door and Frank, Dave's dad, shouted the door was open. Dave sat in the kitchen with a block of cheddar and half a loaf in front of him. When he saw Pink, he put his fingers to his lips, picked up his plate and motioned for Pink to follow him into the back yard.

Astonishingly, the windows connection reared it's ugly head again. Dave had wandered down by the canal towpath and had come across a white van not unlike Jimmy Glover's. Without even thinking about it, he had pelted the windscreen with stones until it succumbed to his will. No one came to investigate despite all the noise, so he then set about all the other windows. Now, he was regretting his actions and only hoped the owner was covered by insurance. Pink told him about the other strange connections and he agreed there was something to the theory. With that off his chest, he asked for a lift to the ferry port the following night, it was time he was out of there.

A good few of the shoots had poked their heads through the thin layer of sharp sand and Pink gave them a generous feed of piss and fresh water, scanning his surroundings to make sure no one was spying on him as he poured. The smell of the treatment plant tended to keep all but the brave away, anyway.

Next, he filled a couple of bags with mushrooms and drove out to see Ash. The market would be closed by now, but Ash would be able to make use of them what with it being the weekend.

Ash wouldn't entertain the acid, politely declining a free trip and explaining only natural produce would enter his body, nothing manufactured, thank you. Pink picked his brains about Indian weddings, how he should behave and such. Ash told him some weddings could run for days on end, but these days tended to be much shorter. The bride and groom would draw up an itinerary of how they wanted it to go and everyone would be obliged to fit in with their plans. Pink saw now why he would be taking the girls down. Obviously, the happy couple had settled for just the one day. As for his behaviour, he had been entrusted with the safe delivery of the bride, which meant he was highly thought of. He should be himself, oh, and make sure he washed behind his ears.

Ash very kindly made him up a takeaway, enough for three, it would be rude of Pink not to visit the flatmates while he was in the area. The girls had another girlfriend round and were glad of the food, making it stretch four ways instead of three. Pink had the feeling his amorous intentions had been scuppered by the cuckoo in the nest and resignedly tucked into his meal. However, Elise acted the minx by playing footsie with him under the table, giving him fresh hope in the loin department.

The other girl, Angie, had only called round to invite Jenny over to see her new flat, Elise had already taken the grand tour which went a long way towards explaining the under table foreplay. Ten minutes later, they were alone and tearing clothes from flesh in a frenzy, Jenny having stoked the fire by giving him an intimate squeeze on her way out.

It felt strange having Elise one on one. Not that he gave it more than a passing thought, preferring to concentrate on what was before him. She had put on a little weight, but he was diplomatic enough not to mention this, even though it looked good on her; a little more to catch hold of.

They worked up a sweat and let the neighbours know what was going on; there could surely have been no doubt in their minds, no doubt at all.

They were sharing a joint when Jenny returned, but gave the game away by still breathing heavily. Jenny seemed slightly miffed until Elise stuck her head up her short skirt and released some of the pressure. True to form, Pink felt the early twitches of arousal and soon all three were writhing on the floor in a tangled mess of limbs and flesh.

A cup of coffee and another cocktail later, he was out of there; promising to meet them in the Albatross later, but drawing the line at staying the night with them, for now.

Angie lived five doors away from the girls and waved from her window as he drove past. He hadn't paid her too much attention earlier, but slowed to have a good look now. Not bad, not at all bad.

The Rapati sisters ignored their one and only customer and descended upon Pink en masse, all talking at once and pushing each other out of the way to be heard first. Wedding talk, what else?

He held his hands up for silence, at the same time wandering behind the counter and asking the old Indian lady if he could help her. She saw the funny side of it, ordered a loaf and some savouries, handed over her cash and left smiling.

Pink was to keep Friday afternoon clear; all three girls were to be painted, whatever that meant. Before he could ask, the subject had been changed to what he would be wearing, only because Mira wanted him in some of the photographs, just so he knew.

Kira had him by the hand now, would he take her to the restaurant? All this wedding talk was doing her head in and she needed a break from it. Having only just returned from there, he had to disappoint her, besides, time was getting on, he had people to see and a number of beers to drink. Kira took it on the chin, apologised for trying to monopolize his time and made him promise to take her for a ride soon.

Eight Ball gave him the once over as he would a stranger. Violet laughed at his attitude and at Pink's reaction when he threw his eyes heavenward.

"He's been waiting in all day for you, Honey."

"More fool him. He must be short of something to do."

"He-he. A more neurotic cat would take offence at that. Good job he knows you love him."

"What about you?"

"Oh yes .... he knows I love him too."

"You're learning, Kitten. Very good."

"And I love you too, Pinkee. Very, very much."

"Good girl, you know it makes sense."

Loud banging on the door interrupted them. Pink looked down from the window, but couldn't see anyone. It turned out to be Pon, he had tried the other night, or to be more precise, the other morning. He had been playing cards and drinking with the local priest and had fancied a smoke on his way home. Pink told him he was lucky not to have been arrested at that early hour, then went on to tell of his recent trip. Pon's eyes lit up at the mention of acid, it had been a long, long time. Pink obliged, but rammed home his point about the windows, telling him to be careful. Pon stayed for a joint and a cup of tea, kicking off his shoes and slipping into a groove around the good music. Violet was strangely quiet. Eight Ball wrestled with one of Pon's shoes for a while then settled under Violet's wall like in the old days.

Pink had a quick shower then offered to take Pon home. He drove to the shop front and pipped the horn, bringing Kira at the run, her smile lighting up the night as she clambered into the back seat.

She talked non stop, asking Pon about his work, his faith, how did he know Pink, what was Pink like at school?

Pon told her stories Pink had half forgotten, making her laugh and ask for more. She liked meeting Pink's friends and felt she was getting one over on her sisters when he took her for a spin.

Pon blushed when she kissed him, then blushed again when she clambered into the seat he had vacated, showing what she'd had for breakfast in her haste. Pink reminded him to be careful, shook his hand and promised to see him soon.

Kira talked and talked all the way home, almost demanding to meet more of his friends. Pink wasn't daft enough to promise her anything, it wouldn't be fair to introduce her to some of the people he knew. When he dropped her off, he gave her the twenty pound notes and asked her to iron them. She wouldn't allow herself to ask why, or why she shouldn't mention it to her sisters. The puzzled look on her face tickled him pink and for once she was quiet.

It cost him dearly the moment he strolled into the Albatross. Around one long table sat Jenny, Elise, their friend Angie, Gloria, Jenny the waitress and Katy J. Six ladies of his recent intimate acquaintance. All, except maybe for Angie, had eyes only for him. Playing it cool, he bought them a drink each, saw there wasn't room for him at the table and decided to stand with Brat, see if he could determine the mood. They all seemed to be integrating famously, laughing and joking among themselves and grooving to the music. He threw a cocktail into the mix, let them pass it round then squeezed in between Gloria and Angie when they made room for him. Fuck it, if the shit hit the fan he always had Violet to fall back on. Oh and Louise, oh and Sarah, then there was Gwynneth, and not forgetting Bea. He hadn't realised his love life had become so complicated, too busy having a good time for that.

It surprised him how amicably the evening passed; it also surprised him how outrageous the seemingly demure Angie could be, her hands were all over him at any given opportunity. She actually tried to follow him into the gents at one point. Nice girl.

Last orders found him in a bit of a dilemma, six women and only the one dick. Gloria eased the strain a little by offering to walk Jenny the waitress home, it was on her way. Katy J lived between the pub and the three other girls' homes so he offered all of them a lift. Brat was highly amused by all this, shaking his head and probably half wishing he had the same problem.

Angie claimed the front passenger seat to the distaste of the others, more or less forcing him to declare he was tired and would be heading for home after dropping everyone off. That would be the fairest way to do it, no arguments.

Katy J went with a goodnight to all and a peck on the cheek for Pink. Jenny and Elise lingered by his open window before kissing him goodnight. All that remained was for Angie to take her leave, he hadn't seen her flat, had he? She had only been in residence for a couple of days, how would he like a nice cup of coffee?

With it being reduced to just the two of them, Angie was back to her original demure self. Pink played along, played it cool, flicked through her record collection before tuning the radio when he couldn't find anything interesting. Angie was in the kitchen so he crept in behind her, scooped a tit in each hand and worked his groin into her pert behind. That was it, the gloves were off, they were naked within seconds and joined at the hip shortly thereafter, adjourning quickly to the comfort of the living room so as to get to know each other that little bit better. In a matter of minutes, Angie managed to elevate herself to the dizzy heights of his number one girl, all down to the fact she proved to be double jointed. The positions she twisted herself into added another dimension to his technique, the highlight being when she found herself able to watch as he penetrated her without the aid of a mirror, unreal.

Without wishing to upset his girls farther up the road, he made his excuses and left. They both knew he'd be back, it would be rude of him not to return for more.

Johan was pleased to see him and laughed his head off at his tales of tripping and shagging. He was now looking forward to the wedding and revealed he had popped the question himself, having bought a ring from his smuggling profits. He and Sira planned to announce their intentions later in the day at Kira's wedding as previously planned. Pink pumped his hand warmly. If his friend was happy, he was happy. They took couple of hours to catch up before Pink started yawning, his bed was calling him and he couldn't for the life of him ignore the call.

"You look tired, Pinkee."

"Got it in one, Kitten."

"He-he. Let's pour you into bed, then."

"Lead on, Violet. Take me there."

CHAPTER 45

People in glass houses

Pink should have slept soundly; should have, but he didn't. Instead, he tried to subject Violet to the contortions and positions Angie had assumed earlier. Violet was having none of it, though, and left the bed in a huff. He woke in a sweat to find her hovering on the wall.

"You ok, Pinkee?"

"Come back to bed."

"He-he. Whatever do you mean?"

"Must have been dreaming."

"I'll say you were dreaming, look at the state of the bed. What was the dream about?"

"Can't remember."

"Go back to sleep, Honey."

"Care to join me?"

"Ok, but no funny business. You're tired."

"Deal."

Violet caused him to go back on his word, almost immediately it seemed. Her tongue was in his ear and her hands were everywhere. He could feel her nipples pressing urgently into his back and turned to face his tormentor. He kissed the face off her, kissed her all over, delighting as she giggled and wriggled. He let her dictate the pace now, mindful of her objections when he had tried to bend her every which way before. She straddled him and rode him for all she was worth, probing his mouth with her hungry tongue and talking him through her orgasm.

Again, he woke in a sweat. This time Violet gazed down on him from the ceiling, an innocent smile on her face like butter wouldn't melt. His hand rested on a damp patch, something new, something different, evidence. What the hell, he ignored it and dropped off to sleep again. No erotic dreams this time, no dreams at all, only the deep sleep of a contented man.

He didn't need to look at the clock, the call to prayers coinciding with his need for a piss. Eight Ball clattered in through the kitchen window, wove between his legs while he peed into the bottle then headed for the warmth of the bed. Pink nudged him over a bit and tried to go back to sleep. Surprisingly, he was successful, grabbing another hour and seriously contemplating doing the same again.

With no plans for the day until he had to take Dave to the ferry, he decided on a lazy interlude, a couple of beers, a couple of cocktails and a stroll down to his garden plot. Smooth.

No milk to go with his breakfast and Eight Ball was loitering with intent, waiting for his cream. Pink descended the stairs and wandered to the back of the bakery. Sunday was cleaning day, all four Rapati ladies had their sleeves rolled up and were getting stuck in to their chores. As soon as Pink stuck his head round the door, everyone stopped what they were doing and flashed their teeth at him. Only one topic, wedding plans, no stone left unturned in a meticulous, almost military build up to next weekend. Pink was impressed and told them so, the attention to detail was no more than Mira deserved. The phone rang and Moraji answered, giving whoever was on the other end an earbashing in her native tongue. Pink caught the tone of her voice and playfully covered Kira's ears to protect her from the diatribe. Her sisters covered their own ears so as not to be left out.

Eight Ball padded in to see what was keeping Pink with his cream, took one look at the strange goings on and turned tail. Pink swore he was shaking his head in bewilderment, but chose to ignore him, happy to show the cat he didn't have exclusive rights to odd behaviour.

With Moraji finished on the phone, it was back to all four women talking at once. Pink headed for the fridge in the shop proper and they followed him as one, there was no escape, nothing for it but to sit down and listen.

Half an hour later he was allowed to leave, but only after he'd promised to take Kira for a ride out, anywhere away from the shop.

Eight Ball sat on the worktop and waited patiently for his treat. Violet tried to distract him, but he was having none of it, knowing full well where his loyalties lay at such times.

Pink ate cornflakes while his eggs boiled, wondering where this attack of the munchies had come from. Usually, a couple of joints started it off, but he hadn't touched any yet. He knew it wouldn't be too long before he did, though.

Violet suggested Alex Harvey should serenade them and Pink couldn't see why not, it had been a while and fitted his mood to a T.

A quick tidy up, followed by a cocktail then a shower; it was time to tend to his plants. Carrying the bottle of piss in a plastic bag, he rapped on the shop window for Kira and walked her down to his patch. She linked his arm and talked non stop until the stench from the treatment plant filled her nostrils. Pink smiled and carried on walking, half dragging her into the stink ahead. She got over it quite quickly, picking up where she had left off and bending his ear further than any woman had ever done. At his garden plot, he produced the bottle and fed the shoots, explaining to Kira it was special feed for special plants. He sent her to the edge of the canal to fill the bottle with water and saw a look of understanding on her face when she returned; the penny had dropped. He didn't have to tell her no one was to know about the place, she knew when to keep her mouth shut.

They strolled back through the park. She had wanted a ride in the Range Rover, but told him this was much better, he was easily a better listener when he wasn't concentrating on driving.

Donny Boot's woman met them where the paths crossed, she was pushing the pram and seemed in something of a hurry. No time to chat, but had he heard about the windows? No? Donny would explain.

With that she was gone, leaving Pink curious, more than curious if truth be told.

He pushed Kira through the back door and shouted see you later to the ladies, jumped into the vehicle and pointed it in the direction of the Boot house, intrigued by his meeting with Donny's woman.

Cowboy responded to the secret knock on the back door, a huge, turban-like bandage on his head.

Inside, Donny, Reg and Bongo had the look of men on the receiving end of a great shock, unable or unwilling to speak of it.

Pink found the makings and sat down to roll a joint, the others visibly relaxed, but still no words were forthcoming. Eventually, Bongo found his tongue and started in on the tale. Reg scored some acid, he wasn't at liberty to divulge where from. Pink waived the need for this information and asked Bongo to continue.

Reg turned up with four tabs of acid, blotting paper depicting a window on each square. They'd had a couple of joints of best black and some beers. Around half past ten and with the kids safely tucked up in bed, all four dropped one each and settled down to enjoy, looking forward to it since it had been a long time. An hour later, they were buzzing, playing the weirdest music they could find, pulling faces at each other, trying to follow what was on the telly and generally having fun with it. Reg went out the back door for a piss so as not to disturb the kids and came back in to report he could hear music, a party, and quite close to hand at that. All four went to investigate, walking along the backs in the darkness in pursuit of the sounds and landed at the nurseries at the end of the road. The greenhouses were in complete darkness, but that was where the music was coming from. One by one they climbed the fence and tiptoed towards the biggest greenhouse. Bongo tried the door, it was open, they poured in, walked along the narrow pathway between tables of tomatoes and found the source of the music, a radio.

They exchanged puzzled looks, then all hell broke loose, glass everywhere as missiles rained in on them. Stones, half bricks, one of which knocked Cowboy for a sixer. Off their heads on acid and as confused as it was possible to be, they panicked. Bongo didn't mind admitting as much, they panicked, no other word for it. Only one purpose in mind and that was to get the fuck out of there by any means open to them. Easier said than done, they were still being bombarded by fuck knows who and in the pitch dark at that. Reg found the nous to upset one of the tables and use it as a battering ram, taking out even more glass than the bombardment had and making an exit in the side of the greenhouse for the rest of them. Cowboy was bleeding badly, but their ordeal wasn't over, not by a long chalk. It was hard to tell how many outlaws were throwing missiles, easy to exaggerate in the dark and under the influence of the acid. Stones were raining in from all angles, stopping only when a police car wailed past with siren blaring and affording them a chance to make good their escape.

Donny, Bongo and Cowboy made use of the ceasefire and got the fuck out of there. Reg, Reg wasn't at all happy about being ambushed and determined to find out who his assailants were. He picked up the tale from Bongo and ran with it.

He sneaked his way to the roadside, followed the hedge round to the corner and took cover. He didn't have long to wait, which pleased him no end. As accustomed as he had been to taking acid, being apart from his compadres had him seeing all manner of things in the hedgerow; his imagination working double overtime, but his resolve holding fast.

Six youths swaggered out of the darkness, maybe thirteen or fourteen years of age. Reg had only one thought in mind now, revenge. He crept after them, back into the nurseries, wishing his friends were with him, but determined to put an end to the matter at his earliest convenience.

The kids followed their leader into the by now almost glassless greenhouse. Reg looked around for a way to get back at them and saw a huge rain barrel mounted on a tripod towering above the greenhouse. He knew he had to topple it, drop it while they were still inside. At the base of the tripod he stopped to make sure they hadn't moved. They were still having a good laugh at their achievements when Reg put a dampener on their evening by removing one of the tripod legs, watching in slow motion as the barrel teetered unsteadily before dropping like a stone on its intended target. Reg didn't hang about to see if they escaped or not, he didn't care a fuck, he knew any survivors would think twice about messing with him again.

Bongo took over again, rolling his shirt up to show lacerations across his back and shoulders, Donny did likewise. Cowboy's injuries were evident, there for all to see, but Reg was remarkably unscathed. All four swore to a man they were finished with acid, but wouldn't take the bet Pink offered at generous odds.

Donny's woman had been sent on a scouting mission, see if she couldn't find out who the kids were. Reg was happy with his retribution, but the others were seething still.

Pink built another joint using Donny's gear and told them his own tale of the acid. There was definitely something to his theory, no argument and no coincidence. He insisted it had all started with Doc, but Bongo chipped in with the scrotes' episode. Pink admitted to bearing witness to that one, but hadn't known acid was involved. Reg told him the scrotes were in court tomorrow along with the Blunts, maybe they could all meet up and give them a proper send off?

Pink left them to it, deciding to swing round by the nurseries to view the damage instead of doing a U turn and going back the way he had come in. Sure enough, there were police cars and stripey tape and a lone policewoman keeping the traffic flowing. Louise.

Pink stopped and gave her his best smile, asked her what was going on and when she finished work. Louise told him what she knew, kids and high jinks. One of them was still in hospital, touch and go whether he kept his left foot as it had almost been severed when the rain barrel crashed in on him. His friends had deserted him and left him to face the music so he hadn't been long in letting on who they were to the cops. As for when she would be finished, if Pink could hang about for half an hour he could drive her home. Did he have any hash? She could do with a nice relaxing joint.

Pink turned back to Donny's, landing back at the same time as his woman and letting the gang know what he had found out. He didn't want to go home now in case he missed Louise so he borrowed a couple of joints. Donny's woman had centre stage as she told what she had discovered on her travels. Several other acquaintances had suffered altercations with windows while tripping. Pink wasn't in the least surprised and the others nodded respectfully in agreement, there was definitely something to what he said.

Louise hopped in beside him and kicked her shoes off. Pink asked her to put them back on again and was awarded a playful slap for his trouble.

He skinned up while she ran a bath, then washed her back for her when she immersed herself. Before long, he was concentrating on her front and standing to attention in her honour, a condition she wasn't long in taking notice of. They made it to the bed with Louise only partially dry, neither of them noticed. They made love slowly, achingly, it had been a while and both felt it deserved to be savoured. Climaxing together, they fell asleep, still entangled and without having sparked up the smoke.

Pink woke with a start and grabbed Louise's alarm clock, fuck, he had to pick Dave up for the eleven o'clock crossing. The sense of relief he felt when he realised it was only five o'clock soon turned to lust. Louise purred appreciatively when he set about her again, this time there was a little more urgency to his method. Louise joined in heartily, giving him all the encouragement he would ever need both vocally and physically.

She apologised for having nothing in to feed him on. He checked the time again and told her to dress quickly.

Ash gave him the bear hug, kissed Louise's hand and showed them to a quiet corner table. They had smoked the joint on the way, which only served to increase their hunger. Four courses later, Pink undid his belt a notch, let out an appreciative belch and went to the kitchen for a word with his host, coming away with another couple of joints worth of hash.

Another bear hug, an outright refusal from Ash when offered payment for the meal and they were gone.

Pink apologised for dumping Louise on her doorstep and promised to see her soon. She accepted his apology graciously and told him she'd be waiting, with bells on.

Dave had been pacing according to Lily. His dad, Frank, had been standing by and was pleased to see Pink roll up, happy now he could have what was left of his Sunday evening in the club.

They set off at eight o'clock to give themselves plenty of time, Dave laughing his head off when told about Reg and co's trip. He himself had news of another friend, again with a windows connection. A sidecar passenger, the driver wasn't tripping, but he was. A bolt sheared and the sidecar separated from the bike, sending it freewheeling down a hill and through a plate glass shop window. The poor bugger came to in the ambulance and broke a window in an attempt to escape, spending the remainder of his trip tied to a gurney.

Dave had been thinking about Pink's theory all day, no doubt about it, an astute observation.

They landed in time to grab a couple of pints. Pink reminded Dave to say hello to Mad Frank and to warn him about the acid. Then it was a firm handshake and a hug before the sailing, with mutual orders to hang loose.

Pink watched the ferry sail. He would miss Dave, the scene would be a whole lot quieter without him.

He decided he wasn't tired and turned into Louise's street on the way home. A police car was parked outside so he stuck his vehicle in reverse and was about to leave when Louise's door opened. Out stepped another female police officer. Pink had never laid eyes on her, but was immediately interested, the uniform unable to disguise her gorgeous figure.

He let her drive away then scampered up the path. Louise came to the door in her dressing gown, out of breath and blushing when she saw who was there.

Pink showed her no mercy, realising he had caught her on the back foot so to speak and diving in for the kill. Yes, she was a friend from work, a good friend, a very, very good friend. Pink wanted details and coaxed an admission from her along with a blow by blow account of their relationship. When she saw he was ok with it, she proceeded to give him chapter and verse, tugging the clothes from him as she went. Of course he had seen it all for himself at first hand with Jenny and Elise, but this was different. Having Louise talk him through her worship of another female had him at his horniest ever, struggling to contain himself in an effort to let her finish her account.

The picture she had planted in his brain would stay with him forever, her husky voice adding to the tingling excitement. They made love for the third time that day, Pink asking if her friend might be into a threesome as he stroked inside her. Louise wasn't sure, she herself was definitely up for it, leave it with her and she would see what she could do.

Another joint, a cup of tea and he was gone. Louise had an early start, but she knew he would be in touch; now, more than ever.

Johan and Eight Ball were fast asleep. Pink checked the ovens, poured a glass of milk and read half of an old newspaper, reflecting on an eventful day. Not bad since he had planned a lazy one.

Johan stirred, listened to further tales of tripping, shared his food with Pink and rolled a joint. For once, Pink didn't want a smoke, it was past his bedtime. Yes, it had been an eventful day.

"Had a good day, Honey?"

"I was just about to say that."

"He-he. That means yes, doesn't it?"

"I suppose so .... Have you ever been with a woman, Kitten?"

"Wow! Where did that come from?"

"Just curious. Answer the question."

"Well .... no .... Well, nearly. I think."

"Good God, woman. You either did or you didn't. Explain."

"It was my last year at school and my best friend and I were in the shower, kissing, experimenting. My sister came in and almost caught us. I think we would have taken it further."

"Tell me more."

"Not much more to tell. Her father took a job abroad shortly afterwards and the whole family moved away. We lost touch."

"Shame."

"Yes, shame. It's the closest I've ever been to another woman, but why do you ask?"

"Like I said, curious."

"Have you ever? .... No, I don't need to ask, do I?"

"Come to bed, Violet Hiccup."

"He-he. Right behind you, Pinkee."

CHAPTER 46

Time, gentlemen, please. Deserved

Pink leaned against the bedroom wall, legs crossed and arms folded across his chest in classic rock star, couldn't give a shit, pose. On the bed in front of him, Violet and Louise were in the sixty nine position, licking and slurping for all they were worth. Sarah flitted around them anxiously seeking a way in, somewhere to put her hands, somewhere to put her tongue. Pink unbuckled his belt and motioned for her to kneel in front of him, she had been getting in the way of his enjoyment. Now, everyone was happy. The girls writhed all over the bed and Sarah attended to his most urgent of requirements. His turn to pleasure Sarah now, and he used his tongue with a relish, making her moan and groan in tune with her friends on the bed.

He woke with Eight Ball's tail in his mouth, another dream, ruined this time by a stupid cat and not helped by Violet's laughter.

"He's lucky you didn't bite his tail off."

"Did you put him up to it?"

"No. He was asleep and dreaming, like you."

"How did you know I was dreaming?"

"I always know when you're dreaming, Honey, but not what you're dreaming about."

"Good job."

"He-he. Go back to sleep."

The night passed without further interruption, even the call to prayers didn't interfere with his sleep. No dreams either, he had been hoping to return to the exact same place and felt let down he hadn't.

Breakfast consisted of French toast, orange juice and loud music, followed by a cocktail of oil and black. Violet sang along and swayed in time to the music, the sight and sound of which he swore he would never ever tire.

His housework was done in what seemed like an instant. In fact, it had taken the best part of an album and a half; an effort which had included cleaning the windows, reminding him of the acid.

He took the bike to his garden plot, making the most of the sunny morning. The Doobie Brothers accompanied him until the batteries failed as he gathered mushrooms. He bought some on his way home, placed the two bags of mushrooms on the back seat of the Range Rover and set sail for the market and Ash's friend.

A little bartering, he had been told to expect that. Money changed hands and he was heading back towards town.

The Boulder looked like a building site with every window on the ground floor boarded up. Pink went to the back gate, climbed onto a nearby post and shouted for the landlord to let him in. His initial fear it had something to do with trippers, night trippers, was groundless.

Apparently, the Blunts and the scrotes had recognised Sunday night as their last night of freedom and decided to make the most of it. The pub was a shambles inside. The pool table was on its side and in pieces, glass strewn everywhere, liquid of one form or another covered the floor and walls. Blood spattered the bar and the gantry was a thing of the past. Stools and tables were reduced to matchwood and the carpet was fit only for the fire.

The police had been called, but much too late to prevent the carnage. Bones had been broken, the Blunts had been carted away in the meat wagon, still laughing by all accounts.

Pink rolled his sleeves up and offered to help with the clean up. Sarah's dad thanked him, but he'd been advised not to touch anything until the insurance assessor had reckoned up the damage. Sarah appeared when she heard his voice and apologized, she wouldn't be able to attend Sandy's funeral now, her dad would need her help.

Pink made his way to the people's gallery in the courthouse, he wasn't on his own. Half of the town's male population had the same idea as he did. Watch the Blunts get their comeuppance, see if they were still laughing when they were sentenced.

The charges regarding the Boulder couldn't be read out and added to their previous, but Pink had a feeling the judge had been made aware of them. In all, seven of them, including the scrotes, were given between five years and eighteen months in prison. A good result, the shocked looks on their faces alone being well worth the entrance fee.

Pink was given a blow by blow account of the goings on in the Boulder by some who had witnessed it at first hand. His name had been mentioned in dispatches, the Blunts and the scrotes seemingly having put two and two together and connecting Pink to their plight. Whatever.

More stories about the acid and windows followed, some minor, and others more serious. Pink was convinced now if he hadn't been before, no doubt Gwynneth would have more of the same to tell.

While the court case was still fresh in his mind, he drove out to Fester's place, remembering being told about how he knew some dangerous people on the inside. Towser made a fuss of him then retired to his bed. Fester listened with interest and vowed to ensure those mentioned wouldn't have an easy time of it in jail, Pink had his solemn word on that.

Gwyneth had sold every last square of the acid and handed over a wad of notes to prove it. Yes, she had heard many stories connecting it to windows, Pink had been first to spot it and his theory was now proven beyond all doubt.

He spent the last hour with her and helped clean up. Gwynneth locked the door, furnished him with another beer and hurriedly disrobed, a girl after his own heart. They worked up a good sweat together, comfortable with how they were with each other; no commitment, just a good old time.

He took her home, but didn't go in, he would never have been allowed to leave if he had.

At the Marlborough Club he heard what the Waites had to say. They had been in the Boulder, and yes, Mickey Blunt had been looking for him. When the shit hit the fan, he approached Light with murder in his eyes. Light didn't hesitate, smashing his nose with the butt of a pool cue. He wasn't the best of pool players, but he could make use of the cue in other ways.

The police didn't pick anyone else up. Sarah's dad pointed out every man Jack responsible for the carnage and told them he wanted to press charges, letting them know to their faces they were barred for life and to keep out of his way when they were released from jail. Good on him.

Pink picked up two rolls of fancy wrapping paper, checked the time and made his way to Kira's school, give her a surprise.

She pushed two boys out of her way when she saw the Range Rover, jumped in the front seat and showed off to her friends by throwing her arms round Pink's neck and kissing him full on.

She had ironed the pound notes for him, but still wouldn't ask him why, however much she wanted to.

Moraji asked him if he'd eaten and sat him at the table when he answered in the negative. Five minutes later he was tucking into one of Sira's curries, it being her turn in the kitchen. No matter to him who's turn it was, there wouldn't be much left by the time he was done.

Mr Rapati entered and joined him at the table. Pink winked at Moraji and apologised to the baker, telling him he'd eaten his dinner.

Moraji and Kira played along, but he was alive to Pink by now and didn't bite; he only wanted to talk about the wedding and hoped he hadn't left anything out. Moraji shushed him, no stone had been left unturned, he was to relax now and let it happen.

Kira appeared with an envelope, handing it over without a word. No one dared to ask what was in it. After all, this was a time of secrets.

Kira asked for and was given permission to go to the shop, even though it was a school night. She was as excited as her sisters about the wedding, but she didn't want them to know that. Pink said nothing. If they hadn't recognised as much for themselves, they weren't the girls he knew and loved.

He spent half an hour with them, the wedding plans had levelled out so all they could do now was wait patiently; a suggestion they took on board, but would hardly be able to act upon.

Upstairs, he wrapped two boxes of cutlery, one lined with pound notes and the other as itself. He had decided to present the bride's mother with a set as a token of his esteem, or maybe just to get rid of them.

"I don't understand about the pound notes, Honey. What's all that about?"

"It's Mira's wedding on Saturday. I'm told it's customary to give money so I'm hedging my bets."

"Very generous of you."

"Mira's been good to me and her intended's a decent bloke. I want them to be happy."

"You've a kind heart, Pinkee. Truly you have."

"When it's deserved I do."

"Who's the other set for?"

"Her mother, so she doesn't feel left out."

"You're so kind. A lovely, lovely man."

"What are you after, Violet? Spill."

"He-he. Fleetwood Mac, please."

Pink sang along in the shower, his audience downstairs clapping and cheering for all they were worth long before he was done.

He was fidgety, a joint of oil failing to subdue him in any way. Throwing some clothes on, he motored out to see if Jenny the waitress was available for some fun, armed with two bottles of chilled cider and a couple of cocktails. It was the night before a funeral and he didn't want to be alone for some reason. Not that Violet wasn't good company, but he had a real need to knead some flesh. His luck was in, Jenny was pleased to see him and put her waitress outfit on to please him. They smoked a joint and shared a bottle, taking their time with it, listening to the radio, talking and groping. She sensed a touch of sadness about him and tried her best to coax a smile, succeeding in snapping him out of it with a bit of role playing; licking the end of her pencil seductively as she took his order, his hand fondling her knickerless backside as he played along.

Before they knew it, the clock had struck midnight, the witching hour. He had a long drive in the morning and bade Jenny goodnight, thanking her for cheering him up.

Johan was upbeat, fascinated by more tales of the acid and of the justice meted out to the Blunts and co. Then it was two o'clock, time for bed. The clock had stopped ticking days ago, he would have to find it and wind it. Johan wished him luck for the morrow and said goodnight.

"You've an early start tomorrow, Honey."

"I know it. Have you seen the clock?"

"In the kitchen cupboard."

"How the fuck did it get there?"

"Well, I didn't put it there so it must have been you. He-he."

"You ready for bed, Kitten? Have you seen Eight Ball?"

"Yes, and yes."

"Ok. C'mon then, let's be having you."

"He-he. You're such a charmer, Pinkee."

CHAPTER 47

Sandy: Rest in peace

Pink had Pon's dog collar on and was resplendent in black frock coat and trousers. His feet were cold, though, and he soon found out why when he happened to look down. He was barefoot, up to his ankles in mud, how the fuck was he supposed to conduct a funeral service with no shoes on? Heads would roll when he found out who was responsible for this oversight, his word on that.

Mr Rapati stood by the coffin and the mourners formed an orderly queue. The smell of freshly baked bread filled the air as he took the lid from the coffin and began selling his wares. No shortage of customers. Pink hoped to hell there would be some left for him as they were miles from the bakery and the length of the queue looked to be never ending.

Another coffin appeared from nowhere and Ash's mate, Malki the market trader, set about selling his mushrooms. Now, there was two queues snaking into the distance as far as the eye could see.

Pink despaired of them all, heathens to a man. He closed his bible with a thump and squelched his way to the grass verge, lighting up a spliff in an effort to control his rage. Suddenly, he had friends, all hanging for a toke on the joint. He reopened his book and began spouting at them in a loud, clear voice; letting them know they were all blasphemers, all destined for hell, or worse.

Not to be outdone, Mr Rapati and the market man raised their own voices in an effort to shift even more produce. Pink gave it up as a bad job, now he knew how Jesus felt when the shitheads wouldn't listen to a word he said. He walked across the canal to the horse field and started picking magic mushrooms, ignoring the deafening silence of the newly converted who had witnessed him walking on water. Fuck them, they had their chance and they blew it; fuck them all, another Messiah would be along in a millennium or two.

He woke strangely refreshed, ready to face the day, and before the alarm sounded at that.

"When was the last time you read the bible, Honey?"

"Why do you ask?"

"It sounded like scripture you were quoting in your sleep."

"God help us all."

"He-he. You're not right in the head, you."

"Let's see now. I'm talking to a ghost. When I'm not talking to a ghost I have conversations with a black cat, when I'm not doing that I'm quoting the bible. You're quite right Violet, I'm not right in the head, me."

"He-he. As long as you're aware of it."

"Have you polished my shoes? I don't want to leave without them."

"Why would you do that, Pinkee?"

"It's a long story. Suffice to say I'll be double checking I've got them on."

"Play some music, please, your choice. And eat some breakfast, will you?"

"Ok, coming up. Will cornflakes be ok?"

"Have some toast, too. It might be a long day, especially since you're not welcome."

"Ok, done deal."

He had been looking forward to Sarah's company on the drive and thought of swinging by the Boulder to see if he couldn't change her mind. Forget that, the poor girl had enough on her plate, half a dozen tapes would keep him occupied.

He stopped for two rather attractive hitchhikers on the outskirts of town and waited patiently for the obligatory boyfriends to appear from behind the bushes. They weren't forthcoming, more fool them. The girls squeezed into the front with him and decided they were going where he was going, that would do for starters.

They hinted there was a reward in it for him at the end of the road, but his heart wasn't in it. They were just a little too young for him, he was going to a funeral and his love life was complicated enough. All this went against them; they could have a free ride, no strings attached.

Bev and Linda were free spirits, or at least had ambitions to be so. A couple of weekends practice at hitchhiking and they reckoned they were ready to face the big wide world. Both had recently lost their jobs, been dumped by their boyfriends and had come up with the idea of travelling for a while, see where it took them. They must have taken Pink to be a man of knowledge, picking his brains for ideas on how to get by on a shoestring budget, where to look for work, who to trust and who to give a wide berth to. He gave them the benefit of his street-smarts. They would likely find work in the hotels, the summer season was fast approaching. Fruit picking, there was another good source of income, and vitamin C to boot. Also, don't trust a man whose eyebrows meet in the middle, very important that one. His final two pieces of advice had them thinking beyond the warm, summer weather. Cuddle up together for warmth, and don't eat the yellow snow.

He treated them to a late breakfast at a transport café, both girls going at their plates like someone was about to take it from them. He had stopped mainly for directions, and to have a piss. Sandy lived, or used to live in a tiny village which hardly seemed worth a mention on the map. The girls had gone in to use the toilets and he noticed them salivating at the sight and smell of frying food.

They liked his music, insisting he should rewind the 'Cry Tough' tape to the beginning and play it again. They were a little apprehensive when he produced a spliff, but soon warmed to the idea when he got half of it down his neck with no apparent harm coming to him. Then the giggles kicked in. Here he was, travelling to bury his friend and laughing his head off with a couple of itinerants; probably the best medicine.

He stopped again for directions, knowing he couldn't be very far from his destination. He managed to secure another lift for the girls at the same time. They would be safe; the driver's eyebrows didn't meet, and besides, she was a woman. The girls hugged and kissed him as thanks for the ride, he wished them well and turned off for the village, maybe just a little apprehensive about what sort of welcome he was walking into.

He had the right place, cars parked in every available space; pavements, grass verges and all around the tiny church. The two sons saw him walking towards the venue and made to bar his way. A girl, a woman in her early thirties, faced them down, snarled something at them and turned to greet Pink, a broad smile on her face.

She introduced herself as Suzanne, Sandy's ex secretary. She had recognised him from Sandy's description, would have known him anyway by the reaction of the sons. She took his arm and led him into the church, thanking him all the while for coming. All Pink knew was she looked and smelled good. Not lavender, patchouli, but not overpowering like the hippie chicks tended wear it. Suzanne wouldn't have other odours to disguise by the look of her.

They got better acquainted as they waited for the coffin to arrive and she let him know she had found another job away from the area. The boys, Sandy's sons, had begged her to stay on, but it would never be the same. Pink sympathised and understood, squeezing her arm to comfort her and catching the dazzling smile in return.

There was to be a send off bunfight at one of the local pubs, not that Pink would be made welcome. If he liked, he and Suzanne could form their own send off party at the other pub. It would be a shame for him to have travelled all this way and not have a drink to see his friend off. Sandy had spoken very fondly of him and Suzanne was beginning to see why. Settled, that would be very nice.

He was aware of someone staring and had a look around the church. Mac caught his eye and gave him a wave, upsetting the sons by changing sides to sit with Pink and Suzanne.

The service went well. One or two business acquaintances spoke highly of Sandy, then, Suzanne excused herself and made her way to the pulpit. In a firm, clear voice, she spoke of her time working for the man. How he didn't suffer fools, was wary of who he trusted and how, late in his life he had made a friend of Pink; couldn't wait to spend time with him, 'something of a maverick', being his exact words.

Pink blushed as all eyes feasted on him, he hadn't expected this; but still, it was good to hear.

At the graveside, the sons took the time to invite Suzanne and Pink to the send off, no hard feelings. Pink suspected Mac had something to do with that one, but it could have been down to Suzanne's eulogy alone.

Suzanne advised him to park the Range Rover in her drive for safety. He had left it on what served the village as a main road and the local farmers weren't at all mindful of what happened to be in the way of their tractors.

At the pub, strangers queued to shake his hand. Suzanne knew most of them and made the introductions so he felt like a visiting dignitary. The eldest son asked how he had come about the Range Rover, not in any way nasty, merely curious. He seemed happy with Pink's explanation, doubly so when Suzanne backed him up. He then rounded on the woman and asked her again to stay with the firm, but she had made the break.

The beer flowed for free, a huge buffet was uncovered and it seemed the entire village took an interest in it. Having eaten two breakfasts, Pink was more for the liquid refreshment to the extent Suzanne insisted he couldn't possibly drive home on all he had consumed. He was to stay at her place and go home in the morning, no argument.

In truth, what he really needed was a joint. He had taken the precaution of rolling a couple of single skinners and stashing them in his tobacco tin. A bench under the front window of the pub allowed him to indulge himself.

Just for badness, he asked Mac why Jimmy Glover hadn't attended the funeral. A sharp intake of breath gave Mac's feelings for the man away. He had been invited, but failed to show, much to the relief of many there. Enough said.

Early evening, the mourners slowly dispersed, leaving Suzanne, Mac, the two sons and Pink still drinking. The eldest son, Steve, dropped a bombshell, albeit in a whisper. All three non relatives had been mentioned in Sandy's will, which was a shock to Pink if not to the others. The will was to be read on Thursday, it would be best if they could attend.

That sent Pink spinning, he had only known Sandy for a matter of weeks; he couldn't see how he deserved a mention, couldn't see it at all.

Suzanne took him to the only restaurant in the village, her house was practically empty in anticipation of her move. They both had the Dover Sole. Pink insisted on paying in lieu of Suzanne's hospitality, she thanked him graciously and squeezed his arm maybe a little longer than was the norm for new acquaintances.

With full bellies, they hit the pub again, the other pub this time, the mourning had taken its toll on them. Now, it was time for some fun; the pool table was available and Suzanne challenged him to a game.

The more they played, the closer they became, Pink wrapping himself around her to demonstrate a shot and Suzanne rubbing her back end into his groin suggestively. Anyone watching them would take them for long term lovers and Pink had a fair idea he was on for the short term at least.

They lasted the pace until chucking out time and left arm in arm. Pink led her to the graveside and helped her out of her frillies. She was a little apprehensive at first, but soon came round to his way of thinking, freaking only when a car caught them in its headlights. Whoever it was didn't slow down or stop and they soon picked up where they left off, Pink whispering to Sandy that this one was for him.

Suzanne hadn't been lying, her house was all but bare. No furniture in the living room, a kettle and a toaster in the kitchen, a bed and a radio in the bedroom. Most of her clothes had been sent on to her new place, with a few outfits hanging in the wardrobe to tide her over. Pink toyed with the radio while she made a coffee and brought it upstairs, there was nowhere else to sit, not that he was bothered. They drank their coffee and talked about Sandy. Suzanne had been his secretary for over six years and knew as much about the business as he did, which was why the sons wanted her to stay. Her heart wouldn't have been in it, though, which was why she had made the decision to give it up. Pink had reminded Sandy of himself as a younger man and that was the reason he had taken a shine to him. Pink was suitably flattered, almost abashed at the revelation.

Suzanne stood in front of the full length wardrobe mirror and looked herself up and down. Pink was soon in behind her, running his hands over the contours of her body, kneading and squeezing and probing for all he was worth. She melted into his arms, at the same time unbuckling his belt and helping his trousers on their way to the floor. She stayed there on her knees, looked up into his eyes and proceeded to suck the marrow from him, aware he was watching her every thrust in the mirror. If anything, this spurred her on to where he couldn't have separated himself from her if he had wanted to.

Needless to say he didn't want to and let her have all he had to give her as she gobbled greedily, almost choking her when he unleashed his load with a loud roar of satisfaction.

Lying in bed later, Suzanne revealed she had instantly liked the sound of his voice when he phoned for the first time, and had fantasised about him ever since. Pink allowed himself a little self satisfied smile at that, telling her something similar had crossed his own mind. He didn't dare tell her she sounded younger on the phone, that would have spoiled the moment .... if not the fantasy.

They woke in the night and wrestled some more, a mutual thing, then slept until whatever time the cock crowed. They then made good use of the mirror again before bathing leisurely together. Pink wasn't too bothered at having to wear the same clothes. He had certainly done worse in the past.

He found the local shop easily, bought bread, milk, bacon and eggs for the breakfast, spoke to one or two locals he recognised from the pub and wandered back to Suzanne's place.

They got on like a house on fire over breakfast, so much so that Suzanne invited him to spend the night to save him driving home and back for the reading of the will. Tempted as he was, and without a change of clothes, he declined her kind offer. Seeing the look of dejection on her pretty face, he asked her what she was doing for the rest of the day. That was that, she was coming with him, she could shop around his home town while he threw a few clothes in a bag, then they could drive back and spend the night, how did that sound?

A cunning move on his part, it meant he would have company, the best kind of company.

Suzanne changed her clothes three times, plumping for the mini skirt and tight white woollen top, thus assuring him he had made the right decision.

She was good company, certainly more on his wavelength than the hitchhikers. The journey took no time at all, the only dicy moment coming when Suzanne asked why she couldn't go to his place and wait for him there. He didn't really want her to know where he lived for the same reason he didn't want any of his lady friends to know. He liked to come and go as he pleased, and besides, he didn't think Violet was quite ready for female guests. He told her it was a shithole, he was ashamed of it and was on the lookout for something better; best if she went shopping as planned, he wouldn't be long.

Suzanne accepted his reasons and he breathed a sigh of relief, glad to have been quick enough to come up with the excuse.

He dropped her off in the town centre, pointed out the Greek café as a meeting place and went home to change.

"How did it go, Honey?"

"Surprisingly well, but I've got to go back."

"Go back? Why?"

"Sandy left me something in his will and it's being read tomorrow."

"Ooh, don't you know what it is? Do you think it's a lot of money?"

"Dunno, Kitten. All I know is he's remembered me in his will. I'll see you tomorrow, ok?"

"Ok, Honey. Drive carefully, wont you?"

"I will."

He took the bottle of piss and fed his plants while it was on the way, leaving the bottle there so as not to stink out the vehicle.

Jenny was admiring Suzanne's top when he entered the café. Both girls flashed their teeth at him and Jenny brought him a cup of coffee, on the house.

They started back straight away to avoid the tea time traffic. Suzanne invited him to put his hand into her shopping bag and he felt a smooth, silky fabric. She had bought underwear since her best stuff had been packed up and shipped out. Pink found himself looking forward to the evening more than ever.

With that in mind, he stopped at a garage for petrol and dragged her into the toilets, banging into her hard from behind for all he was worth. She didn't put up anything resembling a struggle.

They ate in the same restaurant as last night, steaks this time, both had the feeling they would need as much protein as they could absorb.

Again, they cavorted round the pub's pool table, no doubt now in anyone's mind they were lovers. The landlady offered them after time, a lock in. They stayed for an hour or so to be polite then went to see Sandy again, Suzanne's idea this time.

Her knickers were wet and sticky from before. Pink rolled them up in a ball and put them in his pocket, a souvenir, a reminder of his time with Suzanne.

For the first time in a long time he had gone a full day without a joint, not that the girl would have objected although she was a non smoker. He simply hadn't felt the need to get high.

The mirror let Suzanne have a good look at her new underwear, pink, in his honour. He told her it suited her as he ran his hands up and down her firm body. He wasn't lying and she knew it, she knew she looked good.

It must have been the country air, neither of them seemed to be tired. They had a bath surrounded by burning candles, made love in the kitchen while the kettle almost boiled dry, then sat naked under the stars in the warm night air for an hour before going at it again on the lawn.

They must have nodded off, the first rain in weeks waking them with a start. Suzanne ran another bath and Pink was on her again as she bent over to test the temperature of the water, he couldn't seem to get enough of her and she wasn't complaining.

Another snooze. Suzanne started the ball rolling this time, disappearing to the bathroom and returning dressed in her pink underwear. Pink asked her to dance to the still playing radio and she gyrated sexily for his pleasure. It wasn't long before he dragged her back to bed and ravished her, and the underwear stayed on this time.

Not surprisingly, they didn't hear the cock crow in the morning. The first thing Pink heard was the bath running and he went to investigate. No prizes for guessing what happened next.

CHAPTER 48

A quarter the odds

Pink shook hands with the brothers, Mac and the lawyer and Suzanne did the same. He had never been in such a position before. Neither, by the looks of them, had any of the others.

A lot of legal mumbo jumbo followed, about twenty minutes worth and Pink was losing interest fast. The bulk of the estate had been left to the brothers, equal partners. A housekeeper, who was too upset to attend, was bequeathed some ornaments she had polished for centuries, plus the sum of five thousand pounds. Suzanne gasped when she was awarded five thousand pounds and a glowing reference if she should ever leave the company. Generously, the brothers embraced her and shook her hand. Mac choked back tears when given two thousand five hundred pounds and a guaranteed job for life. Pink was up next, one thousand pounds, and again the brothers were diplomatic, shaking his hand and wishing him good luck. The lawyer wasn't finished, though. He handed Pink a legal looking document and closed the folder, saying that concluded his business. Pink couldn't focus on the document, aware curious eyes were on him. The lawyer had vacated the room before he could make any sense of the page in front of him.

Sandy had only gone and left him a quarter share in a race horse, a thoroughbred, no less. The document gave all relevant details of the trainer, the pedigree and contact phone numbers.

Suzanne laughed nervously, she knew of the betting exchanges between the two and explained it to the others. They were quick to wish him every success with the horse, genuine smiles, the old man had a real sense of humour. Furthermore, each of them wrote down their own phone numbers so he could inform them of when the horse was running.

Mac shouted lunch at the restaurant and was amused to find Pink was on first name terms with the staff; amused, but not surprised.

They drank to Sandy's memory. Pink was offered work at another site, but turned it down, lightening the mood by claiming he wanted to concentrate on his fledgling racing career.

Suzanne dragged him back to her place for one more roll in the hay and he didn't let her down. She had a tear in her eye when he left her, it had been fun, she had been pleased to know him. Pink blew her a kiss and was gone, a cheque for one thousand pounds and a quarter of a horse better off.

He was in no particular hurry to be anywhere and stuck to the back roads, enjoying the scenery and stopping off at a couple of little pubs on the way.

At one pub he was approached by a young couple looking for a lift. They were headed for the city and he told them to jump in, he would drop them near the main road, they wouldn't have much trouble hitching from there.

When the girl asked him what he did for a living, he impressed them by claiming he was in the racing business. Not training, more on the ownership side. They passed a pleasant hour together before he dropped them off at a transport café and waited until a wagon driver picked them up. The girl blew a kiss and winked as they passed, leaving him feeling good all over.

Taking to the back roads again, he found a pub in an idyllic setting and smoked a spliff before making it the venue for his evening meal. Not much of a menu to go at, but he was starving hungry, probably as a result of his exertions with the lovely Suzanne.

The locals eyed him suspiciously, they didn't see many strangers round here, he could have been from Mars. A chicken casserole with seasonal vegetables and three pints of beer later, everyone seemed comfortable in his company. The buxom barmaid, especially, had more than a little time for him. If the place had rooms he would have dug in for the night, but instead, he hit the road again. The barmaid slipped the pub's phone number to him with her name scribbled on the back and he put it in the glove compartment for future reference. He liked the look of her, but didn't want to appear too keen.

He was dying for a piss as he neared Gwynneth's pub and decided to call in. Fester was propping up the bar and shouted him a pint, laughing when he wrestled with the toilet door in his hurry to take a leak.

Gwynneth howled with laughter at the acid stories he had gathered. Fester had to be filled in on the finer points, but soon caught up with the joke. Gwynneth had a few window tales of her own, some serious, others hilarious. They agreed it was a good thing no one other than Doc was killed, that no one had come up with the same connection.

Gwynneth had some money for him, but that wasn't why he was there, the barmaid from the pub earlier had inadvertently set his juices flowing. He needed some female company and Gwynneth fitted the bill perfectly.

At mention of the forthcoming nuptials, Fester offered him the use of an upmarket camera. Not the cheap crap from the catalogue warehouse, but top of the range as used by the professionals. Pink arranged to call round in the morning, as long as he kept that brute of a dog tied up while he was there.

He told them about his horse, his bit of a horse. Fester struggled to comprehend how he could own a quarter of an animal. Pink talked him through it, slowly, before Fester had it on a French butcher's hook.

With there being only the three of them present as last orders approached, Pink went to the chip shop and scored their supper.

Gwynneth locked the doors and set up some after hours drinks. All three hoovered up their fish and chips like they hadn't eaten for days.

Pink caught himself in the toilet mirror, his waistline seemed to be expanding at an alarming rate, he needed some exercise badly. There and then he vowed to use the bike more after the wedding, save the Range Rover for anything long haul or over, say, six miles in distance.

His promises were interrupted by the sound of breaking glass, what the fuck was that all about?

Gwynneth was bleeding, not badly. Fester was wrestling with the bolts on the front door and Pink got there just in time to follow him into the street.

Standing there like a spare prick at a whore's wedding was a spotty youth who Pink recognised as a regular. Fester wanted to kill him, but Pink managed to dive between them, recognising the sheer terror of a bad trip in the kid's eyes.

They could have kicked his arse and left him to the night, but Pink coaxed him into the pub; against Fester's better judgement it should be noted.

Gwynneth recognised him straight away, still cleaning blood from her pretty face, just a scratch, one of those scratches that bleeds forever.

The kid was horrified at the sight of the blood and tried to turn back out again. Fester blocked his path and changed his mind for him. Still, his eyes were on the lookout for an escape route, the good cop, bad cop routine sitting uneasily with him in his altered state.

Gwynneth managed to calm him down a little, enough to convince him to sit down and pay attention to what she had to say.

While she attended to him, Pink cleared up the glass, it had been the smallest window in the pub. Fester found some hardboard to block it off until the glazier could attend to it.

With everything calmed, they had some fun with the kid as he came out of his trip, convincing him he had signed up for the army when he let it be known he had encountered soldiers somewhere in the night. They kicked him at four o'clock, sure he was over the worst and equally sure he was still in for a rough time of it with no downers to help his descent.

Pink told Fester it would be after lunchtime before he could call for the camera. That suited his friend, he had only called for a quiet pint with Gwynneth and now look at the time.

Pink took Gwynneth home, ran her a bath, rolled a joint and turned down the bed, they wouldn't need much rocking between them.

She worried about the scratch spoiling her film star looks. Pink promised her it would heal ok and assured her scars could be a big turn on. That didn't go far towards allaying her fears so he dried her off and dragged her into bed for a good seeing to, a surefire method of bringing her round to his way of thinking.

It worked at the second time of asking. He didn't think he had it in him being so tired and all. Amazing what a little bit of role playing can do for a man, Gwynneth's old school uniform still fitted a treat.

He lay awake for a while, going over the last few weeks in his head; his luck was holding out, better than ever, in fact. Sleep came eventually, punctuated by strange dreams of horses, funerals and country pubs; all mixed in with fireworks, smoke rings and coloured ribbons. Weird. Weirder than usual.

CHAPTER 49

An introduction to The Movies

Pink could have been forgiven for thinking he was dreaming again. Someone was fondling his nether regions to the point where he was at attention and ready to go. No lavender aroma, though, so it couldn't be Violet. Slowly, the realisation came to him it could only be Gwynneth, he knew her touch, knew how she handled him.

He let her play for a while, happy to lie back and let it happen. He opened one eye in search of the scratch on her face, gone, she had rubbed some sort of make up into it and made it disappear.

The ensuing rough stuff brought it back to light however, her face in the pillow rubbing the foundation cream away. Pink ran his finger along it to let her know it was still there, then told her he had some cream for it. Gwynneth squealed with laughter as he sprayed her face with his love juice and smoothed it into the offending scar. She had only just stopped laughing when he suggested she should repeat the dose once a day.

Another bath, a breakfast and a joint set him up for the day. He dropped Gwynneth at the Flat Iron and made his way home.

Sira met him at the front door, he hadn't forgotten he had to take the girls for their artwork, had he?

Indeed he had, but she didn't need to know that. What he admitted to was that he had forgotten what time; a little white lie between friends, no harm done.

He had four hours to kill before picking Mira and Sira up then off to school for the youngest; four hours and all he had to do in that time was call round to Fester's place, he could manage that.

"So, are we rich? Richer than in our wildest dreams?"

"That very much depends on how fast a quarter of a horse can run."

"Stop with the conundrums, Pinkee. Spell it out in layman's terms."

"I've been gifted a quarter of a horse."

"What does that mean, Honey? I still don't understand."

"Sandy left me a quarter share in a race horse, a proper thoroughbred."

"Where are we going to keep it? Don't tell me we'll have to move?"

"Give me strength, Violet, I only own it on paper. I might never even lay eyes on it."

"That'll be a relief to Eight Ball."

"Why so?"

"Well, he's your pet. I think another would put his nose out of joint."

"He-he. Sometimes I wonder what you're on, Kitten."

"Did I say something funny?"

"Fuck, you were serious, weren't you?"

"Tell me more about this bit of a horse, what's its name? Has it won any races?"

"Reading between the lines, he's only recently gone into training at a highly respectable yard. His first race will be near the end of the flat season. It looks like I have to chuck in for his bed and board until he can earn his own corn."

"And the name? I asked you for his name."

"It's a bit embarrassing, really. I'm sure Sandy was having a laugh when he latched onto it."

"Tell."

"Well......"

"Tell. C'mon, don't be shy, Pinkee. It doesn't suit you."

"Powder Puff Pink."

Violet was on the floor laughing. Eight Ball padded in from the bedroom to see what all the fuss was about, but didn't hang around to ask.

Pink busied himself by building a joint. True enough, who had ever heard of a race horse called Powder Puff Pink? The commentators would have a field day with that one.

"Sorry, Pinkee, but you must admit, it's hilarious. No other word for it."

"You might not think so when it makes me a lot of money."

"Maybe not, but I can see now why you reckon you might never lay eyes on it."

Towser let Fester know there was someone at the door before Pink could even knock, then almost bowled him over when Fester answered. He then tried to lick him to death when he had him cornered. Fester cracked open a couple of beers and Towser settled down, everything still but his tail and eyes.

Pink had a wander round the Aladdin's cave which was home to Fester, he could have opened a shop with what was lying around. Fester brought the camera, complete with case and tripod. Pink gave an appreciative whistle, it was a beauty. Fester ran through what he knew about the workings of the thing. Nothing to it really, just point and press. Easy.

A box of records caught his eye and he had a rifle through them. Most of them he knew of and either had or didn't wish to own. Two albums by the same band took his interest and Fester offered to let him have a listen. Two tracks in he was sold. Fester wouldn't put a price on them, they were Pink's as a gift. He listened to side one in its entirety, sure in the knowledge he had come across a real bargain.

He stopped off in town and bought four rolls of film for the camera. If he was to be all day at this wedding, he might as well be busy; that was his thinking on the matter, anyway.

A huge builders' skip took up half the road outside the Boulder. The front door was ajar so he stuck his head in for a nosy. Sarah's dad saw him and called him in, the brewery had come up with a complete refit on the strength of the insurance, the planned re- opening would be in a fortnight. Sarah heard him talking and joined them, asking how the funeral had gone. Pink put a smile on her face when he told her about the racehorse and luckily, she didn't ask for the name.

He still had an hour to himself so he popped into the Greek café for a drink. Jenny the waitress was on him in a flash, the coffee was on the house and Pink was on for later that night, could he bring some dope for her? He arranged to meet her at the Albatross around nine.

He had time to check on his garden plot; no bottle of piss to pour, but he rectified that little problem by supplying it right from the source; the sprouting shoots didn't complain.

He dumped the records and the camera before Violet could get a word in, the girls were pacing the pavement outside like a couple of forty dollar whores. He wouldn't dare tell them that, it was simply what sprang to mind when he saw them, a prime example of his warped sense of humour.

Mira and Sira stepped straight into the back seat. Pink was puzzled momentarily until he realised it would save any arguments when they picked Kira up. It would appear the youngest Rapati ruled the roost.

He had never given any thought as to why the girls would need a lift, their destination being the other end of the estate and not five minutes drive away. He was given a cup of tea while the bride to be was pattern painted with henna; her ears, neck, the entire length of her arms, hands, feet and ankles. It caught the eye and looked good on her. Sira was up next, not so extensive a covering for her, she wasn't the one being married. The same for Kira, who giggled throughout.

Pink stood to leave, but Mira took his arm and led him to the artist's chair, it was his turn; it was tradition, he was told as he tried to talk his way out of it. He wouldn't want to upset the bride, now would he?

Pink shrugged in submission, what the hell, anything for a quiet life. He too had his earlobes painted, then his hands and arms to his elbows.

Pink dropped the girls at home and managed his escape after the customary hugs and kisses, stopping at the end of the street and reversing back to their door, just to confirm their departure time for the morning. Three voices chimed at once and he reminded them all to make sure they washed behind their ears. That brought about the giggles, a quite delightful sound.

He had Johan to pick up first in the morning, better make it an earlyish night, he was home before he remembered the cutlery sets in the back of the car. Fuck it, he would hand them over tomorrow.

"What's happened to your hands, Pinkee?"

"Tattoos. I fancied a couple of tattoos, do you like them?"

"I'm not sure. Did they hurt?"

"Nah."

"Let me see, come closer and put the big light on."

"I've had my ears done, too. All included in the price."

"He-he. You can't fool me. Someone's been drawing on you, right?"

"Correct. Apparently, it's a traditional thing for the wedding."

"Really? I've never heard of that."

"Well, now you know, unless those girls are taking the piss out of me."

"He-he. There's always that possibility."

He tested the assurances the henna wouldn't wash off in the shower, playing side one of the other album donated by Fester, merely to test the band's consistency. No audience downstairs, but Violet was impressed and so was he. The henna stayed where it was.

'The Movies' made a most welcome addition to his collection, their first, self titled album and another called 'Double A'. He would let Brat in on the secret, but not tonight, maybe next week when he had played them to death. Mind you, he wouldn't be at all surprised if Brat was aware of them. The number of bands he had turned Pink onto was unbelievable.

He took the Range Rover to the Albatross and parked up in a side street, he wouldn't be out all night and he wouldn't be drinking much.

Jenny had saved him a seat. When he squeezed in with the drinks she took his right hand and showed she had no underwear on, top or bottom. Maybe she could borrow some from Suzanne? Suzanne had some very nice underwear.

Then, Jenny noticed his hands and thought he had a skin complaint. She laughed when he explained how he had come about the markings.

The evening passed like he wasn't there, but to be fair he had the wedding on his mind. He fielded one or two questions as to Dave's whereabouts, listened to more acid anecdotes and quizzed Brat regarding 'The Movies'. Of course he had heard of them, but hadn't actually heard anything by them. Pink told him he was in for a real treat.

At chucking out time, he drove down to the canal bank and sorted Jenny out al fresco. She loved it, loved it to be different, loved it to be Pink. She left an imprint of her breasts and hands across the bonnet and the budding photographer in him wouldn't have minded a picture of it as a keepsake. They smoked a final joint and chatted for ten minutes. He took her home and promised to see her soon, very soon.

The shop had a strange look about it and he realised there was no light sneaking through from the kitchen and bakery. Eight Ball crept round from the side with confusion written all over his face, he couldn't understand why the back door was closed.

He followed Pink upstairs and Violet explained it to him. Apparently, he didn't believe Pink's version.

Unable to sleep, Pink put both 'Movies' albums back to back on a tape, he could have a good listen on the drive down to the wedding.

Violet was very taken with them, her actual comment being they were 'like a breath of fresh air'.

Sleep came eventually, he remembered seeing two o'clock go by. No dreams as such, but the overwhelming feeling Violet was keeping him warm to compensate for the absence of the oven heat.

CHAPTER 50

Snap, snap, snap. SMACK.
Snap, snap, snap

Pink stepped into the shower just as the alarm went off. Eight Ball leapt at the clock and gave it a hard time for disturbing his catnap and Violet howled with laughter.

The tape was given an airing while he ate his breakfast, the more they heard it the more they liked it. Pink dressed carefully, checked himself in the mirror and brushed a few stray cat hairs from his neatly pressed trousers. Making sure he had everything necessary for the trip, he blew Violet a kiss, took the tape from the deck and put the radio on for her.

"Bye, Pinkee. Drive carefully, and try to enjoy yourself."

"I will and I will, Kitten. See you later."

His hair was still wet from the shower, Sira had promised to plait it for him on the way down.

Johan stood on his front doorstep, more used to finishing work at this time of day than going off on a day out, his body clock would be all over the place.

The Rapati girls appeared as he drove up, jaw droppingly gorgeous, especially Mira. Pink had to try the camera, lining them against the house then changing the shot to against the Range Rover;

the colours in their traditional outfits would challenge the worth of any camera.

Meanwhile, Johan loaded the boot with already presented gifts and it was time they weren't there.

Kira claimed the front seat beside him and the others didn't seem too bothered about that., there wouldn't have been much point in complaining. Sira plaited his hair, Mira looked slightly nervous, Johan asked for the music to be turned up a notch.

The early start provided an almost empty road and Pink made good use of it, reaching the halfway stage well ahead of schedule. The dust on the bonnet showed Jenny's hands and breasts off to startling effect and he decided he would stop at the next car wash to clean it.

Kira squealed with delight on the way through the car wash and wanted to do it again. Pink eyed the bonnet and decided that wouldn't be necessary, resuming the trip and finding himself driving behind Ash and the catering staff.

The ever increasingly nervous Mira wanted to stop at the next place with toilet facilities. Pink overtook the caterer's van and turned into a roadside café half a mile later.

Ash followed them in and told Pink he was glad to have dropped on them, he was unsure of the road so Pink could lead them on.

The venue was a converted school. Kira asked for directions when they hit town and they rolled up half an hour early.

Since the groom hadn't arrived, Mr Rapati asked Pink to drive Mira around for ten minutes or so. Sira and Johan stepped out, but Kira wanted to stay with her sister.

Pink parked up a few streets away and helped Kira calm Mira as best they could. When she assured them she was ready and had no last minute doubts, they made their way back to the school.

Inside was like walking into an Indian temple. Pink hadn't really known what to expect and was blown away by the spectacle. Reams of multicoloured fabric festooned the walls and tables, he could tell a lot of money had been spent; and to great effect.

Mira was taken from him and ushered into an annexe, throwing him a little nervous smile as she went

Pink took a three-sixty degree scan of the main hall and gave Ash and his men a wave. Then, he went for his camera, Kira bobbing along by his side like a little faithful puppy. He set the tripod and camera up on a little stage at the far end of the hall and messed around with a panel of light switches, trying his level best to look as though he knew what he was doing.

Kira served as his model as he focused and refocused, suddenly aware of an Indian man about his own age staring at him. Pink nodded hello and was given a sour look, followed by what sounded very much like an angry tirade. Not wishing to spoil Mira's big day by getting involved in any argy bargy, Pink smiled at the man and carried on with what he was doing. Not Kira, Kira let him have both barrels and would have taken up arms against the guy if Pink hadn't calmed her down.

Apparently, he was upset at Pink's presence for some reason, Kira translating his words to mean it should be an Indian photographer and not him.

Pink ignored it, took snaps of the decor, the ever increasing buffet, arriving guests and Kira. Kira managed to appear in every shot. He even took one of the offending man, who was still staring in his direction and, as fate would have it, with an Indian photographer setting up behind him. Pink gave another wave in their general direction.

Happy with his work so far, he left Kira in charge of the equipment and went for a piss; only because the Indian dude had headed that way. They were the only two inside the toilet. Pink asked if he spoke English and he told Pink to fuck off. Pink smacked him once, connecting beautifully with his left eye and dropping him to his knees. He washed his hands, asked the Indian if they had any further business and turned on his heel at his negative response.

The room was filling nicely. Mr Rapati introduced him to the celebrant and posed for a picture and this time he removed Kira from the shot.

Suddenly, it was game on. The celebrant raised his arms and went into a long, long speech, all in Indian which Kira, his lovely assistant, translated as best she could while Pink busied himself with the camera; being as unobtrusive as was humanly possible.

Applause, then a procession led by both sets of parents, closely followed by the bride and groom and their respective attendants. Kira had abandoned him for this part of the ceremony, fussing around her sister and making sure her outfit was shown off to its best. Pink had the floor to himself and managed to take close ups and group shots without standing on anyone's toes. In his element, he was loving it, believing to have found a new career for himself; although he wouldn't say for definite until he viewed the final results.

Kira rejoined him when the bride and groom stood before the celebrant, this was the formal introduction with family members extolling the virtues of the betrothed in turn. At least that's how Kira explained it.

He snapped Moraji with her eyes full of tears, her husband with his chest puffed out with pride, and Sira looking almost as beautiful as her sister. He also captured Sanjeev's family, equally tearful, equally elegant and equally proud.

The celebrant broke into song, read from the holy book, called for anyone with any objections to the union to speak up, read from the book again and let rip with another song.

It was quite a long, drawn out process which had Pink gagging for a gargle of some sort. Thankfully, a recess was called, the bride and groom were separated again and Pink headed for the kitchen. Ash passed him a cold beer and he ran off a few snaps of the workers, his mouth watering at the wonderful aromas escaping from the huge range in the corner. Kira was by his side, asking Ash for a run down of the menu and letting him know she would have done it differently; all in good humour, of course.

Under starters orders again, this time for the actual union of bride and groom. Yet more reading and singing by the celebrant, who reached an almost fitful trance like state before making the declaration which finally bonded the couple in marriage.

Gifts were then presented in a sort of free for all, which gave Pink time to reload and take stock. He sent Kira out to the boot for his own gift to the happy couple, thinking Moraji could wait until tomorrow for hers.

He slipped into the kitchen for another liquid refreshment and found Johan there with Ash and the lads. Pointing the camera, he was about to take the picture when they rushed towards him wielding knives and empty pans.

He truly thought his number was up, thought he had committed some sort of faux pas regarding etiquette.

They were past him in a flash; his barracking friend from earlier had gathered a few amigos from the throng and had a notion to do Pink some damage. From the look on their leader's good eye there was murder in the air.

The catering staff corralled them in a corner of the kitchen and asked Pink what he would like to do with them. Bearing in mind they were at a celebration, he sent Johan into the main hall with the instruction to bring Sanjeev discreetly to the scene.

Sanjeev went berserk and gave them the rounds of the kitchen. The main protagonist turned out to be his second cousin and an employee to boot. They were banished from the reception via the back kitchen door, with the promise of further punishment for bringing disgrace to his family.

Sanjeev thanked Pink for bringing it to his attention, for keeping it under wraps, he couldn't apologize enough. Pink told him to forget it and go back to his new bride before she came looking for him.

Pink made the catering staff pose with their weapons raised for a fun snap, Mira would get a shock when she looked through her wedding album.

Kira stood in line with his present for Mira. When she saw Pink, she started dancing, indicating, not very subtly, that she needed a pee. Pink gave her his best puzzled look and snapped her response; contorted face, legs crossed and eyes popping.

He slipped into her place in the line and watched her run for the toilets.

Moraji approached with a worried look on her face, wringing her hands and furrowing her brow. With all the fuss over the wedding, she had forgotten to buy a gift for Sanjeev's parents. They had presented Mr Rapati with a pair of his and her watches and she had nothing to give in return.

He was almost at the front of the line, but stepped away to attend to Moraji, telling her to follow him.

They grabbed Kira as she left the rest room and took the car keys from her. Then Pink sent her to whisper in her sister's ear that his gift to them was at home, led Moraji to the Range Rover and swapped Mira's gift for hers.

Moraji was crying, how could she ever thank him? Pink explained it was intended for her, she could do what she wished with it, besides, he needed a new watch, anyway.

Moraji skipped to her husband's side carrying the heavy cutlery set and told him of Pink's rescue act. A huge smile of relief crept over his face as he gave Pink the thumbs up and another picture was born.

When he crept in close to snap the happy couple receiving gifts, his assistant and her other sister threw their arms around his neck and kissed him since Moraji had informed them of his heroics.

The band started up, with lively music and the newlyweds were manhandled on to the dance floor where they were encouraged to cut a rug. Before Pink knew it, Kira had him up, complete with camera. He wasn't much of a dancer, at least not without a drink or some drugs in him, but he gave it a shot, relieved when the floor filled quickly. Half an hour of dancing and the speeches began; the groom's father, the bride's father, all manner of uncles and the celebrant, again. Eyes rolled heavenward as he rambled on and on and on. Pink hadn't a clue what he was talking about, but saw the consternation on guests faces; the man would have to be stopped.

Ash appeared behind him and cleared his throat. The celebrant turned to see who had the temerity to interrupt him and Ash leaned forward to announce that dinner was served. The speeches were over, the mood changed instantly, the stampede followed shortly thereafter.

Pink snapped away while Kira joined the scrum with instructions to bring him a plate, she knew what he liked. Moraji threw her arms round him and Mr Rapati pumped his hand, how could they ever thank him?

Sanjeev's mother was over the moon with the cutlery and had invited her new in-laws to dinner so she could make use of it, everybody happy.

Johan and Sira brought him a beer just as Kira turned up with his food. They were becoming increasingly nervous about making their own announcement so Pink told them he would sort it out.

Mira and her new husband joined them, still breathless with the excitement of it all. Pink took Sanjeev to one side, had a word then gathered them all in for a group shot. The band, who had been playing since the speeches ceased, were invited to help themselves to the spread. Sanjeev took advantage of the comparative silence to make a brief announcement.

On behalf of himself and his new bride, he thanked everyone for coming and making their wedding day such a memorable occasion. He then announced how proud he was to be asked to let the assembly know of the engagement of his sister in law, Sira, to his good friend, Johan. Pink was on hand to be the first to congratulate the couple amid rapturous applause from the floor. Mira kicked off with the tears again, closely followed by Moraji and Kira.

Pink brought the camera back into play; running make up made for good pictures, more natural than a forced smile any day, he was getting the hang of this photography lark.

Mr Rapati was all over Johan, partly because he couldn't get anywhere near his middle daughter and partly because she was marrying into royalty.

The catering staff formed an orderly line to offer their congratulations to the Prince. Johan played the adulation down, insisting he was just plain Johan.

The band set about what Pink took to be the Indian equivalent of 'Congratulations' and the dancefloor filled once more. He snapped at the harmonium player as he soared into his solo, then the sitar player showed what he could do, two drummers, a flautist, a guitarist and male and female vocalists were equally proficient and were consigned to film as they performed.

With only one shot left on the second roll, his lovely assistant took the camera from him and handed it to Johan. She wanted a picture of herself with Pink, using the highly animated band as a backdrop.

Pink sloped outside for a cigarette and to change film rolls. Kira brought him a beer and some more food then sat beside him and linked his arm. She was asleep on his shoulder when Moraji found them and had her picture taken unawares, one she wouldn't remember and one she would never be allowed to forget. She stirred after half an hour and followed Pink inside, the sun was on its way to bed and she felt the chill.

She dogged Pink as he snapped the party breaking up, people hugging and kissing newly made friends, exchanging phone numbers and in one instance, exchanging entire outfits.

Sanjeev's father handed Ash an envelope which he tried to refuse. Mr Rapati and Johan stepped in and persuaded him to accept on pain of death, or some other such threat. Sanjeev's father then shook the hand of every member of the catering staff, all captured on film.

Mira had one more favour to ask of Pink. The newlyweds would be honeymooning in Holland with relatives of Sanjeev, could Pink possibly take them to the ferry in the morning?

Kira was suddenly his spokesperson, of course he would; and whatsmore, she would be coming along for the ride.

The catering staff followed him as far as the main road then set off like a bat out of hell, Ash planned to put a couple of hours in at the restaurant. He had prepared more than enough food for the masses and didn't want it to go to waste.

Mira and Sanjeev travelled with Mira's parents, Kira slept on Pink's shoulder, Sira and Johan grooved to the Movies in the back seat, or at least that's what Pink thought they were doing.

They arrived at the Rapati household just before ten. Kira opened one eye to see why they had stopped, promptly snuggled up to Pink and went back to sleep. Sira woke her and took her indoors. Pink handed Mira's present over, let the lovers have five minutes, then took Johan to the bakery. He had volunteered to knock a few orders out, earning a fair number of Brownie points with his future father in law; not that he needed them.

Pink drove to the Albatross in his finery, attracting a crescendo of wolf whistles when he entered.

He sat with Brat, who just happened to have a couple of joints of excellent grass on him. It stunk the pub out, but since everyone seemed to be smoking it, no one appeared to be bothered.

Although it had been a long day, he still wasn't tired so drove out to Jenny and Elise's flat at chucking out time.

No light on and no answer at the door, maybe they were at the restaurant. He didn't make it that far, there was a light on at his favourite contortionist's house, be rude of him not to say hello.

Angie would have fucked him on the doorstep if he hadn't more or less manhandled her into the flat. To say she was happy to see him would be something of an understatement. She looked him up and down in his Sunday best then made a start at disrobing him. He marvelled at the positions she folded herself into, at one point her willing mouth was no more than six inches from her warm, moist pussy. It was like having two women at once, an experience he had enjoyed a few doors down the street. He slipped in and out of each orifice in turn, working himself into a frenzy before spraying his juices all over her.

Now he was tired, felt he could sleep, he had a coffee with Angie and promised to see her soon, promised to take her for a meal at a charming little restaurant he knew.

He checked on Johan at the bakery, he was asleep with Eight Ball on his knee, the ovens were still warm, but cooling down. Johan's night's work over.

He woke when Eight Ball did and accepted a lift home. Eight Ball came along for the ride, sitting between them on the front seat.

"How are my two favourite males?"

"Don't know about Eight Ball, but I'm absolutely shattered. I've an early start at that. Ferry run."

"Let's get you into bed, then. How did the wedding go? Don't answer that, Honey. I'm sorry, tell me tomorrow."

"I'll show you the snaps when I've had them developed, how's that?"

"That'll do for starters."

"Good night, Violet."

"Night night, Pinkee. Sweet dreams."

CHAPTER 51

A whole new ball game

Pink wielded the camera like a veteran. Model after beautiful model posed and pouted for him, took instruction and willingly shed clothes at the drop of a hat. His trusty assistant, Kira, altered lighting to suit the mood, made copious amounts of tea and dusted the models with make up for effect.

In the dark room he couldn't work out why every shot was of Kira, Kira and Eight Ball, maybe the camera was faulty; or maybe the alarm clock was trying to tell him something?

It was, it was telling him to wake the fuck up, it was telling him he was having another of his vivid dreams; it was asking to be launched out of the window.

He made short work of a bowl of cereal and had a quick shower, half singing along with 'She's a be-bopper' from The Movies' 'Double A' album.

Mira launched herself at him, expressing her thanks for their wedding gift. Sanjeev pumped his hand and asked where he had come about the new pound notes since most of those in circulation were scruffy to say the least. Kira butted in with the answer to that one, she had spent hours ironing them.

It looked like they were going for six months with three large suitcases waiting to be loaded. Sanjeev explained half of the contents were gifts for his family in Holland.

Mr Rapati and Moraji came out to see them off, while Sira waved and blew kisses from an upstairs bedroom window.

Kira claimed her place in the front seat and they were away, just as the sun rose; another warm, clear day in prospect.

They made good time. Pink and the girls headed for the dockside café while Sanjeev picked up the pre-booked tickets.

For all the wedding was now well and truly over, it was still the main topic of conversation, had been all the way to the port and would be until the happy couple set sail. Mira went to the rest room and Kira carefully unfurled her umbrella, showing Pink it was full of confetti, just for a laugh. If they dared to give her any grief about it on their return, she told Pink she would point the finger and blame him.

With all aboard who were going aboard, Kira linked his arm and waited for the sailing. The sun was making its presence felt, so much so he had to remove a couple of layers of clothing. They waved and blew kisses from the dockside and waited 'til the ferry turned out of the harbour before setting sail themselves for home.

They stopped off at a roadside café for another drink and the young lady on his arm turned heads wherever they went. It was the same with her sisters,

Kira talked and laughed and joked all the way to the Rapati house. She wanted to stay with him all day, but he had plans to visit Louise; see if she could find out how the new inmates were faring, see if they were having a hard time of it as promised by Fester.

Armed with a couple of cocktails, he knocked on Louise's door, no answer, the bedroom curtains were open so she wasn't in bed. He left his calling card in the shape of a joint to let her know he had called.

He had better luck at Gwynneth's, catching her in her dressing gown. Needless to say she didn't have it on for long. He bent her over the kitchen table and poked at her from behind, letting the neighbours know via the open window that they were having a fun time of it.

Gwynneth had taken delivery of some bush all the way from Acapulco and wanted his opinion.

Always ready to help, he built a joint and fired it up. It smelled good, tasted good and did them good; the second joint did them even more good.

She wanted him to stay for the day, but he was restless and made up the story he had places to be, things to do. He did leave with half an ounce of the grass, though. It made a very pleasant change from the black and the oil.

He called in at the Boulder to see how the renovations were coming along. The place was stripped bare and smelled of fresh plaster. Sarah made him a coffee and asked how the wedding had gone. He promised to show her the snaps, if they turned out. Depending on how they looked, he was considering taking up photography as a means of making money. Sarah blushed bright pink when he said she was to be his first model, his first nude model.

No signs of life at the bakery. Usually, the girls cleaned on a Sunday, but Mr Rapati must have given them a day off. The next shift would probably be Johan's later that night.

As good as his word, he gave the bike an airing, loading up with ready made joints, cider and music; plus, the Movies tape from the car. He couldn't get enough of it.

He rode first to Donny Boot's house and turned him on with a joint of the grass, it made him dry, but he refused a drink and would wait until he had gone a few miles on the bike. He asked about the injuries sustained on the night of their trip and was assured everyone was on the mend. No one had mentioned acid since.

Change of plan. He rode to his garden plot, peed on his ever larger plants and necked a bottle of the cider, checking on his mushroom beds while he was in the area.

He cycled along the canal towpath and turned off near to where Jenny the waitress lived, not so much in need of female company as a desire to share another joint with someone.

They sat in her back yard, a secluded area and a veritable sun trap. Pink stripped off his T-shirt while Jenny made a pot of tea. He could have slept there where he lay, but Jenny altered his plans by slipping her dress off then sitting astride him. She had a lovely firm body and he told her so, which was all the encouragement she needed. Another set of neighbours were treated to the sounds of abandonment.

It was only one o'clock in the day when he left Jenny. Promising to see her soon, he leapt on his bike and cycled to town, he would call at Patsy's pub, see how he was getting on.

Patsy was pleased enough to see him, shouting him a pint and showing a genuine interest in his well-being. It turned out he was one of the very few who had managed to stay on the right side of Jimmy Glover, but he wasn't at all sure how long that would last. His wife joined them after a couple of pints, even uglier than Patsy, Pink wouldn't ask if they had any kids; God help the poor brats if they did.

They played pool for half an hour. Pink was offered to join them for a Sunday roast, but thanked them and declined, somewhere he had to be.

With a thirty bob sway on, he rode to the Rapati house and invited himself in to eat, they were one short at the table. Moraji told him he had done the right thing, there was always plenty of food.

He spent a pleasant hour in their company, mainly talking about how smoothly the wedding had gone. Kira waited on him hand and foot. Sira laughed and told him to watch out, her younger sister had a huge crush on him, he was all she ever talked about. Pink this, that and the other.

Mr Rapati verified his theory that Johan would be working later, then asked him wasn't it about time he called him by his forename, Rupesh?

Moraji explained it meant 'Lord of beauty' in Sanskrit. Pink bit his tongue and stifled an off the cuff comment, Rupesh it would be, then. Rupesh Rapati. It had a kind of ring to it.

Full of vegetable Madras and full of beer, he wobbled away on his bike. The sun had gained in strength, inviting him to go and lie in it. Sun worshipper that he was, he couldn't refuse the call.

Finding a quiet corner at the local park, he smoked his last but one joint, stripped off to where he was barely legal, used his haversack for a pillow and promptly fell asleep.

Kira had the camera now. Eight Ball was definitely in charge, though, since he was wearing the hat. He directed where Kira should point and shoot, then cornered a couple of huge rats for a fight to the death. Kira captured every move he made, moving in close, but not so close as to come between him and the rats. Big as the rats were, it wasn't a fair fight, more like sport for the black cat; a breeze, a walk in the park.

Pink was freezing. The sun had disappeared behind some trees on its way down and now he was cold. He quickly pulled his clothes on, gathered up his belongings, stuck the last joint in his mouth and pushed the bike towards the footpath. The batteries had gone on his walkman, but the earphones remained in place.

As cold as he was, he froze. Was he still dreaming? He flicked his lighter on and put the flame under his hand. No, fuck, he was awake. So why was Violet Hiccup sitting on the park bench he was approaching? Ok, she had her back to him, but he would recognise that hairstyle and that outline in a pea souper fog. Also, the strong odour of lavender was a dead giveaway, no pun intended.

"Violet?"

Violet turned towards him, startled, she had obviously been crying.

"I'm Violet's sister .... Saffron .... Did you know her?"

"Her sister? .... Her *twin* sister?"

"Yes. Did you know her? Today's our birthday. I've come round here to be near her. How well did you know her?"

"I'm .... I'm in her old flat .... I thought you were Violet. I'm sorry, you'll have to excuse me, this is a bit of a shock. Do you mind if I sit down?"

"Please do. Are you ok? You've gone very pale. I hope you're going to light that joint? It might relax you a bit."

Pink fumbled with the lighter. Violet .... Saffron was wearing a short sleeved top and had a jacket on the bench beside her. He gave her the joint to light, picked up the jacket in an act of chivalry and deviousness; one way to find out if she was Violet or not. He helped her left arm into a sleeve and caused her to raise her right arm for the other. No birthmark. Fuck, what should he do now?

Saffron toked long and hard on the joint, she too had a puzzled look about her.

"Would you like to see the flat?"

"You're a fast worker, aren't you?"

"I meant .... I thought it might help what with you being upset and all."

"I know what you meant. I'm sorry. I was trying to be funny." "That's ok. It's a bit awkward. I'm struggling for words here, which is unusual for me."

"Thanks for the invite. I'm not really sure. tell me how you knew my sister."

"I didn't know it had been her flat until after I moved in, the landlord's daughters filled me in."

"Would it have made a difference?"

"What?"

"If you'd known?"

"Nah. You going to smoke the whole joint? I don't mind, really. I've had a good smoke all day, so enjoy."

"Thanks, it's good stuff. I haven't had a smoke in ages."

"Another reason for having a look at the flat. I have plenty, although I keep my shit outside. Safer that way."

"Safe from what?"

"Drug squad. I'm one of their favourite people, like a pet."

"He-he."

Pink had goosebumps now. Saffron had the exact same laugh as Violet, same mannerisms as far as he could see; her voice, her eyes, her absolute everything.

"It's getting dark, cold too. Tell you what, I'm going to pick some more grass up then head out to my friend's restaurant. Why don't you join me? We can talk some more there."

"On the bike? How far away is it?"

"You have a great sense of humour, I like that. We'll take the car."

Pink pushed the bike and Saffron strolled alongside him. Just outside the park gates she hesitated for a split second, took a deep breath then carried on walking and talking.

At the flat door she decided she wanted to come up, then decided against it, then decided she didn't know what to do. Pink took her hand and got an electric shock for his trouble. By the looks of her, Saffron felt it too.

"It's ok, Saffron, it was only a suggestion, no pressure. I don't want you being uncomfortable with it."

"Thanks for that, you're very sensitive. I can't say I've met many sensitive men."

"I'm almost sure I'm a lesbian."

"What makes you say that?"

"I keep fancying women."

Her laughter was like sweet music to his ears.

"You got me back."

They were behind the bakery now, so dark they had to play it by ear. Of course Pink knew his way around and expertly opened the bike shed, stashed the bike and helped himself to a selection of hash. It somehow didn't matter that Saffron knew where he kept his dope. He had only known her for ten minutes, but it didn't matter a jot.

Then, she heard a noise and clung to him. The electric shock was slightly reduced, but still evident to both.

"It's ok, just restless natives. C'mon, let's go and get stoned." Saffron clung to him all the same as they returned to the flat door. He felt her stiffen, then opened the passenger door of the Range Rover and helped her in.

"Nice car. What do you do for a living?"

"I've recently taken up photography. Might see if I can make some sort of a career of that for a while."

"And before that?"

"Building trade, but that turned out to be a little too dangerous."

Pink stopped in a lay-by on the outskirts of town and threw a joint together and the Movies entertained as he passed it to Saffron to spark up.

"That was really fast. And in the dark, too."

"Years of practice skinning up in pubs where the drug squad might pop in at any moment, you had to be quick.

"Do you only smoke grass?"

"No, not at all. Whatever's going, although I've managed to be a little more selective of late."

"How so?"

"Here. You're not police, or drug squad, are you?"

"No, why?"

"You ask an awful lot of questions>"

"It's a woman thing, Nice strong grass, that."

Pink took the joint from her and turned back onto the road, the music having temporarily taken away any need for further questions until he turned off the main road once again.

"Where are we going? I used to live out this way."

"You'll see. Not far to go now."

"Wow! This used to be a youth club and disco when Violet and I were younger."

Ash had him in the usual bear hug as soon as they entered, then daintily shook Saffron's hand. The restaurant was quiet and they found a table in the corner near the kitchen.

"What did he call you?"

"What did you hear?"

"Sounded like Pink. Couldn't possibly have been Pink. Could it?"

"Something wrong with that?"

"You weren't born Pink, were you?"

"Yes."

"I don't believe you."

"My mate Ash there was born brown, but I was born pink; a little jaundiced, but apparently that's perfectly normal.

Saffron's laughter lit the room up and set his pulse racing, uncannily like her sister's.

"I meant Pink's not your given name …. but I'm sure you knew that?"

"It's a nickname, My surname's Lynt, so I was Pink Lynt from an early age."

"Thank God for that. Imagine going through life with a name like Pink."

"I don't need to imagine."

"No, you don't, do you?"

A couple of the waiters came over and shook his hand, another brought a pint of cider without being asked and inquired as to what Saffron would like to drink. Pink could tell she was bemused by all this; bemused, but impressed.

They took their time, talked all through the meal, had their drinks replenished as soon as their glasses were near empty and were waited upon hand and foot.

Ash closed the doors behind the last of his paying guests, produced a cocktail of black and oil and pulled up a chair. He told Saffron of Pink's guile in bringing his good friend Johan and his girl Sira together when it looked like her parents wouldn't approve. He also told of his efforts at the recent wedding, he seemed to understand this girl was perhaps higher up the pecking order than the other girls Pink had dined with.

Saffron listened intently, smiling and nodding at the appropriate times and throwing admiring glances in his direction at random intervals. For his part, Pink couldn't take his eyes from her. Violet had always been his favourite girl, but this was different, a whole new ball game.

496

Suddenly, it was three o'clock in the morning. Where had the time gone?

Saffron linked his arm after the bear hug from Ash and his nostrils filled with lavender as they hit the night air.

At the car, she turned to face him.

"I've had a wonderful time, Pink. Much nicer than I expected before you turned up. You've been a Godsend. Thank you."

"It's been a real pleasure, Saffron. Just glad I could take your mind off things for a while."

"You did that alright."

"It's late, let's take you home."

"I'm not tired."

"In that case, neither am I."

"He-he. Are you always so agreeable?"

"Yes."

"He-he."

Pink loaded her into the vehicle again and headed back to town, the black and the oil working in tandem to reduce the conversation and heighten the listening factor.

He pulled up outside Donny Boot's house, saw a faint light escaping form the front room, led Saffron round the back and gave the secret knock.

Two minutes later Donny himself opened the door, his woman must have been in bed, or unconscious. Donny had been about to retire, but skinned a joint up to be sociable. They spent half an hour with him, Saffron looking slightly uncomfortable at the state of the place and relieved to hit the fresh air when they exited.

"I think I'm ready." She whispered.

"But, we've only just met."

"He-he. To see the flat, I meant."

"Oh, ok. Are you sure? We can leave it for another time."

"You mean you want to see me again?"

"You're a mindreader."

At the front door she baulked again. Pink was nervous enough as to Violet's reaction, but Saffron seemed doubly so; for perhaps a different reason to his.

He took her hand and led her round the back. It was a warm night and the bakery door was ajar. Johan was pleased to see him, and pleased to see he had a young lady in tow other than one of the Rapati sisters. He offered Saffron a seat, put the kettle on for a coffee and passed Pink the makings.

Saffron giggled as she tried to follow his hand movements as he built a spliff, and gasped at the speed of the action.

Eight Ball padded in, took one look at her and did a back somersault, high tailing it out of the door with an accompanying screech. Johan looked puzzled, Saffron looked equally puzzled, only Pink and Eight Ball fully understood the cat's actions.

Hearing the subsequent laughter, Eight Ball returned, albeit cagily, and had a nervous sniff at Saffron. His charm worked its magic on her as it tended to do with everyone and soon he was on her knee and being made a fuss of. Pink breathed a sigh of relief; that was phase one taken care of, now for phase two.

Saffron let him put the key in the door and followed him upstairs, she was carrying Eight Ball. How the fuck would Violet react to this? Let's see, let's just see if his luck was still holding out. Fingers crossed.

ABOUT THE AUTHOR

Angus Shoor Caan

Angus Shoor Caan was born and raised in the coastal town of Saltcoats on Scotland's beautiful, North Ayrshire coast. Aged fifteen, he set off on his travels around the world before returning some forty years later to try his hand at writing.

Author of thirteen novels, a good number of short stories and a collection of McLimericks numbering 6,000 plus, Caan is determined to keep on with the writing until his muse decrees otherwise.

Also, he posts a daily McLimerick to his own and other FB pages, each accompanied by a video of same. The videos can be viewed on YouTube, too.

All publications can be found via Amazon books.

BOOKS BY THIS AUTHOR

Umpteen.

Other books by this author.

Scoosh
Scoosh. The G AP years.
Violet Hiccup.
Larry Kynn (A case study in misadventure)
Life of Riley.
Lucky Tallis Mann.
The Reader.
Dhu Lally and the Bampots.
Zachary Bleu.
Parallel Lives.
Easter Vedan.
Lew Skannon.
And, coming soon. Hash Browne: (Here's the sketch)

Short stories.

Other People's Houses.
Tattie Zkowen's Perfect Days.

Poetry.

Board Bill's Hot 100
Coont Thum. Volumes 1-23